The Little Lady of the Big House

Jack London

All rights reserved © 2019 by Jack London (Public Domain)

© 2019 Les prairies numériques
Cover design and layout © 2019 by FGM
Legal deposit : may 2019
ISBN : 9782953652383

Chapter 1

He awoke in the dark. His awakening was simple, easy, without movement save for the eyes that opened and made him aware of darkness. Unlike most, who must feel and grope and listen to, and contact with, the world about them, he knew himself on the moment of awakening, instantly identifying himself in time and place and personality. After the lapsed hours of sleep he took up, without effort, the interrupted tale of his days. He knew himself to be Dick Forrest, the master of broad acres, who had fallen asleep hours before after drowsily putting a match between the pages of "Road Town" and pressing off the electric reading lamp.

Near at hand there was the ripple and gurgle of some sleepy fountain. From far off, so faint and far that only a keen ear could catch, he heard a sound that made him smile with pleasure. He knew it for the distant, throaty bawl of King Polo—King Polo, his champion Short Horn bull, thrice Grand Champion also of all bulls at Sacramento at the California State Fairs. The smile was slow in easing from Dick Forrest's face, for he dwelt a moment on the new triumphs he had destined that year for King Polo on the Eastern livestock circuits. He would show them that a bull, California born and finished, could compete with the cream of bulls corn-fed in Iowa or imported overseas from the immemorial home of Short Horns.

Not until the smile faded, which was a matter of seconds, did he reach out in the dark and press the first of a row of buttons. There were three rows of such buttons. The concealed lighting that spilled from the huge bowl under the ceiling revealed a sleeping-porch, three sides of which were fine-meshed copper screen. The fourth side was the house wall, solid concrete, through which French windows gave access.

He pressed the second button in the row and the bright light concentered at a particular place on the concrete wall, illuminating, in a row, a clock, a barometer, and centigrade and Fahrenheit thermometers. Almost in a sweep of glance he read the messages of the dials: time 4:30; air pressure, 29:80, which was normal at that altitude and season; and temperature, Fahrenheit, 36°. With another press, the gauges of time and heat and air were sent back into the darkness.

A third button turned on his reading lamp, so arranged that the light fell from above and behind without shining into his eyes. The first button turned off the concealed lighting overhead. He reached a mass of proofsheets from the reading stand, and, pencil in hand, lighting a cigarette, he began to correct.

The place was clearly the sleeping quarters of a man who worked. Efficiency was its key note, though comfort, not altogether Spartan, was also manifest. The bed was of gray enameled iron to tone with the concrete wall. Across the foot of the bed, an extra coverlet, hung a gray robe of wolfskins with every tail a-dangle. On the floor, where rested a pair of slippers, was spread a thick-coated skin of mountain goat.

Heaped orderly with books, magazines and scribble-pads, there was room on the big reading stand for matches, cigarettes, an ashtray, and a thermos bottle. A phonograph, for purposes of dictation, stood on a hinged and swinging bracket. On the wall, under the barometer and thermometers, from a round wooden frame laughed the face of a girl. On the wall, between the rows of buttons and a switchboard, from an open holster, loosely projected the butt of a .44 Colt's automatic.

At six o'clock, sharp, after gray light had begun to filter through the wire netting, Dick Forrest, without raising his eyes from the proofsheets, reached out his right hand and pressed a button in the second row. Five minutes later a soft-slippered Chinese emerged on the sleeping-porch. In his hands he bore a small tray of burnished copper on which rested a cup and saucer, a tiny coffee pot of silver, and a correspondingly tiny silver cream pitcher.

"Good morning, Oh My," was Dick Forrest's greeting, and his eyes smiled and his lips smiled as he uttered it.

"Good morning, Master," Oh My returned, as he busied himself with making room on the reading stand for the tray and with pouring the coffee and cream.

This done, without waiting further orders, noting that his master was already sipping coffee with one hand while he made a correction on the proof with the other, Oh My picked up a rosy, filmy, lacy boudoir cap from the floor and departed. His exit was noiseless. He ebbed away like a shadow through the open French windows.

At six-thirty, sharp to the minute, he was back with a larger tray.

Dick Forrest put away the proofs, reached for a book entitled "Commercial Breeding of Frogs," and prepared to eat. The breakfast was simple yet fairly substantial—more coffee, a half grape-fruit, two soft-boiled eggs made ready in a glass with a dab of butter and piping hot, and a sliver of bacon, not over-cooked, that he knew was of his own raising and curing.

By this time the sunshine was pouring in through the screening and across the bed. On the outside of the wire screen clung a number of house-flies, early-hatched for the season and numb with the night's cold. As Forrest ate he watched the hunting of the meat-eating yellow- jackets. Sturdy, more frost-resistant than bees, they were already on the wing and preying on the benumbed flies. Despite the rowdy noise of their flight, these yellow hunters of the air, with rarely ever a miss, pounced on their helpless victims and sailed away with them. The last fly was gone ere Forrest had sipped his last sip of coffee, marked "Commercial Breeding of Frogs" with a match, and taken up his proofsheets.

After a time, the liquid-mellow cry of the meadow-lark, first vocal for the day, caused him to desist. He looked at the clock. It marked seven. He set aside the proofs and began a series of conversations by means of the switchboard, which he manipulated with a practiced hand.

"Hello, Oh Joy," was his first talk. "Is Mr. Thayer up?... Very well. Don't disturb him. I don't think he'll breakfast in bed, but find out... . That's right, and show him how to work the hot water. Maybe he doesn't know... Yes, that's right. Plan for one more boy as soon as you can get him. There's always a crowd when the good weather comes on.... Sure. Use your judgment. Good-by."

"Mr. Hanley?... Yes," was his second conversation, over another switch. "I've been thinking about the dam on the Buckeye. I want the figures on the gravel-haul and on the rock-crushing... . Yes, that's it. I imagine that the gravel-haul will cost anywhere between six and ten cents a yard more than the crushed rock. That last pitch of hill is what eats up the gravel-teams. Work out the figures... . No, we won't be able to start for a fortnight... . Yes, yes; the new tractors, if they ever deliver, will release the horses from the plowing, but they'll have to go back for the checking... . No, you'll have to see Mr. Everan about that. Good-by."

And his third call:

"Mr. Dawson? Ha! Ha! Thirty-six on my porch right now. It must be white with frost down on the levels. But it's most likely the last this year... . Yes, they swore the tractors would be delivered two days ago... . Call up the station agent... . By the way, you catch Hanley for me. I forgot to tell him to start the 'rat-catchers' out with the second instalment of fly-traps... . Yes, pronto. There were a couple of dozen roosting on my screen this morning... . Yes... . Good- by."

At this stage, Forrest slid out of bed in his pajamas, slipped his feet into the slippers, and strode through the French windows to the bath, already drawn by Oh My. A dozen minutes afterward, shaved as well, he was back in bed, reading his frog book while Oh My, punctual to the minute, massaged his legs.

They were the well-formed legs of a well-built, five-foot-ten man who weighed a hundred and eighty pounds. Further, they told a tale of the man. The left thigh was marred by a scar ten inches in length. Across the left ankle, from instep to heel, were scattered half a dozen scars the size of half-dollars. When Oh My prodded and pulled the left knee a shade too severely, Forrest was guilty of a wince. The right shin was colored with several dark scars, while a big scar, just under the knee, was a positive dent in the bone. Midway between knee and groin was the mark of an ancient three-inch gash, curiously dotted with the minute scars of stitches.

A sudden, joyous nicker from without put the match between the pages of the frog book, and, while Oh My proceeded partly to dress his master in bed, including socks and shoes, the master, twisting partly on his side, stared out in the direction of the nicker. Down the road, through the swaying purple of the early lilacs, ridden by a picturesque cowboy, paced a great horse, glinting ruddy in the morning sun-gold, flinging free the snowy foam of his mighty fetlocks, his noble crest tossing, his eyes roving afield, the trumpet of his love- call echoing through the springing land.

Dick Forrest was smitten at the same instant with joy and anxiety —joy in the glorious beast pacing down between the lilac hedges; anxiety in that the stallion might have awakened the girl who laughed from the round wooden frame on his wall. He glanced quickly across the two- hundred-foot court to the long, shadowy jut of her wing of the house. The shades of her sleeping-porch were down. They did not stir. Again the stallion nickered, and all that moved was a flock of wild canaries, upspringing from the flowers and shrubs of the court, rising like a green-gold spray of light flung from the sunrise.

He watched the stallion out of sight through the lilacs, seeing visions of fair Shire colts mighty of bone and frame and free from blemish, then turned, as ever he turned to the immediate thing, and spoke to his body servant.

"How's that last boy, Oh My? Showing up?"

"Him pretty good boy, I think," was the answer. "Him young boy. Everything new. Pretty slow. All the same bime by him show up good."

"Why? What makes you think so?"

"I call him three, four morning now. Him sleep like baby. Him wake up smiling just like you. That very good."

"Do I wake up smiling?" Forrest queried.

Oh My nodded his head violently.

"Many times, many years, I call you. Always your eyes open, your eyes smile, your mouth smile, your face smile, you smile all over, just like that, right away quick. That very good. A man wake up that way got plenty good sense. I know. This new boy like that. Bime by, pretty soon, he make fine boy. You see. His name Chow Gam. What name you call him this place?"

Dick Forrest meditated.

"What names have we already?" he asked.

"Oh Joy, Ah Well, Ah Me, and me; I am Oh My," the Chinese rattled off. "Oh Joy him say call new boy—"

He hesitated and stared at his master with a challenging glint of eye. Forrest nodded.

"Oh Joy him say call new boy 'Oh Hell.'"

"Oh ho!" Forrest laughed in appreciation. "Oh Joy is a josher. A good name, but it won't do. There is the Missus. We've got to think another name."

"Oh Ho, that very good name."

Forrest's exclamation was still ringing in his consciousness so that he recognized the source of Oh My's inspiration.

"Very well. The boy's name is Oh Ho."

Oh My lowered his head, ebbed swiftly through the French windows, and as swiftly returned with the rest of Forrest's clothes-gear, helping him into undershirt and shirt, tossing a tie around his neck for him to knot, and, kneeling, putting on his leggings and spurs. A Baden Powell hat and a quirt completed his appareling— the quirt, Indian- braided of rawhide, with ten ounces of lead braided into the butt that hung from his wrist on a loop of leather.

But Forrest was not yet free. Oh My handed him several letters, with the explanation that they had come up from the station the previous night after Forrest had gone to bed. He tore the right-hand ends across and glanced at the contents of all but one with speed. The latter he dwelt upon for a moment, with an irritated indrawing of brows, then swung out the phonograph from the wall, pressed the button that made the cylinder revolve, and swiftly dictated, without ever a pause for word or idea:

"In reply to yours of March 14, 1914, I am indeed sorry to learn that you were hit with hog cholera. I am equally sorry that you have seen fit to charge me with the responsibility. And just as equally am I sorry that the boar we sent you is dead.

"I can only assure you that we are quite clear of cholera here, and that we have been clear of cholera for eight years, with the exception of two Eastern importations, the last two years ago, both of which, according to our custom, were segregated on arrival and were destroyed before the contagion could be communicated to our herds.

"I feel that I must inform you that in neither case did I charge the sellers with having sent me diseased stock. On the contrary, as you should know, the incubation of hog cholera being nine days, I consulted the shipping dates of the animals and knew that they had been healthy when shipped.

"Has it ever entered your mind that the railroads are largely responsible for the spread of cholera? Did you ever hear of a railroad fumigating or disinfecting a car which had carried cholera? Consult the dates: First, of shipment by me; second, of receipt of the boar by you; and, third, of appearance of symptoms in the boar. As you say, because of washouts, the boar was five days on the way. Not until the seventh day after you receipted for same did the first symptoms appear. That makes twelve days after it left my hands.

"No; I must disagree with you. I am not responsible for the disaster that overtook your herd. Furthermore, doubly to assure you, write to the State Veterinary as to whether or not my place is free of cholera.

"Very truly yours… "

Chapter 2

When Forrest went through the French windows from his sleeping-porch, he crossed, first, a comfortable dressing room, window-divaned, many- lockered, with a generous fireplace, out of which opened a bathroom; and, second, a long office room, wherein was all the paraphernalia of business—desks, dictaphones, filing cabinets, book cases, magazine files, and drawer-pigeonholes that tiered to the low, beamed ceiling.

Midway in the office room, he pressed a button and a series of book- freightened shelves swung on a pivot, revealing a tiny spiral stairway of steel, which he descended with care that his spurs might not catch, the bookshelves swinging into place behind him.

At the foot of the stairway, a press on another button pivoted more shelves of books and gave him entrance into a long low room shelved with books from floor to ceiling. He went directly to a case, directly to a shelf, and unerringly laid his hand on the book he sought. A minute he ran the pages, found the passage he was after, nodded his head to himself in vindication, and replaced the book.

A door gave way to a pergola of square concrete columns spanned with redwood logs and interlaced with smaller trunks of redwood, all rough and crinkled velvet with the ruddy purple of the bark.

It was evident, since he had to skirt several hundred feet of concrete walls of wandering house, that he had not taken the short way out. Under wide-spreading ancient oaks, where the long hitching-rails, bark-chewed, and the hoof-beaten gravel showed the stamping place of many horses, he found a pale-golden, almost tan-golden, sorrel mare. Her well-groomed spring coat was alive and flaming in the morning sun that slanted straight under the edge of the roof of trees. She was herself alive and flaming. She was built like a stallion, and down her backbone ran a narrow dark strip of hair that advertised an ancestry of many range mustangs.

"How's the Man-Eater this morning?" he queried, as he unsnapped the tie-rope from her throat.

She laid back the tiniest ears that ever a horse possessed—ears that told of some thoroughbred's wild loves with wild mares among the hills—and snapped at Forrest with wicked teeth and wicked-gleaming eyes.

She sidled and attempted to rear as he swung into the saddle, and, sidling and attempting to rear, she went off down the graveled road. And rear she would have, had it not been for the martingale that held her head down and that, as well, saved the rider's nose from her angry-tossing head.

So used was he to the mare, that he was scarcely aware of her antics. Automatically, with slightest touch of rein against arched neck, or with tickle of spur or press of knee, he kept the mare to the way he willed. Once, as she whirled and danced, he caught a glimpse of the Big House. Big it was in all seeming, and yet, such was the vagrant nature of it, it was not so big as it seemed. Eight hundred feet across the front face, it stretched. But much of this eight hundred feet was composed of mere corridors, concrete-walled, tile-roofed, that connected and assembled the various parts of the building. There were patios and pergolas in proportion, and all the walls, with their many right-angled juts and recessions, arose out of a bed of greenery and bloom.

Spanish in character, the architecture of the Big House was not of the California-Spanish type which had been introduced by way of Mexico a hundred years before, and which had been modified by modern architects to the California-Spanish architecture of the day. Hispano-Moresque more technically classified the Big House in all its hybridness, although there were experts who heatedly quarreled with the term.

Spaciousness without austerity and beauty without ostentation were the fundamental impressions the Big House gave. Its lines, long and horizontal, broken only by lines that were vertical and by the lines of juts and recesses that were always right-angled, were as chaste as those of a monastery. The irregular roof-line, however, relieved the hint of monotony.

Low and rambling, without being squat, the square upthrusts of towers and of towers over-topping towers gave just proportion of height without being sky-aspiring. The sense of the Big House was solidarity. It defied earthquakes. It was planted for a thousand years. The honest concrete was overlaid by a cream-stucco of honest cement. Again, this very sameness of color might have proved monotonous to the eye had it not been saved by the many flat roofs of warm-red Spanish tile.

In that one sweeping glance while the mare whirled unduly, Dick

Forrest's eyes, embracing all of the Big House, centered for a quick solicitous instant on the great wing across the two-hundred-foot court, where, under climbing groups of towers, red-snooded in the morning sun, the drawn shades of the sleeping-porch tokened that his lady still slept.

About him, for three quadrants of the circle of the world, arose low- rolling hills, smooth, fenced, cropped, and pastured, that melted into higher hills and steeper wooded slopes that merged upward, steeper, into mighty mountains. The fourth quadrant was unbounded by mountain walls and hills. It faded away, descending easily to vast far flatlands, which, despite the clear brittle air of frost, were too vast and far to scan across.

The mare under him snorted. His knees tightened as he straightened her into the road and forced her to one side. Down upon him, with a pattering of feet on the gravel, flowed a river of white shimmering silk. He knew it at sight for his prize herd of Angora goats, each with a pedigree, each with a history. There had to be a near two hundred of them, and he knew, according to the rigorous selection he commanded, not having been clipped in the fall, that the shining mohair draping the sides of the least of them, as fine as any human new-born baby's hair and finer, as white as any human albino's thatch and whiter, was longer than the twelve-inch staple, and that the mohair of the best of them would dye any color into twenty-inch switches for women's heads and sell at prices unreasonable and profound.

The beauty of the sight held him as well. The roadway had become a flowing ribbon of silk, gemmed with yellow cat-like eyes that floated past wary and curious in their regard for him and his nervous horse. Two Basque herders brought up the rear. They were short, broad, swarthy men, black-eyed, vivid-faced, contemplative and philosophic of expression. They pulled off their hats and ducked their heads to him. Forrest lifted his right hand, the quirt dangling from wrist, the straight forefinger touching the rim of his Baden Powell in semi- military salute.

The mare, prancing and whirling again, he held her with a touch of rein and threat of spur, and gazed after the four-footed silk that filled the road with shimmering white. He knew the significance of their presence. The time for kidding was approaching and they were being brought down from their brush-pastures to the brood-pens and shelters for jealous care and generous feed through the period of increase. And as he gazed, in his mind, comparing, was a vision of all the best of Turkish and South African mohair he had ever seen, and his flock bore the comparison well. It looked good.

It looked very good.

He rode on. From all about arose the clacking whir of manure-spreaders. In the distance, on the low, easy-sloping hills, he saw team after team, and many teams, three to a team abreast, what he knew were his Shire mares, drawing the plows back and forth across, contour-plowing, turning the green sod of the hillsides to the rich dark brown of humus-filled earth so organic and friable that it would almost melt by gravity into fine-particled seed-bed. That was for the corn—and sorghum-planting for his silos. Other hill-slopes, in the due course of his rotation, were knee-high in barley; and still other slopes were showing the good green of burr clover and Canada pea.

Everywhere about him, large fields and small were arranged in a system of accessibility and workability that would have warmed the heart of the most meticulous efficiency-expert. Every fence was hog-tight and bull-proof, and no weeds grew in the shelters of the fences. Many of the level fields were in alfalfa. Others, following the rotations, bore crops planted the previous fall, or were in preparation for the spring-planting. Still others, close to the brood barns and pens, were being grazed by rotund Shropshire and French-Merino ewes, or were being hogged off by white Gargantuan brood-sows that brought a flash of pleasure in his eyes as he rode past and gazed.

He rode through what was almost a village, save that there were neither shops nor hotels. The houses were bungalows, substantial, pleasing to the eye, each set in the midst of gardens where stouter blooms, including roses, were out and smiling at the threat of late frost. Children were already astir, laughing and playing among the flowers or being called in to breakfast by their mothers.

Beyond, beginning at a half-mile distant to circle the Big House, he passed a row of shops. He paused at the first and glanced in. One smith was working at a forge. A second smith, a shoe fresh-nailed on the fore-foot of an elderly Shire mare that would disturb the scales at eighteen hundred weight, was rasping down the outer wall of the hoof to smooth with the toe of the shoe. Forrest saw, saluted, rode on, and, a hundred feet away, paused and scribbled a memorandum in the notebook he drew from his hip-pocket.

He passed other shops—a paint-shop, a wagon-shop, a plumbing shop, a carpenter-shop. While he glanced at the last, a hybrid machine, half- auto, half-truck, passed him at speed and took the main road for the railroad station eight miles away. He knew it for the morning butter- truck freighting from the separator house the daily output of the dairy.

The Big House was the hub of the ranch organization. Half a mile from it, it was encircled by the various ranch centers. Dick Forrest, saluting continually his people, passed at a gallop the dairy center, which was almost a sea of buildings with batteries of silos and with litter carriers emerging on overhead tracks and automatically dumping into waiting manure-spreaders. Several times, business-looking men, college-marked, astride horses or driving carts, stopped him and conferred with him. They were foremen, heads of departments, and they were as brief and to the point as was he. The last of them, astride a Palomina three-year-old that was as graceful and wild as a half-broken Arab, was for riding by with a bare salute, but was stopped by his employer.

"Good morning, Mr. Hennessy, and how soon will she be ready for Mrs. Forrest?" Dick Forrest asked.

"I'd like another week," was Hennessy's answer. "She's well broke now, just the way Mrs. Forrest wanted, but she's over-strung and sensitive and I'd like the week more to set her in her ways."

Forrest nodded concurrence, and Hennessy, who was the veterinary, went on:

"There are two drivers in the alfalfa gang I'd like to send down the hill."

"What's the matter with them?"

"One, a new man, Hopkins, is an ex-soldier. He may know government mules, but he doesn't know Shires."

Forrest nodded.

"The other has worked for us two years, but he's drinking now, and he takes his hang-overs out on his horses—"

"That's Smith, old-type American, smooth-shaven, with a cast in his left eye?" Forrest interrupted.

The veterinary nodded.

"I've been watching him," Forrest concluded. "He was a good man at first, but he's slipped a cog recently. Sure, send him down the hill. And send that other fellow—Hopkins, you said?—along with him. By the way, Mr. Hennessy." As he spoke, Forrest drew forth his pad book, tore off the last note scribbled, and crumpled it in his hand. "You've a new horse-shoer in the shop. How does he strike you?"

"He's too new to make up my mind yet."

"Well, send him down the hill along with the other two. He can't take your orders. I observed him just now fitting a shoe to old Alden Bessie by rasping off half an inch of the toe of her hoof."

"He knew better."

"Send him down the hill," Forrest repeated, as he tickled his

14

champing mount with the slightest of spur-tickles and shot her out along the road, sidling, head-tossing, and attempting to rear.

Much he saw that pleased him. Once, he murmured aloud, "A fat land, a fat land." Divers things he saw that did not please him and that won a note in his scribble pad. Completing the circle about the Big House and riding beyond the circle half a mile to an isolated group of sheds and corrals, he reached the objective of the ride: the hospital. Here he found but two young heifers being tested for tuberculosis, and a magnificent Duroc Jersey boar in magnificent condition. Weighing fully six hundred pounds, its bright eyes, brisk movements, and sheen of hair shouted out that there was nothing the matter with it. Nevertheless, according to the ranch practice, being a fresh importation from Iowa, it was undergoing the regular period of quarantine. Burgess Premier was its name in the herd books of the association, age two years, and it had cost Forrest five hundred dollars laid down on the ranch.

Proceeding at a hand gallop along a road that was one of the spokes radiating from the Big House hub, Forrest overtook Crellin, his hog manager, and, in a five-minute conference, outlined the next few months of destiny of Burgess Premier, and learned that the brood sow, Lady Isleton, the matron of all matrons of the O. I. C.'s and blue- ribbonner in all shows from Seattle to San Diego, was safely farrowed of eleven. Crellin explained that he had sat up half the night with her and was then bound home for bath and breakfast.

"I hear your oldest daughter has finished high school and wants to enter Stanford," Forrest said, curbing the mare just as he had half- signaled departure at a gallop.

Crellin, a young man of thirty-five, with the maturity of a long-time father stamped upon him along with the marks of college and the youthfulness of a man used to the open air and straight-living, showed his appreciation of his employer's interest as he half-flushed under his tan and nodded.

"Think it over," Forrest advised. "Make a statistic of all the college girls—yes, and State Normal girls—you know. How many of them follow career, and how many of them marry within two years after their degrees and take to baby farming."

"Helen is very seriously bent on the matter," Crellin urged.

"Do you remember when I had my appendix out?" Forrest queried. "Well, I had as fine a nurse as I ever saw and as nice a girl as ever walked on two nice legs. She was just six months a full-fledged nurse, then. And four months after that I had to send her a wedding present. She married an automobile agent. She's lived in hotels ever since. She's never had a chance to nurse—never a child of her own to bring through a bout with colic. But... she has hopes... and, whether or not her hopes materialize, she's confoundedly happy. But... what good was her nursing apprenticeship?"

Just then an empty manure-spreader passed, forcing Crellin, on foot, and Forrest, on his mare, to edge over to the side of the road. Forrest glanced with kindling eye at the off mare of the machine, a huge, symmetrical Shire whose own blue ribbons, and the blue ribbons of her progeny, would have required an expert accountant to enumerate and classify.

"Look at the Fotherington Princess," Forrest said, nodding at the mare that warmed his eye. "She is a normal female. Only incidentally, through thousands of years of domestic selection, has man evolved her into a draught beast breeding true to kind. But being a draught-beast is secondary. Primarily she is a female. Take them by and large, our own human females, above all else, love us men and are intrinsically maternal. There is no biological sanction for all the hurly burly of woman to-day for suffrage and career."

"But there is an economic sanction," Crellin objected.

"True," his employer agreed, then proceeded to discount. "Our present industrial system prevents marriage and compels woman to career. But, remember, industrial systems come, and industrial systems go, while biology runs on forever."

"It's rather hard to satisfy young women with marriage these days," the hog-manager demurred.

Dick Forrest laughed incredulously.

"I don't know about that," he said. "There's your wife for an instance. She with her sheepskin—classical scholar at that—well, what has she done with it?... Two boys and three girls, I believe? As I remember your telling me, she was engaged to you the whole last half of her senior year."

"True, but—" Crellin insisted, with an eye-twinkle of appreciation of the point, "that was fifteen years ago, as well as a love-match. We just couldn't help it. That far, I agree. She had planned unheard-of achievements, while I saw nothing else than the deanship of the College of Agriculture. We just couldn't help it. But that was fifteen years ago, and fifteen years have made all the difference in the world in the ambitions and ideals of our young women."

"Don't you believe it for a moment. I tell you, Mr. Crellin, it's a statistic. All contrary things are transient. Ever woman remains Avoman, everlasting, eternal. Not until our girl-children cease from playing with dolls and from looking at their own enticingness in mirrors, will woman ever be otherwise than what she has always been: first, the mother, second, the mate of man. It is a statistic. I've been looking up the girls who graduate from the State Normal. You will notice that those who marry by the way before graduation are excluded. Nevertheless, the average length of time the graduates actually teach school is little more than two years. And when you consider that a lot of them, through ill looks and ill luck, are foredoomed old maids and are foredoomed to teach all their lives, you can see how they cut down the period of teaching of the marriageable ones."

"A woman, even a girl-woman, will have her way where mere men are concerned," Crellin muttered, unable to dispute his employer's figures but resolved to look them up.

"And your girl-woman will go to Stanford," Forrest laughed, as he prepared to lift his mare into a gallop, "and you and I and all men, to the end of time, will see to it that they do have their way."

Crellin smiled to himself as his employer diminished down the road; for Crellin knew his Kipling, and the thought that caused the smile was: "But where's the kid of your own, Mr. Forrest?" He decided to repeat it to Mrs. Crellin over the breakfast coffee.

Once again Dick Forrest delayed ere he gained the Big House. The man he stopped he addressed as Mendenhall, who was his horse-manager as well as pasture expert, and who was reputed to know, not only every blade of grass on the ranch, but the length of every blade of grass and its age from seed-germination as well.

At signal from Forrest, Mendenhall drew up the two colts he was driving in a double breaking-cart. What had caused Forrest to signal was a glance he had caught, across the northern edge of the valley, of great, smooth-hill ranges miles beyond, touched by the sun and deeply green where they projected into the vast flat of the Sacramento Valley.

The talk that followed was quick and abbreviated to terms of understanding between two men who knew. Grass was the subject. Mention was made of the winter rainfall and of the chance for late spring rains to come. Names occurred, such as the Little Coyote and Los Cuatos creeks, the Yolo and the Miramar hills, the Big Basin, Round Valley, and the San Anselmo and Los Banos ranges. Movements of herds and droves, past, present, and to come, were discussed, as well as the outlook for cultivated hay in far upland pastures and the estimates of such hay that still remained over the winter in remote barns in the sheltered mountain valleys where herds had wintered and been fed.

Under the oaks, at the stamping posts, Forrest was saved the trouble of tying the Man-Eater. A stableman came on the run to take the mare, and Forrest, scarce pausing for a word about a horse by the name of Duddy, was clanking his spurs into the Big House.

Chapter 3

Forrest entered a section of the Big House by way of a massive, hewn- timber, iron-studded door that let in at the foot of what seemed a donjon keep. The floor was cement, and doors let off in various directions. One, opening to a Chinese in the white apron and starched cap of a chef, emitted at the same time the low hum of a dynamo. It was this that deflected Forrest from his straight path. He paused, holding the door ajar, and peered into a cool, electric-lighted cement room where stood a long, glass-fronted, glass-shelved refrigerator flanked by an ice-machine and a dynamo. On the floor, in greasy overalls, squatted a greasy little man to whom his employer nodded.

"Anything wrong, Thompson?" he asked.

"There *was*," was the answer, positive and complete.

Forrest closed the door and went on along a passage that was like a tunnel. Narrow, iron-barred openings, like the slits for archers in medieval castles, dimly lighted the way. Another door gave access to a long, low room, beam-ceilinged, with a fireplace in which an ox could have been roasted. A huge stump, resting on a bed of coals, blazed brightly. Two billiard tables, several card tables, lounging corners, and a miniature bar constituted the major furnishing. Two young men chalked their cues and returned Forrest's greeting.

"Good morning, Mr. Naismith," he bantered. "—More material for the *Breeders' Gazette*?"

Naismith, a youngish man of thirty, with glasses, smiled sheepishly and cocked his head at his companion.

"Wainwright challenged me," he explained.

"Which means that Lute and Ernestine must still be beauty-sleeping," Forrest laughed.

Young Wainwright bristled to acceptance of the challenge, but before he could utter the retort on his lips his host was moving on and addressing Naismith over his shoulder.

"Do you want to come along at eleven:thirty? Thayer and I are running out in the machine to look over the Shropshires. He wants about ten carloads of rams. You ought to find good stuff in this matter of Idaho shipments. Bring your camera along.—Seen Thayer this morning?"

"Just came in to breakfast as we were leaving," Bert Wainwright volunteered.

"Tell him to be ready at eleven-thirty if you see him. You're not invited, Bert... out of kindness. The girls are sure to be up then."

"Take Rita along with you anyway," Bert pleaded.

"No fear," was Forrest's reply from the door. "We're on business. Besides, you can't pry Rita from Ernestine with block-and-tackle."

"That's why I wanted to see if you could," Bert grinned.

"Funny how fellows never appreciate their own sisters." Forrest paused for a perceptible moment. "I always thought Rita was a real nice sister. What's the matter with her?"

Before a reply could reach him, he had closed the door and was jingling his spurs along the passage to a spiral stairway of broad concrete steps. As he left the head of the stairway, a dance-time piano measure and burst of laughter made him peep into a white morning room, flooded with sunshine. A young girl, in rose-colored kimono and boudoir cap, was at the instrument, while two others, similarly accoutered, in each other's arms, were parodying a dance never learned at dancing school nor intended by the participants for male eyes to see.

The girl at the piano discovered him, winked, and played on. Not for another minute did the dancers spy him. They gave startled cries, collapsed, laughing, in each other's arms, and the music stopped. They were gorgeous, healthy young creatures, the three of them, and Forrest's eye kindled as he looked at them in quite the same way that it had kindled when he regarded the Fotherington Princess.

Persiflage, of the sort that obtains among young things of the human kind, flew back and forth.

"I've been here five minutes," Dick Forrest asserted.

The two dancers, to cover their confusion, doubted his veracity and instanced his many well-known and notorious guilts of mendacity. The girl at the piano, Ernestine, his sister-in-law, insisted that pearls of truth fell from his lips, that she had seen him from the moment he began to look, and that as she estimated the passage of time he had been looking much longer than five minutes.

"Well, anyway," Forrest broke in on their babel, "Bert, the sweet innocent, doesn't think you are up yet."

"We're not... to him," one of the dancers, a vivacious young Venus, retorted. "Nor are we to you either. So run along, little boy. Run along."

"Look here, Lute," Forrest began sternly. "Just because I am a decrepit old man, and just because you are eighteen, just eighteen, and happen to be my wife's sister, you needn't presume to put the high and mighty over on me. Don't forget—and I state the fact, disagreeable as it may be, for Rita's sake—don't forget that in the past ten years I've paddled you more disgraceful times than you care to dare me to enumerate.

"It is true, I am not so young as I used to was, but—" He felt the biceps of his right arm and made as if to roll up the sleeve. "—But, I'm not all in yet, and for two cents... "

"What?" the young woman challenged belligerently.

"For two cents," he muttered darkly. "For two cents... Besides, and it grieves me to inform you, your cap is not on straight. Also, it is not a very tasteful creation at best. I could make a far more becoming cap with my toes, asleep, and... yes, seasick as well."

Lute tossed her blond head defiantly, glanced at her comrades in solicitation of support, and said:

"Oh, I don't know. It seems humanly reasonable that the three of us can woman-handle a mere man of your elderly and insulting avoirdupois. What do you say, girls? Let's rush him. He's not a minute under forty, and he has an aneurism. Yes, and though loath to divulge family secrets, he's got Meniere's Disease."

Ernestine, a small but robust blonde of eighteen, sprang from the piano and joined her two comrades in a raid on the cushions of the deep window seats. Side by side, a cushion in each hand, and with proper distance between them cannily established for the swinging of the cushions, they advanced upon the foe.

Forrest prepared for battle, then held up his hand for parley.

"'Fraid cat!" they taunted, in several at first, and then in chorus.

He shook his head emphatically.

"Just for that, and for all the rest of your insolences, the three of you are going to get yours. All the wrongs of a lifetime are rising now in my brain in a dazzling brightness. I shall go Berserk in a moment. But first, and I speak as an agriculturist, and I address myself to you, Lute, in all humility, in heaven's name what is Meniere's Disease? Do sheep catch it?"

"Meniere's Disease is," Lute began,... "is what you've got. Sheep are the only known living creatures that get it."

Ensued red war and chaos. Forrest made a football rush of the sort that obtained in California before the adoption of Rugby; and the girls broke the line to let him through, turned upon him, flanked him on either side, and pounded him with cushions.

He turned, with widespread arms, extended fingers, each finger a hook, and grappled the three. The battle became a whirlwind, a bespurred man the center, from which radiated flying draperies of flimsy silk, disconnected slippers, boudoir caps, and hairpins. There were thuds from the cushions, grunts from the man, squeals, yelps and giggles from the girls, and from the totality of the combat inextinguishable laughter and a ripping and tearing of fragile textures.

Dick Forrest found himself sprawled on the floor, the wind half knocked out of him by shrewdly delivered cushions, his head buzzing from the buffeting, and, in one hand, a trailing, torn, and generally disrupted girdle of pale blue silk and pink roses.

In one doorway, cheeks flaming from the struggle, stood Rita, alert as a fawn and ready to flee. In the other doorway, likewise flame- checked, stood Ernestine in the commanding attitude of the Mother of the Gracchi, the wreckage of her kimono wrapped severely about her and held severely about her by her own waist-pressing arm. Lute, cornered behind the piano, attempted to run but was driven back by the menace of Forrest, who, on hands and knees, stamped loudly with the palms of his hands on the hardwood floor, rolled his head savagely, and emitted bull-like roars.

"And they still believe that old prehistoric myth," Ernestine proclaimed from safety, "that once he, that wretched semblance of a man-thing prone in the dirt, captained Berkeley to victory over Stanford."

Her breasts heaved from the exertion, and he marked the pulsating of the shimmering cherry-colored silk with delight as he flung his glance around to the other two girls similarly breathing.

The piano was a miniature grand—a dainty thing of rich white and gold to match the morning room. It stood out from the wall, so that there was possibility for Lute to escape around either way of it. Forrest gained his feet and faced her across the broad, flat top of the instrument. As he threatened to vault it, Lute cried out in horror:

"But your spurs, Dick! Your spurs!"

"Give me time to take them off," he offered.

As he stooped to unbuckle them, Lute darted to escape, but was herded back to the shelter of the piano.

"All right," he growled. "On your head be it. If the piano's scratched I'll tell Paula."

"I've got witnesses," she panted, indicating with her blue joyous eyes the young things in the doorways.

"Very well, my dear." Forrest drew back his body and spread his resting palms. "I'm coming over to you."

Action and speech were simultaneous. His body, posited sidewise from his hands, was vaulted across, the perilous spurs a full foot above the glossy white surface. And simultaneously Lute ducked and went under the piano on hands and knees. Her mischance lay in that she bumped her head, and, before she could recover way, Forrest had circled the piano and cornered her under it.

"Come out!" he commanded. "Come out and take your medicine!"

"A truce," she pleaded. "A truce, Sir Knight, for dear love's sake and all damsels in distress."

"I ain't no knight," Forrest announced in his deepest bass. "I'm an ogre, a filthy, debased and altogether unregenerate ogre. I was born in the tule-swamps. My father was an ogre and my mother was more so. I was lulled to slumber on the squalls of infants dead, foreordained, and predamned. I was nourished solely on the blood of maidens educated in Mills Seminary. My favorite chophouse has ever been a hardwood floor, a loaf of Mills Seminary maiden, and a roof of flat piano. My father, as well as an ogre, was a California horse-thief. I am more reprehensible than my father. I have more teeth. My mother, as well as an ogress, was a Nevada book-canvasser. Let all her shame be told. She even solicited subscriptions for ladies' magazines. I am more terrible than my mother. I have peddled safety razors."

"Can naught soothe and charm your savage breast?" Lute pleaded in soulful tones while she studied her chances for escape.

"One thing only, miserable female. One thing only, on the earth, over the earth, and under its ruining waters—"

A squawk of recognized plagiarism interrupted him from Ernestine.

"See Ernest Dowson, page seventy-nine, a thin book of thin verse ladled out with porridge to young women detentioned at Mills Seminary," Forrest went on. "As I had already enunciated before I was so rudely interrupted, the one thing only that can balm and embalm this savage breast is the 'Maiden's Prayer.' Listen, with all your ears ere I chew them off in multitude and gross! Listen, silly, unbeautiful, squat, short-legged and ugly female under the piano! Can you recite the 'Maiden's Prayer'?"

Screams of delight from the young things in the doorways prevented the proper answer and Lute, from under the piano, cried out to young Wainwright, who had appeared:

"A rescue, Sir Knight! A rescue!"

"Unhand the maiden!" was Bert's challenge.

"Who art thou?" Forrest demanded.

"King George, sirrah!—I mean, er, Saint George."

"Then am I thy dragon," Forrest announced with due humility. "Spare this ancient, honorable, and only neck I have."

"Off with his head!" the young things encouraged.

"Stay thee, maidens, I pray thee," Bert begged. "I am only a Small Potato. Yet am I unafraid. I shall beard the dragon. I shall beard him in his gullet, and, while he lingeringly chokes to death over my unpalatableness and general spinefulness, do you, fair damsels, flee to the mountains lest the valleys fall upon you. Yolo, Petaluma, and West Sacramento are about to be overwhelmed by a tidal wave and many big fishes."

"Off with his head!" the young things chanted. "Slay him in his blood and barbecue him!"

"Thumbs down," Forrest groaned. "I am undone. Trust to the unstrained quality of mercy possessed by Christian young women in the year 1914 who will vote some day if ever they grow up and do not marry foreigners. Consider my head off, Saint George. I am expired. Further deponent sayeth not."

And Forrest, with sobs and slubberings, with realistic shudders and kicks and a great jingling of spurs, lay down on the floor and expired.

Lute crawled out from under the piano, and was joined by Rita and Ernestine in an extemporized dance of the harpies about the slain.

In the midst of it, Forrest sat up, protesting. Also, he was guilty of a significant and privy wink to Lute.

"The hero!" he cried. "Forget him not. Crown him with flowers."

And Bert was crowned with flowers from the vases, unchanged from the day before. When a bunch of water-logged stems of early tulips, propelled by Lute's vigorous arm, impacted soggily on his neck under the ear, he fled. The riot of pursuit echoed along the hall and died out down the stairway toward the stag room. Forrest gathered himself together, and, grinning, went jingling on through the Big House.

He crossed two patios on brick walks roofed with Spanish tile and swamped with early foliage and blooms, and gained his wing of the house, still breathing from the fun, to find, in the office, his secretary awaiting him.

"Good morning, Mr. Blake," he greeted. "Sorry I was delayed." He glanced at his wrist-watch. "Only four minutes, however. I just couldn't get away sooner."

Chapter 4

From nine till ten Forrest gave himself up to his secretary, achieving a correspondence that included learned societies and every sort of breeding and agricultural organization and that would have compelled the average petty business man, unaided, to sit up till midnight to accomplish.

For Dick Forrest was the center of a system which he himself had built and of which he was secretly very proud. Important letters and documents he signed with his ragged fist. All other letters were rubber-stamped by Mr. Blake, who, also, in shorthand, in the course of the hour, put down the indicated answers to many letters and received the formula designations of reply to many other letters. Mr. Blake's private opinion was that he worked longer hours than his employer, although it was equally his private opinion that his employer was a wonder for discovering work for others to perform.

At ten, to the stroke of the clock, as Pittman, Forrest's show-manager, entered the office, Blake, burdened with trays of correspondence, sheafs of documents, and phonograph cylinders, faded away to his own office.

From ten to eleven a stream of managers and foremen flowed in and out. All were well disciplined in terseness and time-saving. As Dick Forrest had taught them, the minutes spent with him were not minutes of cogitation. They must be prepared before they reported or suggested. Bonbright, the assistant secretary, always arrived at ten to replace Blake; and Bonbright, close to shoulder, with flying pencil, took down the rapid-fire interchange of question and answer, statement and proposal and plan. These shorthand notes, transcribed and typed in duplicate, were the nightmare and, on occasion, the Nemesis, of the managers and foremen. For, first, Forrest had a remarkable memory; and, second, he was prone to prove its worth by reference to those same notes of Bonbright.

A manager, at the end of a five or ten minute session, often emerged sweating, limp and frazzled. Yet for a swift hour, at high tension, Forrest met all comers, with a master's grip handling them and all the multifarious details of their various departments. He told Thompson, the machinist, in four flashing minutes, where the fault lay in the dynamo to the Big House refrigerator, laid the fault home to Thompson, dictated a note to Bonbright, with citation by page and chapter to a volume from the library to be drawn by Thompson, told Thompson that Parkman, the dairy manager, was not satisfied with the latest wiring up of milking machines, and that the refrigerating plant at the slaughter house was balking at its accustomed load.

Each man was a specialist, yet Forrest was the proved master of their specialties. As Paulson, the head plowman, complained privily to Dawson, the crop manager: "I've worked here twelve years and never have I seen him put his hands to a plow, and yet, damn him, he somehow seems to know. He's a genius, that's what he is. Why, d'ye know, I've seen him tear by a piece of work, his hands full with that Man-Eater of his a-threatenin' sudden funeral, an', next morning, had 'm mention casually to a half-inch how deep it was plowed an' what plows'd done the plowin'!—Take that plowin' of the Poppy Meadow, up above Little Meadow, on Los Cuatos. I just couldn't see my way to it, an' had to cut out the cross-sub-soiling, an' thought I could slip it over on him. After it was all finished he kind of happened up that way—I was lookin' an' he didn't seem to look—an', well, next A.M. I got mine in the office. No; I didn't slip it over. I ain't tried to slip nothing over since."

At eleven sharp, Wardman, his sheep manager, departed with an engagement scheduled at eleven: thirty to ride in the machine along with Thayer, the Idaho buyer, to look over the Shropshire rams. At eleven, Bonbright having departed with Wardman to work up his notes, Forrest was left alone in the office. From a wire tray of unfinished business—one of many wire trays superimposed in groups of five—he drew a pamphlet issued by the State of Iowa on hog cholera and proceeded to scan it.

Five feet, ten inches in height, weighing a clean-muscled one hundred and eighty pounds, Dick Forrest was anything but insignificant for a forty years' old man. The eyes were gray, large, over-arched by bone of brow, and lashes and brows were dark. The hair, above an ordinary forehead, was light brown to chestnut. Under the forehead, the cheeks showed high-boned, with underneath the slight hollows that necessarily accompany such formation. The jaws were strong without massiveness, the nose, large-nostriled, was straight enough and prominent enough without being too straight or prominent, the chin square without harshness and uncleft, and the mouth girlish and sweet to a degree that did not hide the firmness to which the lips could set on due provocation. The skin was smooth and well-tanned, although, midway between eyebrows and hair, the tan of forehead faded in advertisement of the rim of the Baden Powell interposed between him and the sun.

Laughter lurked in the mouth corners and eye-corners, and there were cheek lines about the mouth that would seem to have been formed by laughter. Equally strong, however, every line of the face that meant blended things carried a notice of surety. Dick Forrest was sure— sure, when his hand reached out for any object on his desk, that the hand would straightly attain the object without a fumble or a miss of a fraction of an inch; sure, when his brain leaped the high places of the hog cholera text, that it was not missing a point; sure, from his balanced body in the revolving desk-chair to the balanced back-head of him; sure, in heart and brain, of life and work, of all he possessed, and of himself.

He had reason to be sure. Body, brain, and career were long-proven sure. A rich man's son, he had not played ducks and drakes with his father's money. City born and reared, he had gone back to the land and made such a success as to put his name on the lips of breeders wherever breeders met and talked. He was the owner, without encumbrance, of two hundred and fifty thousand acres of land—land that varied in value from a thousand dollars an acre to a hundred dollars, that varied from a hundred dollars to ten cents an acre, and that, in stretches, was not worth a penny an acre. The improvements on that quarter of a million acres, from drain-tiled meadows to dredge- drained tule swamps, from good roads to developed water-rights, from farm buildings to the Big House itself, constituted a sum gaspingly ungraspable to the country-side.

Everything was large-scale but modern to the last tick of the clock. His managers lived, rent-free, with salaries commensurate to ability, in five—and ten-thousand-dollar houses—but they were the cream of specialists skimmed from the continent from the Atlantic to the Pacific. When he ordered gasoline-tractors for the cultivation of the flat lands, he ordered a round score. When he dammed water in his mountains he dammed it by the hundreds of millions of gallons. When he ditched his tule-swamps, instead of contracting the excavation, he bought the huge dredgers outright, and, when there was slack work on his own marshes, he contracted for the draining of the marshes of neighboring big farmers, land companies, and corporations for a hundred miles up and down the Sacramento River.

He had brain sufficient to know the need of buying brains and to pay a tidy bit over the current market price for the most capable brains. And he had brain sufficient to direct the brains he bought to a profitable conclusion.

And yet, he was just turned forty was clear-eyed, calm-hearted, hearty-pulsed, man-strong; and yet, his history, until he was thirty, had been harum-scarum and erratic to the superlative. He had run away from a millionaire home when he was thirteen. He had won enviable college honors ere he was twenty-one and after that he had known all the purple ports of the purple seas, and, with cool head, hot heart, and laughter, played every risk that promised and provided in the wild world of adventure that he had lived to see pass under the sobriety of law.

In the old days of San Francisco Forrest had been a name to conjure with. The Forrest Mansion had been one of the pioneer palaces on Nob Hill where dwelt the Floods, the Mackays, the Crockers, and the O'Briens. "Lucky" Richard Forrest, the father, had arrived, via the Isthmus, straight from old New England, keenly commercial, interested before his departure in clipper ships and the building of clipper ships, and interested immediately after his arrival in water-front real estate, river steamboats, mines, of course, and, later, in the draining of the Nevada Comstock and the construction of the Southern Pacific.

He played big, he won big, he lost big; but he won always more than he lost, and what he paid out at one game with one hand, he drew back with his other hand at another game. His winnings from the Comstock he sank into the various holes of the bottomless Daffodil Group in Eldorado County. The wreckage from the Benicia Line he turned into the Napa Consolidated, which was a quicksilver venture, and it earned him five thousand per cent. What he lost in the collapse of the Stockton boom was more than balanced by the realty appreciation of his key- holdings at Sacramento and Oakland.

And, to cap it all, when "Lucky" Richard Forrest had lost everything in a series of calamities, so that San Francisco debated what price his Nob Hill palace would fetch at auction, he grubstaked one, Del Nelson, to a prospecting in Mexico. As soberly set down in history, the result of the said Del Nelson's search for quartz was the Harvest Group, including the fabulous and inexhaustible Tattlesnake, Voice, City, Desdemona, Bullfrog, and Yellow Boy claims. Del Nelson, astounded by his achievement, within the year drowned himself in an enormous quantity of cheap whisky, and, the will being incontestible through lack of kith and kin, left his half to Lucky Richard Forrest.

Dick Forrest was the son of his father. Lucky Richard, a man of boundless energy and enterprise, though twice married and twice widowed, had not been blessed with children. His third marriage occurred in 1872, when he was fifty-eight, and in 1874, although he lost the mother, a twelve-pound boy, stout-barreled and husky-lunged, remained to be brought up by a regiment of nurses in the palace on Nob Hill.

Young Dick was precocious. Lucky Richard was a democrat. Result: Young Dick learned in a year from a private teacher what would have required three years in the grammar school, and used all of the saved years in playing in the open air. Also, result of precocity of son and democracy of father, Young Dick was sent to grammar school for the last year in order to learn shoulder-rubbing democracy with the sons and daughters of workmen, tradesmen, saloon-keepers and politicians.

In class recitation or spelling match his father's millions did not aid him in competing with Patsy Halloran, the mathematical prodigy whose father was a hod-carrier, nor with Mona Sanguinetti who was a wizard at spelling and whose widowed mother ran a vegetable store. Nor were his father's millions and the Nob Hill palace of the slightest assistance to Young Dick when he peeled his jacket and, bareknuckled, without rounds, licking or being licked, milled it to a finish with Jimmy Botts, Jean Choyinsky, and the rest of the lads that went out over the world to glory and cash a few years later, a generation of prizefighters that only San Francisco, raw and virile and yeasty and young, could have produced.

The wisest thing Lucky Richard did for his boy was to give him this democratic tutelage. In his secret heart, Young Dick never forgot that he lived in a palace of many servants and that his father was a man of power and honor. On the other hand, Young Dick learned two-legged, two-fisted democracy. He learned it when Mona Sanguinetti spelled him down in class. He learned it when Berney Miller out-dodged and out-ran him when running across in Black Man.

And when Tim Hagan, with straight left for the hundredth time to bleeding nose and mangled mouth, and with ever reiterant right hook to stomach, had him dazed and reeling, the breath whistling and sobbing through his lacerated lips—was no time for succor from palaces and bank accounts. On his two legs, with his two fists, it was either he or Tim. And it was right there, in sweat and blood and iron of soul, that Young Dick learned how not to lose a losing fight. It had been uphill from the first blow, but he stuck it out until in the end it was agreed that neither could best the other, although this agreement was not reached until they had first lain on the ground in nausea and exhaustion and with streaming eyes wept their rage and defiance at each other. After that, they became chums and between them ruled the schoolyard.

Lucky Richard died the same month Young Dick emerged from grammar school. Young Dick was thirteen years old, with twenty million dollars, and without a relative in the world to trouble him. He was the master of a palace of servants, a steam yacht, stables, and, as well, of a summer palace down the Peninsula in the nabob colony at Menlo. One thing, only, was he burdened with: guardians.

On a summer afternoon, in the big library, he attended the first session of his board of guardians. There were three of them, all elderly, and successful, all legal, all business comrades of his father. Dick's impression, as they explained things to him, was that, although they meant well, he had no contacts with them. In his judgment, their boyhood was too far behind them. Besides that, it was patent that him, the particular boy they were so much concerned with, they did not understand at all. Furthermore, in his own sure way he decided that he was the one person in the world fitted to know what was best for himself.

Mr. Crockett made a long speech, to which Dick listened with alert and becoming attention, nodding his head whenever he was directly addressed or appealed to. Messrs. Davidson and Slocum also had their say and were treated with equal consideration. Among other things, Dick learned what a sterling, upright man his father had been, and the program already decided upon by the three gentlemen which would make him into a sterling and upright man.

When they were quite done, Dick took it upon himself to say a few things.

"I have thought it over," he announced, "and first of all I shall go traveling."

"That will come afterward, my boy," Mr. Slocum explained soothingly. "When—say—when you are ready to enter the university. At that time a year abroad would be a very good thing... a very good thing indeed."

"Of course," Mr. Davidson volunteered quickly, having noted the annoyed light in the lad's eyes and the unconscious firm-drawing and setting of the lips, "of course, in the meantime you could do some traveling, a limited amount of traveling, during your school vacations. I am sure my fellow guardians will agree—under the proper management and safeguarding, of course—that such bits of travel sandwiched between your school-terms, would be advisable and beneficial."

"How much did you say I am worth?" Dick asked with apparent irrelevance.

"Twenty millions—at a most conservative estimate—that is about the sum," Mr. Crockett answered promptly.

"Suppose I said right now that I wanted a hundred dollars!" Dick went on.

"Why—er—ahem." Mr. Slocum looked about him for guidance.

"We would be compelled to ask what you wanted it for," answered Mr. Crockett.

"And suppose," Dick said very slowly, looking Mr. Crockett squarely in the eyes, "suppose I said that I was very sorry, but that I did not care to say what I wanted it for?"

"Then you wouldn't get it," Mr. Crockett said so immediately that there was a hint of testiness and snap in his manner.

Dick nodded slowly, as if letting the information sink in.

"But, of course, my boy," Mr. Slocum took up hastily, "you understand you are too young to handle money yet. We must decide that for you."

"You mean I can't touch a penny without your permission?"

"Not a penny," Mr. Crockett snapped.

Dick nodded his head thoughtfully and murmured, "Oh, I see."

"Of course, and quite naturally, it would only be fair, you know, you will have a small allowance for your personal spending," Mr. Davidson said. "Say, a dollar, or, perhaps, two dollars, a week. As you grow older this allowance will be increased. And by the time you are twenty-one, doubtlessly you will be fully qualified—with advice, of course—to handle your own affairs."

"And until I am twenty-one my twenty million wouldn't buy me a hundred dollars to do as I please with?" Dick queried very subduedly.

Mr. Davidson started to corroborate in soothing phrases, but was waved to silence by Dick, who continued:

"As I understand it, whatever money I handle will be by agreement between the four of us?"

The Board of Guardians nodded.

"That is, whatever we agree, goes?"

Again the Board of Guardians nodded.

"Well, I'd like to have a hundred right now," Dick announced.

"What for?" Mr. Crockett demanded.

"I don't mind telling you," was the lad's steady answer. "To go traveling."

"You'll go to bed at eight:thirty this evening," Mr. Crockett retorted. "And you don't get any hundred. The lady we spoke to you about will be here before six. She is to have, as we explained, daily and hourly charge of you. At six-thirty, as usual, you will dine, and she will dine with you and see you to bed. As we told you, she will have to serve the place of a mother to you—see that your ears are clean, your neck washed—"

"And that I get my Saturday night bath," Dick amplified meekly for him.

"Precisely."

"How much are you—am I—paying the lady for her services?" Dick questioned in the disconcerting, tangential way that was already habitual to him, as his school companions and teachers had learned to their cost.

Mr. Crockett for the first time cleared his throat for pause.

"I'm paying her, ain't I?" Dick prodded. "Out of the twenty million, you know."

"The spit of his father," said Mr. Slocum in an aside.

"Mrs. Summerstone, the lady as you elect to call her, receives one hundred and fifty a month, eighteen hundred a year in round sum," said Mr. Crockett.

"It's a waste of perfectly good money," Dick sighed. "And board and lodging thrown in!"

He stood up—not the born aristocrat of the generations, but the reared aristocrat of thirteen years in the Nob Hill palace. He stood up with such a manner that his Board of Guardians left their leather chairs to stand up with him. But he stood up as no Lord Fauntleroy ever stood up; for he was a mixer. He had knowledge that human life was many-faced and many-placed. Not for nothing had he been spelled down by Mona Sanguinetti. Not for nothing had he fought Tim Hagan to a standstill and, co-equal, ruled the schoolyard roost with him.

He was birthed of the wild gold-adventure of Forty-nine. He was a reared aristocrat and a grammar-school-trained democrat. He knew, in his precocious immature way, the differentiations between caste and mass; and, behind it all, he was possessed of a will of his own and of a quiet surety of self that was incomprehensible to the three elderly gentlemen who had been given charge of his and his destiny and who had pledged themselves to increase his twenty millions and make a man of him in their own composite image.

"Thank you for your kindness," Young Dick said generally to the three. "I guess we'll get along all right. Of course, that twenty millions is mine, and of course you've got to take care of it for me, seeing I know nothing of business—"

"And we'll increase it for you, my boy, we'll increase it for you in safe, conservative ways," Mr. Slocum assured him.

"No speculation," Young Dick warned. "Dad's just been lucky— I've heard him say that times have changed and a fellow can't take the chances everybody used to take."

From which, and from much which has already passed, it might erroneously be inferred that Young Dick was a mean and money-grubbing soul. On the contrary, he was at that instant entertaining secret thoughts and plans so utterly regardless and disdainful of his twenty millions as to place him on a par with a drunken sailor sowing the beach with a three years' pay-day.

"I am only a boy," Young Dick went on. "But you don't know me very well yet. We'll get better acquainted by and by, and, again thanking you... ."

He paused, bowed briefly and grandly as lords in Nob Hill palaces early learn to bow, and, by the quality of the pause, signified that the audience was over. Nor did the impact of dismissal miss his guardians. They, who had been co-lords with his father, withdrew confused and perplexed. Messrs. Davidson and Slocum were on the point of resolving their perplexity into wrath, as they went down the great stone stairway to the waiting carriage, but Mr. Crockett, the testy and snappish, muttered ecstatically: "The son of a gun! The little son of a gun!"

The carriage carried them down to the old Pacific Union Club, where, for another hour, they gravely discussed the future of Young Dick Forrest and pledged themselves anew to the faith reposed in them by Lucky Richard Forrest. And down the hill, on foot, where grass grew on the paved streets too steep for horse-traffic, Young Dick hurried. As the height of land was left behind, almost immediately the palaces and spacious grounds of the nabobs gave way to the mean streets and wooden warrens of the working people. The San Francisco of 1887 as incontinently intermingled its slums and mansions as did the old cities of Europe. Nob Hill arose, like any medieval castle, from the mess and ruck of common life that denned and laired at its base.

Young Dick came to pause alongside a corner grocery, the second story of which was rented to Timothy Hagan Senior, who, by virtue of being a policeman with a wage of a hundred dollars a month, rented this high place to dwell above his fellows who supported families on no more than forty and fifty dollars a month.

In vain Young Dick whistled up through the unscreened, open windows. Tim Hagan Junior was not at home. But Young Dick wasted little wind in the whistling. He was debating on possible adjacent places where Tim Hagan might be, when Tim himself appeared around the corner, bearing a lidless lard-can that foamed with steam beer. He grunted greeting, and Young Dick grunted with equal roughness, just as if, a brief space before, he had not, in most lordly fashion, terminated an audience with three of the richest merchant-kings of an imperial city. Nor did his possession of twenty increasing millions hint the slightest betrayal in his voice or mitigate in the slightest the gruffness of his grunt.

"Ain't seen yeh since yer old man died," Tim Hagan commented.

"Well, you're seein' me now, ain't you?" was Young Dick's retort. "Say, Tim, I come to see you on business."

"Wait till I rush the beer to the old man," said Tim, inspecting the state of the foam in the lard-can with an experienced eye. "He'll roar his head off if it comes in flat."

"Oh, you can shake it up," Young Dick assured him. "Only want to see you a minute. I'm hitting the road to-night. Want to come along?"

Tim's small, blue Irish eyes flashed with interest.

"Where to?" he queried.

"Don't know. Want to come? If you do, we can talk it over after we start? You know the ropes. What d'ye say?"

"The old man'll beat the stuffin' outa me," Tim demurred.

"He's done that before, an' you don't seem to be much missing," Young Dick callously rejoined. "Say the word, an' we'll meet at the Ferry Building at nine to-night. What d'ye say? I'll be there."

"Supposin' I don't show up?" Tim asked.

"I'll be on my way just the same." Young Dick turned as if to depart, paused casually, and said over his shoulder, "Better come along."

Tim shook up the beer as he answered with equal casualness, "Aw right. I'll be there."

After parting from Tim Hagan Young Dick spent a busy hour or so looking up one, Marcovich, a Slavonian schoolmate whose father ran a chop-house in which was reputed to be served the finest twenty-cent meal in the city. Young Marcovich owed Young Dick two dollars, and Young Dick accepted the payment of a dollar and forty cents as full quittance of the debt.

Also, with shyness and perturbation, Young Dick wandered down Montgomery Street and vacillated among the many pawnshops that graced that thoroughfare. At last, diving desperately into one, he managed to exchange for eight dollars and a ticket his gold watch that he knew was worth fifty at the very least.

Dinner in the Nob Hill palace was served at six-thirty. He arrived at six-forty-five and encountered Mrs. Summerstone. She was a stout, elderly, decayed gentlewoman, a daughter of the great Porter-Rickington family that had shaken the entire Pacific Coast with its financial crash in the middle seventies. Despite her stoutness, she suffered from what she called shattered nerves.

"This will never, never do, Richard," she censured. "Here is dinner waiting fifteen minutes already, and you have not yet washed your face and hands."

"I am sorry, Mrs. Summerstone," Young Dick apologized. "I won't keep you waiting ever again. And I won't bother you much ever."

At dinner, in state, the two of them alone in the great dining room, Young Dick strove to make things easy for the lady, whom, despite his knowledge that she was on his pay-roll, he felt toward as a host must feel toward a guest.

"You'll be very comfortable here," he promised, "once you are settled down. It's a good old house, and most of the servants have been here for years."

"But, Richard," she smiled seriously to him; "it is not the servants who will determine my happiness here. It is you."

"I'll do my best," he said graciously. "Better than that. I'm sorry I came in late for dinner. In years and years you'll never see me late again. I won't bother you at all. You'll see. It will be just as though I wasn't in the house."

When he bade her good night, on his way to bed, he added, as a last thought:

"I'll warn you of one thing: Ah Sing. He's the cook. He's been in our house for years and years—oh, I don't know, maybe twenty-five or thirty years he's cooked for father, from long before this house was built or I was born. He's privileged. He's so used to having his own way that you'll have to handle him with gloves. But once he likes you he'll work his fool head off to please you. He likes me that way. You get him to like you, and you'll have the time of your life here. And, honest, I won't give you any trouble at all. It'll be a regular snap, just as if I wasn't here at all."

Chapter 5

AT nine in the evening, sharp to the second, clad in his oldest clothes, Young Dick met Tim Hagan at the Ferry Building.

"No use headin' north," said Tim. "Winter'll come on up that way and make the sleepin' crimpy. D'ye want to go East—that means Nevada and the deserts."

"Any other way?" queried Young Dick. "What's the matter with south? We can head for Los Angeles, an' Arizona, an' New Mexico—oh, an' Texas."

"How much money you got?" Tim demanded.

"What for?" Young Dick countered.

"We gotta get out quick, an' payin' our way at the start is quickest. Me—I'm all hunkydory; but you ain't. The folks that's lookin' after you'll raise a roar. They'll have more detectives out than you can shake at stick at. We gotta dodge 'em, that's what."

"Then we will dodge," said Young Dick. "We'll make short jumps this way and that for a couple of days, layin' low most of the time, paying our way, until we can get to Tracy. Then we'll quit payin' an' beat her south."

All of which program was carefully carried out. They eventually went through Tracy as pay passengers, six hours after the local deputy sheriff had given up his task of searching the trains. With an excess of precaution Young Dick paid beyond Tracy and as far as Modesto. After that, under the teaching of Tim, he traveled without paying, riding blind baggage, box cars, and cow-catchers. Young Dick bought the newspapers, and frightened Tim by reading to him the lurid accounts of the kidnapping of the young heir to the Forrest millions.

Back in San Francisco the Board of Guardians offered rewards that totaled thirty thousand dollars for the recovery of their ward. And Tim Hagan, reading the same while they lay in the grass by some water- tank, branded forever the mind of Young Dick with the fact that honor beyond price was a matter of neither place nor caste and might outcrop in the palace on the height of land or in the dwelling over a grocery down on the flat.

"Gee!" Tim said to the general landscape. "The old man wouldn't raise a roar if I snitched on you for that thirty thousand. It makes me scared to think of it."

And from the fact that Tim thus openly mentioned the matter, Young Dick concluded that there was no possibility of the policeman's son betraying him.

Not until six weeks afterward, in Arizona, did Young Dick bring up the subject.

"You see, Tim," he said, "I've got slathers of money. It's growing all the time, and I ain't spending a cent of it, not so as you can notice... though that Mrs. Summerstone is getting a cold eighteen hundred a year out of me, with board and carriages thrown in, while you an' I are glad to get the leavings of firemen's pails in the round-houses. Just the same, my money's growing. What's ten per cent, on twenty dollars?"

Tim Hagan stared at the shimmering heat-waves of the desert and tried to solve the problem.

"What's one-tenth of twenty million?" Young Dick demanded irritably.

"Huh!—two million, of course."

"Well, five per cent's half of ten per cent. What does twenty million earn at five per cent, for one year?"

Tim hesitated.

"Half of it, half of two million!" Young Dick cried. "At that rate I'm a million richer every year. Get that, and hang on to it, and listen to me. When I'm good and willing to go back—but not for years an' years—we'll fix it up, you and I. When I say the word, you'll write to your father. He'll jump out to where we are waiting, pick me up, and cart me back. Then he'll collect the thirty thousand reward from my guardians, quit the police force, and most likely start a saloon."

"Thirty thousand's a hell of a lot of money," was Tim's nonchalant way of expressing his gratitude.

"Not to me," Young Dick minimized his generosity. "Thirty thousand goes into a million thirty-three times, and a million's only a year's turnover of my money."

But Tim Hagan never lived to see his father a saloon keeper. Two days later, on a trestle, the lads were fired out of an empty box-car by a brake-man who should have known better. The trestle spanned a dry ravine. Young Dick looked down at the rocks seventy feet below and demurred.

"There's room on the trestle," he said; "but what if the train starts up?"

"It ain't goin' to start—beat it while you got time," the brakeman insisted. "The engine's takin' water at the other side. She always takes it here."

But for once the engine did not take water. The evidence at the inquest developed that the engineer had found no water in the tank and started on. Scarcely had the two boys dropped from the side-door of the box-car, and before they had made a score of steps along the narrow way between the train and the abyss, than the train began to move. Young Dick, quick and sure in all his perceptions and adjustments, dropped on the instant to hands and knees on the trestle. This gave him better holding and more space, because he crouched beneath the overhang of the box-cars. Tim, not so quick in perceiving and adjusting, also overcome with Celtic rage at the brakeman, instead of dropping to hands and knees, remained upright to flare his opinion of the brakeman, to the brakeman, in lurid and ancestral terms.

"Get down!—drop!" Young Dick shouted.

But the opportunity had passed. On a down grade, the engine picked up the train rapidly. Facing the moving cars, with empty air at his back and the depth beneath, Tim tried to drop on hands and knees. But the first twist of his shoulders brought him in contact with the car and nearly out-balanced him. By a miracle he recovered equilibrium. But he stood upright. The train was moving faster and faster. It was impossible to get down.

Young Dick, kneeling and holding, watched. The train gathered way. The cars moved more swiftly. Tim, with a cool head, his back to the fall, his face to the passing cars, his arms by his sides, with nowhere save under his feet a holding point, balanced and swayed. The faster the train moved, the wider he swayed, until, exerting his will, he controlled himself and ceased from swaying.

And all would have been well with him, had it not been for one car. Young Dick knew it, and saw it coming. It was a "palace horse-car," projecting six inches wider than any car on the train. He saw Tim see it coming. He saw Tim steel himself to meet the abrupt subtraction of half a foot from the narrow space wherein he balanced. He saw Tim slowly and deliberately sway out, sway out to the extremest limit, and yet not sway out far enough. The thing was physically inevitable. An inch more, and Tim would have escaped the car. An inch more and he would have fallen without impact from the car. It caught him, in that margin of an inch, and hurled him backward and side-twisting. Twice he whirled sidewise, and two and a half times he turned over, ere he struck on his head and neck on the rocks.

He never moved after he struck. The seventy-foot fall broke his neck and crushed his skull. And right there Young Dick learned death—not the ordered, decent death of civilization, wherein doctors and nurses and hypodermics ease the stricken one into the darkness, and ceremony and function and flowers and undertaking institutions conspire to give a happy leave-taking and send-off to the departing shade, but sudden death, primitive death, ugly and ungarnished, like the death of a steer in the shambles or a fat swine stuck in the jugular.

And right there Young Dick learned more—the mischance of life and fate; the universe hostile to man; the need to perceive and to act, to see and know, to be sure and quick, to adjust instantly to all instant shiftage of the balance of forces that bear upon the living. And right there, beside the strangely crumpled and shrunken remnant of what had been his comrade the moment before, Young Dick learned that illusion must be discounted, and that reality never lied.

In New Mexico, Young Dick drifted into the Jingle-bob Ranch, north of Roswell, in the Pecos Valley. He was not yet fourteen, and he was accepted as the mascot of the ranch and made into a "sure-enough" cowboy by cowboys who, on legal papers, legally signed names such as Wild Horse, Willie Buck, Boomer Deacon, and High Pockets.

Here, during a stay of six months, Young Dick, soft of frame and unbreakable, achieved a knowledge of horses and horsemanship, and of men in the rough and raw, that became a life asset. More he learned. There was John Chisum, owner of the Jingle-bob, the Bosque Grande, and of other cattle ranches as far away as the Black River and beyond. John Chisum was a cattle king who had foreseen the coming of the farmer and adjusted from the open range to barbed wire, and who, in order to do so, had purchased every forty acres carrying water and got for nothing the use of the millions of acres of adjacent range that was worthless without the water he controlled. And in the talk by the camp-fire and chuck wagon, among forty-dollar-a-month cowboys who had not foreseen what John Chisum foresaw, Young Dick learned precisely why and how John Chisum had become a cattle king while a thousand of his contemporaries worked for him on wages.

But Young Dick was no cool-head. His blood was hot. He had passion, and fire, and male pride. Ready to cry from twenty hours in the saddle, he learned to ignore the thousand aching creaks in his body and with the stoic brag of silence to withstain from his blankets until the hard-bitten punchers led the way. By the same token he straddled the horse that was apportioned him, insisted on riding night-herd, and knew no hint of uncertainty when it came to him to turn the flank of a stampede with a flying slicker. He could take a chance. It was his joy to take a chance. But at such times he never failed of due respect for reality. He was well aware that men were soft-shelled and cracked easily on hard rocks or under pounding hoofs. And when he rejected a mount that tangled its legs in quick action and stumbled, it was not because he feared to be cracked, but because, when he took a chance on being cracked, he wanted, as he told John Chisum himself, "an even break for his money."

It was while at the Jingle-bob, but mailed by a cattleman from Chicago, that Young Dick wrote a letter to his guardians. Even then, so careful was he, that the envelope was addressed to Ah Sing. Though unburdened by his twenty millions, Young Dick never forgot them, and, fearing his estate might be distributed among remote relatives who might possibly inhabit New England, he warned his guardians that he was still alive and that he would return home in several years. Also, he ordered them to keep Mrs. Summerstone on at her regular salary.

But Young Dick's feet itched. Half a year, he felt, was really more than he should have spent at the Jingle-bob. As a boy hobo, or road- kid, he drifted on across the United States, getting acquainted with its peace officers, police judges, vagrancy laws, and jails. And he learned vagrants themselves at first hand, and floating laborers and petty criminals. Among other things, he got acquainted with farms and farmers, and, in New York State, once picked berries for a week with a Dutch farmer who was experimenting with one of the first silos erected in the United States. Nothing of what he learned came to him in the spirit of research. He had merely the human boy's curiosity about all things, and he gained merely a huge mass of data concerning human nature and social conditions that was to stand him in good stead in later years, when, with the aid of the books, he digested and classified it.

His adventures did not harm him. Even when he consorted with jail- birds in jungle camps, and listened to their codes of conduct and measurements of life, he was not affected. He was a traveler, and they were alien breeds. Secure in the knowledge of his twenty millions, there was neither need nor temptation for him to steal or rob. All things and all places interested him, but he never found a place nor a situation that could hold him. He wanted to see, to see more and more, and to go on seeing.

At the end of three years, nearly sixteen, hard of body, weighing a hundred and thirty pounds, he judged it time to go home and open the books. So he took his first long voyage, signing on as boy on a windjammer bound around the Horn from the Delaware Breakwater to San Francisco. It was a hard voyage, of one hundred and eighty days, but at the end he weighed ten pounds the more for having made it.

Mrs. Summerstone screamed when he walked in on her, and Ah Sing had to be called from the kitchen to identify him. Mrs. Summerstone screamed a second time. It was when she shook hands with him and lacerated her tender skin in the fisty grip of his rope-calloused palms.

He was shy, almost embarrassed, as he greeted his guardians at the hastily summoned meeting. But this did not prevent him from talking straight to the point.

"It's this way," he said. "I am not a fool. I know what I want, and I want what I want. I am alone in the world, outside of good friends like you, of course, and I have my own ideas of the world and what I want to do in it. I didn't come home because of a sense of duty to anybody here. I came home because it was time, because of my sense of duty to myself. I'm all the better from my three years of wandering about, and now it's up to me to go on with my education —my book education, I mean."

"The Belmont Academy," Mr. Slocum suggested. "That will fit you for the university—"

Dick shook his head decidedly.

"And take three years to do it. So would a high school. I intend to be in the University of California inside one year. That means work. But my mind's like acid. It'll bite into the books. I shall hire a coach, or half a dozen of them, and go to it. And I'll hire my coaches myself—hire and fire them. And that means money to handle."

"A hundred a month," Mr. Crockett suggested.

Dick shook his head.

"I've taken care of myself for three years without any of my money. I guess. I can take care of myself along with some of my money here in San Francisco. I don't care to handle my business affairs yet, but I do want a bank account, a respectable-sized one. I want to spend it as I see fit, for what I see fit."

The guardians looked their dismay at one another.

"It's ridiculous, impossible," Mr. Crockett began. "You are as unreasonable as you were before you went away."

"It's my way, I guess," Dick sighed. "The other disagreement was over my money. It was a hundred dollars I wanted then."

"Think of our position, Dick," Mr. Davidson urged. "As your guardians, how would it be looked upon if we gave you, a lad of sixteen, a free hand with money."

"What's the *Freda* worth, right now?" Dick demanded irrelevantly.

"Can sell for twenty thousand any time," Mr. Crockett answered.

"Then sell her. She's too large for me, and she's worth less every year. I want a thirty-footer that I can handle myself for knocking around the Bay, and that won't cost a thousand. Sell the *Freda* and put the money to my account. Now what you three are afraid of is that I'll misspend my money—taking to drinking, horse-racing, and running around with chorus girls. Here's my proposition to make you easy on that: let it be a drawing account for the four of us. The moment any of you decide I am misspending, that moment you can draw out the total balance. I may as well tell you, that just as a side line I'm going to get a business college expert to come here and cram me with the mechanical side of the business game."

Dick did not wait for their acquiescence, but went on as from a matter definitely settled.

"How about the horses down at Menlo?—never mind, I'll look them over and decide what to keep. Mrs. Summerstone will stay on here in charge of the house, because I've got too much work mapped out for myself already. I promise you you won't regret giving me a free hand with my directly personal affairs. And now, if you want to hear about the last three years, I'll spin the yarn for you."

Dick Forrest had been right when he told his guardians that his mind was acid and would bite into the books. Never was there such an education, and he directed it himself—but not without advice. He had learned the trick of hiring brains from his father and from John Chisum of the Jingle-bob. He had learned to sit silent and to think while cow men talked long about the campfire and the chuck wagon. And, by virtue of name and place, he sought and obtained interviews with professors and college presidents and practical men of affairs; and he listened to their talk through many hours, scarcely speaking, rarely asking a question, merely listening to the best they had to offer, content to receive from several such hours one idea, one fact, that would help him to decide what sort of an education he would go in for and how.

Then came the engaging of coaches. Never was there such an engaging and discharging, such a hiring and firing. He was not frugal in the matter. For one that he retained a month, or three months, he discharged a dozen on the first day, or the first week. And invariably he paid such dischargees a full month although their attempts to teach him might not have consumed an hour. He did such things fairly and grandly, because he could afford to be fair and grand.

He, who had eaten the leavings from firemen's pails in roundhouses and "scoffed" mulligan-stews at water-tanks, had learned thoroughly the worth of money. He bought the best with the sure knowledge that it was the cheapest. A year of high school physics and a year of high school chemistry were necessary to enter the university. When he had crammed his algebra and geometry, he sought out the heads of the physics and chemistry departments in the University of California. Professor Carey laughed at him... at the first.

"My dear boy," Professor Carey began.

Dick waited patiently till he was through. Then Dick began, and concluded.

"I'm not a fool, Professor Carey. High school and academy students are children. They don't know the world. They don't know what they want, or why they want what is ladled out to them. I know the world. I know what I want and why I want it. They do physics for an hour, twice a week, for two terms, which, with two vacations, occupy one year. You are the top teacher on the Pacific Coast in physics. The college year is just ending. In the first week of your vacation, giving every minute of your time to me, I can get the year's physics. What is that week worth to you?"

"You couldn't buy it for a thousand dollars," Professor Carey rejoined, thinking he had settled the matter.

"I know what your salary is—" Dick began.

"What is it?" Professor Carey demanded sharply.

"It's not a thousand a week," Dick retorted as sharply. "It's not five hundred a week, nor two-fifty a week—" He held up his hand to stall off interruption. "You've just told me I couldn't buy a week of your time for a thousand dollars. I'm not going to. But I am going to buy that week for two thousand. Heavens!—I've only got so many years to live—"

"And you can buy years?" Professor Carey queried slyly.

"Sure. That's why I'm here. I buy three years in one, and the week from you is part of the deal."

"But I have not accepted," Professor Carey laughed.

"If the sum is not sufficient," Dick said stiffly, "why name the sum you consider fair."

And Professor Carey surrendered. So did Professor Barsdale,

head of the department of chemistry.

Already had Dick taken his coaches in mathematics duck hunting for weeks in the sloughs of the Sacramento and the San Joaquin. After his bout with physics and chemistry he took his two coaches in literature and history into the Curry County hunting region of southwestern Oregon. He had learned the trick from his father, and he worked, and played, lived in the open air, and did three conventional years of adolescent education in one year without straining himself. He fished, hunted, swam, exercised, and equipped himself for the university at the same time. And he made no mistake. He knew that he did it because his father's twenty millions had invested him with mastery. Money was a tool. He did not over-rate it, nor under-rate it. He used it to buy what he wanted.

"The weirdest form of dissipation I ever heard," said Mr. Crockett, holding up Dick's account for the year. "Sixteen thousand for education, all itemized, including railroad fares, porters' tips, and shot-gun cartridges for his teachers."

"He passed the examinations just the same," quoth Mr. Slocum.

"And in a year," growled Mr. Davidson. "My daughter's boy entered Belmont at the same time, and, if he's lucky, it will be two years yet before he enters the university."

"Well, all I've got to say," proclaimed Mr. Crockett, "is that from now on what that boy says in the matter of spending his money goes."

"And now I'll have a snap," Dick told his guardians. "Here I am, neck and neck again, and years ahead of them in knowledge of the world. Why, I know things, good and bad, big and little, about men and women and life that sometimes I almost doubt myself that they're true. But I know them.

"From now on, I'm not going to rush. I've caught up, and I'm going through regular. All I have to do is to keep the speed of the classes, and I'll be graduated when I'm twenty-one. From now on I'll need less money for education—no more coaches, you know— and more money for a good time."

Mr. Davidson was suspicious.

"What do you mean by a good time?"

"Oh, I'm going in for the frats, for football, hold my own, you know— and I'm interested in gasoline engines. I'm going to build the first ocean-going gasoline yacht in the world—"

"You'll blow yourself up," Mr. Crockett demurred. "It's a fool notion all these cranks are rushing into over gasoline."

"I'll make myself safe," Dick answered, "and that means experimenting, and it means money, so keep me a good drawing account—same old way— all four of us can draw."

Chapter 6

Dick Forrest proved himself no prodigy at the university, save that he cut more lectures the first year than any other student. The reason for this was that he did not need the lectures he cut, and he knew it. His coaches, while preparing him for the entrance examinations, had carried him nearly through the first college year. Incidentally, he made the Freshman team, a very scrub team, that was beaten by every high school and academy it played against.

But Dick did put in work that nobody saw. His collateral reading was wide and deep, and when he went on his first summer cruise in the ocean-going gasoline yacht he had built no gay young crowd accompanied him. Instead, his guests, with their families, were professors of literature, history, jurisprudence, and philosophy. It was long remembered in the university as the "high-brow" cruise. The professors, on their return, reported a most enjoyable time. Dick returned with a greater comprehension of the general fields of the particular professors than he could have gained in years at their class-lectures. And time thus gained, enabled him to continue to cut lectures and to devote more time to laboratory work.

Nor did he miss having his good college time. College widows made love to him, and college girls loved him, and he was indefatigable in his dancing. He never cut a smoker, a beer bust, or a rush, and he toured the Pacific Coast with the Banjo and Mandolin Club.

And yet he was no prodigy. He was brilliant at nothing. Half a dozen of his fellows could out-banjo and out-mandolin him. A dozen fellows were adjudged better dancers than he. In football, and he gained the Varsity in his Sophomore year, he was considered a solid and dependable player, and that was all. It seemed never his luck to take the ball and go down the length of the field while the Blue and Gold host tore itself and the grandstand to pieces. But it was at the end of heart-breaking, grueling slog in mud and rain, the score tied, the second half imminent to its close, Stanford on the five-yard line, Berkeley's ball, with two downs and three yards to gain—it was then that the Blue and Gold arose and chanted its demand for Forrest to hit the center and hit it hard.

He never achieved super-excellence at anything. Big Charley Everson drank him down at the beer busts. Harrison Jackson, at hammer- throwing, always exceeded his best by twenty feet. Carruthers out- pointed him at boxing. Anson Burge could always put his shoulders to the mat, two out of three, but always only by the hardest work. In English composition a fifth of his class excelled him. Edlin, the Russian Jew, out-debated him on the contention that property was robbery. Schultz and Debret left him with the class behind in higher mathematics; and Otsuki, the Japanese, was beyond all comparison with him in chemistry.

But if Dick Forrest did not excel at anything, he failed in nothing. He displayed no superlative strength, he betrayed no weakness nor deficiency. As he told his guardians, who, by his unrelenting good conduct had been led into dreaming some great career for him; as he told them, when they asked what he wanted to become:

"Nothing. Just all around. You see, I don't have to be a specialist. My father arranged that for me when he left me his money. Besides, I couldn't be a specialist if I wanted to. It isn't me."

And thus so well-keyed was he, that he expressed clearly his key. He had no flare for anything. He was that rare individual, normal, average, balanced, all-around.

When Mr. Davidson, in the presence of his fellow guardians, stated his pleasure in that Dick had shown no wildness since he had settled down, Dick replied:

"Oh, I can hold myself when I want to."

"Yes," said Mr. Slocum gravely. "It's the finest thing in the world that you sowed your wild oats early and learned control."

Dick looked at him curiously.

"Why, that boyish adventure doesn't count," he said. "That wasn't wildness. I haven't gone wild yet. But watch me when I start. Do you know Kipling's 'Song of Diego Valdez'? Let me quote you a bit of it. You see, Diego Valdez, like me, had good fortune. He rose so fast to be High Admiral of Spain that he found no time to take the pleasure he had merely tasted. He was lusty and husky, but he had no time, being too busy rising. But always, he thought, he fooled himself with the thought, that his lustiness and huskiness would last, and, after he became High Admiral he could then have his pleasure. Always he remembered:

"'—comrades— Old playmates on new seas— When as we traded orpiment Among the savages— A thousand leagues to south'ard And thirty years removed— They knew not noble Valdez, But me they knew and loved.

"'Then they that found good liquor They drank it not alone, And they that found fair plunder, They told us every one, Behind our chosen islands Or secret shoals between, When, walty from far voyage, We gathered to careen.

"'There burned our breaming-fagots, All pale along the shore: There rose our worn pavilions— A sail above an oar: As flashed each yearning anchor Through mellow seas afire, So swift our careless captains Rowed each to his desire.

"'Where lay our loosened harness? Where turned our naked feet? Whose tavern mid the palm-trees? What quenchings of what heat? Oh fountain in the desert! Oh cistern in the waste! Oh bread we ate in secret! Oh cup we spilled in haste!

"'The youth new-taught of longing, The widow curbed and wan — The good wife proud at season, And the maid aware of man; All souls, unslaked, consuming, Defrauded in delays, Desire not more than quittance Than I those forfeit days!'

"Oh, get him, get him, you three oldsters, as I've got him! Get what he saws next:

"'I dreamed to wait my pleasure, Unchanged my spring would bide: Wherefore, to wait my pleasure, I put my spring aside, Till, first in face of Fortune, And last in mazed disdain, I made Diego Valdez High Admiral of Spain!'

"Listen to me, guardians!" Dick cried on, his face a flame of passion. "Don't forget for one moment that I am anything but unslaked, consuming. I am. I burn. But I hold myself. Don't think I am a dead one because I am a darn nice, meritorious boy at college. I am young. I am alive. I am all lusty and husky. But I make no mistake. I hold myself. I don't start out now to blow up on the first lap. I am just getting ready. I am going to have my time. I am not going to spill my cup in haste. And in the end I am not going to lament as Diego Valdez did:

"'There walks no wind 'neath heaven Nor wave that shall restore The old careening riot And the clamorous, crowded shore— The fountain in the desert, The cistern in the waste, The bread we ate in secret, The cup we spilled in haste.'

"Listen, guardians! Do you know what it is to hit your man, to hit him in hot blood—square to the jaw—and drop him cold? I want that. And I want to love, and kiss, and risk, and play the lusty, husky fool. I want to take my chance. I want my careening riot, and I want it while I am young, but not while I am too young. And I'm going to have it. And in the meantime I play the game at college, I hold myself, I equip myself, so that when I turn loose I am going to have the best chance of my best. Oh, believe me, I do not always sleep well of nights."

"You mean?" queried Mr. Crockett.

"Sure. That's just what I mean. I haven't gone wild yet, but just watch me when I start."

"And you will start when you graduate?"

The remarkable youngster shook his head.

"After I graduate I'm going to take at least a year of post-graduate courses in the College of Agriculture. You see, I'm developing a hobby—farming. I want to do something ... something constructive. My father wasn't constructive to amount to anything. Neither were you fellows. You struck a new land in pioneer days, and you picked up money like a lot of sailors shaking out nuggets from the grass roots in a virgin placer—"

"My lad, I've some little experience in Californian farming," Mr. Crockett interrupted in a hurt way.

"Sure you have, but you weren't constructive. You were—well, facts are facts—you were destructive. You were a bonanza farmer. What did you do? You took forty thousand acres of the finest Sacramento Valley soil and you grew wheat on it year after year. You never dreamed of rotation. You burned your straw. You exhausted your humus. You plowed four inches and put a plow-sole like a cement sidewalk just four inches under the surface. You exhausted that film of four inches and now you can't get your seed back.

"You've destroyed. That's what my father did. They all did it. Well, I'm going to take my father's money and construct. I'm going to take worked-out wheat-land that I can buy as at a fire-sale, rip out the plow-sole, and make it produce more in the end than it did when you fellows first farmed it."

It was at the end of his Junior year that Mr. Crockett again mentioned Dick's threatened period of wildness.

"Soon as I'm done with cow college," was his answer. "Then I'm going to buy, and stock, and start a ranch that'll be a ranch. And then I'll set out after my careening riot."

"About how large a ranch will you start with?" Mr. Davidson asked.

"Maybe fifty thousand acres, maybe five hundred thousand. It all depends. I'm going to play unearned increment to the limit. People haven't begun to come to California yet. Without a tap of my hand or a turn over, fifteen years from now land that I can buy for ten dollars an acre will be worth fifty, and what I can buy for fifty will

50

be worth five hundred."

"A half million acres at ten dollars an acre means five million dollars," Mr. Crockett warned gravely.

"And at fifty it means twenty-five million," Dick laughed.

But his guardians never believed in the wild oats pilgrimage he threatened. He might waste his fortune on new-fangled farming, but to go literally wild after such years of self-restraint was an unthinkable thing.

Dick took his sheepskin with small honor. He was twenty-eighth in his class, and he had not set the college world afire. His most notable achievement had been his resistance and bafflement of many nice girls and of the mothers of many nice girls. Next, after that, he had signalized his Senior year by captaining the Varsity to its first victory over Stanford in five years. It was in the day prior to large- salaried football coaches, when individual play meant much; but he hammered team-work and the sacrifice of the individual into his team, so that on Thanksgiving Day, over a vastly more brilliant eleven, the Blue and Gold was able to serpentine its triumph down Market Street in San Francisco.

In his post-graduate year in cow college, Dick devoted himself to laboratory work and cut all lectures. In fact, he hired his own lecturers, and spent a sizable fortune on them in mere traveling expenses over California. Jacques Ribot, esteemed one of the greatest world authorities on agricultural chemistry, who had been seduced from his two thousand a year in France by the six thousand offered by the University of California, who had been seduced to Hawaii by the ten thousand of the sugar planters, Dick Forrest seduced with fifteen thousand and the more delectable temperate climate of California on a five years' contract.

Messrs. Crockett, Slocum, and Davidson threw up their hands in horror and knew that this was the wild career Dick Forrest had forecast.

But this was only one of Dick Forrest's similar dissipations. He stole from the Federal Government, at a prodigal increase of salary, its star specialist in livestock breeding, and by similar misconduct he robbed the University of Nebraska of its greatest milch cow professor, and broke the heart of the Dean of the College of Agriculture of the University of California by appropriating Professor Nirdenhammer, the wizard of farm management.

"Cheap at the price, cheap at the price," Dick explained to his guardians. "Wouldn't you rather see me spend my money in buying professors than in buying race horses and actresses? Besides, the trouble with you fellows is that you don't know the game of buying brains. I do. That's my specialty. I'm going to make money out of them, and, better than that, I'm going to make a dozen blades of grass grow where you fellows didn't leave room for half a blade in the soil you gutted."

So it can be understood how his guardians could not believe in his promise of wild career, of kissing and risking, and hitting men hot on the jaw. "One year more," he warned, while he delved in agricultural chemistry, soil analysis, farm management, and traveled California with his corps of high-salaried experts. And his guardians could only apprehend a swift and wide dispersal of the Forrest millions when Dick attained his majority, took charge of the totality of his fortune, and actually embarked on his agricultural folly.

The day he was twenty-one the purchase of his principality, that extended west from the Sacramento River to the mountain tops, was consummated.

"An incredible price," said Mr. Crockett.

"Incredibly cheap," said Dick. "You ought to see my soil reports. You ought to see my water-reports. And you ought to hear me sing. Listen, guardians, to a song that is a true song. I am the singer and the song."

Whereupon, in the queer quavering falsetto that is the sense of song to the North American Indian, the Eskimo, and the Mongol, Dick sang:

"Hu'-tim yo'-kim koi-o-di'! Wi'-hi yan'-ning koi-o-di'! Lo'-whi yan'-ning koi-o-di'! Yo-ho' Nai-ni', hal-u'-dom yo nai, yo-ho' nai-nim'!"

"The music is my own," he murmured apologetically, "the way I think it ought to have sounded. You see, no man lives who ever heard it sung. The Nishinam got it from the Maidu, who got it from the Konkau, who made it. But the Nishinam and the Maidu and the Konkau are gone. Their last rancheria is not. You plowed it under, Mr. Crockett, with you bonanza gang-plowing, plow-soling farming. And I got the song from a certain ethnological report, volume three, of the United States Pacific Coast Geographical and Geological Survey. Red Cloud, who was formed out of the sky, first sang this song to the stars and the mountain flowers in the morning of the world. I shall now sing it for you in English."

And again, in Indian falsetto, ringing with triumph, vernal and bursting, slapping his thighs and stamping his feet to the accent, Dick sang:

"The acorns come down from heaven! I plant the short acorns in the valley! I plant the long acorns in the valley! I sprout, I, the black-oak acorn, sprout, I sprout!"

Dick Forrest's name began to appear in the newspapers with appalling frequency. He leaped to instant fame by being the first man in California who paid ten thousand dollars for a single bull. His livestock specialist, whom he had filched from the Federal Government, in England outbid the Rothschilds' Shire farm for Hillcrest Chieftain, quickly to be known as Forrest's Folly, paying for that kingly animal no less than five thousand guineas.

"Let them laugh," Dick told his ex-guardians. "I am importing forty Shire mares. I'll write off half his price the first twelvemonth. He will be the sire and grandsire of many sons and grandsons for which the Californians will fall over themselves to buy of me at from three to five thousand dollars a clatter."

Dick Forrest was guilty of many similar follies in those first months of his majority. But the most unthinkable folly of all was, after he had sunk millions into his original folly, that he turned it over to his experts personally to develop along the general broad lines laid down by him, placed checks upon them that they might not go catastrophically wrong, bought a ticket in a passenger brig to Tahiti, and went away to run wild.

Occasionally his guardians heard from him. At one time he was owner and master of a four-masted steel sailing ship that carried the English flag and coals from Newcastle. They knew that much, because they had been called upon for the purchase price, because they read Dick's name in the papers as master when his ship rescued the passengers of the ill-fated *Orion*, and because they collected the insurance when Dick's ship was lost with most of all hands in the great Fiji hurricane. In 1896, he was in the Klondike; in 1897, he was in Kamchatka and scurvy-stricken; and, next, he erupted with the American flag into the Philippines. Once, although they could never learn how nor why, he was owner and master of a crazy tramp steamer, long since rejected by Lloyd's, which sailed under the aegis of Siam.

From time to time business correspondence compelled them to hear from him from various purple ports of the purple seas. Once, they had to bring the entire political pressure of the Pacific Coast to bear upon Washington in order to get him out of a scrape in Russia, of which affair not one line appeared in the daily press, but which affair was secretly provocative of ticklish joy and delight in all the chancellories of Europe.

Incidentally, they knew that he lay wounded in Mafeking; that he pulled through a bout with yellow fever in Guayaquil; and that he stood trial for brutality on the high seas in New York City. Thrice they read in the press dispatches that he was dead: once, in battle, in Mexico; and twice, executed, in Venezuela. After such false flutterings, his guardians refused longer to be thrilled when he crossed the Yellow Sea in a sampan, was "rumored" to have died of beri-beri, was captured from the Russians by the Japanese at Mukden, and endured military imprisonment in Japan.

The one thrill of which they were still capable, was when, true to promise, thirty years of age, his wild oats sown, he returned to California with a wife to whom, as he announced, he had been married several years, and whom all his three guardians found they knew. Mr. Slocum had dropped eight hundred thousand along with the totality of her father's fortune in the final catastrophe at the Los Cocos mine in Chihuahua when the United States demonetized silver. Mr. Davidson had pulled a million out of the Last Stake along with her father when he pulled eight millions from that sunken, man-resurrected, river bed in Amador County. Mr. Crockett, a youth at the time, had "spooned" the Merced bottom with her father in the late 'fifties, had stood up best man with him at Stockton when he married her mother, and, at Grant's Pass, had played poker with him and with the then Lieutenant U.S. Grant when all the little the western world knew of that young lieutenant was that he was a good Indian fighter but a poor poker player.

And Dick Forrest had married the daughter of Philip Desten! It was not a case of wishing Dick luck. It was a case of garrulous insistence on the fact that he did not know how lucky he was. His guardians forgave him all his wildness. He had made good. At last he had performed a purely rational act. Better; it was a stroke of genius. Paula Desten! Philip Desten's daughter! The Desten blood! The Destens and the Forrests! It was enough. The three aged comrades of Forrest and Desten of the old Gold Days, of the two who had played and passed on, were even severe with Dick. They warned him of the extreme value of his treasure, of the sacred duty such wedlock imposed on him, of all the traditions and virtues of the Desten and Forrest blood, until Dick laughed and broke in with the disconcerting statement that they were talking like a bunch of fanciers or eugenics cranks—which was precisely what they were talking like, although they did not care to be told so crassly.

At any rate, the simple fact that he had married a Desten made them nod unqualified approbation when he showed them the plans and building estimates of the Big House. Thanks to Paula Desten, for once they were agreed that he was spending wisely and well. As for his farming, it was incontestible that the Harvest Group was unfalteringly producing, and he might be allowed his hobbies.

Nevertheless, as Mr. Slocum put it: "Twenty-five thousand dollars for a mere work-horse stallion is a madness. Work-horses are work-horses; now had it been running stock... ."

Chapter 7

While Dick Forrest scanned the pamphlet on hog cholera issued by the State of Iowa, through his open windows, across the wide court, began to come sounds of the awakening of the girl who laughed from the wooden frame by his bed and who had left on the floor of his sleeping porch, not so many hours before, the rosy, filmy, lacy, boudoir cap so circumspectly rescued by Oh My.

Dick heard her voice, for she awoke, like a bird, with song. He heard her trilling, in and out through open windows, all down the long wing that was hers. And he heard her singing in the patio garden, where, also, she desisted long enough to quarrel with her Airedale and scold the collie pup unholily attracted by the red-orange, divers-finned, and many-tailed Japanese goldfish in the fountain basin.

He was aware of pleasure that she was awake. It was a pleasure that never staled. Always, up himself for hours, he had a sense that the Big House was not really awake until he heard Paula's morning song across the patio.

But having tasted the pleasure of knowing her to be awake, Dick, as usual, forgot her in his own affairs. She went out of his consciousness as he became absorbed again in the Iowa statistics on hog cholera.

"Good morning, Merry Gentleman," was the next he heard, always adorable music in his ears; and Paula flowed in upon him, all softness of morning kimono and stayless body, as her arm passed around his neck and she perched, half in his arms, on one accommodating knee of his. And he pressed her, and advertised his awareness of her existence and nearness, although his eyes lingered a full half minute longer on the totals of results of Professor Kenealy's hog inoculations on Simon Jones' farm at Washington, Iowa.

"My!" she protested. "You are too fortunate. You are sated with riches. Here is your Lady Boy, your 'little haughty moon,' and you haven't even said, 'Good morning, Little Lady Boy, was your sleep sweet and gentle?'"

And Dick Forrest forsook the statistical columns of Professor Kenealy's inoculations, pressed his wife closer, kissed her, but with insistent right fore-finger maintained his place in the pages of the pamphlet.

Nevertheless, the very terms of her "reproof prevented him from asking what he should have asked—the prosperity of her night since the boudoir cap had been left upon his sleeping porch. He shut the pamphlet on his right fore-finger, at the place he intended to resume, and added his right arm to his left about her.

"Oh!" she cried. "Oh! Oh! Listen!"

From without came the flute-calls of quail. She quivered against him with the joy she took in the mellow-sweet notes.

"The coveys are breaking up," he said.

"It means spring," Paula cried.

"And the sign that good weather has come."

"And love!"

"And nest-building and egg-laying," Dick laughed. "Never has the world seemed more fecund than this morning. Lady Isleton is farrowed of eleven. The angoras were brought down this morning for the kidding. You should have seen them. And the wild canaries have been discussing matrimony in the patio for hours. I think some free lover is trying to break up their monogamic heaven with modern love-theories. It's a wonder you slept through the discussion. Listen! There they go now. Is that applause? Or is it a riot?"

Arose a thin twittering, like elfin pipings, with sharp pitches and excited shrillnesses, to which Dick and Paula lent delighted ears, till, suddenly, with the abruptness of the trump of doom, all the microphonic chorus of the tiny golden lovers was swept away, obliterated, in a Gargantuan blast of sound—no less wild, no less musical, no less passionate with love, but immense, dominant, compelling by very vastitude of volume.

The eager eyes of the man and woman sought instantly the channel past open French windows and the screen of the sleeping porch to the road through the lilacs, while they waited breathlessly for the great stallion to appear who trumpeted his love-call before him. Again, unseen, he trumpeted, and Dick said:

"I will sing you a song, my haughty moon. It is not my song. It is the Mountain Lad's. It is what he nickers. Listen! He sings it again. This is what he says: 'Hear me! I am Eros. I stamp upon the hills. I fill the wide valleys. The mares hear me, and startle, in quiet pastures; for they know me. The grass grows rich and richer, the land is filled with fatness, and the sap is in the trees. It is the spring. The spring is mine. I am monarch of my kingdom of the spring. The mares remember my voice. They know me aforetime through their mothers before them. Hear me! I am Eros. I stamp upon the hills, and the wide valleys are my heralds, echoing the sound of my approach.'"

And Paula pressed closer to her husband, and was pressed, as her lips touched his forehead, and as the pair of them, gazing at the empty road among the lilacs, saw it filled with the eruptive vision of Mountain Lad, majestic and mighty, the gnat-creature of a man upon his back absurdly small; his eyes wild and desirous, with the blue sheen that surfaces the eyes of stallions; his mouth, flecked with the froth and fret of high spirit, now brushed to burnished knees of impatience, now tossed skyward to utterance of that vast, compelling call that shook the air.

Almost as an echo, from afar off, came a thin-sweet answering whinney.

"It is the Fotherington Princess," Paula breathed softly.

Again Mountain Lad trumpeted his call, and Dick chanted:

"Hear me! I am Eros! I stamp upon the hills!"

And almost, for a flash of an instant, circled soft and close in his arms, Paula knew resentment of her husband's admiration for the splendid beast. And the next instant resentment vanished, and, in acknowledgment of due debt, she cried gaily:

"And now, Red Cloud! the Song of the Acorn!" Dick glanced half absently to her from the pamphlet folded on his finger, and then, with equal pitch of gaiety, sang:

"The acorns come down from heaven! I plant the short acorns in the valley! I plant the long acorns in the valley! I sprout, I, the black-oak acorn, sprout, I sprout!"

She had impressed herself very close against him during his moment of chanting, but, in the first moments that succeeded she felt the restless movement of the hand that held the finger-marked hog-pamphlet and caught the swift though involuntary flash of his eye to the clock on his desk that marked 11:25. Again she tried to hold him, although, with equal involuntariness, her attempt was made in mild terms of resentment.

"You are a strange and wonderful Red Cloud," she said slowly. "Sometimes almost am I convinced that you are utterly Red Cloud, planting your acorns and singing your savage joy of the planting. And, sometimes, almost you are to me the ultramodern man, the last word of the two-legged, male human that finds Trojan adventures in sieges of statistics, and, armed with test tubes and hypodermics, engages in gladiatorial contests with weird microorganisms. Almost, at times, it seems you should wear glasses and be bald-headed; almost, it seems... ."

"That I have no right of vigor to possess an armful of girl," he completed for her, drawing her still closer. "That I am a silly scientific brute who doesn't merit his 'vain little breath of sweet rose-colored dust.' Well, listen, I have a plan. In a few days... ."

But his plan died in birth, for, at their backs, came a discreet cough of warning, and, both heads turning as one they saw Bonbright, the assistant secretary, with a sheaf of notes on yellow sheets in his hand.

"Four telegrams," he murmured apologetically. "Mr. Blake is confident that two of them are very important. One of them concerns that Chile shipment of bulls... ."

And Paula, slowly drawing away from her husband and rising to her feet, could feel him slipping from her toward his tables of statistics, bills of lading, and secretaries, foremen, and managers.

"Oh, Paula," Dick called, as she was fading through the doorway; "I've christened the last boy—he's to be known as 'Oh Ho.' How do you like it?"

Her reply began with a hint of forlornness that vanished with her smile, as she warned:

"You *will* play ducks and drakes with the house-boys' names."

"I never do it with pedigreed stock," he assured her with a solemnity belied by the challenging twinkle in his eyes.

"I didn't mean that," was her retort. "I meant that you were exhausting the possibilities of the language. Before long you'll have to be calling them Oh Bel, Oh Hell, and Oh Go to Hell. Your 'Oh' was a mistake. You should have started with 'Red.' Then you could have had Red Bull, Red Horse, Red Dog, Red Frog, Red Fern—and, and all the rest of the reds."

She mingled her laughter with his, as she vanished, and, the next moment, the telegram before him, he was immersed in the details of the shipment, at two hundred and fifty dollars each, F. O. B., of three hundred registered yearling bulls to the beef ranges of Chile. Even so, vaguely, with vague pleasure, he heard Paula sing her way back across the patio to her long wing of house; though he was unaware that her voice was a trifle, just the merest trifle, subdued.

Chapter 8

Five minutes after Paula had left him, punctual to the second, the four telegrams disposed of, Dick was getting into a ranch motor car, along with Thayer, the Idaho buyer, and Naismith, the special correspondent for the *Breeders' Gazette*. Wardman, the sheep manager, joined them at the corrals where several thousand young Shropshire rams had been assembled for inspection.

There was little need for conversation. Thayer was distinctly disappointed in this, for he felt that the purchase of ten carloads of such expensive creatures was momentous enough to merit much conversation.

"They speak for themselves," Dick had assured him, and turned aside to give data to Naismith for his impending article on Shropshires in California and the Northwest.

"I wouldn't advise you to bother to select them," Dick told Thayer ten minutes later. "The average is all top. You could spend a week picking your ten carloads and have no higher grade than if you had taken the first to hand."

This cool assumption that the sale was already consummated so perturbed Thayer, that, along with the sure knowledge that he had never seen so high a quality of rams, he was nettled into changing his order to twenty carloads.

As he told Naismith, after they had regained the Big House and as they chalked their cues to finish the interrupted game:

"It's my first visit to Forrest's. He's a wizard. I've been buying in the East and importing. But those Shropshires won my judgment. You noticed I doubled my order. Those Idaho buyers will be wild for them. I only had buying orders straight for six carloads, and contingent on my judgment for two carloads more; but if every buyer doesn't double his order, straight and contingent, when he sees them rams, and if there isn't a stampede for what's left, I don't know sheep. They're the goods. If they don't jump up the sheep game of Idaho ... well, then Forrest's no breeder and I'm no buyer, that's all."

As the warning gong for lunch rang out—a huge bronze gong from Korea that was never struck until it was first indubitably ascertained that Paula was awake—Dick joined the young people at the goldfish fountain in the big patio. Bert Wainwright, variously advised and commanded by his sister, Rita, and by Paula and her sisters, Lute and Ernestine, was striving with a dip-net to catch a particularly gorgeous flower of a fish whose size and color and multiplicity of fins and tails had led Paula to decide to segregate him for the special breeding tank in the fountain of her own secret patio. Amid high excitement, and much squealing and laughter, the deed was accomplished, the big fish deposited in a can and carried away by the waiting Italian gardener.

"And what have you to say for yourself?" Ernestine challenged, as Dick joined them.

"Nothing," he answered sadly. "The ranch is depleted. Three hundred beautiful young bulls depart to-morrow for South America, and Thayer— you met him last night—is taking twenty carloads of rams. All I can say is that my congratulations are extended to Idaho and Chile."

"Plant more acorns," Paula laughed, her arms about her sisters, the three of them smilingly expectant of an inevitable antic.

"Oh, Dick, sing your acorn song," Lute begged.

He shook his head solemnly.

"I've got a better one. It's purest orthodoxy. It's got Red Cloud and his acorn song skinned to death. Listen! This is the song of the little East-sider, on her first trip to the country under the auspices of her Sunday School. She's quite young. Pay particular attention to her lisp."

And then Dick chanted, lisping:

"The goldfish thwimmeth in the bowl, The robin thiths upon the tree; What maketh them thit so eathily? Who stuckth the fur upon their breasths? God! God! He done it!"

"Cribbed," was Ernestine's judgment, as the laughter died away.

"Sure," Dick agreed. "I got it from the *Rancher and Stockman,* that got it from the *Swine Breeders' Journal*, that got it from the *Western Advocate*, that got it from *Public Opinion*, that got it, undoubtedly, from the little girl herself, or, rather from her Sunday School teacher. For that matter I am convinced it was first printed in *Our Dumb Animals*."

The bronze gong rang out its second call, and Paula, one arm around Dick, the other around Rita, led the way into the house, while, bringing up the rear, Bert Wainwright showed Lute Ernestine a new tango step.

"One thing, Thayer," Dick said in an aside, after releasing himself from the girls, as they jostled in confusion where they met Thayer and Naismith at the head of the stairway leading down to the dining room. "Before you leave us, cast your eyes over those Merinos. I really have to brag about them, and American sheepmen will have to come to them. Of course, started with imported stock, but I've made a California strain that will make the French breeders sit up. See Wardman and take your pick. Get Naismith to look them over with you. Stick half a dozen of them in your train-load, with my compliments, and let your Idaho sheepmen get a line on them."

They seated at a table, capable of indefinite extension, in a long, low dining room that was a replica of the hacienda dining rooms of the Mexican land-kings of old California. The floor was of large brown tiles, the beamed ceiling and the walls were whitewashed, and the huge, undecorated, cement fireplace was an achievement in massiveness and simplicity. Greenery and blooms nodded from without the deep- embrasured windows, and the room expressed the sense of cleanness, chastity, and coolness.

On the walls, but not crowded, were a number of canvases— most ambitious of all, in the setting of honor, all in sad grays, a twilight Mexican scene by Xavier Martinez, of a peon, with a crooked- stick plow and two bullocks, turning a melancholy furrow across the foreground of a sad, illimitable, Mexican plain. There were brighter pictures, of early Mexican-Californian life, a pastel of twilight eucalyptus with a sunset-tipped mountain beyond, by Reimers, a moonlight by Peters, and a Griffin stubble-field across which gleamed and smoldered California summer hills of tawny brown and purple- misted, wooded canyons.

"Say," Thayer muttered in an undertone across to Naismith, while Dick and the girls were in the thick of exclamatory and giggling banter, "here's some stuff for that article of yours, if you touch upon the Big House. I've seen the servants' dining room. Forty head sit down to it every meal, including gardeners, chauffeurs, and outside help. It's a boarding house in itself. Some head, some system, take it from me. That Chiney boy, Oh Joy, is a wooz. He's housekeeper, or manager, of the whole shebang, or whatever you want to call his job—and, say, it runs that smooth you can't hear it."

"Forrest's the real wooz," Naismith nodded. "He's the brains that picks brains. He could run an army, a campaign, a government, or even a three-ring circus."

"Which last is some compliment," Thayer concurred heartily.

"Oh, Paula," Dick said across to his wife. "I just got word that

Graham arrives to-morrow morning. Better tell Oh Joy to put him in the watch-tower. It's man-size quarters, and it's possible he may carry out his threat and work on his book."

"Graham?—Graham?" Paula queried aloud of her memory. "Do I know him?"

"You met him once two years ago, in Santiago, at the Café Venus. He had dinner with us."

"Oh, one of those naval officers?"

Dick shook his head.

"The civilian. Don't you remember that big blond fellow—you talked music with him for half an hour while Captain Joyce talked our heads off to prove that the United States should clean Mexico up and out with the mailed fist."

"Oh, to be sure," Paula vaguely recollected. "He'd met you somewhere before... South Africa, wasn't it? Or the Philippines?"

"That's the chap. South Africa, it was. Evan Graham. Next time we met was on the *Times* dispatch boat on the Yellow Sea. And we crossed trails a dozen times after that, without meeting, until that night in the Café Venus.

"Heavens—he left Bora-Bora, going east, two days before I dropped anchor bound west on my way to Samoa. I came out of Apia, with letters for him from the American consul, the day before he came in. We missed each other by three days at Levuka—I was sailing the *Wild Duck* then. He pulled out of Suva as guest on a British cruiser. Sir Everard Im Thurm, British High Commissioner of the South Seas, gave me more letters for Graham. I missed him at Port Resolution and at Vila in the New Hebrides. The cruiser was junketing, you see. I beat her in and out of the Santa Cruz Group. It was the same thing in the Solomons. The cruiser, after shelling the cannibal villages at Langa-Langa, steamed out in the morning. I sailed in that afternoon. I never did deliver those letters in person, and the next time I laid eyes on him was at the Café Venus two years ago."

"But who about him, and what about him?" Paula queried. "And what's the book?"

"Well, first of all, beginning at the end, he's broke—that is, for him, he's broke. He's got an income of several thousand a year left, but all that his father left him is gone. No; he didn't blow it. He got in deep, and the 'silent panic' several years ago just about cleaned him. But he doesn't whimper.

"He's good stuff, old American stock, a Yale man. The book—he expects to make a bit on it—covers last year's trip across South America, west coast to east coast. It was largely new ground. The

Brazilian government voluntarily voted him a honorarium of ten thousand dollars for the information he brought out concerning unexplored portions of Brazil. Oh, he's a man, all man. He delivers the goods. You know the type—clean, big, strong, simple; been everywhere, seen everything, knows most of a lot of things, straight, square, looks you in the eyes—well, in short, a man's man."

Ernestine clapped her hands, flung a tantalizing, man-challenging, man-conquering glance at Bert Wainwright, and exclaimed: "And he comes tomorrow!"

Dick shook his head reprovingly.

"Oh, nothing in that direction, Ernestine. Just as nice girls as you have tried to hook Evan Graham before now. And, between ourselves, I couldn't blame them. But he's had good wind and fast legs, and they've always failed to run him down or get him into a corner, where, dazed and breathless, he's mechanically muttered 'Yes' to certain interrogatories and come out of the trance to find himself, roped, thrown, branded, and married. Forget him, Ernestine. Stick by golden youth and let it drop its golden apples. Pick them up, and golden youth with them, making a noise like stupid failure all the time you are snaring swift-legged youth. But Graham's out of the running. He's old like me—just about the same age—and, like me, he's run a lot of those queer races. He knows how to make a get-away. He's been cut by barbed wire, nose-twitched, neck-burnt, cinched to a fare-you-well, and he remains subdued but uncatchable. He doesn't care for young things. In fact, you may charge him with being wobbly, but I plead guilty, by proxy, that he is merely old, hard bitten, and very wise."

Chapter 9

"Where's my Boy in Breeches?" Dick shouted, stamping with jingling spurs through the Big House in quest of its Little Lady.

He came to the door that gave entrance to her long wing. It was a door without a knob, a huge panel of wood in a wood-paneled wall. But Dick shared the secret of the hidden spring with his wife, pressed the spring, and the door swung wide.

"Where's my Boy in Breeches?" he called and stamped down the length of her quarters.

A glance into the bathroom, with its sunken Roman bath and descending marble steps, was fruitless, as were the glances he sent into Paula's wardrobe room and dressing room. He passed the short, broad stairway that led to her empty window-seat divan in what she called her Juliet Tower, and thrilled at sight of an orderly disarray of filmy, pretty, lacy woman's things that he knew she had spread out for her own sensuous delight of contemplation. He fetched up for a moment at a drawing easel, his reiterant cry checked on his lips, and threw a laugh of recognition and appreciation at the sketch, just outlined, of an awkward, big-boned, knobby, weanling colt caught in the act of madly whinneying for its mother.

"Where's my Boy in Breeches?" he shouted before him, out to the sleeping porch; and found only a demure, brow-troubled Chinese woman of thirty, who smiled self-effacing embarrassment into his eyes.

This was Paula's maid, Oh Dear, so named by Dick, many years before, because of a certain solicitous contraction of her delicate brows that made her appear as if ever on the verge of saying, "Oh dear!" In fact, Dick had taken her, as a child almost, for Paula's service, from a fishing village on the Yellow Sea where her widow-mother earned as much as four dollars in a prosperous year at making nets for the fishermen. Oh Dear's first service for Paula had been aboard the three-topmast schooner, *All Away*, at the same time that Oh Joy, cabin-boy, had begun to demonstrate the efficiency that enabled him, through the years, to rise to the majordomoship of the Big House.

"Where is your mistress, Oh Dear?" Dick asked.

Oh Dear shrank away in an agony of bashfulness.

Dick waited.

"She maybe with 'm young ladies—I don't know," Oh Dear stammered; and Dick, in very mercy, swung away on his heel.

"Where's my Boy in Breeches?" he shouted, as he stamped out under the porte cochère just as a ranch limousine swung around the curve among the lilacs.

"I'll be hanged if I know," a tall, blond man in a light summer suit responded from the car; and the next moment Dick Forrest and Evan Graham were shaking hands.

Oh My and Oh Ho carried in the hand baggage, and Dick accompanied his guest to the watch tower quarters.

"You'll have to get used to us, old man," Dick was explaining. "We run the ranch like clockwork, and the servants are wonders; but we allow ourselves all sorts of loosenesses. If you'd arrived two minutes later there'd have been no one to welcome you but the Chinese boys. I was just going for a ride, and Paula—Mrs. Forrest —has disappeared."

The two men were almost of a size, Graham topping his host by perhaps an inch, but losing that inch in the comparative breadth of shoulders and depth of chest. Graham was, if anything, a clearer blond than Forrest, although both were equally gray of eye, equally clear in the whites of the eyes, and equally and precisely similarly bronzed by sun and weather-beat. Graham's features were in a slightly larger mold; his eyes were a trifle longer, although this was lost again by a heavier droop of lids. His nose hinted that it was a shade straighter as well as larger than Dick's, and his lips were a shade thicker, a shade redder, a shade more bowed with fulsomeness.

Forrest's hair was light brown to chestnut, while Graham's carried a whispering advertisement that it would have been almost golden in its silk had it not been burned almost to sandiness by the sun. The cheeks of both were high-boned, although the hollows under Forrest's cheek- bones were more pronounced. Both noses were large-nostriled and sensitive. And both mouths, while generously proportioned, carried the impression of girlish sweetness and chastity along with the muscles that could draw the lips to the firmness and harshness that would not give the lie to the square, uncleft chins beneath.

But the inch more in height and the inch less in chest-girth gave Evan Graham a grace of body and carriage that Dick Forrest did not possess. In this particular of build, each served well as a foil to the other. Graham was all light and delight, with a hint—but the slightest of hints—of Prince Charming. Forrest's seemed a more efficient and formidable organism, more dangerous to other life, stouter-gripped on its own life.

Forrest threw a glance at his wrist watch as he talked, but in that glance, without pause or fumble of focus, with swift certainty of correlation, he read the dial.

"Eleven-thirty," he said. "Come along at once, Graham. We don't eat till twelve-thirty. I am sending out a shipment of bulls, three hundred of them, and I'm downright proud of them. You simply must see them. Never mind your riding togs. Oh Ho—fetch a pair of my leggings. You, Oh Joy, order Altadena saddled.—What saddle do you prefer, Graham?"

"Oh, anything, old man."

"English?—Australian?—McClellan?—Mexican?" Dick insisted.

"McClellan, if it's no trouble," Graham surrendered.

They sat their horses by the side of the road and watched the last of the herd beginning its long journey to Chili disappear around the bend.

"I see what you're doing—it's great," Graham said with sparkling eyes. "I've fooled some myself with the critters, when I was a youngster, down in the Argentine. If I'd had beef-blood like that to build on, I mightn't have taken the cropper I did."

"But that was before alfalfa and artesian wells," Dick smoothed for him. "The time wasn't ripe for the Shorthorn. Only scrubs could survive the droughts. They were strong in staying powers but light on the scales. And refrigerator steamships hadn't been invented. That's what revolutionized the game down there."

"Besides, I was a mere youngster," Graham added. "Though that meant nothing much. There was a young German tackled it at the same time I did, with a tenth of my capital. He hung it out, lean years, dry years, and all. He's rated in seven figures now."

They turned their horses back for the Big House. Dick flirted his wrist to see his watch.

"Lots of time," he assured his guest. "I'm glad you saw those yearlings. There was one reason why that young German stuck it out. He had to. You had your father's money to fall back on, and, I imagine not only that your feet itched, but that your chief weakness lay in that you could afford to solace the itching."

"Over there are the fish ponds," Dick said, indicating with a nod of his head to the right an invisible area beyond the lilacs. "You'll have plenty of opportunity to catch a mess of trout, or bass, or even catfish. You see, I'm a miser. I love to make things work. There may be a justification for the eight-hour labor day, but I make the work- day of water just twenty-four hours' long. The ponds are in series, according to the nature of the fish. But the water starts working up in the mountains. It irrigates a score of mountain meadows before it makes the plunge and is clarified to crystal clearness in the next few rugged miles; and at the plunge from the highlands it generates half the power and all the lighting used on the ranch. Then it sub- irrigates lower levels, flows in here to the fish ponds, and runs out and irrigates miles of alfalfa farther on. And, believe me, if by that time it hadn't reached the flat of the Sacramento, I'd be pumping out the drainage for more irrigation."

"Man, man," Graham laughed, "you could make a poem on the wonder of water. I've met fire-worshipers, but you're the first real water- worshiper I've ever encountered. And you're no desert-dweller, either. You live in a land of water—pardon the bull—but, as I was saying… "

Graham never completed his thought. From the right, not far away, came the unmistakable ring of shod hoofs on concrete, followed by a mighty splash and an outburst of women's cries and laughter. Quickly the cries turned to alarm, accompanied by the sounds of a prodigious splashing and floundering as of some huge, drowning beast. Dick bent his head and leaped his horse through the lilacs, Graham, on Altadena, followed at his heels. They emerged in a blaze of sunshine, on an open space among the trees, and Graham came upon as unexpected a picture as he had ever chanced upon in his life.

Tree-surrounded, the heart of the open space was a tank, four-sided of concrete. The upper end of the tank, full width, was a broad spillway, sheened with an inch of smooth-slipping water. The sides were perpendicular. The lower end, roughly corrugated, sloped out gently to solid footing. Here, in distress that was consternation, and in fear that was panic, excitedly bobbed up and down a cowboy in bearskin chaps, vacuously repeating the exclamation, "Oh God! Oh God!"—the first division of it rising in inflection, the second division inflected fallingly with despair. On the edge of the farther side, facing him, in bathing suits, legs dangling toward the water, sat three terrified nymphs.

And in the tank, the center of the picture, a great horse, bright bay and wet and ruddy satin, vertical in the water, struck upward and outward into the free air with huge fore-hoofs steel-gleaming in the wet and sun, while on its back, slipping and clinging, was the white form of what Graham took at first to be some glorious youth. Not until the stallion, sinking, emerged again by means of the powerful beat of his legs and hoofs, did Graham realize that it was a woman who rode him—a woman as white as the white silken slip of a bathing suit that molded to her form like a marble-carven veiling of drapery. As marble was her back, save that the fine delicate muscles moved and crept under the silken suit as she strove to keep her head above water. Her slim round arms were twined in yards of half-drowned stallion-mane, while her white round knees slipped on the sleek, wet, satin pads of the great horse's straining shoulder muscles. The white toes of her dug for a grip into the smooth sides of the animal, vainly seeking a hold on the ribs beneath.

In a breath, or the half of a breath, Graham saw the whole breathless situation, realized that the white wonderful creature was a woman, and sensed the smallness and daintiness of her despite her gladiatorial struggles. She reminded him of some Dresden china figure set absurdly small and light and strangely on the drowning back of a titanic beast. So dwarfed was she by the bulk of the stallion that she was a midget, or a tiny fairy from fairyland come true.

As she pressed her cheek against the great arching neck, her golden- brown hair, wet from being under, flowing and tangled, seemed tangled in the black mane of the stallion. But it was her face that smote Graham most of all. It was a boy's face; it was a woman's face; it was serious and at the same time amused, expressing the pleasure it found woven with the peril. It was a white woman's face—and modern; and yet, to Graham, it was all-pagan. This was not a creature and a situation one happened upon in the twentieth century. It was straight out of old Greece. It was a Maxfield Parrish reminiscence from the Arabian Nights. Genii might be expected to rise from those troubled depths, or golden princes, astride winged dragons, to swoop down out of the blue to the rescue.

The stallion, forcing itself higher out of water, missed, by a shade, from turning over backward as it sank. Glorious animal and glorious rider disappeared together beneath the surface, to rise together, a second later, the stallion still pawing the air with fore-hoofs the size of dinner plates, the rider still clinging to the sleek, satin- coated muscles. Graham thought, with a gasp, what might have happened had the stallion turned over. A chance blow from any one of those four enormous floundering hoofs could have put out and quenched forever the light and sparkle of that superb, white-bodied, fire-animated woman.

"Ride his neck!" Dick shouted. "Catch his foretop and get on his neck till he balances out!"

The woman obeyed, digging her toes into the evasive muscle-pads for the quick effort, and leaping upward, one hand twined in the wet mane, the other hand free and up-stretched, darting between the ears and clutching the foretop. The next moment, as the stallion balanced out horizontally in obedience to her shiftage of weight, she had slipped back to the shoulders. Holding with one hand to the mane, she waved a white arm in the air and flashed a smile of acknowledgment to Forrest; and, as Graham noted, she was cool enough to note him on his horse beside Forrest. Also, Graham realized that the turning of her head and the waving of her arm was only partly in bravado, was more in aesthetic wisdom of the picture she composed, and was, most of all, sheer joy of daring and emprise of the blood and the flesh and the life that was she.

"Not many women'd tackle that," Dick said quietly, as Mountain Lad, easily retaining his horizontal position once it had been attained, swam to the lower end of the tank and floundered up the rough slope to the anxious cowboy.

The latter swiftly adjusted the halter with a turn of chain between the jaws. But Paula, still astride, leaned forward, imperiously took the lead-part from the cowboy, whirled Mountain Lad around to face Forrest, and saluted.

"Now you will have to go away," she called. "This is our hen party, and the stag public is not admitted."

Dick laughed, saluted acknowledgment, and led the way back through the lilacs to the road.

"Who ... who was it?" Graham queried.

"Paula—Mrs. Forrest—the boy girl, the child that never grew up, the grittiest puff of rose-dust that was ever woman."

"My breath is quite taken away," Graham said. "Do your people do such stunts frequently?"

"First time she ever did that," Forrest replied. "That was Mountain Lad. She rode him straight down the spill-way—tobogganed with him, twenty-two hundred and forty pounds of him."

"Risked his neck and legs as well as her own," was Graham's comment.

"Thirty-five thousand dollars' worth of neck and legs," Dick smiled. "That's what a pool of breeders offered me for him last year after he'd cleaned up the Coast with his get as well as himself. And as for Paula, she could break necks and legs at that price every day in the year until I went broke—only she doesn't. She never has accidents."

"I wouldn't have given tuppence for her chance if he'd turned over."

"But he didn't," Dick answered placidly. "That's Paula's luck. She's tough to kill. Why, I've had her under shell-fire where she was actually disappointed because she didn't get hit, or killed, or near- killed. Four batteries opened on us, shrapnel, at mile-range, and we had to cover half a mile of smooth hill-brow for shelter. I really felt I was justified in charging her with holding back. She did admit a 'trifle.' We've been married ten or a dozen years now, and, d'ye know, sometimes it seems to me I don't know her at all, and that nobody knows her, and that she doesn't know herself—just the same way as you and I can look at ourselves in a mirror and wonder who the devil we are anyway. Paula and I have one magic formula: *Damn the expense when fun is selling.* And it doesn't matter whether the price is in dollars, hide, or life. It's our way and our luck. It works. And, d'ye know, we've never been gouged on the price yet."

Chapter 10

It was a stag lunch. As Forrest explained, the girls were "hen-partying."

"I doubt you'll see a soul of them till four o'clock, when Ernestine, that's one of Paula's sisters, is going to wallop me at tennis—at least so she's threatened and pledged."

And Graham sat through the lunch, where only men sat, took his part in the conversation on breeds and breeding, learned much, contributed a mite from his own world-experiences, and was unable to shake from his eyes the persistent image of his hostess, the vision of the rounded and delicate white of her against the dark wet background of the swimming stallion. And all the afternoon, looking over prize Merinos and Berkshire gilts, continually that vision burned up under his eyelids. Even at four, in the tennis court, himself playing against Ernestine, he missed more than one stroke because the image of the flying ball would suddenly be eclipsed by the image of a white marble figure of a woman that strove and clung on the back of a great horse.

Graham, although an outlander, knew his California, and, while every girl of the swimming suits was gowned for dinner, was not surprised to find no man similarly accoutered. Nor had he made the mistake of so being himself, despite the Big House and the magnificent scale on which it operated.

Between the first and second gongs, all the guests drifted into the long dining room. Sharp after the second gong, Dick Forrest arrived and precipitated cocktails. And Graham impatiently waited the appearance of the woman who had worried his eyes since noon. He was prepared for all manner of disappointment. Too many gorgeous stripped athletes had he seen slouched into conventional garmenting, to expect too much of the marvelous creature in the white silken swimming suit when it should appear garbed as civilized women garb.

He caught his breath with an imperceptible gasp when she entered. She paused, naturally, for just the right flash of an instant in the arched doorway, limned against the darkness behind her, the soft glow of the indirect lighting full upon her. Graham's lips gasped apart, and remained apart, his eyes ravished with the beauty and surprise of her he had deemed so small, so fairy-like. Here was no delicate midget of a child-woman or boy-girl on a stallion, but a grand lady, as only a small woman can be grand on occasion.

Taller in truth was she, as well as in seeming, than he had judged her, and as finely proportioned in her gown as in her swimming suit. He noted her shining gold-brown hair piled high; the healthy tinge of her skin that was clean and clear and white; the singing throat, full and round, incomparably set on a healthy chest; and the gown, dull blue, a sort of medieval thing with half-fitting, half-clinging body, with flowing sleeves and trimmings of gold-jeweled bands.

She smiled an embracing salutation and greeting. Graham recognized it as kin to the one he had seen when she smiled from the back of the stallion. When she started forward, he could not fail to see the inimitable way she carried the cling and weight of her draperies with her knees—round knees, he knew, that he had seen press desperately into the round muscle-pads of Mountain Lad. Graham observed, also, that she neither wore nor needed corseting. Nor could he fail, as she crossed the floor, to see two women: one, the grand lady, the mistress of the Big House; one, the lovely equestrienne statue beneath the dull-blue, golden-trimmed gown, that no gowning could ever make his memory forget.

She was upon them, among them, and Graham's hand held hers in the formal introduction as he was made welcome to the Big House and all the hacienda in a voice that he knew was a singing voice and that could proceed only from a throat that pillared, such as hers, from a chest deep as hers despite her smallness.

At table, across the corner from her, he could not help a surreptitious studying of her. While he held his own in the general fun and foolishness, it was his hostess that mostly filled the circle of his eye and the content of his mind.

It was as bizarre a company as Graham had ever sat down to dinner with. The sheep-buyer and the correspondent for the *Breeders' Gazette* were still guests. Three machine-loads of men, women, and girls, totaling fourteen, had arrived shortly before the first gong and had remained to ride home in the moonlight. Graham could not remember their names; but he made out that they came from some valley town thirty miles away called Wickenberg, and that they were of the small-town banking, professional, and wealthy-farmer class. They were full of spirits, laughter, and the latest jokes and catches sprung in the latest slang.

"I see right now," Graham told Paula, "if your place continues to be the caravanserai which it has been since my arrival, that I might as well give up trying to remember names and people."

"I don't blame you," she laughed concurrence. "But these are neighbors. They drop in any time. Mrs. Watson, there, next to Dick, is of the old land-aristocracy. Her grandfather, Wicken, came across the Sierras in 1846. Wickenberg is named after him. And that pretty dark- eyed girl is her daughter... ."

And while Paula gave him a running sketch of the chance guests, Graham heard scarce half she said, so occupied was he in trying to sense his way to an understanding of her. Naturalness was her keynote, was his first judgment. In not many moments he had decided that her key-note was joy. But he was dissatisfied with both conclusions, and knew he had not put his finger on her. And then it came to him—pride. That was it! It was in her eye, in the poise of her head, in the curling tendrils of her hair, in her sensitive nostrils, in the mobile lips, in the very pitch and angle of the rounded chin, in her hands, small, muscular and veined, that he knew at sight to be the hard-worked hands of one who had spent long hours at the piano. Pride it was, in every muscle, nerve, and quiver of her—conscious, sentient, stinging pride.

She might be joyous and natural, boy and woman, fun and frolic; but always the pride was there, vibrant, tense, intrinsic, the basic stuff of which she was builded. She was a woman, frank, outspoken, straight- looking, plastic, democratic; but toy she was not. At times, to him, she seemed to glint an impression of steel—thin, jewel-like steel. She seemed strength in its most delicate terms and fabrics. He fondled the impression of her as of silverspun wire, of fine leather, of twisted hair-sennit from the heads of maidens such as the Marquesans make, of carven pearl-shell for the lure of the bonita, and of barbed ivory at the heads of sea-spears such as the Eskimos throw.

"All right, Aaron," they heard Dick Forrest's voice rising, in a lull, from the other end of the table. "Here's something from Phillips Brooks for you to chew on. Brooks said that no man 'has come to true greatness who has not felt in some degree that his life belongs to his race, and that what God gives him, he gives him for mankind.'"

"So at last you believe in God?" the man, addressed Aaron, genially sneered back. He was a slender, long-faced olive-brunette, with brilliant black eyes and the blackest of long black beards.

"I'm hanged if I know," Dick answered. "Anyway, I quoted only figuratively. Call it morality, call it good, call it evolution."

"A man doesn't have to be intellectually correct in order to be great," intruded a quiet, long-faced Irishman, whose sleeves were threadbare and frayed. "And by the same token many men who are most correct in sizing up the universe have been least great."

"True for you, Terrence," Dick applauded.

"It's a matter of definition," languidly spoke up an unmistakable Hindoo, crumbling his bread with exquisitely slender and small-boned fingers. "What shall we mean as *great*?"

"Shall we say *beauty*?" softly queried a tragic-faced youth, sensitive and shrinking, crowned with an abominably trimmed head of long hair.

Ernestine rose suddenly at her place, hands on table, leaning forward with a fine simulation of intensity.

"They're off!" she cried. "They're off! Now we'll have the universe settled all over again for the thousandth time. Theodore"—to the youthful poet—"it's a poor start. Get into the running. Ride your father ion and your mother ion, and you'll finish three lengths ahead."

A roar of laughter was her reward, and the poet blushed and receded into his sensitive shell.

Ernestine turned on the black-bearded one:

"Now, Aaron. He's not in form. You start it. You know how. Begin: 'As Bergson so well has said, with the utmost refinement of philosophic speech allied with the most comprehensive intellectual outlook that... .'"

More laughter roared down the table, drowning Ernestine's conclusion as well as the laughing retort of the black-bearded one.

"Our philosophers won't have a chance to-night," Paula stole in an aside to Graham.

"Philosophers?" he questioned back. "They didn't come with the Wickenberg crowd. Who and what are they? I'm all at sea."

"They—" Paula hesitated. "They live here. They call themselves the jungle-birds. They have a camp in the woods a couple of miles away, where they never do anything except read and talk. I'll wager, right now, you'll find fifty of Dick's latest, uncatalogued books in their cabins. They have the run of the library, as well, and you'll see them drifting in and out, any time of the day or night, with their arms full of books—also, the latest magazines. Dick says they are responsible for his possessing the most exhaustive and up-to-date library on philosophy on the Pacific Coast. In a way, they sort of digest such things for him. It's great fun for Dick, and, besides, it saves him time. He's a dreadfully hard worker, you know."

"I understand that they… that Dick takes care of them?" Graham asked, the while he pleasured in looking straight into the blue eyes that looked so straight into his.

As she answered, he was occupied with noting the faintest hint of bronze—perhaps a trick of the light—in her long, brown lashes. Perforce, he lifted his gaze to her eyebrows, brown, delicately stenciled, and made sure that the hint of bronze was there. Still lifting his gaze to her high-piled hair, he again saw, but more pronounced, the bronze note glinting from the brown-golden hair. Nor did he fail to startle and thrill to a dazzlement of smile and teeth and eye that frequently lived its life in her face. Hers was no thin smile of restraint, he judged. When she smiled she smiled all of herself, generously, joyously, throwing the largess of all her being into the natural expression of what was herself and which domiciled somewhere within that pretty head of hers.

"Yes," she was saying. "They have never to worry, as long as they live, over mere bread and butter. Dick is most generous, and, rather immoral, in his encouragement of idleness on the part of men like them. It's a funny place, as you'll find out until you come to understand us. They… they are appurtenances, and—and hereditaments, and such things. They will be with us always until we bury them or they bury us. Once in a while one or another of them drifts away—for a time. Like the cat, you know. Then it costs Dick real money to get them back. Terrence, there—Terrence McFane—he's an epicurean anarchist, if you know what that means. He wouldn't kill a flea. He has a pet cat I gave him, a Persian of the bluest blue, and he carefully picks her fleas, not injuring them, stores them in a vial, and turns them loose in the forest on his long walks when he tires of human companionship and communes with nature.

"Well, only last year, he got a bee in his bonnet—the alphabet. He started for Egypt—without a cent, of course—to run the alphabet down in the home of its origin and thereby to win the formula that would explain the cosmos. He got as far as Denver, traveling as tramps travel, when he mixed up in some I. W. W. riot for free speech or something. Dick had to hire lawyers, pay fines, and do just about everything to get him safe home again.

"And the one with a beard—Aaron Hancock. Like Terrence, he won't work. Aaron's a Southerner. Says none of his people ever did work, and that there have always been peasants and fools who just couldn't be restrained from working. That's why he wears a beard. To shave, he holds, is unnecessary work, and, therefore, immoral. I remember, at Melbourne, when he broke in upon Dick and me, a sunburnt wild man from out the Australian bush. It seems he'd been making original researches in anthropology, or folk-lore-ology, or something like that. Dick had known him years before in Paris, and Dick assured him, if he ever drifted back to America, of food and shelter. So here he is."

"And the poet?" Graham asked, glad that she must still talk for a while, enabling him to study the quick dazzlement of smile that played upon her face.

"Oh, Theo—Theodore Malken, though we call him Leo. He won't work, either. His people are old Californian stock and dreadfully wealthy; but they disowned him and he disowned them when he was fifteen. They say he is lunatic, and he says they are merely maddening. He really writes some remarkable verse... when he does write; but he prefers to dream and live in the jungle with Terrence and Aaron. He was tutoring immigrant Jews in San Francisco, when Terrence and Aaron rescued him, or captured him, I don't know which. He's been with us two years now, and he's actually filling out, despite the facts that Dick is absurdly generous in furnishing supplies and that they'd rather talk and read and dream than cook. The only good meals they get is when they descend upon us, like to-night."

"And the Hindoo, there—who's he?"

"That's Dar Hyal. He's their guest. The three of them invited him up, just as Aaron first invited Terrence, and as Aaron and Terrence invited Leo. Dick says, in time, three more are bound to appear, and then he'll have his Seven Sages of the Madroño Grove. Their jungle camp is in a madroño grove, you know. It's a most beautiful spot, with living springs, a canyon—but I was telling you about Dar Hyal.

"He's a revolutionist, of sorts. He's dabbled in our universities, studied in France, Italy, Switzerland, is a political refugee from India, and he's hitched his wagon to two stars: one, a new synthetic system of philosophy; the other, rebellion against the tyranny of British rule in India. He advocates individual terrorism and direct mass action. That's why his paper, *Kadar*, or *Badar*, or something like that, was suppressed here in California, and why he narrowly escaped being deported; and that's why he's up here just now, devoting himself to formulating his philosophy.

"He and Aaron quarrel tremendously—that is, on philosophical matters. And now—" Paula sighed and erased the sigh with her smile—"and now, I'm done. Consider yourself acquainted. And, oh, if you encounter our sages more intimately, a word of warning, especially if the encounter be in the stag room: Dar Hyal is a total abstainer; Theodore Malken can get poetically drunk, and usually does, on one cocktail; Aaron Hancock is an expert wine-bibber; and Terrence McFane, knowing little of one drink from another, and caring less, can put ninety-nine men out of a hundred under the table and go right on lucidly expounding epicurean anarchy."

One thing Graham noted as the dinner proceeded. The sages called Dick Forrest by his first name; but they always addressed Paula as "Mrs. Forrest," although she called them by their first names. There was nothing affected about it. Quite unconsciously did they, who respected few things under the sun, and among such few things not even work— quite unconsciously, and invariably, did they recognize the certain definite aloofness in Dick Forrest's wife so that her given name was alien to their lips. By such tokens Evan Graham was not slow in learning that Dick Forrest's wife had a way with her, compounded of sheerest democracy and equally sheer royalty.

It was the same thing, after dinner, in the big living room. She dared as she pleased, but nobody assumed. Before the company settled down, Paula seemed everywhere, bubbling over with more outrageous spirits than any of them. From this group or that, from one corner or another, her laugh rang out. And her laugh fascinated Graham. There was a fibrous thrill in it, most sweet to the ear, that differentiated it from any laugh he had ever heard. It caused Graham to lose the thread of young Mr. Wombold's contention that what California needed was not a Japanese exclusion law but at least two hundred thousand Japanese coolies to do the farm labor of California and knock in the head the threatened eight-hour day for agricultural laborers. Young Mr. Wombold, Graham gleaned, was an hereditary large land-owner in the vicinity of Wickenberg who prided himself on not yielding to the trend of the times by becoming an absentee landlord.

From the piano, where Eddie Mason was the center of a group of girls, came much noise of ragtime music and slangtime song. Terrence McFane and Aaron Hancock fell into a heated argument over the music of futurism. And Graham was saved from the Japanese situation with Mr. Wombold by Dar Hyal, who proceeded to proclaim Asia for the Asiatics and California for the Californians.

Paula, catching up her skirts for speed, fled down the room in some romp, pursued by Dick, who captured her as she strove to dodge around the Wombold group.

"Wicked woman," Dick reproved her in mock wrath; and, the

next moment, joined her in persuading Dar Hyal to dance.

And Dar Hyal succumbed, flinging Asia and the Asiatics to the winds, along with his arms and legs, as he weirdly parodied the tango in what he declared to be the "blastic" culmination of modern dancing.

"And now, Red Cloud, sing Mr. Graham your Acorn Song," Paula commanded Dick.

Forrest, his arm still about her, detaining her for the threatened punishment not yet inflicted, shook his head somberly.

"The Acorn Song!" Ernestine called from the piano; and the cry was taken up by Eddie Mason and the girls.

"Oh, do, Dick," Paula pleaded. "Mr. Graham is the only one who hasn't heard it."

Dick shook his head.

"Then sing him your Goldfish Song."

"I'll sing him Mountain Lad's song," Dick bullied, a whimsical sparkle in his eyes. He stamped his feet, pranced, nickered a not bad imitation of Mountain Lad, tossed an imaginary mane, and cried:

"Hear me! I am Eros! I stamp upon the hills!"

"The Acorn Song," Paula interrupted quickly and quietly, with just the hint of steel in her voice.

Dick obediently ceased his chant of Mountain Lad, but shook his head like a stubborn colt.

"I have a new song," he said solemnly. "It is about you and me, Paula. I got it from the Nishinam."

"The Nishinam are the extinct aborigines of this part of California," Paula shot in a swift aside of explanation to Graham.

Dick danced half a dozen steps, stiff-legged, as Indians dance, slapped his thighs with his palms, and began a new chant, still retaining his hold on his wife.

"Me, I am Ai-kut, the first man of the Nishinam. Ai-kut is the short for Adam, and my father and my mother were the coyote and the moon. And this is Yo-to-to-wi, my wife. She is the first woman of the Nishinam. Her father and her mother were the grasshopper and the ring- tailed cat. They were the best father and mother left after my father and mother. The coyote is very wise, the moon is very old; but who ever heard much of anything of credit to the grasshopper and the ring- tailed cat? The Nishinam are always right. The mother of all women had to be a cat, a little, wizened, sad-faced, shrewd ring-tailed cat."

Whereupon the song of the first man and woman was interrupted by protests from the women and acclamations from the men.

"This is Yo-to-to-wi, which is the short for Eve," Dick chanted on, drawing Paula bruskly closer to his side with a semblance of savage roughness. "Yo-to-to-wi is not much to look at. But be not hard upon her. The fault is with the grasshopper and the ring-tailed cat. Me, I am Ai-kut, the first man; but question not my taste. I was the first man, and this, I saw, was the first woman. Where there is but one choice, there is not much to choose. Adam was so circumstanced. He chose Eve. Yo-to-to-wi was the one woman in all the world for me, so I chose Yo-to-to-wi."

And Evan Graham, listening, his eyes on that possessive, encircling arm of all his hostess's fairness, felt an awareness of hurt, and arose unsummoned the thought, to be dismissed angrily, "Dick Forrest is lucky—too lucky."

"Me, I am Ai-kut," Dick chanted on. "This is my dew of woman. She is my honey-dew of woman. I have lied to you. Her father and her mother were neither hopper nor cat. They were the Sierra dawn and the summer east wind of the mountains. Together they conspired, and from the air and earth they sweated all sweetness till in a mist of their own love the leaves of the chaparral and the manzanita were dewed with the honey-dew.

"Yo-to-to-wi is my honey-dew woman. Hear me! I am Ai-kut. Yo-to-to-wi is my quail woman, my deer-woman, my lush-woman of all soft rain and fat soil. She was born of the thin starlight and the brittle dawn- light before the sun ...

"And," Forrest concluded, relapsing into his natural voice and enunciation, having reached the limit of extemporization,—"and if you think old, sweet, blue-eyed Solomon has anything on me in singing the Song of Songs, just put your names down for the subscription edition of *my* Song of Songs."

Chapter 11

It was Mrs. Mason who first asked that Paula play; but it was Terrence McFane and Aaron Hancock who evicted the rag-time group from the piano and sent Theodore Malken, a blushing ambassador, to escort Paula.

"'Tis for the confounding of this pagan that I'm askin' you to play 'Reflections on the Water,'" Graham heard Terrence say to her.

"And 'The Girl with Flaxen Hair,' after, please," begged Hancock, the indicted pagan. "It will aptly prove my disputation. This wild Celt has a bog-theory of music that predates the cave-man—and he has the unadulterated stupidity to call himself ultra-modern."

"Oh, Debussy!" Paula laughed. "Still wrangling over him, eh? I'll try and get around to him. But I don't know with what I'll begin."

Dar Hyal joined the three sages in seating Paula at the concert grand which, Graham decided, was none too great for the great room. But no sooner was she seated than the three sages slipped away to what were evidently their chosen listening places. The young poet stretched himself prone on a deep bearskin forty feet from the piano, his hands buried in his hair. Terrence and Aaron lolled into a cushioned embrasure of a window seat, sufficiently near to each other to nudge the points of their respective contentions as Paula might expound them. The girls were huddled in colored groups on wide couches or garlanded in twos and threes on and in the big koa-wood chairs.

Evan Graham half-started forward to take the honor of turning Paula's music, but saw in time that Dar Hyal had already elected to himself that office. Graham glimpsed the scene with quiet curious glances. The grand piano, under a low arch at the far-end of the room, was cunningly raised and placed as on and in a sounding board. All jollity and banter had ceased. Evidently, he thought, the Little Lady had a way with her and was accepted as a player of parts. And from this he was perversely prepared for disappointment.

Ernestine leaned across from a chair to whisper to him:

"She can do anything she wants to do. And she doesn't work ... much. She studied under Leschetizky and Madame Carreno, you know, and she abides by their methods. She doesn't play like a woman, either. Listen to that!"

Graham knew that he expected disappointment from her confident hands, even as she rippled them over the keys in little chords and runs with which he could not quarrel but which he had heard too often before from technically brilliant but musically mediocre performers. But whatever he might have fancied she would play, he was all unprepared for Rachmaninoff's sheerly masculine Prelude, which he had heard only men play when decently played.

She took hold of the piano, with the first two ringing bars, masterfully, like a man; she seemed to lift it, and its sounding wires, with her two hands, with the strength and certitude of maleness. And then, as only he had heard men do it, she sank, or leaped—he could scarcely say which—to the sureness and pureness and ineffable softness of the *Andante* following.

She played on, with the calm and power of anything but the little, almost girlish woman he glimpsed through half-closed lids across the ebony board of the enormous piano, which she commanded, as she commanded herself, as she commanded the composer. Her touch was definite, authoritative, was his judgment, as the Prelude faded away in dying chords hauntingly reminiscent of its full vigor that seemed still to linger in the air.

While Aaron and Terrence debated in excited whispers in the window seat, and while Dar Hyal sought other music at Paula's direction, she glanced at Dick, who turned off bowl after bowl of mellow light till Paula sat in an oasis of soft glow that brought out the dull gold lights in her dress and hair.

Graham watched the lofty room grow loftier in the increasing shadows. Eighty feet in length, rising two stories and a half from masonry walls to tree-trunked roof, flung across with a flying gallery from the rail of which hung skins of wild animals, hand-woven blankets of Oaxaca and Ecuador, and tapas, woman-pounded and vegetable-dyed, from the islands of the South Pacific, Graham knew it for what it was—a feast-hall of some medieval castle; and almost he felt a poignant sense of lack of the long spread table, with pewter below the salt and silver above the salt, and with huge hound-dogs scuffling beneath for bones.

Later, when Paula had played sufficient Debussy to equip Terrence and Aaron for fresh war, Graham talked with her about music for a few vivid moments. So well did she prove herself aware of the philosophy of music, that, ere he knew it, he was seduced into voicing his own pet theory.

"And so," he concluded, "the true psychic factor of music took nearly three thousand years to impress itself on the Western mind. Debussy more nearly attains the idea-engendering and suggestive serenity—say of the time of Pythagoras—than any of his fore-runners—"

Here, Paula put a pause in his summary by beckoning over Terrence and Aaron from their battlefield in the windowseat.

"Yes, and what of it?" Terrence was demanding, as they came up side by side. "I defy you, Aaron, I defy you, to get one thought out of Bergson on music that is more lucid than any thought he ever uttered in his 'Philosophy of Laughter,' which is not lucid at all."

"Oh!—listen!" Paula cried, with sparkling eyes. "We have a new prophet. Hear Mr. Graham. He's worthy of your steel, of both your steel. He agrees with you that music is the refuge from blood and iron and the pounding of the table. That weak souls, and sensitive souls, and high-pitched souls flee from the crassness and the rawness of the world to the drug-dreams of the over-world of rhythm and vibration—"

"Atavistic!" Aaron Hancock snorted. "The cave-men, the monkey-folk, and the ancestral bog-men of Terrence did that sort of thing—"

"But wait," Paula urged. "It's his conclusions and methods and processes. Also, there he disagrees with you, Aaron, fundamentally. He quoted Pater's 'that all art aspires toward music'—"

"Pure prehuman and micro-organic chemistry," Aaron broke in. "The reactions of cell-elements to the doggerel punch of the wave-lengths of sunlight, the foundation of all folk-songs and rag-times. Terrence completes his circle right there and stultifies all his windiness. Now listen to me, and I will present—"

"But wait," Paula pleaded. "Mr. Graham argues that English puritanism barred music, real music, for centuries... ."

"True," said Terrence.

"And that England had to win to its sensuous delight in rhythm through Milton and Shelley—"

"Who was a metaphysician." Aaron broke in.

"A lyrical metaphysician," Terrence defined instantly. "*That* you must acknowledge, Aaron."

"And Swinburne?" Aaron demanded, with a significance that tokened former arguments.

"He says Offenbach was the fore-runner of Arthur Sullivan,"

Paula cried challengingly. "And that Auber was before Offenbach. And as for Wagner, ask him, just ask him—"

And she slipped away, leaving Graham to his fate. He watched her, watched the perfect knee-lift of her draperies as she crossed to Mrs. Mason and set about arranging bridge quartets, while dimly he could hear Terrence beginning:

"It is agreed that music was the basis of inspiration of all the arts of the Greeks... ."

Later, when the two sages were obliviously engrossed in a heated battle as to whether Berlioz or Beethoven had exposited in their compositions the deeper intellect, Graham managed his escape. Clearly, his goal was to find his hostess again. But she had joined two of the girls in the whispering, giggling seclusiveness of one of the big chairs, and, most of the company being deep in bridge, Graham found himself drifted into a group composed of Dick Forrest, Mr. Wombold, Dar Hyal, and the correspondent of the *Breeders' Gazette*.

"I'm sorry you won't be able to run over with me," Dick was saying to the correspondent. "It would mean only one more day. I'll take you tomorrow."

"Sorry," was the reply. "But I must make Santa Rosa. Burbank has promised me practically a whole morning, and you know what that means. Yet I know the *Gazette* would be glad for an account of the experiment. Can't you outline it?—briefly, just briefly? Here's Mr. Graham. It will interest him, I am sure."

"More water-works?" Graham queried.

"No; an asinine attempt to make good farmers out of hopelessly poor ones," Mr. Wombold answered. "I contend that any farmer to-day who has no land of his own, proves by his lack of it that he is an inefficient farmer."

"On the contrary," spoke up Dar Hyal, weaving his slender Asiatic fingers in the air to emphasize his remarks. "Quite on the contrary. Times have changed. Efficiency no longer implies the possession of capital. It is a splendid experiment, an heroic experiment. And it will succeed."

"What is it, Dick?" Graham urged. "Tell us."

"Oh, nothing, just a white chip on the table," Forrest answered lightly. "Most likely it will never come to anything, although just the same I have my hopes—"

"A white chip!" Wombold broke in. "Five thousand acres of prime valley land, all for a lot of failures to batten on, to farm, if you please, on salary, with food thrown in!"

"The food that is grown on the land only," Dick corrected. "Now

I will have to put it straight. I've set aside five thousand acres midway between here and the Sacramento River."

"Think of the alfalfa it grew, and that you need," Wombold again interrupted.

"My dredgers redeemed twice that acreage from the marshes in the past year," Dick replied. "The thing is, I believe the West and the world must come to intensive farming. I want to do my share toward blazing the way. I've divided the five thousand acres into twenty-acre holdings. I believe each twenty acres should support, comfortably, not only a family, but pay at least six per cent."

"When it is all allotted it will mean two hundred and fifty families," the *Gazette* man calculated; "and, say five to the family, it will mean twelve hundred and fifty souls."

"Not quite," Dick corrected. "The last holding is occupied, and we have only a little over eleven hundred on the land." He smiled whimsically. "But they promise, they promise. Several fat years and they'll average six to the family."

"Who is *we*?" Graham inquired.

"Oh, I have a committee of farm experts on it—my own men, with the exception of Professor Lieb, whom the Federal Government has loaned me. The thing is: they *must* farm, with individual responsibility, according to the scientific methods embodied in our instructions. The land is uniform. Every holding is like a pea in the pod to every other holding. The results of each holding will speak in no uncertain terms. The failure of any farmer, through laziness or stupidity, measured by the average result of the entire two hundred and fifty farmers, will not be tolerated. Out the failures must go, convicted by the average of their fellows.

"It's a fair deal. No farmer risks anything. With the food he may grow and he and his family may consume, plus a cash salary of a thousand a year, he is certain, good seasons and bad, stupid or intelligent, of at least a hundred dollars a month. The stupid and the inefficient will be bound to be eliminated by the intelligent and the efficient. That's all. It will demonstrate intensive farming with a vengeance. And there is more than the certain salary guaranty. After the salary is paid, the adventure must yield six per cent, to me. If more than this is achieved, then the entire hundred per cent, of the additional achievement goes to the farmer."

"Which means that each farmer with go in him will work nights to make good—I see," said the *Gazette* man. "And why not? Hundred- dollar jobs aren't picked up for the asking. The average farmer in the United States doesn't net fifty a month on his own land, especially when his wages of superintendence and of direct personal labor are subtracted. Of course able men will work their heads off to hold to such a proposition, and they'll see to it that every member of the family does the same."

"'Tis the one objection I have to this place," Terrence McFane, who had just joined the group, announced. "Ever one hears but the one thing—work. 'Tis repulsive, the thought of the work, each on his twenty acres, toilin' and moilin', daylight till dark, and after dark — an' for what? A bit of meat, a bit of bread, and, maybe, a bit of jam on the bread. An' to what end? Is meat an' bread an' jam the end of it all, the meaning of life, the goal of existence? Surely the man will die, like a work horse dies, after a life of toil. And what end has been accomplished? Bread an' meat an' jam? Is that it? A full belly and shelter from the cold till one's body drops apart in the dark moldiness of the grave?"

"But, Terrence, you, too, will die," Dick Forrest retorted.

"But, oh, my glorious life of loafing," came the instant answer. "The hours with the stars and the flowers, under the green trees with the whisperings of breezes in the grass. My books, my thinkers and their thoughts. Beauty, music, all the solaces of all the arts. What? When I fade into the dark I shall have well lived and received my wage for living. But these twenty-acre work-animals of two-legged men of yours! Daylight till dark, toil and moil, sweat on the shirts on the backs of them that dries only to crust, meat and bread in their bellies, roofs that don't leak, a brood of youngsters to live after them, to live the same beast-lives of toil, to fill their bellies with the same meat and bread, to scratch their backs with the same sweaty shirts, and to go into the dark knowing only meat and bread, and, mayhap, a bit of jam."

"But somebody must do the work that enables you to loaf," Mr. Wombold spoke up indignantly.

"'Tis true, 'tis sad 'tis true," Terrence replied lugubriously. Then his face beamed. "And I thank the good Lord for it, for the work-beasties that drag and drive the plows up and down the fields, for the bat-eyed miner-beasties that dig the coal and gold, for all the stupid peasant-beasties that keep my hands soft, and give power to fine fellows like Dick there, who smiles on me and shares the loot with me, and buys the latest books for me, and gives me a place at his board that is plenished by the two-legged work-beasties, and a place at his fire that is builded by the same beasties, and a shack and a bed in the jungle under the madroño trees where never work intrudes its monstrous head."

Evan Graham was slow in getting ready for bed that night. He was unwontedly stirred both by the Big House and by the Little

Lady who was its mistress. As he sat on the edge of the bed, half-undressed, and smoked out a pipe, he kept seeing her in memory, as he had seen her in the flesh the past twelve hours, in her varied moods and guises—the woman who had talked music with him, and who had expounded music to him to his delight; who had enticed the sages into the discussion and abandoned him to arrange the bridge tables for her guests; who had nestled in the big chair as girlish as the two girls with her; who had, with a hint of steel, quelled her husband's obstreperousness when he had threatened to sing Mountain Lad's song; who, unafraid, had bestridden the half-drowning stallion in the swimming tank; and who, a few hours later, had dreamed into the dining room, distinctive in dress and person, to meet her many guests.

The Big House, with all its worthy marvels and bizarre novelties, competed with the figure of Paula Forrest in filling the content of his imagination. Once again, and yet again, many times, he saw the slender fingers of Dar Hyal weaving argument in the air, the black whiskers of Aaron Hancock enunciating Bergsonian dogmas, the frayed coat-cuffs of Terrence McFane articulating thanks to God for the two- legged work-beasties that enabled him to loaf at Dick Forrest's board and under Dick Forrest's madroño trees.

Graham knocked out his pipe, took a final sweeping survey of the strange room which was the last word in comfort, pressed off the lights, and found himself between cool sheets in the wakeful dark. Again he heard Paula Forrest laugh; again he sensed her in terms of silver and steel and strength; again, against the dark, he saw that inimitable knee-lift of her gown. The bright vision of it was almost an irk to him, so impossible was it for him to shake it from his eyes. Ever it returned and burned before him, a moving image of light and color that he knew to be subjective but that continually asserted the illusion of reality.

He saw stallion and rider sink beneath the water, and rise again, a flurry of foam and floundering of hoofs, and a woman's face that laughed while she drowned her hair in the drowning mane of the beast. And the first ringing bars of the Prelude sounded in his ears as again he saw the same hands that had guided the stallion lift the piano to all Rachmaninoff's pure splendor of sound.

And when Graham finally fell asleep, it was in the thick of marveling over the processes of evolution that could produce from primeval mire and dust the glowing, glorious flesh and spirit of woman.

Chapter 12

The next morning Graham learned further the ways of the Big House. Oh My had partly initiated him in particular things the preceding day and had learned that, after the waking cup of coffee, he preferred to breakfast at table, rather than in bed. Also, Oh My had warned him that breakfast at table was an irregular affair, anywhere between seven and nine, and that the breakfasters merely drifted in at their convenience. If he wanted a horse, or if he wanted a swim or a motor car, or any ranch medium or utility he desired, Oh My informed him, all he had to do was to call for it.

Arriving in the breakfast room at half past seven, Graham found himself just in time to say good-by to the *Gazette* man and the Idaho buyer, who, finishing, were just ready to catch the ranch machine that connected at Eldorado with the morning train for San Francisco. He sat alone, being perfectly invited by a perfect Chinese servant to order as he pleased, and found himself served with his first desire—an ice-cold, sherried grapefruit, which, the table-boy proudly informed him, was "grown on the ranch." Declining variously suggested breakfast foods, mushes, and porridges, Graham had just ordered his soft-boiled eggs and bacon, when Bert Wainwright drifted in with a casualness that Graham recognized as histrionic, when, five minutes later, in boudoir cap and delectable negligee, Ernestine Desten drifted in and expressed surprise at finding such a multitude of early risers.

Later, as the three of them were rising from table, they greeted Lute Desten and Rita Wainwright arriving. Over the billiard table with Bert, Graham learned that Dick Forrest never appeared for breakfast, that he worked in bed from terribly wee small hours, had coffee at six, and only on unusual occasions appeared to his guests before the twelve-thirty lunch. As for Paula Forrest, Bert explained, she was a poor sleeper, a late riser, lived behind a door without a knob in a spacious wing with a rare and secret patio that even he had seen but once, and only on infrequent occasion was she known to appear before twelve-thirty, and often not then.

"You see, she's healthy and strong and all that," he explained, "but she was born with insomnia. She never could sleep. She couldn't sleep as a little baby even. But it's never hurt her any, because she's got a will, and won't let it get on her nerves. She's just about as tense as they make them, yet, instead of going wild when she can't sleep, she just wills to relax, and she does relax. She calls them her `white nights,' when she gets them. Maybe she'll fall asleep at daybreak, or at nine or ten in the morning; and then she'll sleep the rest of the clock around and get down to dinner as chipper as you please."

"It's constitutional, I fancy," Graham suggested.

Bert nodded.

"It would be a handicap to nine hundred and ninety-nine women out of a thousand. But not to her. She puts up with it, and if she can't sleep one time—she should worry—she just sleeps some other time and makes it up."

More and other things Bert Wainwright told of his hostess, and Graham was not slow in gathering that the young man, despite the privileges of long acquaintance, stood a good deal in awe of her.

"I never saw anybody whose goat she couldn't get if she went after it," he confided. "Man or woman or servant, age, sex, and previous condition of servitude—it's all one when she gets on the high and mighty. And I don't see how she does it. Maybe it's just a kind of light that comes into her eyes, or some kind of an expression on her lips, or, I don't know what—anyway, she puts it across and nobody makes any mistake about it."

"She has a … a way with her," Graham volunteered.

"That's it!" Bert's face beamed. "It's a way she has. She just puts it over. Kind of gives you a chilly feeling, you don't know why. Maybe she's learned to be so quiet about it because of the control she's learned by passing sleepless nights without squealing out or getting sour. The chances are she didn't bat an eye all last night—excitement, you know, the crowd, swimming Mountain Lad and such things. Now ordinary things that'd keep most women awake, like danger, or storm at sea, and such things, Dick says don't faze her. She can sleep like a baby, he says, when the town she's in is being bombarded or when the ship she's in is trying to claw off a lee shore. She's a wonder, and no mistake. You ought to play billiards with her—the English game. She'll go some."

A little later, Graham, along with Bert, encountered the girls in the morning room, where, despite an hour of rag-time song and dancing and chatter, he was scarcely for a moment unaware of a loneliness, a lack, and a desire to see his hostess, in some fresh and unguessed mood and way, come in upon them through the open door.

Still later, mounted on Altadena and accompanied by Bert on a thoroughbred mare called Mollie, Graham made a two hours' exploration of the dairy center of the ranch, and arrived back barely in time to keep an engagement with Ernestine in the tennis court.

He came to lunch with an eagerness for which his keen appetite could not entirely account; and he knew definite disappointment when his hostess did not appear.

"A white night," Dick Forrest surmised for his guest's benefit, and went into details additional to Bert's of her constitutional inaptitude for normal sleep. "Do you know, we were married years before I ever saw her sleep. I knew she did sleep, but I never saw her. I've seen her go three days and nights without closing an eye and keep sweet and cheerful all the time, and when she did sleep, it was out of exhaustion. That was when the *All Away* went ashore in the Carolines and the whole population worked to get us off. It wasn't the danger, for there wasn't any. It was the noise. Also, it was the excitement. She was too busy living. And when it was almost all over, I actually saw her asleep for the first time in my life."

A new guest had arrived that morning, a Donald Ware, whom Graham met at lunch. He seemed well acquainted with all, as if he had visited much in the Big House; and Graham gathered that, despite his youth, he was a violinist of note on the Pacific Coast.

"He has conceived a grand passion for Paula," Ernestine told Graham as they passed out from the dining room.

Graham raised his eyebrows.

"Oh, but she doesn't mind," Ernestine laughed. "Every man that comes along does the same thing. She's used to it. She has just a charming way of disregarding all their symptoms, and enjoys them, and gets the best out of them in consequence. It's lots of fun to Dick. You'll be doing the same before you're here a week. If you don't, we'll all be surprised mightily. And if you don't, most likely you'll hurt Dick's feelings. He's come to expect it as a matter of course. And when a fond, proud husband gets a habit like that, it must hurt terribly to see his wife not appreciated."

"Oh, well, if I am expected to, I suppose I must," Graham sighed. "But just the same I hate to do whatever everybody does just because everybody does it. But if it's the custom—well, it's the custom, that's all. But it's mighty hard on one with so many other nice girls around."

There was a quizzical light in his long gray eyes that affected

92

Ernestine so profoundly that she gazed into his eyes over long, became conscious of what she was doing, dropped her own eyes away, and flushed.

"Little Leo—the boy poet you remember last night," she rattled on in a patent attempt to escape from her confusion. "He's madly in love with Paula, too. I've heard Aaron Hancock chaffing him about some sonnet cycle, and it isn't difficult to guess the inspiration. And Terrence—the Irishman, you know—he's mildly in love with her. They can't help it, you see; and can you blame them?"

"She surely deserves it all," Graham murmured, although vaguely hurt in that the addle-pated, alphabet-obsessed, epicurean anarchist of an Irishman who gloried in being a loafer and a pensioner should even mildly be in love with the Little Lady. "She is most deserving of all men's admiration," he continued smoothly. "From the little I've seen of her she's quite remarkable and most charming."

"She's my half-sister," Ernestine vouchsafed, "although you wouldn't dream a drop of the same blood ran in our veins. She's so different. She's different from all the Destens, from any girl I ever knew— though she isn't exactly a girl. She's thirty-eight, you know —"

"Pussy, pussy," Graham whispered.

The pretty young blonde looked at him in surprise and bewilderment, taken aback by the apparent irrelevance of his interruption.

"Cat," he censured in mock reproof.

"Oh!" she cried. "I never meant it that way. You will find we are very frank here. Everybody knows Paula's age. She tells it herself. I'm eighteen—so, there. And now, just for your meanness, how old are you?"

"As old as Dick," he replied promptly.

"And he's forty," she laughed triumphantly. "Are you coming swimming? —the water will be dreadfully cold."

Graham shook his head. "I'm going riding with Dick."

Her face fell with all the ingenuousness of eighteen.

"Oh," she protested, "some of his eternal green manures, or hillside terracing, or water-pocketing."

"But he said something about swimming at five."

Her face brightened joyously.

"Then we'll meet at the tank. It must be the same party. Paula said swimming at five."

As they parted under a long arcade, where his way led to the tower room for a change into riding clothes, she stopped suddenly and called:

"Oh, Mr. Graham."

He turned obediently.

"You really are not compelled to fall in love with Paula, you know. It was just my way of putting it."

"I shall be very, very careful," he said solemnly, although there was a twinkle in his eye as he concluded.

Nevertheless, as he went on to his room, he could not but admit to himself that the Paula Forrest charm, or the far fairy tentacles of it, had already reached him and were wrapping around him. He knew, right there, that he would prefer the engagement to ride to have been with her than with his old-time friend, Dick.

As he emerged from the house to the long hitching-rails under the ancient oaks, he looked eagerly for his hostess. Only Dick was there, and the stable-man, although the many saddled horses that stamped in the shade promised possibilities. But Dick and he rode away alone. Dick pointed out her horse, an alert bay thoroughbred, stallion at that, under a small Australian saddle with steel stirrups, and double- reined and single-bitted.

"I don't know her plans," he said. "She hasn't shown up yet, but at any rate she'll be swimming later. We'll meet her then."

Graham appreciated and enjoyed the ride, although more than once he found himself glancing at his wrist-watch to ascertain how far away five o'clock might yet be. Lambing time was at hand, and through home field after home field he rode with his host, now one and now the other dismounting to turn over onto its feet rotund and glorious Shropshire and Ramboullet-Merino ewes so hopelessly the product of man's selection as to be unable to get off, of themselves, from their own broad backs, once they were down with their four legs helplessly sky-aspiring.

"I've really worked to make the American Merino," Dick was saying; "to give it the developed leg, the strong back, the well-sprung rib, and the stamina. The old-country breed lacked the stamina. It was too much hand-reared and manicured."

"You're doing things, big things," Graham assured him. "Think of shipping rams to Idaho! That speaks for itself."

Dick Forrest's eyes were sparkling, as he replied:

"Better than Idaho. Incredible as it may sound, and asking forgiveness for bragging, the great flocks to-day of Michigan and Ohio can trace back to my California-bred Ramboullet rams. Take Australia. Twelve years ago I sold three rams for three hundred each to a visiting squatter. After he took them back and demonstrated them he sold them for as many thousand each and ordered a shipload more from me. Australia will never be the worse for my having been. Down there they say that lucerne, artesian wells, refrigerator ships, and Forrest's rams have tripled the wool and mutton production."

Quite by chance, on the way back, meeting Mendenhall, the horse manager, they were deflected by him to a wide pasture, broken by wooded canyons and studded with oaks, to look over a herd of yearling Shires that was to be dispatched next morning to the upland pastures and feeding sheds of the Miramar Hills. There were nearly two hundred of them, rough-coated, beginning to shed, large-boned and large for their age.

"We don't exactly crowd them," Dick Forrest explained, "but Mr. Mendenhall sees to it that they never lack full nutrition from the time they are foaled. Up there in the hills, where they are going, they'll balance their grass with grain. This makes them assemble every night at the feeding places and enables the feeders to keep track of them with a minimum of effort. I've shipped fifty stallions, two-year- olds, every year for the past five years, to Oregon alone. They're sort of standardized, you know. The people up there know what they're getting. They know my standard so well that they'll buy unsight and unseen."

"You must cull a lot, then," Graham ventured.

"And you'll see the culls draying on the streets of San Francisco," Dick answered.

"Yes, and on the streets of Denver," Mr. Mendenhall amplified, "and of Los Angeles, and—why, two years ago, in the horse-famine, we shipped twenty carloads of four-year geldings to Chicago, that averaged seventeen hundred each. The lightest were sixteen, and there were matched pairs up to nineteen hundred. Lord, Lord, that was a year for horse-prices—blue sky, and then some."

As Mr. Mendenhall rode away, a man, on a slender-legged, head-tossing Palomina, rode up to them and was introduced to Graham as Mr. Hennessy, the ranch veterinary.

"I heard Mrs. Forrest was looking over the colts," he explained to his employer, "and I rode across to give her a glance at The Fawn here. She'll be riding her in less than a week. What horse is she on to-day?"

"The Fop," Dick replied, as if expecting the comment that was prompt as the disapproving shake of Mr. Hennessy's head.

"I can never become converted to women riding stallions," muttered the veterinary. "The Fop is dangerous. Worse—though I take my hat off to his record—he's malicious and vicious. She— Mrs. Forrest ought to ride him with a muzzle—but he's a striker as well, and I don't see how she can put cushions on his hoofs."

"Oh, well," Dick placated, "she has a bit that *is* a bit in his mouth, and she's not afraid to use it—"

"If he doesn't fall over on her some day," Mr. Hennessy grumbled. "Anyway, I'll breathe easier when she takes to The Fawn here. Now *she's* a lady's mount—all the spirit in the world, but nothing vicious. She's a sweet mare, a sweet mare, and she'll steady down from her friskiness. But she'll always be a gay handful—no riding academy proposition."

"Let's ride over," Dick suggested. "Mrs. Forrest'll have a gay handful in The Fop if she's ridden him into that bunch of younglings.—It's her territory, you know," he elucidated to Graham. "All the house horses and lighter stock is her affair. And she gets grand results. I can't understand it, myself. It's like a little girl straying into an experimental laboratory of high explosives and mixing the stuff around any old way and getting more powerful combinations than the graybeard chemists."

The three men took a cross-ranch road for half a mile, turned up a wooded canyon where ran a spring-trickle of stream, and emerged on a wide rolling terrace rich in pasture. Graham's first glimpse was of a background of many curious yearling and two-year-old colts, against which, in the middleground, he saw his hostess, on the back of the bright bay thoroughbred, The Fop, who, on hind legs, was striking his forefeet in the air and squealing shrilly. They reined in their mounts and watched.

"He'll get her yet," the veterinary muttered morosely. "That Fop isn't safe."

But at that moment Paula Forrest, unaware of her audience, with a sharp cry of command and a cavalier thrust of sharp spurs into The Fop's silken sides, checked him down to four-footedness on the ground and a restless, champing quietness.

"Taking chances?" Dick mildly reproached her, as the three rode up.

"Oh, I can manage him," she breathed between tight teeth, as, with ears back and vicious-gleaming eyes, The Fop bared his teeth in a bite that would have been perilously near to Graham's leg had she not reined the brute abruptly away across the neck and driven both spurs solidly into his sides.

The Fop quivered, squealed, and for the moment stood still.

"It's the old game, the white man's game," Dick laughed. "She's not afraid of him, and he knows it. She outgames him, out-savages him, teaches him what savagery is in its intimate mood and tense."

Three times, while they looked on, ready to whirl their own

steeds away if he got out of hand, The Fop attempted to burst into rampage, and three times, solidly, with careful, delicate hand on the bitter bit, Paula Forrest dealt him double spurs in the ribs, till he stood, sweating, frothing, fretting, beaten, and in hand.

"It's the way the white man has always done," Dick moralized, while Graham suffered a fluttery, shivery sensation of admiration of the beast-conquering Little Lady. "He's out-savaged the savage the world around," Dick went on. "He's out-endured him, out-filthed him, out- scalped him, out-tortured him, out-eaten him— yes, out-eaten him. It's a fair wager that the white man, in extremis, has eaten more of the genus homo, than the savage, in extremis, has eaten."

"Good afternoon," Paula greeted her guest, the ranch veterinary, and her husband. "I think I've got him now. Let's look over the colts. Just keep an eye, Mr. Graham, on his mouth. He's a dreadful snapper. Ride free from him, and you'll save your leg for old age."

Now that The Fop's demonstration was over, the colts, startled into flight by some impish spirit amongst them, galloped and frisked away over the green turf, until, curious again, they circled back, halted at gaze, and then, led by one particularly saucy chestnut filly, drew up in half a circle before the riders, with alert pricking ears.

Graham scarcely saw the colts at first. He was seeing his protean hostess in a new role. Would her proteanness never end? he wondered, as he glanced over the magnificent, sweating, mastered creature she bestrode. Mountain Lad, despite his hugeness, was a mild-mannered pet beside this squealing, biting, striking Fop who advertised all the spirited viciousness of the most spirited vicious thoroughbred.

"Look at her," Paula whispered to Dick, in order not to alarm the saucy chestnut filly. "Isn't she wonderful! That's what I've been working for." Paula turned to Evan. "Always they have some fault, some miss, at the best an approximation rather than an achievement. But she's an achievement. Look at her. She's as near right as I shall probably ever get. Her sire is Big Chief, if you know our racing register. He sold for sixty thousand when he was a cripple. We borrowed the use of him. She was his only get of the season. But look at her! She's got his chest and lungs. I had my choices—mares eligible for the register. Her dam wasn't eligible, but I chose her. She was an obstinate old maid, but she was the one mare for Big Chief. This is her first foal and she was eighteen years old when she bred. But I knew it was there. All I had to do was to look at Big Chief and her, and it just had to be there."

"The dam was only half thoroughbred," Dick explained.

"But with a lot of Morgan on the other side," Paula added instantly, "and a streak along the back of mustang. This shall be called Nymph, even if she has no place in the books. She'll be my first unimpeachable perfect saddle horse—I know it—the kind I like—my dream come true at last."

"A hoss has four legs, one on each corner," Mr. Hennessy uttered profoundly.

"And from five to seven gaits," Graham took up lightly,

"And yet I don't care for those many-gaited Kentuckians," Paula said quickly, "—except for park work. But for California, rough roads, mountain trails, and all the rest, give me the fast walk, the fox trot, the long trot that covers the ground, and the not too-long, ground-covering gallop. Of course, the close-coupled, easy canter; but I scarcely call that a gait—it's no more than the long lope reduced to the adjustment of wind or rough ground."

"She's a beauty," Dick admired, his eyes warm in contemplation of the saucy chestnut filly, who was daringly close and alertly sniffing of the subdued Fop's tremulous and nostril-dilated muzzle.

"I prefer my own horses to be near thoroughbred rather than all thoroughbred," Paula proclaimed. "The running horse has its place on the track, but it's too specialized for mere human use."

"Nicely coupled," Mr. Hennessy said, indicating the Nymph. "Short enough for good running and long enough for the long trot. I'll admit I didn't have any faith in the combination; but you've got a grand animal out of it just the same."

"I didn't have horses when I was a young girl," Paula said to Graham; "and the fact that I can now not only have them but breed them and mold them to my heart's desire is always too good to be true. Sometimes I can't believe it myself, and have to ride out and look them over to make sure."

She turned her head and raised her eyes gratefully to Forrest; and Graham watched them look into each other's eyes for a long half-minute. Forrest's pleasure in his wife's pleasure, in her young enthusiasm and joy of life, was clear to Graham's observation. "Lucky devil," was Graham's thought, not because of his host's vast ranch and the success and achievement of it, but because of the possession of a wonder-woman who could look unabashed and appreciative into his eyes as the Little Lady had looked.

Graham was meditating, with skepticism, Ernestine's information that Paula Forrest was thirty-eight, when she turned to the colts and pointed her riding whip at a black yearling nibbling at the spring green.

"Look at that level rump, Dick," she said, "and those trotting feet and pasterns." And, to Graham: "Rather different from Nymph's long wrists, aren't they? But they're just what I was after." She laughed a little, with just a shade of annoyance. "The dam was a bright sorrel— almost like a fresh-minted twenty-dollar piece—and I did so want a pair out of her, of the same color, for my own trap. Well, I can't say that I exactly got them, although I bred her to a splendid, sorrel trotting horse. And this is my reward, this black— and, wait till we get to the brood mares and you'll see the other, a full brother and mahogany brown. I'm so disappointed."

She singled out a pair of dark bays, feeding together: "Those are two of Guy Dillon's get—brother, you know, to Lou Dillon. They're out of different mares, not quite the same bay, but aren't they splendidly matched? And they both have Guy Dillon's coat."

She moved her subdued steed on, skirting the flank of the herd quietly in order not to alarm it; but a number of colts took flight.

"Look at them!" she cried. "Five, there, are hackneys. Look at the lift of their fore-legs as they run."

"I'll be terribly disappointed if you don't get a prize-winning four- in-hand out of them," Dick praised, and brought again the flash of grateful eyes that hurt Graham as he noted it.

"Two are out of heavier mares—see that one in the middle and the one on the far left—and there's the other three to pick from for the leaders. Same sire, five different dams, and a matched and balanced four, out of five choices, all in the same season, is a stroke of luck, isn't it?"

She turned quickly to Mr. Hennessy: "I can begin to see the ones that will have to sell for polo ponies—among the two-year-olds. You can pick them."

"If Mr. Mendenhall doesn't sell that strawberry roan for a clean fifteen hundred, it'll be because polo has gone out of fashion," the veterinary approved, with waxing enthusiasm. "I've had my eye on them. That pale sorrel, there. You remember his set-back. Give him an extra year and he'll—look at his coupling!—watch him turn!—a cow-skin?— he'll turn on a silver dollar! Give him a year to make up, and he'll stand a show for the international. Listen to me. I've had my faith in him from the beginning. Cut out that Burlingame crowd. When he's ripe, ship him straight East."

Paula nodded and listened to Mr. Hennessy's judgment, her eyes kindling with his in the warmth of the sight of the abounding young life for which she was responsible.

"It always hurts, though," she confessed to Graham, "selling such beauties to have them knocked out on the field so quickly."

Her sheer absorption in the animals robbed her speech of any hint of affectation or show—so much so, that Dick was impelled to praise her judgment to Evan.

"I can dig through a whole library of horse practice, and muddle and mull over the Mendelian Law until I'm dizzy, like the clod that I am; but she is the genius. She doesn't have to study law. She just knows it in some witch-like, intuitional way. All she has to do is size up a bunch of mares with her eyes, and feel them over a little with her hands, and hunt around till she finds the right sires, and get pretty nearly what she wants in the result—except color, eh, Paul?" he teased.

She showed her laughing teeth in the laugh at her expense, in which Mr. Hennessy joined, and Dick continued: "Look at that filly there. We all knew Paula was wrong. But look at it! She bred a rickety old thoroughbred, that we wanted to put out of her old age, to a standard stallion; got a filly; bred it back with a thoroughbred; bred its filly foal with the same standard again; knocked all our prognostications into a cocked hat, and—well, look at it, a world-beater polo pony. There is one thing we have to take off our hats to her for: she doesn't let any woman sentimentality interfere with her culling. Oh, she's cold-blooded enough. She's as remorseless as any man when it comes to throwing out the undesirables and selecting for what she wants. But she hasn't mastered color yet. There's where her genius falls down, eh, Paul? You'll have to put up with Duddy and Fuddy for a while longer for your trap. By the way, how is Duddy?"

"He's come around," she answered, "thanks to Mr. Hennessy."

"Nothing serious," the veterinarian added. "He was just off his feed a trifle. It was more a scare of the stableman than anything else."

Chapter 13

From the colt pasture to the swimming tank Graham talked with his hostess and rode as nearly beside her as The Fop's wickedness permitted, while Dick and Hennessy, on ahead, were deep in ranch business.

"Insomnia has been a handicap all my life," she said, while she tickled The Fop with a spur in order to check a threatened belligerence. "But I early learned to keep the irritation of it off my nerves and the weight of it off my mind. In fact, I early came to make a function of it and actually to derive enjoyment from it. It was the only way to master a thing I knew would persist as long as I persisted. Have you—of course you have—learned to win through an undertow?"

"Yes, by never fighting it," Graham answered, his eyes on the spray of color in her cheeks and the tiny beads of sweat that arose from her continuous struggle with the high-strung creature she rode. Thirty- eight! He wondered if Ernestine had lied. Paula Forrest did not look twenty-eight. Her skin was the skin of a girl, with all the delicate, fine-pored and thin transparency of the skin of a girl.

"Exactly," she went on. "By not fighting the undertow. By yielding to its down-drag and out-drag, and working with it to reach air again. Dick taught me that trick. So with my insomnia. If it is excitement from immediate events that holds me back from the City of Sleep, I yield to it and come quicker to unconsciousness from out the entangling currents. I invite my soul to live over again, from the same and different angles, the things that keep me from unconsciousness.

"Take the swimming of Mountain Lad yesterday. I lived it over last night as I had lived it in reality. Then I lived it as a spectator— as the girls saw it, as you saw it, as the cowboy saw it, and, most of all, as my husband saw it. Then I made up a picture of it, many pictures of it, from all angles, and painted them, and framed them, and hung them, and then, a spectator, looked at them as if for the first time. And I made myself many kinds of spectators, from crabbed old maids and lean pantaloons to girls in boarding school and Greek boys of thousands of years ago.

"After that I put it to music. I played it on the piano, and guessed the playing of it on full orchestras and blaring bands. I chanted it, I sang it-epic, lyric, comic; and, after a weary long while, of course I slept in the midst of it, and knew not that I slept until I awoke at twelve to-day. The last time I had heard the clock strike was six. Six unbroken hours is a capital prize for me in the sleep lottery."

As she finished, Mr. Hennessy rode away on a cross path, and Dick Forrest dropped back to squire his wife on the other side.

"Will you sport a bet, Evan?" he queried.

"I'd like to hear the terms of it first," was the answer.

"Cigars against cigars that you can't catch Paula in the tank inside ten minutes—no, inside five, for I remember you're some swimmer."

"Oh, give him a chance, Dick," Paula cried generously. "Ten minutes will worry him."

"But you don't know him," Dicked argued. "And you don't value my cigars. I tell you he is a swimmer. He's drowned kanakas, and you know what that means."

"Perhaps I should reconsider. Maybe he'll slash a killing crawl-stroke at me before I've really started. Tell me his history and prizes."

"I'll just tell you one thing. They still talk of it in the Marquesas. It was the big hurricane of 1892. He did forty miles in forty-five hours, and only he and one other landed on the land. And they were all kanakas. He was the only white man; yet he out-endured and drowned the last kanaka of them—"

"I thought you said there was one other?" Paula interrupted.

"She was a woman," Dick answered. "He drowned the last kanaka."

"And the woman was then a white woman?" Paula insisted.

Graham looked quickly at her, and although she had asked the question of her husband, her head turned to the turn of his head, so that he found her eyes meeting his straightly and squarely in interrogation. Graham held her gaze with equal straightness as he answered: "She was a kanaka."

"A queen, if you please," Dick took up. "A queen out of the ancient chief stock. She was Queen of Huahoa."

"Was it the chief stock that enabled her to out-endure the native men?" Paula asked. "Or did you help her?"

"I rather think we helped each other toward the end," Graham replied. "We were both out of our heads for short spells and long spells. Sometimes it was one, sometimes the other, that was all in. We made the land at sunset—that is, a wall of iron coast, with the surf bursting sky-high. She took hold of me and clawed me in the water to get some sense in me. You see, I wanted to go in, which would have meant finish.

"She got me to understand that she knew where she was; that the current set westerly along shore and in two hours would drift us abreast of a spot where we could land. I swear I either slept or was unconscious most of those two hours; and I swear she was in one state or the other when I chanced to come to and noted the absence of the roar of the surf. Then it was my turn to claw and maul her back to consciousness. It was three hours more before we made the sand. We slept where we crawled out of the water. Next morning's sun burnt us awake, and we crept into the shade of some wild bananas, found fresh water, and went to sleep again. Next I awoke it was night. I took another drink, and slept through till morning. She was still asleep when the bunch of kanakas, hunting wild goats from the next valley, found us."

"I'll wager, for a man who drowned a whole kanaka crew, it was you who did the helping," Dick commented.

"She must have been forever grateful," Paula challenged, her eyes directly on Graham's. "Don't tell me she wasn't young, wasn't beautiful, wasn't a golden brown young goddess."

"Her mother was the Queen of Huahoa," Graham answered. "Her father was a Greek scholar and an English gentleman. They were dead at the time of the swim, and Nomare was queen herself. She *was* young. She was beautiful as any woman anywhere in the world may be beautiful. Thanks to her father's skin, she as not golden brown. She was tawny golden. But you've heard the story undoubtedly—"

He broke off with a look of question to Dick, who shook his head.

Calls and cries and splashings of water from beyond a screen of trees warned them that they were near the tank.

"You'll have to tell me the rest of the story some time," Paula said.

"Dick knows it. I can't see why he hasn't told you."

She shrugged her shoulders.

"Perhaps because he's never had the time or the provocation."

"God wot, it's had wide circulation," Graham laughed. "For know that I was once morganatic—or whatever you call it—king of the cannibal isles, or of a paradise of a Polynesian isle at any rate.

—'By a purple wave on an opal beach in the hush of the Mahim woods,'" he hummed carelessly, in conclusion, and swung off from his horse.

"'The white moth to the closing vine, the bee to the opening clover,'" she hummed another line of the song, while The Fop nearly got his teeth into her leg and she straightened him out with the spur, and waited for Dick to help her off and tie him.

"Cigars!—I'm in on that!—you can't catch her!" Bert Wainwright called from the top of the high dive forty feet above. "Wait a minute! I'm coming!"

And come he did, in a swan dive that was almost professional and that brought handclapping approval from the girls.

"A sweet dive, balanced beautifully," Graham told him as he emerged from the tank.

Bert tried to appear unconscious of the praise, failed, and, to pass it off, plunged into the wager.

"I don't know what kind of a swimmer you are, Graham," he said, "but I just want in with Dick on the cigars."

"Me, too; me, too!" chorused Ernestine, and Lute, and Rita.

"Boxes of candy, gloves, or any truck you care to risk," Ernestine added.

"But I don't know Mrs. Forrest's records, either," Graham protested, after having taken on the bets. "However, if in five minutes—"

"Ten minutes," Paula said, "and to start from opposite ends of the tank. Is that fair? Any touch is a catch." Graham looked his hostess over with secret approval. She was clad, not in the single white silk slip she evidently wore only for girl parties, but in a coquettish imitation of the prevailing fashion mode, a suit of changeable light blue and green silk—almost the color of the pool; the skirt slightly above the knees whose roundedness he recognized; with long stockings to match, and tiny bathing shoes bound on with crossed ribbons. On her head was a jaunty swimming cap no jauntier than herself when she urged the ten minutes in place of five.

Rita Wainwright held the watch, while Graham walked down to the other end of the hundred-and-fifty-foot tank.

"Paula, you'll be caught if you take any chances," Dick warned. "Evan Graham is a real fish man."

"I guess Paula'll show him a few, even without the pipe," Bert bragged loyally. "And I'll bet she can out-dive him."

"There you lose," Dick answered. "I saw the rock he dived from at Huahoa. That was after his time, and after the death of Queen Nomare. He was only a youngster—twenty-two; he had to be to do it. It was off the peak of the Pau-wi Rock—one hundred and twenty-eight feet by triangulation. And he couldn't do it legitimately or technically with a swan-dive, because he had to clear two lower ledges while he was in the air. The upper ledge of the two, by their own traditions, was the highest the best of the kanakas had ever dared since their traditions began. Well, he did it. He became tradition. As long as the kanakas of Huahoa survive he will remain tradition—Get ready, Rita. Start on the full minute."

"It's almost a shame to play tricks on so reputable a swimmer," Paula confided to them, as she faced her guest down the length of the tank and while both waited the signal.

"He may get you before you can turn the trick," Dick warned again. And then, to Bert, with just a shade of anxiety: "Is it working all right? Because if it isn't, Paula will have a bad five seconds getting out of it."

"All O.K.," Bert assured. "I went in myself. The pipe is working. There's plenty of air."

"Ready!" Rita called. "Go!"

Graham ran toward their end like a foot-racer, while Paula darted up the high dive. By the time she had gained the top platform, his hands and feet were on the lower rungs. When he was half-way up she threatened a dive, compelling him to cease from climbing and to get out on the twenty-foot platform ready to follow her to the water. Whereupon she laughed down at him and did not dive. "Time is passing— the precious seconds are ticking off," Ernestine chanted.

When he started to climb, Paula again chased him to the half-way platform with a threat to dive. But not many seconds did Graham waste. His next start was determined, and Paula, poised for her dive, could not send him scuttling back. He raced upward to gain the thirty-foot platform before she should dive, and she was too wise to linger. Out into space she launched, head back, arms bent, hands close to chest, legs straight and close together, her body balanced horizontally on the air as it fell outward and downward.

"Oh you Annette Kellerman!" Bert Wamwright's admiring cry floated up.

Graham ceased pursuit to watch the completion of the dive, and saw his hostess, a few feet above the water, bend her head forward, straighten out her arms and lock the hands to form the arch before her head, and, so shifting the balance of her body, change it from the horizontal to the perfect, water-cleaving angle.

The moment she entered the water, he swung out on the thirty-foot platform and waited. From this height he could make out her body beneath the surface swimming a full stroke straight for the far end of the tank. Not till then did he dive. He was confident that he could outspeed her, and his dive, far and flat, entered him in the water twenty feet beyond her entrance.

But at the instant he was in, Dick dipped two flat rocks into the water and struck them together. This was the signal for Paula to change her course. Graham heard the concussion and wondered. He broke surface in the full swing of the crawl and went down the tank to the far end at a killing pace. He pulled himself out and watched the surface of the tank. A burst of handclapping from the girls drew his eyes to the Little Lady drawing herself out of the tank at the other end.

Again he ran down the side of the tank, and again she climbed the scaffold. But this time his wind and endurance enabled him to cut down her lead, so that she was driven to the twenty-foot platform. She took no time for posturing or swanning, but tilted immediately off in a stiff dive, angling toward the west side of the tank. Almost they were in the air at the same time. In the water and under it, he could feel against his face and arms the agitation left by her progress; but she led into the deep shadow thrown by the low afternoon sun, where the water was so dark he could see nothing.

When he touched the side of the tank he came up. She was not in sight. He drew himself out, panting, and stood ready to dive in at the first sign of her. But there were no signs.

"Seven minutes!" Rita called. "And a half! ... Eight!... And a half!"

And no Paula Forrest broke surface. Graham refused to be alarmed because he could see no alarm on the faces of the others.

"I lose," he announced at Rita's "Nine minutes!"

"She's been under over two minutes, and you're all too blessed calm about it to get me excited," he said. "I've still a minute—maybe I don't lose," he added quickly, as he stepped off feet first into the tank.

As he went down he turned over and explored the cement wall of tank with his hands. Midway, possibly ten feet under the surface he estimated, his hands encountered an opening in the wall. He felt about, learned it Was unscreened, and boldly entered. Almost before he was in, he found he could come up; but he came up slowly, breaking surface in pitchy blackness and feeling about him without splashing.

His fingers touched a cool smooth arm that shrank convulsively at contact while the possessor of it cried sharply with the startle of fright. He held on tightly and began to laugh, and Paula laughed with him. A line from "The First Chanty" flashed into his consciousness— "*Hearing her laugh in the gloom greatly I loved her.*"

"You did frighten me when you touched me," she said. "You came without a sound, and I was a thousand miles away, dreaming... "

"What?" Graham asked.

"Well, honestly, I had just got an idea for a gown—a dusty, musty, mulberry-wine velvet, with long, close lines, and heavy, tarnished gold borders and cords and things. And the only jewelery a ring—one enormous pigeon-blood ruby that Dick gave me years ago when we sailed the *All Away*."

"Is there anything you don't do?" he laughed.

She joined with him, and their mirth sounded strangely hollow in the pent and echoing dark.

"Who told you?" she next asked.

"No one. After you had been under two minutes I knew it had to be something like this, and I came exploring."

"It was Dick's idea. He had it built into the tank afterward. You will find him full of whimsies. He delighted in scaring old ladies into fits by stepping off into the tank with their sons or grandsons and hiding away in here. But after one or two nearly died of shock —old ladies, I mean—he put me up, as to-day, to fooling hardier persons like yourself.—Oh, he had another accident. There was a Miss Coghlan, friend of Ernestine, a little seminary girl. They artfully stood her right beside the pipe that leads out, and Dick went off the high dive and swam in here to the inside end of the pipe. After several minutes, by the time she was in collapse over his drowning, he spoke up the pipe to her in most horrible, sepulchral tones. And right there Miss Coghlan fainted dead away."

"She must have been a weak sister," Graham commented; while he struggled with a wanton desire for a match so that he could strike it and see how Paula Forrest looked paddling there beside him to keep afloat.

"She had a fair measure of excuse," Paula answered. "She was a young thing—eighteen; and she had a sort of school-girl infatuation for Dick. They all get it. You see, he's such a boy when he's playing that they can't realize that he's a hard-bitten, hard-working, deep-thinking, mature, elderly benedict. The embarrassing thing was that the little girl, when she was first revived and before she could gather her wits, exposed all her secret heart. Dick's face was a study while she babbled her—"

"Well?—going to stay there all night?" Bert Wainwright's voice came down the pipe, sounding megaphonically close.

"Heavens!" Graham sighed with relief; for he had startled and clutched Paula's arm. "That's the time I got my fright. The little maiden is avenged. Also, at last, I know what a lead-pipe cinch is."

"And it's time we started for the outer world," she suggested. "It's not the coziest gossiping place in the world. Shall I go first?"

"By all means—and I'll be right behind; although it's a pity the water isn't phosphorescent. Then I could follow your incandescent heel like that chap Byron wrote about—don't you remember?"

He heard her appreciative gurgle in the dark, and then her: "Well, I'm going now."

Unable to see the slightest glimmer, nevertheless, from the few sounds she made he knew she had turned over and gone down head first, and he was not beyond visioning with inner sight the graceful way in which she had done it—an anything but graceful feat as the average swimming woman accomplishes it.

"Somebody gave it away to you," was Bert's prompt accusal, when Graham rose to the surface of the tank and climbed out.

"And you were the scoundrel who rapped stone under water," Graham challenged. "If I'd lost I'd have protested the bet. It was a crooked game, a conspiracy, and competent counsel, I am confident, would declare it a felony. It's a case for the district attorney."

"But you won," Ernestine cried.

"I certainly did, and, therefore, I shall not prosecute you, nor any one of your crooked gang—if the bets are paid promptly. Let me see— you owe me a box of cigars—"

"One cigar, sir!"

"A box! A box!" "Cross tag!" Paula cried. "Let's play cross-tag! — You're IT!"

Suiting action to word, she tagged Graham on the shoulder and plunged into the tank. Before he could follow, Bert seized him, whirled him in a circle, was himself tagged, and tagged Dick before he could escape. And while Dick pursued his wife through the tank and Bert and Graham sought a chance to cross, the girls fled up the scaffold and stood in an enticing row on the fifteen-foot diving platform.

Chapter 14

An indifferent swimmer, Donald Ware had avoided the afternoon sport in the tank; but after dinner, somewhat to the irritation of Graham, the violinist monopolized Paula at the piano. New guests, with the casual expectedness of the Big House, had drifted in—a lawyer, by name Adolph Well, who had come to confer with Dick over some big water- right suit; Jeremy Braxton, straight from Mexico, Dick's general superintendent of the Harvest Group, which bonanza, according to Jeremy Braxton, was as "unpetering" as ever; Edwin O'Hay, a red-headed Irish musical and dramatic critic; and Chauncey Bishop, editor and owner of the *San Francisco Dispatch*, and a member of Dick's class and frat, as Graham gleaned.

Dick had started a boisterous gambling game which he called "Horrible Fives," wherein, although excitement ran high and players plunged, the limit was ten cents, and, on a lucky coup, the transient banker might win or lose as high as ninety cents, such coup requiring at least ten minutes to play out. This game went on at a big table at the far end of the room, accompanied by much owing and borrowing of small sums and an incessant clamor for change.

With nine players, the game was crowded, and Graham, rather than draw cards, casually and occasionally backed Ernestine's cards, the while he glanced down the long room at the violinist and Paula Forrest absorbed in Beethoven Symphonies and Delibes' Ballets. Jeremy Braxton was demanding raising the limit to twenty cents, and Dick, the heaviest loser, as he averred, to the tune of four dollars and sixty cents, was plaintively suggesting the starting of a "kitty" in order that some one should pay for the lights and the sweeping out of the place in the morning, when Graham, with a profound sigh at the loss of his last bet—a nickel which he had had to pay double—announced to Ernestine that he was going to take a turn around the room to change his luck.

"I prophesied you would," she told him under her breath.

"What?" he asked.

She glanced significantly in Paula's direction.

"Just for that I simply must go down there now," he retorted.

"Can't dast decline a dare," she taunted.

"If it were a dare I wouldn't dare do it."

"In which case I dare you," she took up.

He shook his head: "I had already made up my mind to go right down there to that one spot and cut that fiddler out of the running. You can't dare me out of it at this late stage. Besides, there's Mr. O'Hay waiting for you to make your bet."

Ernestine rashly laid ten cents, and scarcely knew whether she won or lost, so intent was she on watching Graham go down the room, although she did know that Bert Wainwright had not been unobservant of her gaze and its direction. On the other hand, neither she nor Bert, nor any other at the table, knew that Dick's quick-glancing eyes, sparkling with merriment while his lips chaffed absurdities that made them all laugh, had missed no portion of the side play.

Ernestine, but little taller than Paula, although hinting of a plus roundness to come, was a sun-healthy, clear blonde, her skin sprayed with the almost transparent flush of maidenhood at eighteen. To the eye, it seemed almost that one could see through the pink daintiness of fingers, hand, wrist, and forearm, neck and cheek. And to this delicious transparency of rose and pink, was added a warmth of tone that did not escape Dick's eyes as he glimpsed her watch Evan Graham move down the length of room. Dick knew and classified her wild imagined dream or guess, though the terms of it were beyond his divination.

What she saw was what she imagined was the princely walk of Graham, the high, light, blooded carriage of his head, the delightful carelessness of the gold-burnt, sun-sanded hair that made her fingers ache to be into with caresses she for the first time knew were possible of her fingers.

Nor did Paula, during an interval of discussion with the violinist in which she did not desist from stating her criticism of O'Hay's latest criticism of Harold Bauer, fail to see and keep her eyes on Graham's progress. She, too, noted with pleasure his grace of movement, the high, light poise of head, the careless hair, the clear bronze of the smooth cheeks, the splendid forehead, the long gray eyes with the hint of drooping lids and boyish sullenness that fled before the smile with which he greeted her.

She had observed that smile often since her first meeting with him. It was an irresistible smile, a smile that lighted the eyes with the radiance of good fellowship and that crinkled the corners into tiny, genial lines. It was provocative of smiles, for she found herself smiling a silent greeting in return as she continued stating to Ware her grievance against O'Hay's too-complacent praise of Bauer.

But her engagement was tacitly with Donald Ware at the piano, and with no more than passing speech, she was off and away in a series of Hungarian dances that made Graham marvel anew as he loafed and smoked in a window-seat.

He marveled at the proteanness of her, at visions of those nimble fingers guiding and checking The Fop, swimming and paddling in submarine crypts, and, falling in swan-like flight through forty feet of air, locking just above the water to make the diver's head-protecting arch of arm.

In decency, he lingered but few minutes, returned to the gamblers, and put the entire table in a roar with a well-acted Yiddisher's chagrin and passion at losing entire nickels every few minutes to the fortunate and chesty mine superintendent from Mexico.

Later, when the game of Horrible Fives broke up, Bert and Lute Desten spoiled the Adagio from Beethoven's *Sonata Pathetique* by exaggeratedly ragging to it in what Dick immediately named "The Loving Slow-Drag," till Paula broke down in a gale of laughter and ceased from playing.

New groupings occurred. A bridge table formed with Weil, Rita, Bishop, and Dick. Donald Ware was driven from his monopoly of Paula by the young people under the leadership of Jeremy Braxton; while Graham and O'Hay paired off in a window-seat and O'Hay talked shop.

After a time, in which all at the piano had sung Hawaiian *hulas*, Paula sang alone to her own accompaniment. She sang several German love-songs in succession, although it was merely for the group about her and not for the room; and Evan Graham, almost to his delight, decided that at last he had found a weakness in her. She might be a magnificent pianist, horsewoman, diver, and swimmer, but it was patent, despite her singing throat, that she was not a magnificent singer. This conclusion he was quickly compelled to modify. A singer she was, a consummate singer. Weakness was only comparative after all. She lacked the magnificent voice. It was a sweet voice, a rich voice, with the same warm-fibered thrill of her laugh; but the volume so essential to the great voice was not there. Ear and voice seemed effortlessly true, and in her singing were feeling, artistry, training, intelligence. But volume—it was scarcely a fair average, was his judgment.

But quality—there he halted. It was a woman's voice. It was haunted with richness of sex. In it resided all the temperament in the world— with all the restraint of discipline, was the next step of his analysis. He had to admire the way she refused to exceed the limitations of her voice. In this she achieved triumphs.

And, while he nodded absently to O'Hay's lecturette on the state of the—opera, Graham fell to wondering if Paula Forrest, thus so completely the mistress of her temperament, might not be equally mistress of her temperament in the deeper, passional ways. There was a challenge there—based on curiosity, he conceded, but only partly so based; and, over and beyond, and, deeper and far beneath, a challenge to a man made in the immemorial image of man.

It was a challenge that bade him pause, and even look up and down the great room and to the tree-trunked roof far above, and to the flying gallery hung with the spoils of the world, and to Dick Forrest, master of all this material achievement and husband of the woman, playing bridge, just as he worked, with all his heart, his laughter ringing loud as he caught Rita in renig. For Graham had the courage not to shun the ultimate connotations. Behind the challenge in his speculations lurked the woman. Paula Forrest was splendidly, deliciously woman, all woman, unusually woman. From the blow between the eyes of his first striking sight of her, swimming the great stallion in the pool, she had continued to witch-ride his man's imagination. He was anything but unused to women; and his general attitude was that of being tired of the mediocre sameness of them. To chance upon the unusual woman was like finding the great pearl in a lagoon fished out by a generation of divers.

"Glad to see you're still alive," Paula laughed to him, a little later.

She was prepared to depart with Lute for bed. A second bridge quartet had been arranged—Ernestine, Bert, Jeremy Braxton, and Graham; while O'Hay and Bishop were already deep in a bout of two-handed pinochle.

"He's really a charming Irishman when he keeps off his one string," Paula went on.

"Which, I think I am fair, is music," Graham said.

"And on music he is insufferable," Lute observed. "It's the only thing he doesn't know the least thing about. He drives one frantic."

"Never mind," Paula soothed, in gurgling tones. "You will all be avenged. Dick just whispered to me to get the philosophers up tomorrow night. You know how they talk music. A musical critic is their awful prey."

"Terrence said the other night that there was no closed season on musical critics," Lute contributed.

"Terrence and Aaron will drive him to drink," Paula laughed her joy of anticipation. "And Dar Hyal, alone, with his blastic theory of art, can specially apply it to music to the confutation of all the first words and the last. He doesn't believe a thing he says about blastism, any more than was he serious when he danced the other evening. It's his bit of fun. He's such a deep philosopher that he has to get his fun somehow."

"And if O'Hay ever locks horns with Terrence," Lute prophesied, "I can see Terrence tucking arm in arm with him, leading him down to the stag room, and heating the argument with the absentest-minded variety of drinks that ever O'Hay accomplished."

"Which means a very sick O'Hay next day," Paula continued her gurgles of anticipation.

"I'll tell him to do it!" exclaimed Lute.

"You mustn't think we're all bad," Paula protested to Graham. "It's just the spirit of the house. Dick likes it. He's always playing jokes himself. He relaxes that way. I'll wager, right now, it was Dick's suggestion, to Lute, and for Lute to carry out, for Terrence to get O'Hay into the stag room. Now, 'fess up, Lute."

"Well, I will say," Lute answered with meticulous circumspection, "that the idea was not entirely original with me."

At this point, Ernestine joined them and appropriated Graham with:

"We're all waiting for you. We've cut, and you and I are partners. Besides, Paula's making her sleep noise. So say good night, and let her go."

Paula had left for bed at ten o'clock. Not till one did the bridge break up. Dick, his arm about Ernestine in brotherly fashion, said good night to Graham where one of the divided ways led to the watch tower, and continued on with his pretty sister-in-law toward her quarters.

"Just a tip, Ernestine," he said at parting, his gray eyes frankly and genially on hers, but his voice sufficiently serious to warn her.

"What have I been doing now?" she pouted laughingly.

"Nothing... as yet. But don't get started, or you'll be laying up a sore heart for yourself. You're only a kid yet—eighteen; and a darned nice, likable kid at that. Enough to make 'most any man sit up and take notice. But Evan Graham is not 'most any man—"

"Oh, I can take care of myself," she blurted out in a fling of quick resentment.

"But listen to me just the same. There comes a time in the affairs of a girl when the love-bee gets a buzzing with a very loud hum in her pretty noddle. Then is the time she mustn't make a mistake and start in loving the wrong man. You haven't fallen in love with Evan Graham yet, and all you have to do is just not to fall in love with him. He's not for you, nor for any young thing. He's an oldster, an ancient, and possibly has forgotten more about love, romantic love, and young things, than you'll ever learn in a dozen lives. If he ever marries again—"

"Again!" Ernestine broke in.

"Why, he's been a widower, my dear, for over fifteen years."

"Then what of it?" she demanded defiantly.

"Just this," Dick continued quietly. "He's lived the young-thing romance, and lived it wonderfully; and, from the fact that in fifteen years he has not married again, means—"

"That he's never recovered from his loss?" Ernestine interpolated. "But that's no proof—"

"—Means that he's got over his apprenticeship to wild young romance," Dick held on steadily. "All you have to do is look at him and realize that he has not lacked opportunities, and that, on occasion, some very fine women, real wise women, mature women, have given him foot-races that tested his wind and endurance. But so far they've not succeeded in catching him. And as for young things, you know how filled the world is with them for a man like him. Think it over, and just keep your heart-thoughts away from him. If you don't let your heart start to warm toward him, it will save your heart from a grievous chill later on."

He took one of her hands in his, and drew her against him, an arm soothingly about her shoulder. For several minutes of silence Dick idly speculated on what her thoughts might be.

"You know, we hard-bitten old fellows—" he began half-apologetically, half-humorously.

But she made a restless movement of distaste, and cried out:

"Are the only ones worth while! The young men are all youngsters, and that's what's the matter with them. They're full of life, and coltish spirits, and dance, and song. But they're not serious. They're not big. They're not—oh, they don't give a girl that sense of all- wiseness, of proven strength, of, of... well, of manhood."

"I understand," Dick murmured. "But please do not forget to glance at the other side of the shield. You glowing young creatures of women must affect the old fellows in precisely similar ways. They may look on you as toys, playthings, delightful things to whom to teach a few fine foolishnesses, but not as comrades, not as equals, not as sharers—full sharers. Life is something to be learned. They have learned it... some of it. But young things like you, Ernestine, have you learned any of it yet?"

"Tell me," she asked abruptly, almost tragically, "about this wild young romance, about this young thing when he was young, fifteen years ago."

"Fifteen?" Dick replied promptly. "Eighteen. They were married three years before she died. In fact—figure it out for yourself—they were actually married, by a Church of England dominie, and living in wedlock, about the same moment that you were squalling your first post-birth squalls in this world."

"Yes, yes—go on," she urged nervously. "What was she like?"

"She was a resplendent, golden-brown, or tan-golden half-caste, a Polynesian queen whose mother had been a queen before her, whose father was an Oxford man, an English gentleman, and a real scholar. Her name was Nomare. She was Queen of Huahoa. She was barbaric. He was young enough to out-barbaric her. There was nothing sordid in their marriage. He was no penniless adventurer. She brought him her island kingdom and forty thousand subjects. He brought to that island his fortune—and it was no inconsiderable fortune. He built a palace that no South Sea island ever possessed before or will ever possess again. It was the real thing, grass-thatched, hand-hewn beams that were lashed with cocoanut sennit, and all the rest. It was rooted in the island; it sprouted out of the island; it *belonged*, although he fetched Hopkins out from New York to plan it.

"Heavens! they had their own royal yacht, their mountain house, their canoe house—the last a veritable palace in itself. I know. I have been at great feasts in it—though it was after their time. Nomare was dead, and no one knew where Graham was, and a king of collateral line was the ruler.

"I told you he out-barbaricked her. Their dinner service was gold.— Oh, what's the use in telling any more. He was only a boy. She was half-English, half-Polynesian, and a really and truly queen. They were flowers of their races. They were a pair of wonderful children. They lived a fairy tale. And... well, Ernestine, the years have passed, and Evan Graham has passed from the realm of the young thing. It will be a remarkable woman that will ever infatuate him now. Besides, he's practically broke. Though he didn't wastrel his money. As much misfortune, and more, than anything else."

"Paula would be more his kind," Ernestine said meditatively.

"Yes, indeed," Dick agreed. "Paula, or any woman as remarkable as Paula, would attract him a thousand times more than all the sweet, young, lovely things like you in the world. We oldsters have our standards, you know."

"And I'll have to put up with the youngsters," Ernestine sighed.

"In the meantime, yes," he chuckled. "Remembering, always, that you, too, in time, may grow into the remarkable, mature woman, who can outfoot a man like Evan in a foot-race of love for possession."

"But I shall be married long before that," she pouted.

"Which will be your good fortune, my dear. And, now, good night. And you are not angry with me?"

She smiled pathetically and shook her head, put up her lips to be kissed, then said as they parted:

"I promise not to be angry if you will only show me the way that in the end will lead me to ancient graybeards like you and Graham."

Dick Forrest, turning off lights as he went, penetrated the library, and, while selecting half a dozen reference volumes on mechanics and physics, smiled as if pleased with himself at recollection of the interview with his sister-in-law. He was confident that he had spoken in time and not a moment too soon. But, half way up the book-concealed spiral staircase that led to his work room, a remark of Ernestine, echoing in his consciousness, made him stop from very suddenness to lean his shoulder against the wall.—"*Paula would be more his kind.*"

"Silly ass!" he laughed aloud, continuing on his way. "And married a dozen years!"

Nor did he think again about it, until, in bed, on his sleeping porch, he took a glance at his barometers and thermometers, and prepared to settle down to the solution of the electrical speculation that had been puzzling him. Then it was, as he peered across the great court to his wife's dark wing and dark sleeping porch to see if she were still waking, that Ernestine's remark again echoed. He dismissed it with a "Silly ass!" of scorn, lighted a cigarette, and began running, with trained eye, the indexes of the books and marking the pages sought with matches.

Chapter 15

It was long after ten in the morning, when Graham, straying about restlessly and wondering if Paula Forrest ever appeared before the middle of the day, wandered into the music room. Despite the fact that he was a several days' guest in the Big House, so big was it that the music room was new territory. It was an exquisite room, possibly thirty-five by sixty and rising to a lofty trussed ceiling where a warm golden light was diffused from a skylight of yellow glass. Red tones entered largely into the walls and furnishing, and the place, to him, seemed to hold the hush of music.

Graham was lazily contemplating a Keith with its inevitable triumph of sun-gloried atmosphere and twilight-shadowed sheep, when, from the tail of his eye, he saw his hostess come in from the far entrance. Again, the sight of her, that was a picture, gave him the little catch-breath of gasp. She was clad entirely in white, and looked very young and quite tall in the sweeping folds of a *holoku* of elaborate simplicity and apparent shapelessness. He knew the *holoku* in the home of its origin, where, on the *lanais* of Hawaii, it gave charm to a plain woman and double-folded the charm of a charming woman.

While they smiled greeting across the room, he was noting the set of her body, the poise of head and frankness of eyes—all of which seemed articulate with a friendly, comradely, "Hello, friends." At least such was the form Graham's fancy took as she came toward him.

"You made a mistake with this room," he said gravely.

"No, don't say that! But how?"

"It should have been longer, much longer, twice as long at least."

"Why?" she demanded, with a disapproving shake of head, while he delighted in the girlish color in her cheeks that gave the lie to her thirty-eight years.

"Because, then," he answered, "you should have had to walk twice as far this morning and my pleasure of watching you would have been correspondingly increased. I've always insisted that the *holoku* is the most charming garment ever invented for women."

"Then it was my *holoku* and not I," she retorted. "I see you are like Dick—always with a string on your compliments, and lo, when we poor sillies start to nibble, back goes the compliment dragging at the end of the string.

"Now I want to show you the room," she hurried on, closing his disclaimer. "Dick gave me a free hand with it. It's all mine, you see, even to its proportions."

"And the pictures?"

"I selected them," she nodded, "every one of them, and loved them onto the walls myself. Although Dick did quarrel with me over that Vereschagin. He agreed on the two Millets and the Corot over there, and on that Isabey; and even conceded that some Vereschagins might do in a music room, but not that particular Vereschagin. He's jealous for our local artists, you see. He wanted more of them, wanted to show his appreciation of home talent."

"I don't know your Pacific Coast men's work very well," Graham said. "Tell me about them. Show me that—Of course, that's a Keith, there; but whose is that next one? It's beautiful."

"A McComas—" she was answering; and Graham, with a pleasant satisfaction, was settling himself to a half-hour's talk on pictures, when Donald Ware entered with questing eyes that lighted up at sight of the Little Lady.

His violin was under his arm, and he crossed to the piano in a brisk, business-like way and proceeded to lay out music.

"We're going to work till lunch," Paula explained to Graham. "He swears I'm getting abominably rusty, and I think he's half right. We'll see you at lunch. You can stay if you care, of course; but I warn you it's really going to be work. And we're going swimming this afternoon. Four o'clock at the tank, Dick says. Also, he says he's got a new song he's going to sing then.—What time is it, Mr. Ware?"

"Ten minutes to eleven," the musician answered briefly, with a touch of sharpness.

"You're ahead of time—the engagement was for eleven. And till eleven you'll have to wait, sir. I must run and see Dick, first. I haven't said good morning to him yet."

Well Paula knew her husband's hours. Scribbled secretly in the back of the note-book that lay always on the reading stand by her couch were hieroglyphic notes that reminded her that he had coffee at six-thirty; might possibly be caught in bed with proof-sheets or books till eight- forty-five, if not out riding; was inaccessible between nine and ten, dictating correspondence to Blake; was inaccessible between ten and eleven, conferring with managers and foremen, while Bonbright, the assistant secretary, took down, like any court reporter, every word uttered by all parties in the rapid-fire interviews.

At eleven, unless there were unexpected telegrams or business, she could usually count on finding Dick alone for a space, although invariably busy. Passing the secretaries' room, the click of a typewriter informed her that one obstacle was removed. In the library, the sight of Mr. Bonbright hunting a book for Mr. Manson, the Shorthorn manager, told her that Dick's hour with his head men was over.

She pressed the button that swung aside a section of filled bookshelves and revealed the tiny spiral of steel steps that led up to Dick's work room. At the top, a similar pivoting section of shelves swung obediently to her press of button and let her noiselessly into his room. A shade of vexation passed across her face as she recognized Jeremy Braxton's voice. She paused in indecision, neither seeing nor being seen.

"If we flood we flood," the mine superintendent was saying. "It will cost a mint—yes, half a dozen mints—to pump out again. And it's a damned shame to drown the old Harvest that way."

"But for this last year the books show that we've worked at a positive loss," Paula heard Dick take up. "Every petty bandit from Huerta down to the last peon who's stolen a horse has gouged us. It's getting too stiff—taxes extraordinary—bandits, revolutionists, and federals. We could survive it, if only the end were in sight; but we have no guarantee that this disorder may not last a dozen or twenty years."

"Just the same, the old Harvest—think of flooding her!" the superintendent protested.

"And think of Villa," Dick replied, with a sharp laugh the bitterness of which did not escape Paula. "If he wins he says he's going to divide all the land among the peons. The next logical step will be the mines. How much do you think we've coughed up to the constitutionalists in the past twelvemonth?"

"Over a hundred and twenty thousand," Braxton answered promptly. "Not counting that fifty thousand cold bullion to Torenas before he retreated. He jumped his army at Guaymas and headed for Europe with it—I wrote you all that."

"If we keep the workings afloat, Jeremy, they'll go on gouging, gouge without end, Amen. I think we'd better flood. If we can make wealth more efficiently than those rapscallions, let us show them that we can destroy wealth with the same facility."

"That's what I tell them. And they smile and repeat that such and such a free will offering, under exigent circumstances, would be very acceptable to the revolutionary chiefs—meaning themselves. The big chiefs never finger one peso in ten of it. Good Lord! I show them what we've done. Steady work for five thousand peons. Wages raised from ten centavos a day to a hundred and ten. I show them peons—ten-centavo men when we took them, and five-peso men when I showed them. And the same old smile and the same old itching palm, and the same old acceptability of a free will offering from us to the sacred cause of the revolution. By God! Old Diaz was a robber, but he was a decent robber. I said to Arranzo: 'If we shut down, here's five thousand Mexicans out of a job—what'll you do with them?' And Arranzo smiled and answered me pat. 'Do with them?' he said. 'Why, put guns in their hands and march 'em down to take Mexico City.'"

In imagination Paula could see Dick's disgusted shrug of shoulders as she heard him say:

"The curse of it is—that the stuff is there, and that we're the only fellows that can get it out. The Mexicans can't do it. They haven't the brains. All they've got is the guns, and they're making us shell out more than we make. There's only one thing for us, Jeremy. We'll forget profits for a year or so, lay off the men, and just keep the engineer force on and the pumping going."

"I threw that into Arranzo," Jeremy Braxton's voice boomed. "And what was his comeback? That if we laid off the peons, he'd see to it that the engineers laid off, too, and the mine could flood and be damned to us.—No, he didn't say that last. He just smiled, but the smile meant the same thing. For two cents I'd a-wrung his yellow neck, except that there'd have been another patriot in his boots and in my office next day proposing a stiffer gouge.

"So Arranzo got his 'bit,' and, on top of it, before he went across to join the main bunch around Juarez, he let his men run off three hundred of our mules—thirty thousand dollars' worth of mule-flesh right there, after I'd sweetened him, too. The yellow skunk!"

"Who is revolutionary chief in our diggings right now?" Paula heard her husband ask with one of his abrupt shifts that she knew of old time tokened his drawing together the many threads of a situation and proceeding to action.

"Raoul Bena."

"What's his rank?"

"Colonel—he's got about seventy ragamuffins."

"What did he do before he quit work?"

"Sheep-herder."

"Very well." Dick's utterance was quick and sharp. "You've got to play-act. Become a patriot. Hike back as fast as God will let you. Sweeten this Raoul Bena. He'll see through your play, or he's no Mexican. Sweeten him and tell him you'll make him a general—a second Villa."

"Lord, Lord, yes, but how?" Jeremy Braxton demanded.

"By putting him at the head of an army of five thousand. Lay off the men. Make him make them volunteer. We're safe, because Huerta is doomed. Tell him you're a real patriot. Give each man a rifle. We'll stand that for a last gouge, and it will prove you a patriot. Promise every man his job back when the war is over. Let them and Raoul Bena depart with your blessing. Keep on the pumping force only. And if we cut out profits for a year or so, at the same time we are cutting down losses. And perhaps we won't have to flood old Harvest after all."

Paula smiled to herself at Dick's solution as she stole back down the spiral on her way to the music room. She was depressed, but not by the Harvest Group situation. Ever since her marriage there had always been trouble in the working of the Mexican mines Dick had inherited. Her depression was due to her having missed her morning greeting to him. But this depression vanished at meeting Graham, who had lingered with Ware at the piano and who, at her coming, was evidencing signs of departure.

"Don't run away," she urged. "Stay and witness a spectacle of industry that should nerve you up to starting on that book Dick has been telling me about."

Chapter 16

On Dick's face, at lunch, there was no sign of trouble over the Harvest Group; nor could anybody have guessed that Jeremy Braxton's visit had boded anything less gratifying than a report of unfailing earnings. Although Adolph Weil had gone on the early morning train, which advertised that the business which had brought him had been transacted with Dick at some unheard of hour, Graham discovered a greater company than ever at the table. Besides a Mrs. Tully, who seemed a stout and elderly society matron, and whom Graham could not make out, there were three new men, of whose identity he gleaned a little: a Mr. Gulhuss, State Veterinary; a Mr. Deacon, a portrait painter of evident note on the Coast; and a Captain Lester, then captain of a Pacific Mail liner, who had sailed skipper for Dick nearly twenty years before and who had helped Dick to his navigation.

The meal was at its close, and the superintendent was glancing at his watch, when Dick said:

"Jeremy, I want to show you what I've been up to. We'll go right now. You'll have time on your way to the train."

"Let us all go," Paula suggested, "and make a party of it. I'm dying to see it myself, Dick's been so obscure about it."

Sanctioned by Dick's nod, she was ordering machines and saddle horses the next moment.

"What is it?" Graham queried, when she had finished.

"Oh, one of Dick's stunts. He's always after something new. This is an invention. He swears it will revolutionize farming—that is, small farming. I have the general idea of it, but I haven't seen it set up yet. It was ready a week ago, but there was some delay about a cable or something concerning an adjustment."

"There's billions in it... if it works," Dick smiled over the table. "Billions for the farmers of the world, and perhaps a trifle of royalty for me... if it works."

"But what is it?" O'Hay asked. "Music in the dairy barns to make the cows give down their milk more placidly?"

"Every farmer his own plowman while sitting on his front porch," Dick baffled back. "In fact, the labor-eliminating intermediate stage between soil production and sheer laboratory production of food. But wait till you see it. Gulhuss, this is where I kill my own business, if it works, for it will do away with the one horse of every ten-acre farmer between here and Jericho."

In ranch machines and on saddle animals, the company was taken a mile beyond the dairy center, where a level field was fenced squarely off and contained, as Dick announced, just precisely ten acres.

"Behold," he said, "the one-man and no-horse farm where the farmer sits on the porch. Please imagine the porch."

In the center of the field was a stout steel pole, at least twenty feet in height and guyed very low.

From a drum on top of the pole a thin wire cable ran to the extreme edge of the field and was attached to the steering lever of a small gasoline tractor. About the tractor two mechanics fluttered. At command from Dick they cranked the motor and started it on its way.

"This is the porch," Dick said. "Just imagine we're all that future farmer sitting in the shade and reading the morning paper while the manless, horseless plowing goes on."

Alone, unguided, the drum on the head of the pole in the center winding up the cable, the tractor, at the circumference permitted by the cable, turned a single furrow as it described a circle, or, rather, an inward trending spiral about the field.

"No horse, no driver, no plowman, nothing but the farmer to crank the tractor and start it on its way," Dick exulted, as the uncanny mechanism turned up the brown soil and continued unguided, ever spiraling toward the field's center. "Plow, harrow, roll, seed, fertilize, cultivate, harvest—all from the front porch. And where the farmer can buy juice from a power company, all he, or his wife, will have to do is press the button, and he to his newspaper, and she to her pie-crust."

"All you need, now, to make it absolutely perfect," Graham praised, "is to square the circle."

"Yes," Mr. Gulhuss agreed. "As it is, a circle in a square field loses some acreage."

Graham's face advertised a mental arithmetic trance for a minute, when he announced: "Loses, roughly, three acres out of every ten."

"Sure," Dick concurred. "But the farmer has to have his front porch somewhere on his ten acres. And the front porch represents the house, the barn, the chicken yard and the various outbuildings.

Very well. Let him get tradition out of his mind, and, instead of building these things in the center of his ten acres, let him build them on the three acres of fringe. And let him plant his fruit and shade trees and berry bushes on the fringe. When you come to consider it, the traditionary method of erecting the buildings in the center of a rectangular ten acres compels him to plow around the center in broken rectangles."

Gulhuss nodded enthusiastically. "Sure. And there's always the roadway from the center out to the county road or right of way. That breaks the efficiency of his plowing. Break ten acres into the consequent smaller rectangles, and it's expensive cultivation."

"Wish navigation was as automatic," was Captain Lester's contribution.

"Or portrait painting," laughed Rita Wainwright with a significant glance at Mr. Deacon.

"Or musical criticism," Lute remarked, with no glance at all, but with a pointedness of present company that brought from O'Hay:

"Or just being a charming young woman."

"What price for the outfit?" Jeremy Braxton asked.

"Right now, we could manufacture and lay down, at a proper profit, for five hundred. If the thing came into general use, with up to date, large-scale factory methods, three hundred. But say five hundred. And write off fifteen per cent, for interest and constant, it would cost the farmer seventy dollars a year. What ten-acre farmer, on two- hundred-dollar land, who keeps books, can keep a horse for seventy dollars a year? And on top of that, it would save him, in labor, personal or hired, at the abjectest minimum, two hundred dollars a year."

"But what guides it?" Rita asked.

"The drum on the post. The drum is graduated for the complete radius— which took some tall figuring, I assure you—and the cable, winding around the drum and shortening, draws the tractor in toward the center."

"There are lots of objections to its general introduction, even among small farmers," Gulhuss said.

Dick nodded affirmation.

"Sure," he replied. "I have over forty noted down and classified. And I've as many more for the machine itself. If the thing is a success, it will take a long time to perfect it and introduce it."

Graham found himself divided between watching the circling tractor and casting glances at the picture Paula Forrest was on her mount. It was her first day on The Fawn, which was the Palomina mare Hennessy had trained for her. Graham smiled with secret approval of her femininity; for Paula, whether she had designed her habit for the mare, or had selected one most peculiarly appropriate, had achieved a triumph.

In place of a riding coat, for the afternoon was warm, she wore a tan linen blouse with white turnback collar. A short skirt, made like the lower part of a riding coat, reached the knees, and from knees to entrancing little bespurred champagne boots tight riding trousers showed. Skirt and trousers were of fawn-colored silk corduroy. Soft white gauntlets on her hands matched with the collar in the one emphasis of color. Her head was bare, the hair done tight and low around her ears and nape of neck.

"I don't see how you can keep such a skin and expose yourself to the sun this way," Graham ventured, in mild criticism.

"I don't," she smiled with a dazzle of white teeth. "That is, I don't expose my face this way more than a few times a year. I'd like to, because I love the sun-gold burn in my hair; but I don't dare a thorough tanning."

The mare frisked, and a breeze of air blew back a flap of skirt, showing an articulate knee where the trouser leg narrowed tightly over it. Again Graham visioned the white round of knee pressed into the round muscles of the swimming Mountain Lad, as he noted the firm knee- grip on her pigskin English saddle, quite new and fawn-colored to match costume and horse.

When the magneto on the tractor went wrong, and the mechanics busied themselves with it in the midst of the partly plowed field, the company, under Paula's guidance, leaving Dick behind with his invention, resolved itself into a pilgrimage among the brood-centers on the way to the swimming tank. Mr. Crellin, the hog-manager, showed them Lady Isleton, who, with her prodigious, fat, recent progeny of eleven, won various naïve encomiums, while Mr. Crellin warmly proclaimed at least four times, "And not a runt, not a runt, in the bunch."

Other glorious brood-sows, of Berkshire, Duroc-Jersey, and O. I. C. blood, they saw till they were wearied, and new-born kids and lambs, and rotund does and ewes. From center to center, Paula kept the telephones warning ahead of the party's coming, so that Mr. Manson waited to exhibit the great King Polo, and his broad-backed Shorthorn harem, and the Shorthorn harems of bulls that were only little less than King Polo in magnificence and record; and Parkman, the Jersey manager, was on hand, with staffed assistants, to parade Sensational Drake, Golden Jolly, Fontaine Royal, Oxford Master, and Karnak's Fairy Boy—blue ribbon bulls, all, and founders and scions of noble houses of butter-fat renown, and Rosaire Queen, Standby's Dam, Golden Jolly's Lass, Olga's Pride, and Gertie of Maitlands—equally blue-ribboned and blue-blooded Jersey matrons in the royal realm of butter-fat; and Mr. Mendenhall, who had charge of the Shires, proudly exhibited a string of mighty stallions, led by the mighty Mountain Lad, and a longer string of matrons, headed by the Fotherington Princess of the silver whinny. Even old Alden Bessie, the Princess's dam, retired to but part-day's work, he sent for that they might render due honor to so notable a dam.

As four o'clock approached, Donald Ware, not keen on swimming, returned in one of the machines to the Big House, and Mr. Gulhuss remained to discuss Shires with Mr. Mendenhall. Dick was at the tank when the party arrived, and the girls were immediately insistent for the new song.

"It isn't exactly a new song," Dick explained, his gray eyes twinkling roguery, "and it's not my song. It was sung in Japan before I was born, and, I doubt not, before Columbus discovered America. Also, it is a duet—a competitive duet with forfeit penalties attached. Paula will have to sing it with me.—I'll teach you. Sit down there, that's right.—Now all the rest of you gather around and sit down."

Still in her riding habit, Paula sat down on the concrete, facing her husband, in the center of the sitting audience. Under his direction, timing her movements to his, she slapped her hands on her knees, slapped her palms together, and slapped her palms against his palms much in the fashion of the nursery game of "Bean Porridge Hot." Then he sang the song, which was short and which she quickly picked up, singing it with him and clapping the accent. While the air of it was orientally catchy, it was chanted slowly, almost monotonously, but it was quickly provocative of excitement to the spectators:

"*Jong-Keena, Jong-Keena, Jong-Jong, Keena-Keena, Yo-ko-ham-a, Nag-a-sak-i, Kobe-mar-o—hoy!!!*"

The last syllable, *hoy*, was uttered suddenly, explosively, and an octave and more higher than the pitch of the melody. At the same moment that it was uttered, Paula's and Dick's hands were abruptly shot toward each other's, either clenched or open. The point of the game was that Paula's hands, open or closed, at the instant of uttering hoy, should match Dick's. Thus, the first time, she did match him, both his and her hands being closed, whereupon he took off his hat and tossed it into Lute's lap.

"My forfeit," he explained. "Come on, Paul, again." And again they sang and clapped:

"*Jong-Keena, Jong-Keena, Jong-Jong, Keena-Keena, Yo-ko-ham-a, Nag-a-sak-i, Kobe-mar-o—hoy!!!*"

This time, with the *hoy*, her hands were closed and his were open.

"Forfeit!—forfeit!" the girls cried.

She looked her costume over with alarm, asking, "What can I give?"

"A hair pin," Dick advised; and one of her turtleshell hair pins joined his hat in Lute's lap.

"Bother it!" she exclaimed, when the last of her hair pins had gone the same way, she having failed seven times to Dick's once. "I can't see why I should be so slow and stupid. Besides, Dick, you're too clever. I never could out-guess you or out-anticipate you."

Again they sang the song. She lost, and, to Mrs. Tully's shocked "Paula!" she forfeited a spur and threatened a boot when the remaining spur should be gone. A winning streak of three compelled Dick to give up his wrist watch and both spurs. Then she lost her wrist watch and the remaining spur.

"Jong-Keena, Jong-Keena," they began again, while Mrs. Tully remonstrated, "Now, Paula, you simply must stop this.—Dick, you ought to be ashamed of yourself."

But Dick, emitting a triumphant "*Hoy!*" won, and joined in the laughter as Paula took off one of her little champagne boots and added it to the heap in Lute's lap.

"It's all right, Aunt Martha," Paula assured Mrs. Tully. "Mr. Ware's not here, and he's the only one who would be shocked.— Come on, Dick. You can't win every time."

"Jong-Keena, Jong-Keena," she chanted on with her husband. The repetition, at first slow, had accelerated steadily, so that now they fairly rippled through with it, while their slapping, striking palms made a continuous patter. The exercise and excitement had added to the sun's action on her skin, so that her laughing face was all a rosy glow.

Evan Graham, a silent spectator, was aware of hurt and indignity. He knew the "Jong-Keena" of old time from the geishas of the tea houses of Nippon, and, despite the unconventionality that ruled the Forrests and the Big House, he experienced shock in that Paula should take part in such a game. It did not enter his head at the moment that he would have been merely curious to see how far the madness would go had the player been Lute, or Ernestine, or Rita. Not till afterward did he realize that his concern and sense of outrage were due to the fact that the player was Paula, and that, therefore, she was bulking bigger in his imagination than he was conscious of. What he was conscious of at the moment was that he was growing angry and that he had deliberately to check himself from protesting.

By this time Dick's cigarette case and matches and Paula's second boot, belt, skirt-pin, and wedding ring had joined the mound of forfeits. Mrs. Tully, her face set in stoic resignation, was silent.

"Jong-Keena, Jong-Keena," Paula laughed and sang on, and Graham heard Ernestine laugh to Bert, "I don't see what she can spare next."

"Well, you know her," he heard Bert answer. "She's game once she gets started, and it certainly looks like she's started."

"*Hoy!*" Paula and Dick cried simultaneously, as they thrust out their hands.

But Dick's were closed, and hers were open. Graham watched her vainly quest her person for the consequent forfeit.

"Come on, Lady Godiva," Dick commanded. "You hae sung, you hae danced; now pay the piper."

"Was the man a fool?" was Graham's thought. "And a man with a wife like that."

"Well," Paula sighed, her fingers playing with the fastenings of her blouse, "if I must, I must."

Raging inwardly, Graham averted his gaze, and kept it averted. There was a pause, in which he knew everybody must be hanging on what she would do next. Then came a giggle from Ernestine, a burst of laughter from all, and, "A frame-up!" from Bert, that overcame Graham's resoluteness. He looked quickly. The Little Lady's blouse was off, and, from the waist up, she appeared in her swimming suit. It was evident that she had dressed over it for the ride.

"Come on, Lute—you next," Dick was challenging.

But Lute, not similarly prepared for *Jong-Keena*, blushingly led the retreat of the girls to the dressing rooms.

Graham watched Paula poise at the forty-foot top of the diving scaffold and swan-dive beautifully into the tank; heard Bert's admiring "Oh, you Annette Kellerman!" and, still chagrined by the trick that had threatened to outrage him, fell to wondering about the wonder woman, the Little Lady of the Big House, and how she had happened so wonderfully to be. As he fetched down the length of tank, under water, moving with leisurely strokes and with open eyes watching the shoaling bottom, it came to him that he did not know anything about her. She was Dick Forrest's wife. That was all he knew. How she had been born, how she had lived, how and where her past had been—of all this he knew nothing.

Ernestine had told him that Lute and she were half sisters of Paula. That was one bit of data, at any rate. (Warned by the increasing brightness of the bottom that he had nearly reached the end of the tank, and recognizing Dick's and Bert's legs intertwined in what must be a wrestling bout, Graham turned about, still under water, and swam back a score or so of feet.) There was that Mrs. Tully whom Paula had addressed as Aunt Martha. Was she truly an aunt? Or was she a courtesy Aunt through sisterhood with the mother of Lute and Ernestine?

He broke surface, was hailed by the others to join in bull-in-the-ring; in which strenuous sport, for the next half hour, he was compelled more than once to marvel at the litheness and agility, as well as strategy, of Paula in her successful efforts at escaping through the ring. Concluding the game through weariness, breathing hard, the entire party raced the length of the tank and crawled out to rest in the sunshine in a circle about Mrs. Tully.

Soon there was more fun afoot, and Paula was contending impossible things with Mrs. Tully.

"Now, Aunt Martha, just because you never learned to swim is no reason for you to take such a position. I am a real swimmer, and I tell you I can dive right into the tank here, and stay under for ten minutes."

"Nonsense, child," Mrs. Tully beamed. "Your father, when he was young, a great deal younger than you, my dear, could stay under water longer than any other man; and his record, as I know, was three minutes and forty seconds, as I very well know, for I held the watch myself and kept the time when he won against Harry Selby on a wager."

"Oh, I know my father was some man in his time," Paula swaggered; "but times have changed. If I had the old dear here right now, in all his youthful excellence, I'd drown him if he tried to stay under water with me. Ten minutes? Of course I can do ten minutes. And I will. You hold the watch, Aunt Martha, and time me. Why, it's as easy as—"

"Shooting fish in a bucket," Dick completed for her.

Paula climbed to the platform above the springboard.

"Time me when I'm in the air," she said.

"Make your turn and a half," Dick called.

She nodded, smiled, and simulated a prodigious effort at filling her lungs to their utmost capacity. Graham watched enchanted. A diver himself, he had rarely seen the turn and a half attempted by women other than professionals. Her wet suit of light blue and green silk clung closely to her, showing the lines of her justly proportioned body. With what appeared to be an agonized gulp for the last cubic inch of air her lungs could contain, she sprang up, out, and down, her body vertical and stiff, her legs straight, her feet close together as they impacted on the springboard end. Flung into the air by the board, she doubled her body into a ball, made a complete revolution, then straightened out in perfect diver's form, and in a perfect dive, with scarcely a ripple, entered the water.

"A Toledo blade would have made more splash," was Graham's verdict.

"If only I could dive like that," Ernestine breathed her admiration. "But I never shall. Dick says diving is a matter of timing, and that's why Paula does it so terribly well. She's got the sense of time—"

"And of abandon," Graham added.

"Of willed abandon," Dick qualified.

"Of relaxation by effort," Graham agreed. "I've never seen a professional do so perfect a turn and a half."

"And I'm prouder of it than she is," Dick proclaimed. "You see, I taught her, though I confess it was an easy task. She coordinates almost effortlessly. And that, along with her will and sense of time — why her first attempt was better than fair."

"Paula is a remarkable woman," Mrs. Tully said proudly, her eyes fluttering between the second hand of the watch and the unbroken surface of the pool. "Women never swim so well as men. But she does.— Three minutes and forty seconds! She's beaten her father!"

"But she won't stay under any five minutes, much less ten," Dick solemnly stated. "She'll burst her lungs first."

At four minutes, Mrs. Tully began to show excitement and to look anxiously from face to face. Captain Lester, not in the secret, scrambled to his feet with an oath and dived into the tank.

"Something has happened," Mrs. Tully said with controlled quietness. "She hurt herself on that dive. Go in after her, you men."

But Graham and Bert and Dick, meeting under water, gleefully grinned and squeezed hands. Dick made signs for them to follow, and led the way through the dark-shadowed water into the crypt, where, treading water, they joined Paula in subdued whisperings and gigglings.

"Just came to make sure you were all right," Dick explained. "And now we've got to beat it.—You first, Bert. I'll follow Evan."

And, one by one, they went down through the dark water and came up on the surface of the pool. By this time Mrs. Tully was on her feet and standing by the edge of the tank.

"If I thought this was one of your tricks, Dick Forrest," she began.

But Dick, paying no attention, acting preternaturally calmly, was directing the men loudly enough for her to hear.

"We've got to make this systematic, fellows. You, Bert, and you, Evan, join with me. We start at this end, five feet apart, and search the bottom across. Then move along and repeat it back."

"Don't exert yourselves, gentlemen," Mrs. Tully called, beginning to laugh. "As for you, Dick, you come right out. I want to box your ears."

"Take care of her, you girls," Dick shouted. "She's got hysterics."

"I haven't, but I will have," she laughed.

"But damn it all, madam, this is no laughing matter!" Captain Lester spluttered breathlessly, as he prepared for another trip to explore the bottom.

"Are you on, Aunt Martha, really and truly on?" Dick asked, after the valiant mariner had gone down.

Mrs. Tully nodded. "But keep it up, Dick, you've got one dupe. Elsie Coghlan's mother told me about it in Honolulu last year."

Not until eleven minutes had elapsed did the smiling face of Paula break the surface. Simulating exhaustion, she slowly crawled out and sank down panting near her aunt. Captain Lester, really exhausted by his strenuous exertions at rescue, studied Paula keenly, then marched to the nearest pillar and meekly bumped his head three times against the concrete.

"I'm afraid I didn't stay down ten minutes," Paula said. "But I wasn't much under that, was I, Aunt Martha?"

"You weren't much under at all," Mrs. Tully replied, "if it's my opinion you were asking. I'm surprised that you are even wet.— There, there, breathe naturally, child. The play-acting is unnecessary. I remember, when I was a young girl, traveling in India, there was a school of fakirs who leaped into deep wells and stayed down much longer than you, child, much longer indeed."

"You knew!" Paula charged.

"But you didn't know I did," her Aunt retorted. "And therefore your conduct was criminal. When you consider a woman of my age, with my heart—"

"And with your blessed, brass-tack head," Paula cried.

"For two apples I'd box your ears."

"And for one apple I'd hug you, wet as I am," Paula laughed back. "Anyway, we did fool Captain Lester.—Didn't we, Captain?"

"Don't speak to me," that doughty mariner muttered darkly. "I'm busy with myself, meditating what form my vengeance shall take.

—As for you, Mr. Dick Forrest, I'm divided between blowing up your dairy, or hamstringing Mountain Lad. Maybe I'll do both. In the meantime I am going out to kick that mare you ride."

Dick on The Outlaw, and Paula on The Fawn, rode back side by side to the Big House.

"How do you like Graham?" he asked.

"Splendid," was her reply. "He's your type, Dick. He's universal, like you, and he's got the same world-marks branded on him—the Seven Seas, the books, and all the rest. He's an artist, too, and pretty well all-around. And he's good fun. Have you noticed his smile? It's irresistible. It makes one want to smile with him."

"And he's got his serious scars, as well," Dick nodded concurrence.

"Yes—right in the corners of the eyes, just after he has smiled, you'll see them come. They're not tired marks exactly, but rather the old eternal questions: Why? What for? What's it worth? What's it all about?"

And bringing up the rear of the cavalcade, Ernestine and Graham talked.

"Dick's deep," she was saying. "You don't know him any too well. He's dreadfully deep. I know him a little. Paula knows him a lot. But very few others ever get under the surface of him. He's a real philosopher, and he has the control of a stoic or an Englishman, and he can play- act to fool the world."

At the long hitching rails under the oaks, where the dismounting party gathered, Paula was in gales of laughter.

"Go on, go on," she urged Dick, "more, more."

"She's been accusing me of exhausting my vocabulary in naming the house-boys by my system," he explained.

"And he's given me at least forty more names in a minute and a half.— Go on, Dick, more."

"Then," he said, striking a chant, "we can have Oh Sin and Oh Pshaw, Oh Sing and Oh Song, Oh Sung and Oh Sang, Oh Last and Oh Least, Oh Ping and Oh Pong, Oh Some, Oh More, and Oh Most, Oh Naught and Oh Nit... "

And Dick jingled away into the house still chanting his extemporized directory.

Chapter 17

A week of dissatisfaction and restlessness ensued for Graham. Torn between belief that his business was to leave the Big House on the first train, and desire to see, and see more of Paula, to be with her, and to be more with her—he succeeded in neither leaving nor in seeing as much of her as during the first days of his visit.

At first, and for the five days that he lingered, the young violinist monopolized nearly her entire time of visibility. Often Graham strayed into the music room, and, quite neglected by the pair, sat for moody half-hours listening to their "work." They were oblivious of his presence, either flushed and absorbed with the passion of their music, or wiping their foreheads and chatting and laughing companionably in pauses to rest. That the young musician loved her with an ardency that was almost painful, was patent to Graham; but what hurt him was the abandon of devotion with which she sometimes looked at Ware after he had done something exceptionally fine. In vain Graham tried to tell himself that all this was mental on her part—purely delighted appreciation of the other's artistry. Nevertheless, being man, it hurt, and continued to hurt, until he could no longer suffer himself to remain.

Once, chancing into the room at the end of a Schumann song and just after Ware had departed, Graham found Paula still seated at the piano, an expression of rapt dreaming on her face. She regarded him almost unrecognizingly, gathered herself mechanically together, uttered an absent-minded commonplace or so, and left the room. Despite his vexation and hurt, Graham tried to think it mere artist-dreaming on her part, a listening to the echo of the just-played music in her soul. But women were curious creatures, he could not help moralizing, and were prone to lose their hearts most strangely and inconsequentially. Might it not be that by his very music this youngster of a man was charming the woman of her?

With the departure of Ware, Paula Forrest retired almost completely into her private wing behind the door without a knob. Nor did this seem unusual, Graham gleaned from the household.

"Paula is a woman who finds herself very good company," Ernestine explained, "and she often goes in for periods of aloneness, when Dick is the only person who sees her."

"Which is not flattering to the rest of the company," Graham smiled.

"Which makes her such good company whenever she is in company," Ernestine retorted.

The driftage through the Big House was decreasing. A few guests, on business or friendship, continued to come, but more departed. Under Oh Joy and his Chinese staff the Big House ran so frictionlessly and so perfectly, that entertainment of guests seemed little part of the host's duties. The guests largely entertained themselves and one another.

Dick rarely appeared, even for a moment, until lunch, and Paula, now carrying out her seclusion program, never appeared before dinner.

"Rest cure," Dick laughed one noon, and challenged Graham to a tournament with boxing gloves, single-sticks, and foils.

"And now's the time," he told Graham, as they breathed between bouts, "for you to tackle your book. I'm only one of the many who are looking forward to reading it, and I'm looking forward hard. Got a letter from Havely yesterday—he mentioned it, and wondered how far along you were."

So Graham, in his tower room, arranged his notes and photographs, schemed out the work, and plunged into the opening chapters. So immersed did he become that his nascent interest in Paula might have languished, had it not been for meeting her each evening at dinner. Then, too, until Ernestine and Lute left for Santa Barbara, there were afternoon swims and rides and motor trips to the pastures of the Miramar Hills and the upland ranges of the Anselmo Mountains. Other trips they made, sometimes accompanied by Dick, to his great dredgers working in the Sacramento basin, or his dam-building on the Little Coyote and Los Cuatos creeks, or to his five-thousand-acre colony of twenty-acre farmers, where he was trying to enable two hundred and fifty heads of families, along with their families, to make good on the soil.

That Paula sometimes went for long solitary rides, Graham knew, and, once, he caught her dismounting from the Fawn at the hitching rails.

"Don't you think you are spoiling that mare for riding in company?" he twitted.

Paula laughed and shook her head.

"Well, then," he asserted stoutly, "I'm spoiling for a ride with you."

"There's Lute, and Ernestine, and Bert, and all the rest."

"This is new country," he contended. "And one learns country through the people who know it. I've seen it through the eyes of Lute, and Ernestine and all the rest; but there is a lot I haven't seen and which I can see only through your eyes."

"A pleasant theory," she evaded. "A—a sort of landscape vampirism."

"But without the ill effects of vampirism," he urged quickly.

Her answer was slow in coming. Her look into his eyes was frank and straight, and he could guess her words were weighed and gauged.

"I don't know about that," was all she said finally; but his fancy leaped at the several words, ranging and conjecturing their possible connotations.

"But we have so much we might be saying to each other," he tried again. "So much we… ought to be saying to each other."

"So I apprehend," she answered quietly; and again that frank, straight look accompanied her speech.

So she did apprehend—the thought of it was flame to him, but his tongue was not quick enough to serve him to escape the cool, provoking laugh as she turned into the house.

Still the company of the Big House thinned. Paula's aunt, Mrs. Tully, much to Graham's disappointment (for he had expected to learn from her much that he wanted to know of Paula), had gone after only a several days' stay. There was vague talk of her return for a longer stay; but, just back from Europe, she declared herself burdened with a round of duty visits which must be performed before her pleasure visiting began.

O'Hay, the critic, had been compelled to linger several days in order to live down the disastrous culmination of the musical raid made upon him by the philosophers. The idea and the trick had been Dick's. Combat had joined early in the evening, when a seeming chance remark of Ernestine had enabled Aaron Hancock to fling the first bomb into the thick of O'Hay's deepest convictions. Dar Hyal, a willing and eager ally, had charged around the flank with his blastic theory of music and taken O'Hay in reverse. And the battle had raged until the hot-headed Irishman, beside himself with the grueling the pair of skilled logomachists were giving him, accepted with huge relief the kindly invitation of Terrence McFane to retire with him to the tranquillity and repose of the stag room, where, over a soothing highball and far from the barbarians, the two of them could have a heart to heart talk on real music. At two in the morning, wild-eyed and befuddled, O'Hay had been led to bed by the upright-walking and unshakably steady Terrence.

"Never mind," Ernestine had told O'Hay later, with a twinkle in her eye that made him guess the plot. "It was only to be expected. Those rattle-brained philosophers would drive even a saint to drink."

"I thought you were safe in Terrence's hands," had been Dick's mock apology. "A pair of Irishmen, you know. I'd forgot Terrence was case- hardened. Do you know, after he said good night to you, he came up to me for a yarn. And he was steady as a rock. He mentioned casually of having had several sips, so I... I... never dreamed ... er... that he had indisposed you."

When Lute and Ernestine departed for Santa Barbara, Bert Wainwright and his sister remembered their long-neglected home in Sacramento. A pair of painters, proteges of Paula, arrived the same day. But they were little in evidence, spending long days in the hills with a trap and driver and smoking long pipes in the stag room.

The free and easy life of the Big House went on in its frictionless way. Dick worked. Graham worked. Paula maintained her seclusion. The sages from the madrono grove strayed in for wordy dinners—and wordy evenings, except when Paula played for them. Automobile parties, from Sacramento, Wickenberg, and other valley towns, continued to drop in unexpectedly, but never to the confusion of Oh Joy and the house boys, whom Graham saw, on occasion, with twenty minutes' warning, seat a score of unexpected guests to a perfect dinner. And there were even nights—rare ones—when only Dick and Graham and Paula sat at dinner, and when, afterward, the two men yarned for an hour before an early bed, while she played soft things to herself or disappeared earlier than they.

But one moonlight evening, when the Watsons and Masons and Wombolds arrived in force, Graham found himself out, when every bridge table was made up. Paula was at the piano. As he approached he caught the quick expression of pleasure in her eyes at sight of him, which as quickly vanished. She made a slight movement as if to rise, which did not escape his notice any more than did her quiet mastery of the impulse that left her seated.

She was immediately herself as he had always seen her—although it was little enough he had seen of her, he thought, as he talked whatever came into his head, and rummaged among her songs with her. Now one and now another song he tried with her, subduing his high baritone to her light soprano with such success as to win cries of more from the bridge players.

"Yes, I am positively aching to be out again over the world with Dick," she told him in a pause. "If we could only start to-morrow! But Dick can't start yet. He's in too deep with too many experiments and adventures on the ranch here. Why, what do you think he's up to now? As if he did not have enough on his hands, he's going to revolutionize the sales end, or, at least, the California and Pacific Coast portion of it, by making the buyers come to the ranch."

"But they do do that," Graham said. "The first man I met here was a buyer from Idaho."

"Oh, but Dick means as an institution, you know—to make them come en masse at a stated time. Not simple auction sales, either, though he says he will bait them with a bit of that to excite interest. It will be an annual fair, to last three days, in which he will be the only exhibitor. He's spending half his mornings now in conference with Mr. Agar and Mr. Pitts. Mr. Agar is his sales manager, and Mr. Pitts his showman."

She sighed and rippled her fingers along the keyboard.

"But, oh, if only we could get away—Timbuctoo, Mokpo, or Jericho."

"Don't tell me you've ever been to Mokpo," Graham laughed.

She nodded. "Cross my heart, solemnly, hope to die. It was with Dick in the *All Away* and in the long ago. It might almost be said we honeymooned in Mokpo."

And while Graham exchanged reminiscences of Mokpo with her, he cudgeled his brain to try and decide whether her continual reference to her husband was deliberate.

"I should imagine you found it such a paradise here," he was saying.

"I do, I do," she assured him with what seemed unnecessary vehemence. "But I don't know what's come over me lately. I feel it imperative to be up and away. The spring fret, I suppose; the Red Gods and their medicine. And if only Dick didn't insist on working his head off and getting tied down with projects! Do you know, in all the years of our marriage, the only really serious rival I have ever had has been this ranch. He's pretty faithful, and the ranch *is* his first love. He had it all planned and started before he ever met me or knew I existed."

"Here, let us try this together," Graham said abruptly, placing the song on the rack before her.

"Oh, but it's the 'Gypsy Trail,'" she protested. "It will only make my mood worse." And she hummed:

"'Follow the Romany patteran West to the sinking sun, Till the junk sails lift through the homeless drift, And the East and the West are one.'

"What is the Romany patteran?" she broke off to ask. "I've always thought of it as patter, or patois, the Gypsy patois, and somehow it strikes me as absurd to follow a language over the world—a sort of philological excursion."

"In a way the patteran is speech," he answered. "But it always says one thing: 'This way I have passed.' Two sprigs, crossed in certain ways and left upon the trail, compose the patteran. But they must always be of different trees or shrubs. Thus, on the ranch here, a patteran could be made of manzanita and madrono, of oak and spruce, of buckeye and alder, of redwood and laurel, of huckleberry and lilac. It is a sign of Gypsy comrade to Gypsy comrade, of Gypsy lover to Gypsy lover." And he hummed:

"'Back to the road again, again, Out of a clear sea track; Follow the cross of the Gypsy trail, Over the world and back.'"

She nodded comprehension, looked for a moment with troubled eyes down the long room to the card-players, caught herself in her momentary absentness, and said quickly:

"Heaven knows there's a lot of Gypsy in some of us. I have more than full share. In spite of his bucolic proclivities, Dick is a born Gypsy. And from what he has told of you, you are hopelessly one."

"After all, the white man is the real Gypsy, the king Gypsy," Graham propounded. "He has wandered wider, wilder, and with less equipment, than any Gypsy. The Gypsy has followed in his trails, but never made trail for him.—Come; let us try it."

And as they sang the reckless words to their merry, careless lilt, he looked down at her and wondered—wondered at her—at himself. This was no place for him by this woman's side, under her husband's roof- tree. Yet here he was, and he should have gone days before. After the years he was just getting acquainted with himself. This was enchantment, madness. He should tear himself away at once. He had known enchantments and madnesses before, and had torn himself away. Had he softened with the years? he questioned himself. Or was this a profounder madness than he had experienced? This meant the violation of dear things—things so dear, so jealously cherished and guarded in his secret life, that never yet had they suffered violation.

And still he did not tear himself away. He stood there beside her, looking down on her brown crown of hair glinting gold and bronze and bewitchingly curling into tendrils above her ears, singing a song that was fire to him—that must be fire to her, she being what she was and feeling what she had already, in flashes, half-unwittingly, hinted to him.

She is a witch, and her voice is not the least of her witchery, he thought, as *her* voice, so richly a woman's voice, so essentially her voice in contradistinction to all women's voices in the world, sang and throbbed in his ear. And he knew, beyond shade of doubt, that she felt some touch of this madness that afflicted him; that she sensed, as he sensed, that the man and the woman were met.

They thrilled together as they sang, and the thought and the sure knowledge of it added fuel to his own madness till his voice warmed unconsciously to the daring of the last lines, as, voices and thrills blending, they sang:

"'The wild hawk to the wind-swept sky, The deer to the wholesome wold, And the heart of a man to the heart of a maid As it was in the days of old— The heart of a man to the heart of a maid, Light of my tents be fleet, Morning waits at the end of the world, And the world is all at our feet.'"

He looked for her to look up as the last notes died away, but she remained quiet a moment, her eyes bent on the keys. And then the face that was turned to his was the face of the Little Lady of the Big House, the mouth smiling mischievously, the eyes filled with roguery, as she said:

"Let us go and devil Dick—he's losing. I've never seen him lose his temper at cards, but he gets ridiculously blue after a long siege of losing.

"And he does love gambling," she continued, as she led the way to the tables. "It's one of his modes of relaxing. It does him good. About once or twice a year, if it's a good poker game, he'll sit in all night to it and play to the blue sky if they take off the limit."

Chapter 18

Almost immediately after the singing of the "Gypsy Trail," Paula emerged from her seclusion, and Graham found himself hard put, in the tower room, to keep resolutely to his work when all the morning he could hear snatches of song and opera from her wing, or laughter and scolding of dogs from the great patio, or the continuous pulse for hours of the piano from the distant music room. But Graham, patterning after Dick, devoted his mornings to work, so that he rarely encountered Paula before lunch.

She made announcement that her spell of insomnia was over and that she was ripe for all gaieties and excursions Dick had to offer her. Further, she threatened, in case Dick grudged these personal diversions, to fill the house with guests and teach him what liveliness was. It was at this time that her Aunt Martha—Mrs. Tully — returned for a several days' visit, and that Paula resumed the driving of Duddy and Fuddy in the high, one-seated Stude-baker trap. Duddy and Fuddy were spirited trotters, but Mrs. Tully, despite her elderliness and avoirdupois, was without timidity when Paula held the reins.

As Mrs. Tully told Graham: "And that is a concession I make to no woman save Paula. She is the only woman I can trust myself to with horses. She has the horse-way about her. When she was a child she was wild over horses. It's a wonder she didn't become a circus rider."

More, much more, Graham learned about Paula in various chats with her aunt. Of Philip Desten, Paula's father, Mrs. Tully could never say enough. Her eldest brother, and older by many years, he had been her childhood prince. His ways had been big ways, princely ways—ways that to commoner folk had betokened a streak of madness. He was continually guilty of the wildest things and the most chivalrous things. It was this streak that had enabled him to win various fortunes, and with equal facility to lose them, in the great gold adventure of Forty-nine. Himself of old New England stock, he had had for great grandfather a Frenchman—a trifle of flotsam from a mid- ocean wreck and landed to grow up among the farmer-sailormen of the coast of Maine.

"And once, and once only, in each generation, that French Desten crops out," Mrs. Tully assured Graham. "Philip was that Frenchman in his generation, and who but Paula, and in full measure, received that same inheritance in her generation. Though Lute and Ernestine are her half- sisters, no one would imagine one drop of the common blood was shared. That's why Paula, instead of going circus-riding, drifted inevitably to France. It was that old original Desten that drew her over."

And of the adventure in France, Graham learned much. Philip Desten's luck had been to die when the wheel of his fortune had turned over and down. Ernestine and Lute, little tots, had been easy enough for Desten's sisters to manage. But Paula, who had fallen to Mrs. Tully, had been the problem—"because of that Frenchman."

"Oh, she is rigid New England," Mrs. Tully insisted, "the solidest of creatures as to honor and rectitude, dependableness and faithfulness. As a girl she really couldn't bring herself to lie, except to save others. In which case all her New England ancestry took flight and she would lie as magnificently as her father before her. And he had the same charm of manner, the same daring, the same ready laughter, the same vivacity. But what is lightsome and blithe in her, was debonaire in him. He won men's hearts always, or, failing that, their bitterest enmity. No one was left cold by him in passing. Contact with him quickened them to love or hate. Therein Paula differs, being a woman, I suppose, and not enjoying man's prerogative of tilting at windmills. I don't know that she has an enemy in the world. All love her, unless, it may well be, there are cat-women who envy her her nice husband."

And as Graham listened, Paula's singing came through the open window from somewhere down the long arcades, and there was that ever-haunting thrill in her voice that he could not escape remembering afterward. She burst into laughter, and Mrs. Tully beamed to him and nodded at the sound.

"There laughs Philip Desten," she murmured, "and all the Frenchwomen behind the original Frenchman who was brought into Penobscot, dressed in homespun, and sent to meeting. Have you noticed how Paula's laugh invariably makes everybody look up and smile? Philip's laugh did the same thing."

"Paula had always been passionately fond of music, painting, drawing. As a little girl she could be traced around the house and grounds by the trail she left behind her of images and shapes, made in whatever medium she chanced upon—drawn on scraps of paper, scratched on bits of wood, modeled in mud and sand.

"She loved everything, and everything loved her," said Mrs. Tully. "She was never timid of animals. And yet she always stood in awe of them; but she was born sense-struck, and her awe was beauty-awe. Yes, she was an incorrigible hero-worshiper, whether the person was merely beautiful or did things. And she never will outgrow that beauty—awe of anything she loves, whether it is a grand piano, a great painting, a beautiful mare, or a bit of landscape.

"And Paula had wanted to do, to make beauty herself. But she was sorely puzzled whether she should devote herself to music or painting. In the full swing of work under the best masters in Boston, she could not refrain from straying back to her drawing. From her easel she was lured to modeling.

"And so, with her love of the best, her soul and heart full of beauty, she grew quite puzzled and worried over herself, as to which talent was the greater and if she had genius at all. I suggested a complete rest from work and took her abroad for a year. And of all things, she developed a talent for dancing. But always she harked back to her music and painting. No, she was not flighty. Her trouble was that she was too talented—"

"Too diversely talented," Graham amplified.

"Yes, that is better," Mrs. Tully nodded. "But from talent to genius is a far cry, and to save my life, at this late day, I don't know whether the child ever had a trace of genius in her. She has certainly not done anything big in any of her chosen things."

"Except to be herself," Graham added.

"Which *is* the big thing," Mrs. Tully accepted with a smile of enthusiasm. "She is a splendid, unusual woman, very unspoiled, very natural. And after all, what does doing things amount to? I'd give more for one of Paula's madcap escapades—oh, I heard all about swimming the big stallion—than for all her pictures if every one was a masterpiece. But she was hard for me to understand at first. Dick often calls her the girl that never grew up. But gracious, she can put on the grand air when she needs to. I call her the most mature child I have ever seen. Dick was the finest thing that ever happened to her. It was then that she really seemed for the first time to find herself. It was this way."

And Mrs. Tully went on to sketch the year of travel in Europe, the resumption of Paula's painting in Paris, and the conviction she finally reached that success could be achieved only by struggle and that her aunt's money was a handicap.

"And she had her way," Mrs. Tully sighed. "She—why, she

dismissed me, sent me home. She would accept no more than the meagerest allowance, and went down into the Latin Quarter on her own, batching with two other American girls. And she met Dick. Dick was a rare one. You couldn't guess what he was doing then. Running a cabaret—oh, not these modern cabarets, but a real students' cabaret of sorts. It was very select. They were a lot of madmen. You see, he was just back from some of his wild adventuring at the ends of the earth, and, as he stated it, he wanted to stop living life for a while and to talk about life instead.

"Paula took me there once. Oh, they were engaged—the day before, and he had called on me and all that. I had known 'Lucky' Richard Forrest, and I knew all about his son. From a worldly standpoint, Paula couldn't have made a finer marriage. It was quite a romance. Paula had seen him captain the University of California eleven to victory over Stanford. And the next time she saw him was in the studio she shared with the two girls. She didn't know whether Dick was worth millions or whether he was running a cabaret because he was hard up, and she cared less. She always followed her heart. Fancy the situation: Dick the uncatchable, and Paula who never flirted. They must have sprung forthright into each other's arms, for inside the week it was all arranged, and Dick made his call on me, as if my decision meant anything one way or the other.

"But Dick's cabaret. It was the Cabaret of the Philosophers—a small pokey place, down in a cellar, in the heart of the Quarter, and it had only one table. Fancy that for a cabaret! But such a table! A big round one, of plain boards, without even an oil-cloth, the wood stained with the countless drinks spilled by the table-pounding of the philosophers, and it could seat thirty. Women were not permitted. An exception was made for Paula and me.

"You've met Aaron Hancock here. He was one of the philosophers, and to this day he swaggers that he owed Dick a bigger bill that never was paid than any of his customers. And there they used to meet, all those wild young thinkers, and pound the table, and talk philosophy in all the tongues of Europe. Dick always had a penchant for philosophers.

"But Paula spoiled that little adventure. No sooner were they married than Dick fitted out his schooner, the All Away, and away the blessed pair of them went, honeymooning from Bordeaux to Hongkong."

"And the cabaret was closed, and the philosophers left homeless and discussionless," Graham remarked.

Mrs. Tully laughed heartily and shook her head.

"He endowed it for them," she gasped, her hand to her side. "Or partially endowed it, or something. I don't know what the arrangement was. And within the month it was raided by the police for an anarchist club."

After having learned the wide scope of her interests and talents, Graham was nevertheless surprised one day at finding Paula all by herself in a corner of a window-seat, completely absorbed in her work on a piece of fine embroidery.

"I love it," she explained. "All the costly needlework of the shops means nothing to me alongside of my own work on my own designs. Dick used to fret at my sewing. He's all for efficiency, you know, elimination of waste energy and such things. He thought sewing was a wasting of time. Peasants could be hired for a song to do what I was doing. But I succeeded in making my viewpoint clear to him.

"It's like the music one makes oneself. Of course I can buy better music than I make; but to sit down at an instrument and evoke the music oneself, with one's own fingers and brain, is an entirely different and dearer satisfaction. Whether one tries to emulate another's performance, or infuses the performance with one's own personality and interpretation, it's all the same. It is soul-joy and fulfilment.

"Take this little embroidered crust of lilies on the edge of this flounce—there is nothing like it in the world. Mine the idea, all mine, and mine the delight of giving form and being to the idea. There are better ideas and better workmanship in the shops; but this is different. It is mine. I visioned it, and I made it. And who is to say that embroidery is not art?"

She ceased speaking and with her eyes laughed the insistence of her question.

"And who is to say," Graham agreed, "that the adorning of beautiful womankind is not the worthiest of all the arts as well as the sweetest?"

"I rather stand in awe of a good milliner or modiste," she nodded gravely. "They really are artists, and important ones, as Dick would phrase it, in the world's economy."

Another time, seeking the library for Andean reference, Graham came upon Paula, sprawled gracefully over a sheet of paper on a big table and flanked by ponderous architectural portfolios, engaged in drawing plans of a log bungalow or camp for the sages of the madroño grove.

"It's a problem," she sighed. "Dick says that if I build it I must build it for seven. We've got four sages now, and his heart is set on seven. He says never mind showers and such things, because what philosopher ever bathes? And he has suggested seriously seven stoves and seven kitchens, because it is just over such mundane things that philosophers always quarrel."

"Wasn't it Voltaire who quarreled with a king over candle-ends?" Graham queried, pleasuring in the sight of her graceful abandon. Thirty-eight! It was impossible. She seemed almost a girl, petulant and flushed over some school task. Then he remembered Mrs. Tully's remark that Paula was the most mature child she had ever known.

It made him wonder. Was she the one, who, under the oaks at the hitching rails, with two brief sentences had cut to the heart of an impending situation? "So I apprehend," she had said. What had she apprehended? Had she used the phrase glibly, without meaning? Yet she it was who had thrilled and fluttered to him and with him when they had sung the "Gypsy Trail." *That* he knew. But again, had he not seen her warm and glow to the playing of Donald Ware? But here Graham's ego had its will of him, for he told himself that with Donald Ware it was different. And he smiled to himself and at himself at the thought.

"What amuses you?" Paula was asking.

"Heaven knows I am no architect. And I challenge you to house seven philosophers according to all the absurd stipulations laid down by Dick."

Back in his tower room with his Andean books unopened before him, Graham gnawed his lip and meditated. The woman was no woman. She was the veriest child. Or—and he hesitated at the thought—was this naturalness that was overdone? Did she in truth apprehend? It must be. It had to be. She was of the world. She knew the world. She was very wise. No remembered look of her gray eyes but gave the impression of poise and power. That was it —strength! He recalled her that first night when she had seemed at times to glint an impression of steel, of thin and jewel-like steel. In his fancy, at the time, he remembered likening her strength to ivory, to carven pearl shell, to sennit twisted of maidens' hair.

And he knew, now, ever since the brief words at the hitching rails and the singing of the "Gypsy Trail," that whenever their eyes looked into each other's it was with a mutual knowledge of unsaid things.

In vain he turned the pages of the books for the information he sought. He tried to continue his chapter without the information, but no words flowed from his pen. A maddening restlessness was upon him. He seized a time table and pondered the departure of trains, changed his mind, switched the room telephone to the house barn, and asked to have Altadena saddled.

It was a perfect morning of California early summer. No breath of wind stirred over the drowsing fields, from which arose the calls of quail and the notes of meadowlarks. The air was heavy with lilac fragrance, and from the distance, as he rode between the lilac hedges, Graham heard the throaty nicker of Mountain Lad and the silvery answering whinney of the Fotherington Princess.

Why was he here astride Dick Forrest's horse? Graham asked himself. Why was he not even then on the way to the station to catch that first train he had noted on the time table? This unaccustomed weakness of decision and action was a new rôle for him, he considered bitterly. But—and he was on fire with the thought of it—this was his one life, and this was the one woman in the world.

He reined aside to let a herd of Angora goats go by. Each was a doe, and there were several hundred of them; and they were moved slowly by the Basque herdsmen, with frequent pauses, for each doe was accompanied by a young kid. In the paddock were many mares with new- born colts; and once, receiving warning in time, Graham raced into a crossroad to escape a drove of thirty yearling stallions being moved somewhere across the ranch. Their excitement was communicated to that entire portion of the ranch, so that the air was filled with shrill nickerings and squealings and answering whinneys, while Mountain Lad, beside himself at sight and sound of so many rivals, raged up and down his paddock, and again and again trumpeted his challenging conviction that he was the most amazing and mightiest thing that had ever occurred on earth in the way of horse flesh.

Dick Forrest pranced and sidled into the cross road on the Outlaw, his face beaming with delight at the little tempest among his many creatures.

"Fecundity! Fecundity!"—he chanted in greeting, as he reined in to a halt, if halt it might be called, with his tan-golden sorrel mare a-fret and a-froth, wickedly reaching with her teeth now for his leg and next for Graham's, one moment pawing the roadway, the next moment, in sheer impotence of resentfulness, kicking the empty air with one hind leg and kicking the air repeatedly, a dozen times.

"Those youngsters certainly put Mountain Lad on his mettle," Dick laughed. "Listen to his song:

"'Hear me! I am Eros. I stamp upon the hills. I fill the wide valleys. The mares hear me, and startle, in quiet pastures; for they know me. The land is filled with fatness, and the sap is in the trees.

It is the spring. The spring is mine. I am monarch of my kingdom of the spring. The mares remember my voice. They knew me aforetime through their mothers before them. Hear me! I am Eros. I stamp upon the hills, and the wide valleys are my heralds, echoing the sound of my approach.'"

Chapter 19

After Mrs. Tully's departure, Paula, true to her threat, filled the house with guests. She seemed to have remembered all who had been waiting an invitation, and the limousine that met the trains eight miles away was rarely empty coming or going. There were more singers and musicians and artist folk, and bevies of young girls with their inevitable followings of young men, while mammas and aunts and chaperons seemed to clutter all the ways of the Big House and to fill a couple of motor cars when picnics took place.

And Graham wondered if this surrounding of herself by many people was not deliberate on Paula's part. As for himself, he definitely abandoned work on his book, and joined in the before-breakfast swims of the hardier younger folk, in the morning rides over the ranch, and in whatever fun was afoot indoors and out.

Late hours and early were kept; and one night, Dick, who adhered to his routine and never appeared to his guests before midday, made a night of it at poker in the stag-room. Graham had sat in, and felt well repaid when, at dawn, the players received an unexpected visit from Paula—herself past one of her white nights, she said, although no sign of it showed on her fresh skin and color. Graham had to struggle to keep his eyes from straying too frequently to her as she mixed golden fizzes to rejuvenate the wan-eyed, jaded players. Then she made them start the round of "jacks" that closed the game, and sent them off for a cold swim before breakfast and the day's work or frolic.

Never was Paula alone. Graham could only join in the groups that were always about her. Although the young people ragged and tangoed incessantly, she rarely danced, and then it was with the young men. Once, however, she favored him with an old-fashioned waltz. "Your ancestors in an antediluvian dance," she mocked the young people, as she stepped out; for she and Graham had the floor to themselves.

Once down the length of the room, the two were in full accord. Paula, with the sympathy Graham recognized that made her the exceptional accompanist or rider, subdued herself to the masterful art of the man, until the two were as parts of a sentient machine that operated without jar or friction. After several minutes, finding their perfect mutual step and pace, and Graham feeling the absolute giving of Paula to the dance, they essayed rhythmical pauses and dips, their feet never leaving the floor, yet affecting the onlookers in the way Dick voiced it when he cried out: "They float! They float!" The music was the "Waltz of Salomé," and with its slow-fading end they postured slower and slower to a perfect close.

There was no need to speak. In silence, without a glance at each other, they returned to the company where Dick was proclaiming:

"Well, younglings, codlings, and other fry, that's the way we old folks used to dance. I'm not saying anything against the new dances, mind you. They're all right and dandy fine. But just the same it wouldn't injure you much to learn to waltz properly. The way you waltz, when you do attempt it, is a scream. We old folks do know a thing or two that is worth while."

"For instance?" queried one of the girls.

"I'll tell you. I don't mind the young generation smelling of gasoline the way it does—"

Cries and protests drowned Dick out for a moment.

"I know I smell of it myself," he went on. "But you've all failed to learn the good old modes of locomotion. There isn't a girl of you that Paula can't walk into the ground. There isn't a fellow of you that Graham and I can't walk into a receiving hospital.—Oh, I know you can all crank engines and shift gears to the queen's taste. But there isn't one of you that can properly ride a horse—a real horse, in the only way, I mean. As for driving a smart pair of roadsters, it's a screech. And how many of you husky lads, hell-scooting on the bay in your speed-boats, can take the wheel of an old-time sloop or schooner, without an auxiliary, and get out of your own way in her?"

"But we get there just the same," the same girl retorted.

"And I don't deny it," Dick answered. "But you are not always pretty. I'll tell you a pretty sight that no one of you can ever present — Paula, there, with the reins of four slashing horses in her hands, her foot on the brake, swinging tally-ho along a mountain road."

On a warm morning, in the cool arcade of the great patio, a chance group of four or five, among whom was Paula, formed about Graham, who had been reading alone. After a time he returned to his magazine with such absorption that he forgot those about him until an awareness of silence penetrated to his consciousness. He looked up. All the others save Paula had strayed off. He could hear their distant laughter from across the patio. But Paula! He surprised the look on her face, in her eyes. It was a look bent on him, concerning him. Doubt, speculation, almost fear, were in her eyes; and yet, in that swift instant, he had time to note that it was a look deep and searching—almost, his quick fancy prompted, the look of one peering into the just-opened book of fate. Her eyes fluttered and fell, and the color increased in her cheeks in an unmistakable blush. Twice her lips moved to the verge of speech; yet, caught so arrantly in the act, she was unable to phrase any passing thought. Graham saved the painful situation by saying casually:

"Do you know, I've just been reading De Vries' eulogy of Luther Burbank's work, and it seems to me that Dick is to the domestic animal world what Burbank is to the domestic vegetable world. You are life- makers here—thumbing the stuff into new forms of utility and beauty."

Paula, by this time herself again, laughed and accepted the compliment.

"I fear me," Graham continued with easy seriousness, "as I watch your achievements, that I can only look back on a misspent life. Why didn't I get in and *make* things? I'm horribly envious of both of you."

"We *are* responsible for a dreadful lot of creatures being born," she said. "It makes one breathless to think of the responsibility."

"The ranch certainly spells fecundity," Graham smiled. "I never before was so impressed with the flowering and fruiting of life. Everything here prospers and multiplies—"

"Oh!" Paula cried, breaking in with a sudden thought. "Some day I'll show you my goldfish. I breed them, too—yea, and commercially. I supply the San Francisco dealers with their rarest strains, and I even ship to New York. And, best of all, I actually make money—profits, I mean. Dick's books show it, and he is the most rigid of bookkeepers. There isn't a tack-hammer on the place that isn't inventoried; nor a horse-shoe nail unaccounted for. That's why he has such a staff of bookkeepers. Why, do you know, calculating every last least item of expense, including average loss of time for colic and lameness, out of fearfully endless columns of figures he has worked the cost of an hour's labor for a draught horse to the third decimal place."

"But your goldfish," Graham suggested, irritated by her constant dwelling on her husband.

"Well, Dick makes his bookkeepers keep track of my goldfish in the same way. I'm charged every hour of any of the ranch or house labor I use on the fish—postage stamps and stationery, too, if you please. I have to pay interest on the plant. He even charges me for the water, just as if he were a city water company and I a householder. And still I net ten per cent., and have netted as high as thirty. But Dick laughs and says when I've deducted the wages of superintendence—my superintendence, he means—that I'll find I am poorly paid or else am operating at a loss; that with my net I couldn't hire so capable a superintendent.

"Just the same, that's why Dick succeeds in his undertakings. Unless it's sheer experiment, he never does anything without knowing precisely, to the last microscopic detail, what it is he is doing."

"He is very sure," Graham observed.

"I never knew a man to be so sure of himself," Paula replied warmly; "and I never knew a man with half the warrant. I know him. He is a genius—but only in the most paradoxical sense. He is a genius because he is so balanced and normal that he hasn't the slightest particle of genius in him. Such men are rarer and greater than geniuses. I like to think of Abraham Lincoln as such a type."

"I must admit I don't quite get you," Graham said.

"Oh, I don't dare to say that Dick is as good, as cosmically good, as Lincoln," she hurried on. "Dick *is* good, but it is not that. It is in their excessive balance, normality, lack of flare, that they are of the same type. Now I am a genius. For, see, I do things without knowing how I do them. I just do them. I get effects in my music that way. Take my diving. To save my life I couldn't tell how I swan-dive, or jump, or do the turn and a half.

"Dick, on the other hand, can't do anything unless he clearly knows in advance *how* he is going to do it. He does everything with balance and foresight. He's a general, all-around wonder, without ever having been a particular wonder at any one thing.—Oh, I know him. He's never been a champion or a record-breaker in any line of athletics. Nor has he been mediocre in any line. And so with everything else, mentally, intellectually. He is an evenly forged chain. He has no massive links, no weak links."

"I'm afraid I'm like you," Graham said, "that commoner and lesser creature, a genius. For I, too, on occasion, flare and do the most unintentional things. And I am not above falling on my knees before mystery."

"And Dick hates mystery—or it would seem he does. Not content with knowing *how*—he is eternally seeking the *why* of the *how*. Mystery is a challenge to him. It excites him like a red rag does a bull. At once he is for ripping the husks and the heart from mystery, so that he will know the *how* and the *why*, when it will be no longer mystery but a generalization and a scientifically demonstrable fact."

Much of the growing situation was veiled to the three figures of it. Graham did not know of Paula's desperate efforts to cling close to her husband, who, himself desperately busy with his thousand plans and projects, was seeing less and less of his company. He always appeared at lunch, but it was a rare afternoon when he could go out with his guests. Paula did know, from the multiplicity of long, code telegrams from Mexico, that things were in a parlous state with the Harvest Group. Also, she saw the agents and emissaries of foreign investors in Mexico, always in haste and often inopportune, arriving at the ranch to confer with Dick. Beyond his complaint that they ate the heart out of his time, he gave her no clew to the matters discussed.

"My! I wish you weren't so busy," she sighed in his arms, on his knees, one fortunate morning, when, at eleven o'clock, she had caught him alone.

It was true, she had interrupted the dictation of a letter into the phonograph; and the sigh had been evoked by the warning cough of Bonbright, whom she saw entering with more telegrams in his hand.

"Won't you let me drive you this afternoon, behind Duddy and Fuddy, just you and me, and cut the crowd?" she begged.

He shook his head and smiled.

"You'll meet at lunch a weird combination," he explained. "Nobody else needs to know, but I'll tell you." He lowered his voice, while Bonbright discreetly occupied himself at the filing cabinets. "They're Tampico oil folk. Samuels himself, President of the Nacisco; and Wishaar, the big inside man of the Pearson-Brooks crowd—the chap that engineered the purchase of the East Coast railroad and the Tiuana Central when they tried to put the Nacisco out of business; and Matthewson—he's the *hi-yu-skookum* big chief this side the Atlantic of the Palmerston interests —you know, the English crowd that fought the Nacisco and the Pearson-Brooks bunch so hard; and, oh, there'll be several others. It shows you that things are rickety down Mexico way when such a bunch stops scrapping and gets together.

"You see, they are oil, and I'm important in my way down there, and they want me to swing the mining interests in with the oil. Truly, big things are in the air, and we've got to hang together and do something or get out of Mexico. And I'll admit, after they gave me the turn-down in the trouble three years ago, that I've sulked in my tent and made them come to see me."

He caressed her and called her his armful of dearest woman, although she detected his eye roving impatiently to the phonograph with its unfinished letter.

"And so," he concluded, with a pressure of his arms about her that seemed to hint that her moment with him was over and she must go, "that means the afternoon. None will stop over. And they'll be off and away before dinner."

She slipped off his knees and out of his arms with unusual abruptness, and stood straight up before him, her eyes flashing, her cheeks white, her face set with determination, as if about to say something of grave importance. But a bell tinkled softly, and he reached for the desk telephone.

Paula drooped, and sighed inaudibly, and, as she went down the room and out the door, and as Bonbright stepped eagerly forward with the telegrams, she could hear the beginning of her husband's conversation:

"No. It is impossible. He's got to come through, or I'll put him out of business. That gentleman's agreement is all poppycock. If it were only that, of course he could break it. But I've got some mighty interesting correspondence that he's forgotten about... . Yes, yes; it will clinch it in any court of law. I'll have the file in your office by five this afternoon. And tell him, for me, that if he tries to put through this trick, I'll break him. I'll put a competing line on, and his steamboats will be in the receiver's hands inside a year... . And... hello, are you there?... And just look up that point I suggested. I am rather convinced you'll find the Interstate Commerce has got him on two counts... ."

Nor did Graham, nor even Paula, imagine that Dick—the keen one, the deep one, who could see and sense things yet to occur and out of intangible nuances and glimmerings build shrewd speculations and hypotheses that subsequent events often proved correct—was already sensing what had not happened but what might happen. He had not heard Paula's brief significant words at the hitching post; nor had he seen Graham catch her in that deep scrutiny of him under the arcade. Dick had heard nothing, seen little, but sensed much; and, even in advance of Paula, had he apprehended in vague ways what she afterward had come to apprehend.

The most tangible thing he had to build on was the night, immersed in bridge, when he had not been unaware of the abrupt leaving of the piano after the singing of the "Gypsy Trail"; nor when, in careless smiling greeting of them when they came down the room to devil him over his losing, had he failed to receive a hint or feeling of something unusual in Paula's roguish teasing face. On the moment, laughing retorts, giving as good as she sent, Dick's own laughing eyes had swept over Graham beside her and likewise detected the unusual. The man was overstrung, had been Dick's mental note at the time. But why should he be overstrung? Was there any connection between his overstrungness and the sudden desertion by Paula of the piano? And all the while these questions were slipping through his thoughts, he had laughed at their sallies, dealt, sorted his hand, and won the bid on no trumps.

Yet to himself he had continued to discount as absurd and preposterous the possibility of his vague apprehension ever being realized. It was a chance guess, a silly speculation, based upon the most trivial data, he sagely concluded. It merely connoted the attractiveness of his wife and of his friend. But—and on occasional moments he could not will the thought from coming uppermost in his mind—why had they broken off from singing that evening? Why had he received the feeling that there was something unusual about it? Why had Graham been overstrung?

Nor did Bonbright, one morning, taking dictation of a telegram in the last hour before noon, know that Dick's casual sauntering to the window, still dictating, had been caused by the faint sound of hoofs on the driveway. It was not the first of recent mornings that Dick had so sauntered to the window, to glance out with apparent absentness at the rush of the morning riding party in the last dash home to the hitching rails. But he knew, on this morning, before the first figures came in sight whose those figures would be.

"Braxton is safe," he went on with the dictation without change of tone, his eyes on the road where the riders must first come into view. "If things break he can get out across the mountains into Arizona. See Connors immediately. Braxton left Connors complete instructions. Connors to-morrow in Washington. Give me fullest details any move— signed."

Up the driveway the Fawn and Altadena clattered neck and neck. Dick had not been disappointed in the figures he expected to see. From the rear, cries and laughter and the sound of many hoofs tokened that the rest of the party was close behind.

"And the next one, Mr. Bonbright, please put in the Harvest code," Dick went on steadily, while to himself he was commenting that Graham was a passable rider but not an excellent one, and that it would have to be seen to that he was given a heavier horse than Altadena. "It is to Jeremy Braxton. Send it both ways. There is a chance one or the other may get through... "

Chapter 20

Once again the tide of guests ebbed from the Big House, and more than one lunch and dinner found only the two men and Paula at the table. On such evenings, while Graham and Dick yarned for their hour before bed, Paula no longer played soft things to herself at the piano, but sat with them doing fine embroidery and listening to the talk.

Both men had much in common, had lived life in somewhat similar ways, and regarded life from the same angles. Their philosophy was harsh rather than sentimental, and both were realists. Paula made a practice of calling them the pair of "Brass Tacks."

"Oh, yes," she laughed to them, "I understand your attitude. You are successes, the pair of you—physical successes, I mean. You have health. You are resistant. You can stand things. You have survived where men less resistant have gone down. You pull through African fevers and bury the other fellows. This poor chap gets pneumonia in Cripple Creek and cashes in before you can get him to sea level. Now why didn't you get pneumonia? Because you were more deserving? Because you had lived more virtuously? Because you were more careful of risks and took more precautions?"

She shook her head.

"No. Because you were luckier—I mean by birth, by possession of constitution and stamina. Why, Dick buried his three mates and two engineers at Guayaquil. Yellow fever. Why didn't the yellow fever germ, or whatever it is, kill Dick? And the same with you, Mr. Broad- shouldered Deep-chested Graham. In this last trip of yours, why didn't you die in the swamps instead of your photographer? Come. Confess. How heavy was he? How broad were his shoulders? How deep his chest?—wide his nostrils?— tough his resistance?"

"He weighed a hundred and thirty-five," Graham admitted ruefully. "But he looked all right and fit at the start. I think I was more surprised than he when he turned up his toes." Graham shook his head. "It wasn't because he was a light weight and small. The small men are usually the toughest, other things being equal. But you've put your finger on the reason just the same. He didn't have the physical stamina, the resistance,—You know what I mean, Dick?"

"In a way it's like the quality of muscle and heart that enables some prizefighters to go the distance—twenty, thirty, forty rounds, say," Dick concurred. "Right now, in San Francisco, there are several hundred youngsters dreaming of success in the ring. I've watched them trying out. All look good, fine-bodied, healthy, fit as fiddles, and young. And their spirits are most willing. And not one in ten of them can last ten rounds. I don't mean they get knocked out. I mean they blow up. Their muscles and their hearts are not made out of first- grade fiber. They simply are not made to move at high speed and tension for ten rounds. And some of them blow up in four or five rounds. And not one in forty can go the twenty-round route, give and take, hammer and tongs, one minute of rest to three of fight, for a full hour of fighting. And the lad who can last forty rounds is one in ten thousand—lads like Nelson, Gans, and Wolgast.

"You understand the point I am making," Paula took up. "Here are the pair of you. Neither will see forty again. You're a pair of hard- bitten sinners. You've gone through hardship and exposure that dropped others all along the way. You've had your fun and folly. You've roughed and rowdied over the world—"

"Played the wild ass," Graham laughed in.

"And drunk deep," Paula added. "Why, even alcohol hasn't burned you. You were too tough. You put the other fellows under the table, or into the hospital or the grave, and went your gorgeous way, a song on your lips, with tissues uncorroded, and without even the morning-after headache. And the point is that you are successes. Your muscles are blond-beast muscles, your vital organs are blond-beast organs. And from all this emanates your blond-beast philosophy. That's why you are brass tacks, and preach realism, and practice realism, shouldering and shoving and walking over lesser and unluckier creatures, who don't dare talk back, who, like Dick's prizefighting boys, would blow up in the first round if they resorted to the arbitrament of force."

Dick whistled a long note of mock dismay.

"And that's why you preach the gospel of the strong," Paula went on. "If you had been weaklings, you'd have preached the gospel of the weak and turned the other cheek. But you—you pair of big-muscled giants— when you are struck, being what you are, you don't turn the other cheek—"

"No," Dick interrupted quietly. "We immediately roar, 'Knock his block off!' and then do it.—She's got us, Evan, hip and thigh. Philosophy, like religion, is what the man is, and is by him made in his own image."

And while the talk led over the world, Paula sewed on, her eyes filled with the picture of the two big men, admiring, wondering, pondering, without the surety of self that was theirs, aware of a slipping and giving of convictions so long accepted that they had seemed part of her.

Later in the evening she gave voice to her trouble.

"The strangest part of it," she said, taking up a remark Dick had just made, "is that too much philosophizing about life gets one worse than nowhere. A philosophic atmosphere is confusing—at least to a woman. One hears so much about everything, and against everything, that nothing is sure. For instance, Mendenhall's wife is a Lutheran. She hasn't a doubt about anything. All is fixed, ordained, immovable. Star-drifts and ice-ages she knows nothing about, and if she did they would not alter in the least her rules of conduct for men and women in this world and in relation to the next.

"But here, with us, you two pound your brass tacks, Terrence does a Greek dance of epicurean anarchism, Hancock waves the glittering veils of Bergsonian metaphysics, Leo makes solemn obeisance at the altar of Beauty, and Dar Hyal juggles his sophistic blastism to no end save all your applause for his cleverness. Don't you see? The effect is that there is nothing solid in any human judgment. Nothing is right. Nothing is wrong. One is left compassless, rudderless, chartless on a sea of ideas. Shall I do this? Must I refrain from that? Will it be wrong? Is there any virtue in it? Mrs. Mendenhall has her instant answer for every such question. But do the philosophers?"

Paula shook her head.

"No. All they have is ideas. They immediately proceed to talk about it, and talk and talk and talk, and with all their erudition reach no conclusion whatever. And I am just as bad. I listen and listen, and talk and talk, as I am talking now, and remain convictionless. There is no test—"

"But there is," Dick said. "The old, eternal test of truth—*Will it work?*"

"Ah, now you are pounding your favorite brass tack," Paula smiled. "And Dar Hyal, with a few arm-wavings and wordwhirrings, will show that all brass tacks are illusions; and Terrence, that brass tacks are sordid, irrelevant and non-essential things at best; and Hancock, that the overhanging heaven of Bergson is paved with brass tacks, only that they are a much superior article to yours; and Leo, that there is only one brass tack in the universe, and that it is Beauty, and that it isn't brass at all but gold."

"Come on, Red Cloud, go riding this afternoon," Paula asked her husband. "Get the cobwebs out of your brain, and let lawyers and mines and livestock go hang."

"I'd like to, Paul," he answered. "But I can't. I've got to rush in a machine all the way to the Buckeye. Word came in just before lunch. They're in trouble at the dam. There must have been a fault in the under-strata, and too-heavy dynamiting has opened it. In short, what's the good of a good dam when the bottom of the reservoir won't hold water?"

Three hours later, returning from the Buckeye, Dick noted that for the first time Paula and Graham had gone riding together alone.

The Wainwrights and the Coghlans, in two machines, out for a week's trip to the Russian River, rested over for a day at the Big House, and were the cause of Paula's taking out the tally-ho for a picnic into the Los Baños Hills. Starting in the morning, it was impossible for Dick to accompany them, although he left Blake in the thick of dictation to go out and see them off. He assured himself that no detail was amiss in the harnessing and hitching, and reseated the party, insisting on Graham coming forward into the box-seat beside Paula.

"Just must have a reserve of man's strength alongside of Paula in case of need," Dick explained. "I've known a brake-rod to carry away on a down grade somewhat to the inconvenience of the passengers. Some of them broke their necks. And now, to reassure you, with Paula at the helm, I'll sing you a song:

"What can little Paula do? Why, drive a phaeton and two. Can little Paula do no more? Yes, drive a tally-ho and four."

All were in laughter as Paula nodded to the grooms to release the horses' heads, took the feel of the four mouths on her hands, and shortened and slipped the reins to adjustment of four horses into the collars and taut on the traces.

In the babel of parting gibes to Dick, none of the guests was aware of aught else than a bright morning, the promise of a happy day, and a genial host bidding them a merry going. But Paula, despite the keen exhilaration that should have arisen with the handling of four such horses, was oppressed by a vague sadness in which, somehow, Dick's being left behind figured. Through Graham's mind Dick's merry face had flashed a regret of conscience that, instead of being seated there beside this one woman, he should be on train and steamer fleeing to the other side of the world.

But the merriness died on Dick's face the moment he turned on his heel to enter the house. It was a few minutes later than ten when he finished his dictation and Mr. Blake rose to go. He hesitated, then said a trifle apologetically:

"You told me, Mr. Forrest, to remind you of the proofs of your Shorthorn book. They wired their second hurry-up yesterday."

"I won't be able to tackle it myself," Dick replied. "Will you please correct the typographical, submit the proofs to Mr. Manson for correction of fact—tell him be sure to verify that pedigree of King of Devon—and ship them off."

Until eleven Dick received his managers and foremen. But not for a quarter of an hour after that did he get rid of his show manager, Mr. Pitts, with the tentative make-up of the catalogue for the first annual stock-sale on the ranch. By that time Mr. Bonbright was on hand with his sheaf of telegrams, and the lunch-hour was at hand ere they were cleaned up.

For the first time alone since he had seen the tally-ho off, Dick stepped out on his sleeping porch to the row of barometers and thermometers on the wall. But he had come to consult, not them, but the girl's face that laughed from the round wooden frame beneath them.

"Paula, Paula," he said aloud, "are you surprising yourself and me after all these years? Are you turning madcap at sober middle age?"

He put on leggings and spurs to be ready for riding after lunch, and what his thoughts had been while buckling on the gear he epitomized to the girl in the frame.

"Play the game," he muttered. And then, after a pause, as he turned to go: "A free field and no favor ... and no favor."

"Really, if I don't go soon, I'll have to become a pensioner and join the philosophers of the madroño grove," Graham said laughingly to Dick.

It was the time of cocktail assembling, and Paula, in addition to Graham, was the only one of the driving party as yet to put in an appearance.

"If all the philosophers together would just make one book!"

Dick demurred. "Good Lord, man, you've just got to complete your book here. I got you started and I've got to see you through with it."

Paula's encouragement to Graham to stay on—mere stereotyped, uninterested phrases—was music to Dick. His heart leapt. After all, might he not be entirely mistaken? For two such mature, wise, middle- aged individuals as Paula and Graham any such foolishness was preposterous and unthinkable. They were not young things with their hearts on their sleeves.

"To the book!" he toasted. He turned to Paula. "A good cocktail," he praised. "Paul, you excel yourself, and you fail to teach Oh Joy the art. His never quite touch yours.—Yes, another, please."

Chapter 21

Graham, riding solitary through the redwood canyons among the hills that overlooked the ranch center, was getting acquainted with Selim, the eleven-hundred-pound, coal-black gelding which Dick had furnished him in place of the lighter Altadena. As he rode along, learning the good nature, the roguishness and the dependableness of the animal, Graham hummed the words of the "Gypsy Trail" and allowed them to lead his thoughts. Quite carelessly, foolishly, thinking of bucolic lovers carving their initials on forest trees, he broke a spray of laurel and another of redwood. He had to stand in the stirrups to pluck a long- stemmed, five-fingered fern with which to bind the sprays into a cross. When the patteran was fashioned, he tossed it on the trail before him and noted that Selim passed over without treading upon it. Glancing back, Graham watched it to the next turn of the trail. A good omen, was his thought, that it had not been trampled.

More five-fingered ferns to be had for the reaching, more branches of redwood and laurel brushing his face as he rode, invited him to continue the manufacture of patterans, which he dropped as he fashioned them. An hour later, at the head of the canyon, where he knew the trail over the divide was difficult and stiff, he debated his course and turned back.

Selim warned him by nickering. Came an answering nicker from close at hand. The trail was wide and easy, and Graham put his mount into a fox trot, swung a wide bend, and overtook Paula on the Fawn.

"Hello!" he called. "Hello! Hello!"

She reined in till he was alongside.

"I was just turning back," she said. "Why did you turn back? I thought you were going over the divide to Little Grizzly."

"You knew I was ahead of you?" he asked, admiring the frank, boyish way of her eyes straight-gazing into his.

"Why shouldn't I? I had no doubt at the second patteran."

"Oh, I'd forgotten about them," he laughed guiltily. "Why did *you* turn back?"

She waited until the Fawn and Selim had stepped over a fallen alder across the trail, so that she could look into Graham's eyes when she answered:

"Because I did not care to follow your trail.—To follow anybody's trail," she quickly amended. "I turned back at the second one."

He failed of a ready answer, and an awkward silence was between them. Both were aware of this awkwardness, due to the known but unspoken things.

"Do you make a practice of dropping patterans?" Paula asked.

"The first I ever left," he replied, with a shake of the head. "But there was such a generous supply of materials it seemed a pity, and, besides, the song was haunting me."

"It was haunting me this morning when I woke up," she said, this time her face straight ahead so that she might avoid a rope of wild grapevine that hung close to her side of the trail.

And Graham, gazing at her face in profile, at her crown of gold-brown hair, at her singing throat, felt the old ache at the heart, the hunger and the yearning. The nearness of her was a provocation. The sight of her, in her fawn-colored silk corduroy, tormented him with a rush of visions of that form of hers—swimming Mountain Lad, swan- diving through forty feet of air, moving down the long room in the dull-blue dress of medieval fashion with the maddening knee-lift of the clinging draperies.

"A penny for them," she interrupted his visioning. His answer was prompt.

"Praise to the Lord for one thing: you haven't once mentioned Dick."

"Do you so dislike him?"

"Be fair," he commanded, almost sternly. "It is because I like him. Otherwise... "

"What?" she queried.

Her voice was brave, although she looked straight before her at the Fawn's pricking ears.

"I can't understand why I remain. I should have been gone long ago."

"Why?" she asked, her gaze still on the pricking ears.

"Be fair, be fair," he warned. "You and I scarcely need speech for understanding."

She turned full upon him, her cheeks warming with color, and, without speech, looked at him. Her whip-hand rose quickly, half way, as if to press her breast, and half way paused irresolutely, then dropped down to her side. But her eyes, he saw, were glad and startled. There was no mistake. The startle lay in them, and also the gladness. And he, knowing as it is given some men to know, changed the bridle rein to his other hand, reined close to her, put his arm around her, drew her till the horses rocked, and, knee to knee and lips on lips, kissed his desire to hers. There was no mistake—pressure to pressure, warmth to warmth, and with an elate thrill he felt her breathe against him.

The next moment she had torn herself loose. The blood had left her face. Her eyes were blazing. Her riding-whip rose as if to strike him, then fell on the startled Fawn. Simultaneously she drove in both spurs with such suddenness and force as to fetch a groan and a leap from the mare.

He listened to the soft thuds of hoofs die away along the forest path, himself dizzy in the saddle from the pounding of his blood. When the last hoof-beat had ceased, he half-slipped, half-sank from his saddle to the ground, and sat on a mossy boulder. He was hard hit—harder than he had deemed possible until that one great moment when he had held her in his arms. Well, the die was cast.

He straightened up so abruptly as to alarm Selim, who sprang back the length of his bridle rein and snorted.

What had just occurred had been unpremeditated. It was one of those inevitable things. It had to happen. He had not planned it, although he knew, now, that had he not procrastinated his going, had he not drifted, he could have foreseen it. And now, going could not mend matters. The madness of it, the hell of it and the joy of it, was that no longer was there any doubt. Speech beyond speech, his lips still tingling with the memory of hers, she had told him. He dwelt over that kiss returned, his senses swimming deliciously in the sea of remembrance.

He laid his hand caressingly on the knee that had touched hers, and was grateful with the humility of the true lover. Wonderful it was that so wonderful a woman should love him. This was no girl. This was a woman, knowing her own will and wisdom. And she had breathed quickly in his arms, and her lips had been live to his. He had evoked what he had given, and he had not dreamed, after the years, that he had had so much to give.

He stood up, made as if to mount Selim, who nozzled his shoulder, then paused to debate.

It was no longer a question of going. That was definitely settled. Dick had certain rights, true. But Paula had her rights, and did he have the right to go, after what had happened, unless ... unless she went with him? To go now was to kiss and ride away. Surely, since the world of sex decreed that often the same men should love the one woman, and therefore that perfidy should immediately enter into such a triangle—surely, it was the lesser evil to be perfidious to the man than to the woman.

It was a real world, he pondered as he rode slowly along; and Paula, and Dick, and he were real persons in it, were themselves conscious realists who looked the facts of life squarely in the face. This was no affair of priest and code, of other wisdoms and decisions. Of themselves must it be settled. Some one would be hurt. But life was hurt. Success in living was the minimizing of pain. Dick believed that himself, thanks be. The three of them believed it. And it was nothing new under the sun. The countless triangles of the countless generations had all been somehow solved. This, then, would be solved. All human affairs reached some solution.

He shook sober thought from his brain and returned to the bliss of memory, reaching his hand to another caress of his knee, his lips breathing again to the breathing of hers against them. He even reined Selim to a halt in order to gaze at the hollow resting place of his bent arm which she had filled.

Not until dinner did Graham see Paula again, and he found her the very usual Paula. Not even his eye, keen with knowledge, could detect any sign of the day's great happening, nor of the anger that had whitened her face and blazed in her eyes when she half-lifted her whip to strike him. In everything she was the same Little Lady of the Big House. Even when it chanced that her eyes met his, they were serene, untroubled, with no hint of any secret in them. What made the situation easier was the presence of several new guests, women, friends of Dick and her, come for a couple of days.

Next morning, in the music room, he encountered them and Paula at the piano.

"Don't you sing, Mr. Graham?" a Miss Hoffman asked.

She was the editor of a woman's magazine published in San Francisco, Graham had learned.

"Oh, adorably," he assured her. "Don't I, Mrs. Forrest?" he appealed.

"It is quite true," Paula smiled, "if for no other reason that he is kind enough not to drown me quite."

"And nothing remains but to prove our words," he volunteered. "There's a duet we sang the other evening—" He glanced at Paula for a sign. "—Which is particularly good for my kind of singing." Again he gave her a passing glance and received no cue to her will or wish. "The music is in the living room. I'll go and get it."

"It's the 'Gypsy Trail,' a bright, catchy thing," he heard her saying to the others as he passed out.

They did not sing it so recklessly as on that first occasion, and much of the thrill and some of the fire they kept out of their voices; but they sang it more richly, more as the composer had intended it and with less of their own particular interpretation. But Graham was thinking as he sang, and he knew, too, that Paula was thinking, that in their hearts another duet was pulsing all unguessed by the several women who applauded the song's close.

"You never sang it better, I'll wager," he told Paula.

For he had heard a new note in her voice. It had been fuller, rounder, with a generousness of volume that had vindicated that singing throat.

"And now, because I know you don't know, I'll tell you what a patteran is," she was saying... .

Chapter 22

"Dick, boy, your position is distinctly Carlylean," Terrence McFane said in fatherly tones.

The sages of the madrono grove were at table, and, with Paula, Dick and Graham, made up the dinner party of seven.

"Mere naming of one's position does not settle it, Terrence," Dick replied. "I know my point is Carlylean, but that does not invalidate it. Hero-worship is a very good thing. I am talking, not as a mere scholastic, but as a practical breeder with whom the application of Mendelian methods is an every-day commonplace."

"And I am to conclude," Hancock broke in, "that a Hottentot is as good as a white man?"

"Now the South speaks, Aaron," Dick retorted with a smile. "Prejudice, not of birth, but of early environment, is too strong for all your philosophy to shake. It is as bad as Herbert Spencer's handicap of the early influence of the Manchester School."

"And Spencer is on a par with the Hottentot?" Dar Hyal challenged.

Dick shook his head.

"Let me say this, Hyal. I think I can make it clear. The average Hottentot, or the average Melanesian, is pretty close to being on a par with the average white man. The difference lies in that there are proportionately so many more Hottentots and negroes who are merely average, while there is such a heavy percentage of white men who are not average, who are above average. These are what I called the pace- makers that bring up the speed of their own race average-men. Note that they do not change the nature or develop the intelligence of the average-men. But they give them better equipment, better facilities, enable them to travel a faster collective pace.

"Give an Indian a modern rifle in place of his bow and arrows and he will become a vastly more efficient game-getter. The Indian hunter himself has not changed in the slightest. But his entire Indian race sported so few of the above-average men, that all of them, in ten thousand generations, were unable to equip him with a rifle."

"Go on, Dick, develop the idea," Terrence encouraged. "I begin to glimpse your drive, and you'll soon have Aaron on the run with his race prejudices and silly vanities of superiority."

"These above-average men," Dick continued, "these pace-makers, are the inventors, the discoverers, the constructionists, the sporting dominants. A race that sports few such dominants is classified as a lower race, as an inferior race. It still hunts with bows and arrows. It is not equipped. Now the average white man, per se, is just as bestial, just as stupid, just as inelastic, just as stagnative, just as retrogressive, as the average savage. But the average white man has a faster pace. The large number of sporting dominants in his society give him the equipment, the organization, and impose the law.

"What great man, what hero—and by that I mean what sporting dominant— has the Hottentot race produced? The Hawaiian race produced only one— Kamehameha. The negro race in America, at the outside only two, Booker T. Washington and Du Bois—and both with white blood in them... ."

Paula feigned a cheerful interest while the exposition went on. She did not appear bored, but to Graham's sympathetic eyes she seemed inwardly to droop. And in an interval of tilt between Terrence and Hancock, she said in a low voice to Graham:

"Words, words, words, so much and so many of them! I suppose Dick is right—he so nearly always is; but I confess to my old weakness of inability to apply all these floods of words to life—to my life, I mean, to my living, to what I should do, to what I must do." Her eyes were unfalteringly fixed on his while she spoke, leaving no doubt in his mind to what she referred. "I don't know what bearing sporting dominants and race-paces have on my life. They show me no right or wrong or way for my particular feet. And now that they've started they are liable to talk the rest of the evening... .

"Oh, I do understand what they say," she hastily assured him; "but it doesn't mean anything to me. Words, words, words—and I want to know what to do, what to do with myself, what to do with you, what to do with Dick."

But the devil of speech was in Dick Forrest's tongue, and before Graham could murmur a reply to Paula, Dick was challenging him for data on the subject from the South American tribes among which he had traveled. To look at Dick's face it would have been unguessed that he was aught but a carefree, happy arguer. Nor did

Graham, nor did Paula, Dick's dozen years' wife, dream that his casual careless glances were missing no movement of a hand, no change of position on a chair, no shade of expression on their faces.

What's up? was Dick's secret interrogation. Paula's not herself. She's positively nervous, and all the discussion is responsible. And Graham's off color. His brain isn't working up to mark. He's thinking about something else, rather than about what he is saying. What is that something else?

And the devil of speech behind which Dick hid his secret thoughts impelled him to urge the talk wider and wilder.

"For once I could almost hate the four sages," Paula broke out in an undertone to Graham, who had finished furnishing the required data.

Dick, himself talking, in cool sentences amplifying his thesis, apparently engrossed in his subject, saw Paula make the aside, although no word of it reached his ears, saw her increasing nervousness, saw the silent sympathy of Graham, and wondered what had been the few words she uttered, while to the listening table he was saying:

"Fischer and Speiser are both agreed on the paucity of unit-characters that circulate in the heredity of the lesser races as compared with the immense variety of unit-characters in say the French, or German, or English... ."

No one at the table suspected that Dick deliberately dangled the bait of a new trend to the conversation, nor did Leo dream afterward that it was the master-craft and deviltry of Dick rather than his own question that changed the subject when he demanded to know what part the female sporting dominants played in the race.

"Females don't sport, Leo, my lad," Terrence, with a wink to the others, answered him. "Females are conservative. They keep the type true. They fix it and hold it, and are the everlasting clog on the chariot of progress. If it wasn't for the females every blessed mother's son of us would be a sporting dominant. I refer to our distinguished breeder and practical Mendelian whom we have with us this evening to verify my random statements."

"Let us get down first of all to bedrock and find out what we are talking about," Dick was prompt on the uptake. "What is woman?" he demanded with an air of earnestness.

"The ancient Greeks said woman was nature's failure to make a man," Dar Hyal answered, the while the imp of mockery laughed in the corners of his mouth and curled his thin cynical lips derisively.

Leo was shocked. His face flushed. There was pain in his eyes and his lips were trembling as he looked wistful appeal to Dick.

"The half-sex," Hancock gibed. "As if the hand of God had been withdrawn midway in the making, leaving her but a half-soul, a groping soul at best."

"No I no!" the boy cried out. "You must not say such things!—Dick, you know. Tell them, tell them."

"I wish I could," Dick replied. "But this soul discussion is vague as souls themselves. We all know, of our selves, that we often grope, are often lost, and are never so much lost as when we think we know where we are and all about ourselves. What is the personality of a lunatic but a personality a little less, or very much less, coherent than ours? What is the personality of a moron? Of an idiot? Of a feeble- minded child? Of a horse? A dog? A mosquito? A bullfrog? A woodtick? A garden snail? And, Leo, what is your own personality when you sleep and dream? When you are seasick? When you are in love? When you have colic? When you have a cramp in the leg? When you are smitten abruptly with the fear of death? When you are angry? When you are exalted with the sense of the beauty of the world and think you think all inexpressible unutterable thoughts?

"I say *think you think* intentionally. Did you really think, then your sense of the beauty of the world would not be inexpressible, unutterable. It would be clear, sharp, definite. You could put it into words. Your personality would be clear, sharp, and definite as your thoughts and words. Ergo, Leo, when you deem, in exalted moods, that you are at the summit of existence, in truth you are thrilling, vibrating, dancing a mad orgy of the senses and not knowing a step of the dance or the meaning of the orgy. You don't know yourself. Your soul, your personality, at that moment, is a vague and groping thing. Possibly the bullfrog, inflating himself on the edge of a pond and uttering hoarse croaks through the darkness to a warty mate, possesses also, at that moment, a vague and groping personality.

"No, Leo, personality is too vague for any of our vague personalities to grasp. There are seeming men with the personalities of women. There are plural personalities. There are two-legged human creatures that are neither fish, flesh, nor fowl. We, as personalities, float like fog-wisps through glooms and darknesses and light-flashings. It is all fog and mist, and we are all foggy and misty in the thick of the mystery."

"Maybe it's mystification instead of mystery—man-made mystification," Paula said.

"There talks the true woman that Leo thinks is not a half-soul," Dick retorted. "The point is, Leo, sex and soul are all interwoven and tangled together, and we know little of one and less of the other."

"But women are beautiful," the boy stammered.

"Oh, ho!" Hancock broke in, his black eyes gleaming wickedly. "So, Leo, you identify woman with beauty?"

The young poet's lips moved, but he could only nod.

"Very well, then, let us take the testimony of painting, during the last thousand years, as a reflex of economic conditions and political institutions, and by it see how man has molded and daubed woman into the image of his desire, and how she has permitted him—"

"You must stop baiting Leo," Paula interfered, "and be truthful, all of you, and say what you do know or do believe."

"Woman is a very sacred subject," Dar Hyal enunciated solemnly.

"There is the Madonna," Graham suggested, stepping into the breach to Paula's aid.

"And the cérébrale," Terrence added, winning a nod of approval from Dar Hyal.

"One at a time," Hancock said. "Let us consider the Madonna-worship, which was a particular woman-worship in relation to the general woman- worship of all women to-day and to which Leo subscribes. Man is a lazy, loafing savage. He dislikes to be pestered. He likes tranquillity, repose. And he finds himself, ever since man began, saddled to a restless, nervous, irritable, hysterical traveling companion, and her name is woman. She has moods, tears, vanities, angers, and moral irresponsibilities. He couldn't destroy her. He had to have her, although she was always spoiling his peace. What was he to do?"

"Trust him to find a way—the cunning rascal," Terrence interjected.

"He made a heavenly image of her," Hancock kept on. "He idealized her good qualities, and put her so far away that her bad qualities couldn't get on his nerves and prevent him from smoking his quiet lazy pipe of peace and meditating upon the stars. And when the ordinary every-day woman tried to pester, he brushed her aside from his thoughts and remembered his heaven-woman, the perfect woman, the bearer of life and custodian of immortality.

"Then came the Reformation. Down went the worship of the Mother. And there was man still saddled to his repose-destroyer. What did he do then?"

"Ah, the rascal," Terrence grinned.

"He said: 'I will make of you a dream and an illusion.' And he did. The Madonna was his heavenly woman, his highest conception of woman. He transferred all his idealized qualities of her to the earthly woman, to every woman, and he has fooled himself into believing in them and in her ever since... like Leo does."

"For an unmarried man you betray an amazing intimacy with the pestiferousness of woman," Dick commented. "Or is it all purely theoretical?" Terrence began to laugh.

"Dick, boy, it's Laura Marholm Aaron's been just reading. He can spout her chapter and verse."

"And with all this talk about woman we have not yet touched the hem of her garment," Graham said, winning a grateful look from Paula and Leo.

"There is love," Leo breathed. "No one has said one word about love."

"And marriage laws, and divorces, and polygamy, and monogamy, and free love," Hancock rattled off.

"And why, Leo," Dar Hyal queried, "is woman, in the game of love, always the pursuer, the huntress?"

"Oh, but she isn't," the boy answered quietly, with an air of superior knowledge. "That is just some of your Shaw nonsense."

"Bravo, Leo," Paula applauded.

"Then Wilde was wrong when he said woman attacks by sudden and strange surrenders?" Dar Hyal asked.

"But don't you see," protested Leo, "all such talk makes woman a monster, a creature of prey." As he turned to Dick, he stole a side glance at Paula and love welled in his eyes. "Is she a creature of prey, Dick?"

"No," Dick answered slowly, with a shake of head, and gentleness was in his voice for sake of what he had just seen in the boy's eyes. "I cannot say that woman is a creature of prey. Nor can I say she is a creature preyed upon. Nor will I say she is a creature of unfaltering joy to man. But I will say that she is a creature of much joy to man— "

"And of much foolishness," Hancock added.

"Of much fine foolishness," Dick gravely amended.

"Let me ask Leo something," Dar Hyal said. "Leo, why is it that a woman loves the man who beats her?"

"And doesn't love the man who doesn't beat her?" Leo countered. "Precisely."

"Well, Dar, you are partly right and mostly wrong.—Oh, I have learned about definitions from you fellows. You've cunningly left them out of your two propositions. Now I'll put them in for you. A man who beats a woman he loves is a low type man. A woman who loves the man who beats her is a low type woman. No high type man beats the woman he loves. No high type woman," and all unconsciously Leo's eyes roved to Paula, "could love a man who beats her."

"No, Leo," Dick said, "I assure you I have never, never beaten Paula."

"So you see, Dar," Leo went on with flushing cheeks, "you are wrong. Paula loves Dick without being beaten."

With what seemed pleased amusement beaming on his face, Dick turned to Paula as if to ask her silent approval of the lad's words; but what Dick sought was the effect of the impact of such words under the circumstances he apprehended. In Paula's eyes he thought he detected a flicker of something he knew not what. Graham's face he found expressionless insofar as there was no apparent change of the expression of interest that had been there.

"Woman has certainly found her St. George tonight," Graham complimented. "Leo, you shame me. Here I sit quietly by while you fight three dragons."

"And such dragons," Paula joined in. "If they drove O'Hay to drink, what will they do to you, Leo?"

"No knight of love can ever be discomfited by all the dragons in the world," Dick said. "And the best of it, Leo, is in this case the dragons are more right than you think, and you are more right than they just the same."

"Here's a dragon that's a good dragon, Leo, lad," Terrence spoke up. "This dragon is going to desert his disreputable companions and come over on your side and be a Saint Terrence. And this Saint Terrence has a lovely question to ask you."

"Let this dragon roar first," Hancock interposed. "Leo, by all in love that is sweet and lovely, I ask you: why do lovers, out of jealousy, so often kill the woman they love?"

"Because they are hurt, because they are insane," came the answer, "and because they have been unfortunate enough to love a woman so low in type that she could be guilty of making them jealous."

"But, Leo, love will stray," Dick prompted. "You must give a more sufficient answer."

"True for Dick," Terrence supplemented. "And it's helping you I am to the full stroke of your sword. Love will stray among the highest types, and when it does in steps the green-eyed monster. Suppose the most perfect woman you can imagine should cease to love the man who does not beat her and come to love another man who loves her and will not beat her—what then? All highest types, mind you. Now up with your sword and slash into the dragons."

"The first man will not kill her nor injure her in any way," Leo asserted stoutly. "Because if he did he would not be the man you describe. He would not be high type, but low type."

"You mean, he would get out of the way?" Dick asked, at the same time busying himself with a cigarette so that he might glance at no one's face.

Leo nodded gravely.

"He would get out of the way, and he would make the way easy for her, and he would be very gentle with her."

"Let us bring the argument right home," Hancock said. "We'll suppose you're in love with Mrs. Forrest, and Mrs. Forrest is in love with you, and you run away together in the big limousine—"

"Oh, but I wouldn't," the boy blurted out, his cheeks burning.

"Leo, you are not complimentary," Paula encouraged.

"It's just supposing, Leo," Hancock urged.

The boy's embarrassment was pitiful, and his voice quivered, but he turned bravely to Dick and said:

"That is for Dick to answer."

"And I'll answer," Dick said. "I wouldn't kill Paula. Nor would I kill you, Leo. That wouldn't be playing the game. No matter what I felt at heart, I'd say, 'Bless you, my children.' But just the same—" He paused, and the laughter signals in the corners of his eyes advertised a whimsey—"I'd say to myself that Leo was making a sad mistake. You see, he doesn't know Paula."

"She would be for interrupting his meditations on the stars," Terrence smiled.

"Never, never, Leo, I promise you," Paula exclaimed.

"There do you belie yourself, Mrs. Forrest," Terrence assured her. "In the first place, you couldn't help doing it. Besides, it'd be your bounden duty to do it. And, finally, if I may say so, as somewhat of an authority, when I was a mad young lover of a man, with my heart full of a woman and my eyes full of the stars, 'twas ever the dearest delight to be loved away from them by the woman out of my heart."

"Terrence, if you keep on saying such lovely things," cried Paula," I'll run away with both you and Leo in the limousine."

"Hurry the day," said Terrence gallantly. "But leave space among your fripperies for a few books on the stars that Leo and I may be studying in odd moments."

The combat ebbed away from Leo, and Dar Hyal and Hancock beset Dick.

"What do you mean by 'playing the game'?" Dar Hyal asked.

"Just what I said, just what Leo said," Dick answered; and he knew that Paula's boredom and nervousness had been banished for some time and that she was listening with an interest almost eager. "In my way of thinking, and in accord with my temperament, the most horrible spiritual suffering I can imagine would be to kiss a woman who endured my kiss."

"Suppose she fooled you, say for old sake's sake, or through desire not to hurt you, or pity for you?" Hancock propounded.

"It would be, to me, the unforgivable sin," came Dick's reply. "It would not be playing the game—for her. I cannot conceive the fairness, nor the satisfaction, of holding the woman one loves a moment longer than she loves to be held. Leo is very right. The drunken artisan, with his fists, may arouse and keep love alive in the breast of his stupid mate. But the higher human males, the males with some shadow of rationality, some glimmer of spirituality, cannot lay rough hands on love. With Leo, I would make the way easy for the woman, and I would be very gentle with her."

"Then what becomes of your boasted monogamic marriage institution of Western civilization?" Dar Hyal asked.

And Hancock: "You argue for free love, then?"

"I can only answer with a hackneyed truism," Dick said. "There can be no love that is not free. Always, please, remember the point of view is that of the higher types. And the point of view answers you, Dar. The vast majority of individuals must be held to law and labor by the monogamic institution, or by a stern, rigid marriage institution of some sort. They are unfit for marriage freedom or love freedom. Freedom of love, for them, would be merely license of promiscuity. Only such nations have risen and endured where God and the State have kept the people's instincts in discipline and order."

"Then you don't believe in the marriage laws for say yourself," Dar Hyal inquired, "while you do believe in them for other men?"

"I believe in them for all men. Children, family, career, society, the State—all these things make marriage, legal marriage, imperative. And by the same token that is why I believe in divorce. Men, all men, and women, all women, are capable of loving more than once, of having the old love die and of finding a new love born. The State cannot control love any more than can a man or a woman. When one falls in love one falls in love, and that's all he knows about it. There it is— throbbing, sighing, singing, thrilling love. But the State can control license."

"It is a complicated free love that you stand for," Hancock criticised. "True, and for the reason that man, living in society, is a most complicated animal."

"But there are men, lovers, who would die at the loss of their loved one," Leo surprised the table by his initiative. "They would die if she died, they would die—oh so more quickly—if she lived and loved another."

"Well, they'll have to keep on dying as they have always died in the past," Dick answered grimly. "And no blame attaches anywhere for their deaths. We are so made that our hearts sometimes stray."

"My heart would never stray," Leo asserted proudly, unaware that all at the table knew his secret. "I could never love twice, I know."

"True for you, lad," Terrence approved. "The voice of all true lovers is in your throat. 'Tis the absoluteness of love that is its joy —how did Shelley put it?—or was it Keats?—'All a wonder and a wild delight.' Sure, a miserable skinflint of a half-baked lover would it be that could dream there was aught in woman form one-thousandth part as sweet, as ravishing and enticing, as glorious and wonderful as his own woman that he could ever love again."

And as they passed out from the dining room, Dick, continuing the conversation with Dar Hyal, was wondering whether Paula would kiss him good night or slip off to bed from the piano. And Paula, talking to Leo about his latest sonnet which he had shown her, was wondering if she could kiss Dick, and was suddenly greatly desirous to kiss him, she knew not why.

Chapter 23

There was little talk that same evening after dinner. Paula, singing at the piano, disconcerted Terrence in the midst of an apostrophe on love. He quit a phrase midmost to listen to the something new he heard in her voice, then slid noiselessly across the room to join Leo at full length on the bearskin. Dar Hyal and Hancock likewise abandoned the discussion, each isolating himself in a capacious chair. Graham, seeming least attracted, browsed in a current magazine, but Dick observed that he quickly ceased turning the pages. Nor did Dick fail to catch the new note in Paula's voice and to endeavor to sense its meaning.

When she finished the song the three sages strove to tell her all at the same time that for once she had forgotten herself and sung out as they had always claimed she could. Leo lay without movement or speech, his chin on his two hands, his face transfigured.

"It's all this talk on love," Paula laughed, "and all the lovely thoughts Leo and Terrence ... and Dick have put into my head."

Terrence shook his long mop of iron-gray hair.

"Into your heart you'd be meaning," he corrected. "'Tis the very heart and throat of love that are yours this night. And for the first time, dear lady, have I heard the full fair volume that is yours. Never again plaint that your voice is thin. Thick it is, and round it is, as a great rope, a great golden rope for the mooring of argosies in the harbors of the Happy Isles."

"And for that I shall sing you the *Gloria*," she answered, "to celebrate the slaying of the dragons by Saint Leo, by Saint Terrence ... and, of course, by Saint Richard."

Dick, missing nothing of the talk, saved himself from speech by crossing to the concealed sideboard and mixing for himself a Scotch and soda.

While Paula sang the *Gloria*, he sat on one of the couches, sipping his drink and remembering keenly. Once before he had heard her sing like that—in Paris, during their swift courtship, and directly afterward, during their honeymoon on the *All Away*.

A little later, using his empty glass in silent invitation to Graham, he mixed highballs for both of them, and, when Graham had finished his, suggested to Paula that she and Graham sing the "Gypsy Trail."

She shook her head and began *Das Kraut Ver-gessenheit*.

"She was not a true woman, she was a terrible woman," the song's close wrung from Leo. "And he was a true lover. She broke his heart, but still he loved her. He cannot love again because he cannot forget his love for her."

"And now, Red Cloud, the Song of the Acorn," Paula said, smiling over to her husband. "Put down your glass, and be good, and plant the acorns."

Dick lazily hauled himself off the couch and stood up, shaking his head mutinously, as if tossing a mane, and stamping ponderously with his feet in simulation of Mountain Lad.

"I'll have Leo know that he is not the only poet and love-knight on the ranch. Listen to Mountain Lad's song, all wonder and wild delight, Terrence, and more. Mountain Lad doesn't moon about the loved one. He doesn't moon at all. He incarnates love, and rears right up in meeting and tells them so. Listen to him!"

Dick filled the room and shook the air with wild, glad, stallion nickering; and then, with mane-tossing and foot-pawing, chanted:

"Hear me! I am Eros! I stamp upon the hills. I fill the wide valleys. The mares hear me, and startle, in quiet pastures; for they know me. The land is filled with fatness, and the sap is in the trees. It is the spring. The spring is mine. I am monarch of my kingdom of the spring. The mares remember my voice. They knew me aforetimes through their mothers before them. Hear me! I am Eros. I stamp upon the hills, and the wide valleys are my heralds, echoing the sound of my approach."

It was the first time the sages of the madrono grove had heard Dick's song, and they were loud in applause. Hancock took it for a fresh start in the discussion, and was beginning to elaborate a biologic Bergsonian definition of love, when he was stopped by Terrence, who had noticed the pain that swept across Leo's face.

"Go on, please, dear lady," Terrence begged. "And sing of love, only of love; for it is my experience that I meditate best upon the stars to the accompaniment of a woman's voice."

A little later, Oh Joy, entering the room, waited till Paula finished a song, then moved noiselessly to Graham and handed him a telegram. Dick scowled at the interruption.

"Very important—I think," the Chinese explained to him.

"Who took it?" Dick demanded.

"Me—I took it," was the answer. "Night clerk at Eldorado call on telephone. He say important. I take it."

"It is, fairly so," Graham spoke up, having finished reading the message. "Can I get a train out to-night for San Francisco, Dick?"

"Oh Joy, come back a moment," Dick called, looking at his watch. "What train for San Francisco stops at Eldorado?"

"Eleven-ten," came the instant information. "Plenty time. Not too much. I call chauffeur?"

Dick nodded.

"You really must jump out to-night?" he asked Graham.

"Really. It is quite important. Will I have time to pack?"

Dick gave a confirmatory nod to Oh Joy, and said to Graham:

"Just time to throw the needful into a grip." He turned to Oh Joy. "Is Oh My up yet?"

"Yessr."

"Send him to Mr. Graham's room to help, and let me know as soon as the machine is ready. No limousine. Tell Saunders to take the racer."

"One fine big strapping man, that," Terrence commented, after Graham had left the room.

They had gathered about Dick, with the exception of Paula, who remained at the piano, listening.

"One of the few men I'd care to go along with, hell for leather, on a forlorn hope or anything of that sort," Dick said. "He was on the *Nethermere* when she went ashore at Pango in the '97 hurricane. Pango is just a strip of sand, twelve feet above high water mark, a lot of cocoanuts, and uninhabited. Forty women among the passengers, English officers' wives and such. Graham had a bad arm, big as a leg— snake bite.

"It was a thundering sea. Boats couldn't live. They smashed two and lost both crews. Four sailors volunteered in succession to carry a light line ashore. And each man, in turn, dead at the end of it, was hauled back on board. While they were untying the last one, Graham, with an arm like a leg, stripped for it and went to it. And he did it, although the pounding he got on the sand broke his bad arm and staved in three ribs. But he made the line fast before he quit. In order to haul the hawser ashore, six more volunteered to go in on Evan's line to the beach. Four of them arrived. And only one woman of the forty was lost—she died of heart disease and fright.

"I asked him about it once. He was as bad as an Englishman. All I could get out of the beggar was that the recovery was uneventful. Thought that the salt water, the exercise, and the breaking of the bone had served as counter-irritants and done the arm good."

Oh Joy and Graham entered the room from opposite ends. Dick saw that Graham's first questing glance was for Paula.

"All ready, sir," Oh Joy announced.

Dick prepared to accompany his guest outside to the car; but Paula evidenced her intention of remaining in the house. Graham started over to her to murmur perfunctory regrets and good-by.

And she, warm with what Dick had just told of him, pleasured at the goodly sight of him, dwelling with her eyes on the light, high poise of head, the careless, sun-sanded hair, and the lightness, almost debonaireness, of his carriage despite his weight of body and breadth of shoulders. As he drew near to her, she centered her gaze on the long gray eyes whose hint of drooping lids hinted of boyish sullenness. She waited for the expression of sullenness to vanish as the eyes lighted with the smile she had come to know so well.

What he said was ordinary enough, as were her regrets; but in his eyes, as he held her hand a moment, was the significance which she had unconsciously expected and to which she replied with her own eyes. The same significance was in the pressure of the momentary handclasp. All unpremeditated, she responded to that quick pressure. As he had said, there was little need for speech between them.

As their hands fell apart, she glanced swiftly at Dick; for she had learned much, in their dozen years together, of his flashes of observance, and had come to stand in awe of his almost uncanny powers of guessing facts from nuances, and of linking nuances into conclusions often startling in their thoroughness and correctness. But Dick, his shoulder toward her, laughing over some quip of Hancock, was just turning his laughter-crinkled eyes toward her as he started to accompany Graham.

No, was her thought; surely Dick had seen nothing of the secret little that had been exchanged between them. It had been very little, very quick—a light in the eyes, a muscular quiver of the fingers, and no lingering. How could Dick have seen or sensed? Their eyes had certainly been hidden from Dick, likewise their clasped hands, for Graham's back had been toward him.

Just the same, she wished she had not made that swift glance at Dick. She was conscious of a feeling of guilt, and the thought of it hurt her as she watched the two big men, of a size and blondness, go down the room side by side. Of what had she been guilty? she asked herself. Why should she have anything to hide? Yet she was honest enough to face the fact and accept, without quibble, that she had something to hide. And her cheeks burned at the thought that she was being drifted into deception.

"I won't be but a couple of days," Graham was saying as he shook hands with Dick at the car.

Dick saw the square, straight look of his eyes, and recognized the firmness and heartiness of his gripping hand. Graham half began to say something, then did not; and Dick knew he had changed his mind when he said:

"I think, when I get back, that I'll have to pack."

"But the book," Dick protested, inwardly cursing himself for the leap of joy which had been his at the other's words.

"That's just why," Graham answered. "I've got to get it finished. It doesn't seem I can work like you do. The ranch is too alluring. I can't get down to the book. I sit over it, and sit over it, but the confounded meadowlarks keep echoing in my ears, and I begin to see the fields, and the redwood canyons, and Selim. And after I waste an hour, I give up and ring for Selim. And if it isn't that, it's any one of a thousand other enchantments."

He put his foot on the running-board of the pulsing car and said, "Well, so long, old man."

"Come back and make a stab at it," urged Dick. "If necessary, we'll frame up a respectable daily grind, and I'll lock you in every morning until you've done it. And if you don't do your work all day, all day you'll stay locked in. I'll make you work.—Got cigarettes?—matches?"

"Right O."

"Let her go, Saunders," Dick ordered the chauffeur; and the car seemed to leap out into the darkness from the brilliantly lighted porte cochére.

Back in the house, Dick found Paula playing to the madrono sages, and ensconced himself on the couch to wait and wonder if she would kiss him good night when bedtime came. It was not, he recognized, as if they made a regular schedule of kissing. It had never been like that. Often and often he did not see her until midday, and then in the presence of guests. And often and often, she slipped away to bed early, disturbing no one with a good night kiss to her husband which might well hint to them that their bedtime had come.

No, Dick concluded, whether or not she kissed him on this particular night it would be equally without significance. But still he wondered.

She played on and sang on interminably, until at last he fell asleep. When he awoke he was alone in the room. Paula and the sages had gone out quietly. He looked at his watch. It marked one o'clock. She had played unusually late, he knew; for he knew she had just gone. It was the cessation of music and movement that had awakened him.

And still he wondered. Often he napped there to her playing, and always, when she had finished, she kissed him awake and sent him to bed. But this night she had not. Perhaps, after all, she was coming back. He lay and drowsed and waited. The next time he looked at his watch, it was two o'clock. She had not come back.

He turned off the lights, and as he crossed the house, pressed off the hall lights as he went, while the many unimportant little nothings, almost of themselves, ranged themselves into an ordered text of doubt and conjecture that he could not refrain from reading.

On his sleeping porch, glancing at his barometers and thermometers, her laughing face in the round frame caught his eyes, and, standing before it, even bending closer to it, he studied her long.

"Oh, well," he muttered, as he drew up the bedcovers, propped the pillows behind him and reached for a stack of proofsheets, "whatever it is I'll have to play it."

He looked sidewise at her picture.

"But, oh, Little Woman, I wish you wouldn't," was the sighed good night.

Chapter 24

As luck would have it, beyond chance guests for lunch or dinner, the Big House was empty. In vain, on the first and second days, did Dick lay out his work, or defer it, so as to be ready for any suggestion from Paula to go for an afternoon swim or drive.

He noted that she managed always to avoid the possibility of being kissed. From her sleeping porch she called good night to him across the wide patio. In the morning he prepared himself for her eleven o'clock greeting. Mr. Agar and Mr. Pitts, with important matters concerning the forthcoming ranch sale of stock still unsettled, Dick promptly cleared out at the stroke of eleven. Up she was, he knew, for he had heard her singing. As he waited, seated at his desk, for once he was idle. A tray of letters before him continued to need his signature. He remembered this morning pilgrimage of hers had been originated by her, and by her, somewhat persistently, had been kept up. And an adorable thing it was, he decided—that soft call of "Good morning, merry gentleman," and the folding of her kimono-clad figure in his arms.

He remembered, further, that he had often cut that little visit short, conveying the impression to her, even while he clasped her, of how busy he was. And he remembered, more than once, the certain little wistful shadow on her face as she slipped away.

Quarter past eleven, and she had not come. He took down the receiver to telephone the dairy, and in the swift rush of women's conversation, ere he hung up, he caught Paula's voice:

"—Bother Mr. Wade. Bring all the little Wades and come, if only for a couple of days—"

Which was very strange of Paula. She had invariably welcomed the intervals of no guests, when she and he were left alone with each other for a day or for several days. And now she was trying to persuade Mrs. Wade to come down from Sacramento. It would seem that Paula did not wish to be alone with him, and was seeking to protect herself with company.

He smiled as he realized that that morning embrace, now that it was not tendered him, had become suddenly desirable. The thought came to him of taking her away with him on one of their travel-jaunts. That would solve the problem, perhaps. And he would hold her very close to him and draw her closer. Why not an Alaskan hunting trip? She had always wanted to go. Or back to their old sailing grounds in the days of the *All Away*—the South Seas. Steamers ran direct between San Francisco and Tahiti. In twelve days they could be ashore in Papeete. He wondered if Lavaina still ran her boarding house, and his quick vision caught a picture of Paula and himself at breakfast on Lavaina's porch in the shade of the mango trees.

He brought his fist down on the desk. No, by God, he was no coward to run away with his wife for fear of any man. And would it be fair to her to take her away possibly from where her desire lay? True, he did not know where her desire lay, nor how far it had gone between her and Graham. Might it not be a spring madness with her that would vanish with the spring? Unfortunately, he decided, in the dozen years of their marriage she had never evidenced any predisposition toward spring madness. She had never given his heart a moment's doubt. Herself tremendously attractive to men, seeing much of them, receiving their admiration and even court, she had remained always her equable and serene self, Dick Forrest's wife—

"Good morning, merry gentleman."

She was peeping in on him, quite naturally from the hall, her eyes and lips smiling to him, blowing him a kiss from her finger tips.

"And good morning, my little haughty moon," he called back, himself equally his natural self.

And now she would come in, he thought; and he would fold her in his arms, and put her to the test of the kiss.

He opened his arms in invitation. But she did not enter. Instead, she startled, with one hand gathered her kimono at her breast, with the other picked up the trailing skirt as if for flight, at the same time looking apprehensively down the hall. Yet his keen ears had caught no sound. She smiled back at him, blew him another kiss, and was gone.

Ten minutes later he had no ears for Bonbright, who, telegrams in hand, startled him as he sat motionless at his desk, as he had sat, without movement, for ten minutes.

And yet she was happy. Dick knew her too long in all the expressions of her moods not to realize the significance of her singing over the house, in the arcades, and out in the patio. He did not leave his workroom till the stroke of lunch; nor did she, as she sometimes did, come to gather him up on the way. At the lunch gong, from across the patio, he heard her trilling die away into the house in the direction of the dining room.

A Colonel Harrison Stoddard—colonel from younger service in the National Guard, himself a retired merchant prince whose hobby was industrial relations and social unrest—held the table most of the meal upon the extension of the Employers' Liability Act so as to include agricultural laborers. But Paula found a space in which casually to give the news to Dick that she was running away for the afternoon on a jaunt up to Wickenberg to the Masons.

"Of course I don't know when I'll be back—you know what the Masons are. And I don't dare ask you to come, though I'd like you along."

Dick shook his head.

"And so," she continued, "if you're not using Saunders—"

Dick nodded acquiescence.

"I'm using Callahan this afternoon," he explained, on the instant planning his own time now that Paula was out of the question. "I never can make out, Paul, why you prefer Saunders. Callahan is the better driver, and of course the safest."

"Perhaps that's why," she said with a smile. "Safety first means slowest most."

"Just the same I'd back Callahan against Saunders on a speed-track," Dick championed.

"Where are you bound?" she asked.

"Oh, to show Colonel Stoddard my one-man and no-horse farm —you know, the automatically cultivated ten-acre stunt I've been frivoling with. A lot of changes have been made that have been waiting a week for me to see tried out. I've been too busy. And after that, I'm going to take him over the colony—what do you think?— five additions the last week."

"I thought the membership was full," Paula said.

"It was, and still is," Dick beamed. "But these are babies. And the least hopeful of the families had the rashness to have twins."

"A lot of wiseacres are shaking their heads over that experiment of yours, and I make free to say that I am merely holding my judgment— you've got to show me by bookkeeping," Colonel Stoddard was saying, immensely pleased at the invitation to be shown over in person.

Dick scarcely heard him, such was the rush of other thoughts. Paula had not mentioned whether Mrs. Wade and the little Wades were coming, much less mentioned that she had invited them. Yet this Dick tried to consider no lapse on her part, for often and often, like himself, she had guests whose arrival was the first he knew of their coming.

It was, however, evident that Mrs. Wade was not coming that day, else Paula would not be running away thirty miles up the valley. That was it, and there was no blinking it. She was running away, and from him. She could not face being alone with him with the consequent perils of intimacy—and perilous, in such circumstances, could have but the significance he feared. And further, she was making the evening sure. She would not be back for dinner, or till long after dinner, it was a safe wager, unless she brought the whole Wickenberg crowd with her. She would be back late enough to expect him to be in bed. Well, he would not disappoint her, he decided grimly, as he replied to Colonel Stoddard:

"The experiment works out splendidly on paper, with decently wide margins for human nature. And there I admit is the doubt and the danger—the human nature. But the only way to test it is to test it, which is what I am doing."

"It won't be the first Dick has charged to profit and loss," Paula said.

"But five thousand acres, all the working capital for two hundred and fifty farmers, and a cash salary of a thousand dollars each a year!" Colonel Stoddard protested. "A few such failures—if it fails—would put a heavy drain on the Harvest."

"That's what the Harvest needs," Dick answered lightly.

Colonel Stoddard looked blank.

"Precisely," Dick confirmed. "Drainage, you know. The mines are flooded—the Mexican situation."

It was during the morning of the second day—the day of Graham's expected return—that Dick, who, by being on horseback at eleven, had avoided a repetition of the hurt of the previous day's "Good morning, merry gentleman" across the distance of his workroom, encountered Ah Ha in a hall with an armful of fresh-cut lilacs. The house-boy's way led toward the tower room, but Dick made sure.

"Where are you taking them, Ah Ha?" he asked.

"Mr. Graham's room—he come to-day."

Now whose thought was that? Dick pondered. Ah Ha's?—Oh Joy's—or Paula's? He remembered having heard Graham more than once express his fancy for their lilacs.

He deflected his course from the library and strolled out through the flowers near the tower room. Through the open windows of it came Paula's happy humming. Dick pressed his lower lip with tight quickness between his teeth and strolled on.

Some great, as well as many admirable, men and women had occupied that room, and for them Paula had never supervised the flower arrangement, Dick meditated. Oh Joy, himself a master of flowers, usually attended to that, or had his house-staff ably drilled to do it.

Among the telegrams Bonbright handed him, was one from Graham, which Dick read twice, although it was simple and unmomentous, being merely a postponement of his return.

Contrary to custom, Dick did not wait for the second lunch-gong. At the sound of the first he started, for he felt the desire for one of Oh Joy's cocktails—the need of a prod of courage, after the lilacs, to meet Paula. But she was ahead of him. He found her—who rarely drank, and never alone—just placing an empty cocktail glass back on the tray.

So she, too, had needed courage for the meal, was his deduction, as he nodded to Oh Joy and held up one finger.

"Caught you at it!" he reproved gaily. "Secret tippling. The gravest of symptoms. Little I thought, the day I stood up with you, that the wife I was marrying was doomed to fill an alcoholic's grave."

Before she could retort, a young man strolled in whom she and Dick greeted as Mr. Winters, and who also must have a cocktail. Dick tried to believe that it was not relief he sensed in Paula's manner as she greeted the newcomer. He had never seen her quite so cordial to him before, although often enough she had met him. At any rate, there would be three at lunch.

Mr. Winters, an agricultural college graduate and special writer for the *Pacific Rural Press*, as well as a sort of protégé of Dick, had come for data for an article on California fish-ponds, and Dick mentally arranged his afternoon's program for him.

"Got a telegram from Evan," he told Paula. "Won't be back till the four o'clock day after to-morrow."

"And after all my trouble!" she exclaimed. "Now the lilacs will be wilted and spoiled."

Dick felt a warm glow of pleasure. There spoke his frank, straightforward Paula. No matter what the game was, or its outcome, at least she would play it without the petty deceptions. She had always been that way—too transparent to make a success of deceit.

Nevertheless, he played his own part by a glance of scarcely interested interrogation.

"Why, in Graham's room," she explained. "I had the boys bring a big armful and I arranged them all myself. He's so fond of them, you know."

Up to the end of lunch, she had made no mention of Mrs. Wade's coming, and Dick knew definitely she was not coming when Paula queried casually:

"Expecting anybody?"

He shook his head, and asked, "Are you doing anything this afternoon?"

"Haven't thought about anything," she answered. "And now I suppose I can't plan upon you with Mr. Winters to be told all about fish."

"But you can," Dick assured her. "I'm turning him over to Mr. Hanley, who's got the trout counted down to the last egg hatched and who knows all the grandfather bass by name. I'll tell you what —" He paused and considered. Then his face lighted as with a sudden idea. "It's a loafing afternoon. Let's take the rifles and go potting squirrels. I noticed the other day they've become populous on that hill above the Little Meadow."

But he had not failed to observe the flutter of alarm that shadowed her eyes so swiftly, and that so swiftly was gone as she clapped her hands and was herself.

"But don't take a rifle for me," she said.

"If you'd rather not—" he began gently.

"Oh, I want to go, but I don't feel up to shooting. I'll take Le Gallienne's last book along—it just came in—and read to you in betweenwhiles. Remember, the last time I did that when we went squirreling it was his 'Quest of the Golden Girl' I read to you."

Chapter 25

Paula on the Fawn, and Dick on the Outlaw, rode out from the Big House as nearly side by side as the Outlaw's wicked perversity permitted. The conversation she permitted was fragmentary. With tiny ears laid back and teeth exposed, she would attempt to evade Dick's restraint of rein and spur and win to a bite of Paula's leg or the Fawn's sleek flank, and with every defeat the pink flushed and faded in the whites of her eyes. Her restless head-tossing and pitching attempts to rear (thwarted by the martingale) never ceased, save when she pranced and sidled and tried to whirl.

"This is the last year of her," Dick announced. "She's indomitable. I've worked two years on her without the slightest improvement. She knows me, knows my ways, knows I am her master, knows when she has to give in, but is never satisfied. She nourishes the perennial hope that some time she'll catch me napping, and for fear she'll miss that time she never lets any time go by."

"And some time she may catch you," Paula said.

"That's why I'm giving her up. It isn't exactly a strain on me, but soon or late she's bound to get me if there's anything in the law of probability. It may be a million-to-one shot, but heaven alone knows where in the series of the million that fatal one is going to pop up."

"You're a wonder, Red Cloud," Paula smiled.

"Why?"

"You think in statistics and percentages, averages and exceptions. I wonder, when we first met, what particular formula you measured me up by."

"I'll be darned if I did," he laughed back. "There was where all signs failed. I didn't have a statistic that applied to you. I merely acknowledged to myself that here was the most wonderful female woman ever born with two good legs, and I knew that I wanted her more than I had ever wanted anything. I just had to have her—"

"And got her," Paula completed for him. "But since, Red Cloud, since. Surely you've accumulated enough statistics on me."

"A few, quite a few," he admitted. "But I hope never to get the last one—"

He broke off at sound of the unmistakable nicker of Mountain Lad. The stallion appeared, the cowboy on his back, and Dick gazed for a moment at the perfect action of the beast's great swinging trot.

"We've got to get out of this," he warned, as Mountain Lad, at sight of them, broke into a gallop.

Together they pricked their mares, whirled them about, and fled, while from behind they heard the soothing "Whoas" of the rider, the thuds of the heavy hoofs on the roadway, and a wild imperative neigh. The Outlaw answered, and the Fawn was but a moment behind her. From the commotion they knew Mountain Lad was getting tempestuous.

Leaning to the curve, they swept into a cross-road and in fifty paces pulled up, where they waited till the danger was past.

"He's never really injured anybody yet," Paula said, as they started back.

"Except when he casually stepped on Cowley's toes. You remember he was laid up in bed for a month," Dick reminded her, straightening out the Outlaw from a sidle and with a flicker of glance catching the strange look with which Paula was regarding him.

There was question in it, he could see, and love in it, and fear—yes, almost fear, or at least apprehension that bordered on dismay; but, most of all, a seeking, a searching, a questioning. Not entirely ungermane to her mood, was his thought, had been that remark of his thinking in statistics.

But he made that he had not seen, whipping out his pad, and, with an interested glance at a culvert they were passing, making a note.

"They missed it," he said. "It should have been repaired a month ago."

"What has become of all those Nevada mustangs?" Paula inquired.

This was a flyer Dick had taken, when a bad season for Nevada pasture had caused mustangs to sell for a song with the alternative of starving to death. He had shipped a trainload down and ranged them in his wilder mountain pastures to the west.

"It's time to break them," he answered. "And I'm thinking of a real old-fashioned rodeo next week. What do you say? Have a barbecue and all the rest, and invite the country side?"

"And then you won't be there," Paula objected.

"I'll take a day off. Is it a go?"

They reined to one side of the road, as she agreed, to pass three farm tractors, all with their trailage of ganged discs and harrows.

"Moving them across to the Rolling Meadows," he explained. "They pay over horses on the right ground."

Rising from the home valley, passing through cultivated fields and wooded knolls, they took a road busy with many wagons hauling road- dressing from the rock-crusher they could hear growling and crunching higher up.

"Needs more exercise than I've been giving her," Dick remarked, jerking the Outlaw's bared teeth away from dangerous proximity to the Fawn's flank.

"And it's disgraceful the way I've neglected Duddy and Fuddy," Paula said. "I've kept their feed down like a miser, but they're a lively handful just the same."

Dick heard her idly, but within forty-eight hours he was to remember with hurt what she had said.

They continued on till the crunch of the rock-crusher died away, penetrated a belt of woodland, crossed a tiny divide where the afternoon sunshine was wine-colored by the manzanita and rose-colored by madronos, and dipped down through a young planting of eucalyptus to the Little Meadow. But before they reached it, they dismounted and tied their horses. Dick took the .22 automatic rifle from his saddle- holster, and with Paula advanced softly to a clump of redwoods on the edge of the meadow. They disposed themselves in the shade and gazed out across the meadow to the steep slope of hill that came down to it a hundred and fifty yards away.

"There they are—three—four of them," Paula whispered, as her keen eyes picked the squirrels out amongst the young grain.

These were the wary ones, the sports in the direction of infinite caution who had shunned the poisoned grain and steel traps of Dick's vermin catchers. They were the survivors, each of a score of their fellows not so cautious, themselves fit to repopulate the hillside.

Dick filled the chamber and magazine with tiny cartridges, examined the silencer, and, lying at full length, leaning on his elbow, sighted across the meadow. There was no sound of explosion when he fired, only the click of the mechanism as the bullet was sped, the empty cartridge ejected, a fresh cartridge flipped into the chamber, and the trigger re-cocked. A big, dun-colored squirrel leaped in the air, fell over, and disappeared in the grain. Dick waited, his eye along the rifle and directed toward several holes around which the dry earth showed widely as evidence of the grain which had been destroyed. When the wounded squirrel appeared, scrambling across the exposed ground to safety, the rifle clicked again and he rolled over on his side and lay still.

At the first click, every squirrel but the stricken one, had made into its burrow. Remained nothing to do but wait for their curiosity to master caution. This was the interval Dick had looked forward to. As he lay and scanned the hillside for curious heads to appear, he wondered if Paula would have something to say to him. In trouble she was, but would she keep this trouble to herself? It had never been her way. Always, soon or late, she brought her troubles to him. But, then, he reflected, she had never had a trouble of this nature before. It was just the one thing that she would be least prone to discuss with him. On the other hand, he reasoned, there was her everlasting frankness. He had marveled at it, and joyed in it, all their years together. Was it to fail her now?

So he lay and pondered. She did not speak. She was not restless. He could hear no movement. When he glanced to the side at her he saw her lying on her back, eyes closed, arms outstretched, as if tired.

A small head, the color of the dry soil of its home, peeped from a hole. Dick waited long minutes, until, assured that no danger lurked, the owner of the head stood full up on its hind legs to seek the cause of the previous click that had startled it. Again the rifle clicked.

"Did you get him?" Paula queried, without opening her eyes.

"Yea, and a fat one," Dick answered. "I stopped a line of generations right there."

An hour passed. The afternoon sun beat down but was not uncomfortable in the shade. A gentle breeze fanned the young grain into lazy wavelets at times, and stirred the redwood boughs above them. Dick added a third squirrel to the score. Paula's book lay beside her, but she had not offered to read.

"Anything the matter?" he finally nerved himself to ask.

"No; headache—a beastly little neuralgic hurt across the eyes, that's all."

"Too much embroidery," he teased.

"Not guilty," was her reply.

All was natural enough in all seeming; but Dick, as he permitted an unusually big squirrel to leave its burrow and crawl a score of feet across the bare earth toward the grain, thought to himself: No, there will be no talk between us this day. Nor will we nestle and kiss lying here in the grass.

His victim was now at the edge of the grain. He pulled trigger. The creature fell over, lay still a moment, then ran in quick awkward fashion toward its hole. Click, click, click, went the mechanism. Puffs of dust leaped from the earth close about the fleeing squirrel, showing the closeness of the misses. Dick fired as rapidly as he could twitch his forefinger on the trigger, so that it was as if he played a stream of lead from a hose.

He had nearly finished refilling the magazine when Paula spoke.

"My! What a fusillade.—Get him?"

"Yea, grandfather of all squirrels, a mighty graineater and destroyer of sustenance for young calves. But nine long smokeless cartridges on one squirrel doesn't pay. I'll have to do better."

The sun dropped lower. The breeze died out. Dick managed another squirrel and sadly watched the hillside for more. He had arranged the time and made his bid for confidence. The situation was as grave as he had feared. Graver it might be, for all he knew, for his world was crumbling about him. Old landmarks were shifting their places. He was bewildered, shaken. Had it been any other woman than Paula! He had been so sure. There had been their dozen years to vindicate his surety... .

"Five o'clock, sun he get low," he announced, rising to his feet and preparing to help her up.

"It did me so much good—just resting," she said, as they started for the horses. "My eyes feel much better. It's just as well I didn't try to read to you."

"And don't be piggy," Dick warned, as lightly as if nothing were amiss with him. "Don't dare steal the tiniest peek into Le Gallienne. You've got to share him with me later on. Hold up your hand.—Now, honest to God, Paul."

"Honest to God," she obeyed.

"And may jackasses dance on your grandmother's grave—"

"And may jackasses dance on my grandmother's grave," she solemnly repeated.

The third morning of Graham's absence, Dick saw to it that he was occupied with his dairy manager when Paula made her eleven o'clock pilgrimage, peeped in upon him, and called her "Good morning, merry gentleman," from the door. The Masons, arriving in several machines with their boisterous crowd of young people, saved Paula for lunch and the afternoon; and, on her urging, Dick noted, she made the evening safe by holding them over for bridge and dancing.

But the fourth morning, the day of Graham's expected return,

Dick was alone in his workroom at eleven. Bending over his desk, signing letters, he heard Paula tiptoe into the room. He did not look up, but while he continued writing his signature he listened with all his soul to the faint, silken swish of her kimono. He knew when she was bending over him, and all but held his breath. But when she had softly kissed his hair and called her "Good morning, merry gentleman," she evaded the hungry sweep of his arm and laughed her way out. What affected him as strongly as the disappointment was the happiness he had seen in her face. She, who so poorly masked her moods, was bright-eyed and eager as a child. And it was on this afternoon that Graham was expected, Dick could not escape making the connection.

He did not care to ascertain if she had replenished the lilacs in the tower room, and, at lunch, which was shared with three farm college students from Davis, he found himself forced to extemporize a busy afternoon for himself when Paula tentatively suggested that she would drive Graham up from Eldorado.

"Drive?" Dick asked.

"Duddy and Fuddy," she explained. "They're all on edge, and I just feel like exercising them and myself. Of course, if you'll share the exercise, we'll drive anywhere you say, and let him come up in the machine."

Dick strove not to think there was anxiety in her manner while she waited for him to accept or decline her invitation.

"Poor Duddy and Fuddy would be in the happy hunting grounds if they had to cover my ground this afternoon," he laughed, at the same time mapping his program. "Between now and dinner I've got to do a hundred and twenty miles. I'm taking the racer, and it's going to be some dust and bump and only an occasional low place. I haven't the heart to ask you along. You go on and take it out of Duddy and Fuddy."

Paula sighed, but so poor an actress was she that in the sigh, intended for him as a customary reluctant yielding of his company, he could not fail to detect the relief at his decision.

"Whither away?" she asked brightly, and again he noticed the color in her face, the happiness, and the brilliance of her eyes.

"Oh, I'm shooting away down the river to the dredging work—Carlson insists I must advise him—and then up in to Sacramento, running over the Teal Slough land on the way, to see Wing Fo Wong."

"And in heaven's name who is this Wing Fo Wong?" she laughingly queried, "that you must trot and see him?"

"A very important personage, my dear. Worth all of two millions

—made in potatoes and asparagus down in the Delta country. I'm leasing three hundred acres of the Teal Slough land to him." Dick addressed himself to the farm students. "That land lies just out of Sacramento on the west side of the river. It's a good example of the land famine that is surely coming. It was tule swamp when I bought it, and I was well laughed at by the old-timers. I even had to buy out a dozen hunting preserves. It averaged me eighteen dollars an acre, and not so many years ago either.

"You know the tule swamps. Worthless, save for ducks and low-water pasturage. It cost over three hundred an acre to dredge and drain and to pay my quota of the river reclamation work. And on what basis of value do you think I am making a ten years' lease to old Wing Fo Wong? TWO thousand an acre. I couldn't net more than that if I truck-farmed it myself. Those Chinese are wizards with vegetables, and gluttons for work. No eight hours for them. It's eighteen hours. The last coolie is a partner with a microscopic share. That's the way Wing Fo Wong gets around the eight hour law."

Twice warned and once arrested, was Dick through the long afternoon. He drove alone, and though he drove with speed he drove with safety. Accidents, for which he personally might be responsible, were things he did not tolerate. And they never occurred. That same sureness and definiteness of adjustment with which, without fumbling or approximating, he picked up a pencil or reached for a door-knob, was his in the more complicated adjustments, with which, as instance, he drove a high-powered machine at high speed over busy country roads.

But drive as he would, transact business as he would, at high pressure with Carlson and Wing Fo Wong, continually, in the middle ground of his consciousness, persisted the thought that Paula had gone out of her way and done the most unusual in driving Graham the long eight miles from Eldorado to the ranch.

"Phew!" he started to mutter a thought aloud, then suspended utterance and thought as he jumped the racer from forty-five to seventy miles an hour, swept past to the left of a horse and buggy going in the same direction, and slanted back to the right side of the road with margin to spare but seemingly under the nose of a run-about coming from the opposite direction. He reduced his speed to fifty and took up his thought:

"Phew! Imagine little Paul's thoughts if I dared that drive with some charming girl!"

He laughed at the fancy as he pictured it, for, most early in their marriage, he had gauged Paula's capacity for quiet jealousy. Never had she made a scene, or dropped a direct remark, or raised a question; but from the first, quietly but unmistakably, she had conveyed the impression of hurt that was hers if he at all unduly attended upon any woman.

He grinned with remembrance of Mrs. Dehameny, the pretty little brunette widow—Paula's friend, not his—who had visited in the long ago in the Big House. Paula had announced that she was not riding that afternoon and, at lunch, had heard him and Mrs. Dehameny arrange to ride into the redwood canyons beyond the grove of the philosophers. And who but Paula, not long after their start, should overtake them and make the party three! He had smiled to himself at the time, and felt immensely tickled with Paula, for neither Mrs. Dehameny nor the ride with her had meant anything to him.

So it was, from the beginning, that he had restricted his attentions to other women. Ever since he had been far more circumspect than Paula. He had even encouraged her, given her a free hand always, had been proud that his wife did attract fine fellows, had been glad that she was glad to be amused or entertained by them. And with reason, he mused. He had been so safe, so sure of her—more so, he acknowledged, than had she any right to be of him. And the dozen years had vindicated his attitude, so that he was as sure of her as he was of the diurnal rotation of the earth. And now, was the form his fancy took, the rotation of the earth was a shaky proposition and old Oom Paul's flat world might be worth considering.

He lifted the gauntlet from his left wrist to snatch a glimpse at his watch, In five minutes Graham would be getting off the train at Eldorado. Dick, himself homeward bound west from Sacramento, was eating up the miles. In a quarter of an hour the train that he identified as having brought Graham, went by. Not until he was well past Eldorado did he overtake Duddy and Fuddy and the trap. Graham sat beside Paula, who was driving. Dick slowed down as he passed, waved a hello to Graham, and, as he jumped into speed again, called cheerily:

"Sorry I've got to give you my dust. I'll beat you a game of billiards before dinner, Evan, if you ever get in."

Chapter 26

"This can't go on. We must do something—at once."

They were in the music room, Paula at the piano, her face turned up to Graham who stood close to her, almost over her.

"You must decide," Graham continued.

Neither face showed happiness in the great thing that had come upon them, now that they considered what they must do.

"But I don't want you to go," Paula urged. "I don't know what I want. You must bear with me. I am not considering myself. I am past considering myself. But I must consider Dick. I must consider you. I... I am so unused to such a situation," she concluded with a wan smile.

"But it must be settled, dear love. Dick is not blind."

"What has there been for him to see?" she demanded. "Nothing, except that one kiss in the canyon, and he couldn't have seen that. Do you think of anything else—I challenge you, sir."

"Would that there were," he met the lighter touch in her mood, then immediately relapsed. "I am mad over you, mad for you. And there I stop. I do not know if you are equally mad. I do not know if you are mad at all."

As he spoke, he dropped his hand to hers on the keys, and she gently withdrew it.

"Don't you see?" he complained. "Yet you wanted me to come back?"

"I wanted you to come back," she acknowledged, with her straight look into his eyes. "I wanted you to come back," she repeated, more softly, as if musing.

"And I'm all at sea," he exclaimed impatiently. "You do love me?"

"I do love you, Evan—you know that. But... " She paused and seemed to be weighing the matter judicially.

"But what?" he commanded. "Go on."

"But I love Dick, too. Isn't it ridiculous?"

He did not respond to her smile, and her eyes delightedly

warmed to the boyish sullenness that vexed his own eyes. A thought was hot on his tongue, but he restrained the utterance of it while she wondered what it was, disappointed not to have had it.

"It will work out," she assured him gravely. "It will have to work out somehow. Dick says all things work out. All is change. What is static is dead, and we're not dead, any of us... are we?"

"I don't blame you for loving Dick, for... for continuing to love Dick," he answered impatiently. "And for that matter, I don't see what you find in me compared with him. This is honest. He is a great man to me, and Great Heart is his name—" she rewarded him with a smile and nod of approval. "But if you continue to love Dick, how about me?"

"But I love you, too."

"It can't be," he cried, tearing himself from the piano to make a hasty march across the room and stand contemplating the Keith on the opposite wall as if he had never seen it before.

She waited with a quiet smile, pleasuring in his unruly impetuousness.

"You can't love two men at once," he flung at her.

"Oh, but I do, Evan. That's what I am trying to work out. Only I don't know which I love more. Dick I have known a long time. You... you are a—"

"Recent acquaintance," he broke in, returning to her with the same angry stride.

"Not that, no, not that, Evan. You have made a revelation to me of myself. I love you as much as Dick. I love you more. I—I don't know."

She broke down and buried her face in her hands, permitting his hand to rest tenderly on her shoulder.

"You see it is not easy for me," she went on. "There is so much involved, so much that I cannot understand. You say you are all at sea. Then think of me all at sea and worse confounded. You—oh, why talk about it—you are a man with a man's experiences, with a man's nature. It is all very simple to you. 'She loves me, she loves me not.' But I am tangled, confused. I—and I wasn't born yesterday —have had no experience in loving variously. I have never had affairs. I loved only one man... and now you. You, and this love for you, have broken into a perfect marriage, Evan—"

"I know—" he said.

"—I don't know," she went on. "I must have time, either to work it out myself or to let it work itself out. If it only weren't for Dick... " her voice trailed off pathetically.

Unconsciously, Graham's hand went farther about her shoulder.

"No, no—not yet," she said softly, as softly she removed it, her own lingering caressingly on his a moment ere she released it. "When you touch me, I can't think," she begged. "I—I can't think."

"Then I must go," he threatened, without any sense of threatening. She made a gesture of protest. "The present situation is impossible, unbearable. I feel like a cur, and all the time I know I am not a cur. I hate deception—oh, I can lie with the Pathan, to the Pathan—but I can't deceive a man like Great Heart. I'd prefer going right up to him and saying: 'Dick, I love your wife. She loves me. What are you going to do about it?'"

"Do so," Paula said, fired for the moment.

Graham straightened up with resolution.

"I will. And now."

"No, no," she cried in sudden panic. "You must go away." Again her voice trailed off, as she said, "But I can't let you go."

If Dick had had any reason to doubt his suspicion of the state of Paula's heart, that reason vanished with the return of Graham. He need look nowhere for confirmation save to Paula. She was in a flushed awakening, burgeoning like the full spring all about them, a happier tone in her happy laugh, a richer song in her throat, a warmness of excitement and a continuous energy of action animating her. She was up early and to bed late. She did not conserve herself, but seemed to live on the champagne of her spirits, until Dick wondered if it was because she did not dare allow herself time to think.

He watched her lose flesh, and acknowledged to himself that the one result was to make her look lovelier than ever, to take on an almost spiritual delicacy under her natural vividness of color and charm.

And the Big House ran on in its frictionless, happy, and remorseless way. Dick sometimes speculated how long it would continue so to run on, and recoiled from contemplation of a future in which it might not so run on. As yet, he was confident, no one knew, no one guessed, but himself. But how long could that continue? Not long, he was certain. Paula was not sufficiently the actress. And were she a master at concealment of trivial, sordid detail, yet the new note and flush of her would be beyond the power of any woman to hide.

He knew his Asiatic servants were marvels of discernment—and discretion, he had to add. But there were the women. Women were cats. To the best of them it would be great joy to catch the radiant, unimpeachable Paula as clay as any daughter of Eve. And any chance woman in the house, for a day, or an evening, might glimpse the situation—Paula's situation, at least, for he could not make out Graham's attitude yet. Trust a woman to catch a woman.

But Paula, different in other ways, was different in this. He had never seen her display cattishness, never known her to be on the lookout for other women on the chance of catching them tripping— except in relation to him. And he grinned again at the deliciousness of the affair with Mrs. Dehameney which had been an affair only in Paula's apprehension.

Among other things of wonderment, Dick speculated if Paula wondered if he knew.

And Paula did wonder, and for a time without avail. She could detect no change in his customary ways and moods or treatment of her. He turned off his prodigious amount of work as usual, played as usual, chanted his songs, and was the happy good fellow. She tried to imagine an added sweetness toward her, but vexed herself with the fear that it was imagined.

But it was not for long that she was in doubt. Sometimes in a crowd, at table, in the living room in the evening, or at cards, she would gaze at him through half-veiled lashes when he was unaware, until she was certain she saw the knowledge in his eyes and face. But no hint of this did she give to Graham. His knowing would not help matters. It might even send him away, which she frankly admitted to herself was the last thing she should want to happen.

But when she came to a realization that she was almost certain Dick knew or guessed, she hardened, deliberately dared to play with the fire. If Dick knew—since he knew, she framed it to herself —why did he not speak? He was ever a straight talker. She both desired and feared that he might, until the fear faded and her earnest hope was that he would. He was the one who acted, did things, no matter what they were. She had always depended upon him as the doer. Graham had called the situation a triangle. Well, Dick could solve it. He could solve anything. Then why didn't he?

In the meantime, she persisted in her ardent recklessness, trying not to feel the conscience-pricks of her divided allegiance, refusing to think too deeply, riding the top of the wave of her life—as she assured herself, living, living, living. At times she scarcely knew what she thought, save that she was very proud in having two such men at heel. Pride had always been one of her dominant key-notes —pride of accomplishment, achievement, mastery, as with her music, her appearance, her swimming. It was all one—to dance, as she well knew, beautifully; to dress with distinction and beauty; to swan-dive, all grace and courage, as few women dared; or, all fragility, to avalanche down the spill-way on the back of Mountain Lad and by the will and steel of her swim the huge beast across the tank.

She was proud, a woman of their own race and type, to watch these two gray-eyed blond men together. She was excited, feverish, but not nervous. Quite coldly, sometimes, she compared the two when they were together, and puzzled to know for which of them she made herself more beautiful, more enticing. Graham she held, and she had held Dick and strove still to hold him.

There was almost a touch of cruelty in the tingles of pride that were hers at thought of these two royal men suffering for her and because of her; for she did not hide from herself the conviction that if Dick knew, or, rather, since he did know, he, too, must be suffering. She assured herself that she was a woman of imagination and purpose in sex matters, and that no part of her attraction toward Graham lay merely in his freshness, newness, difference. And she denied to herself that passion played more than the most minor part. Deep down she was conscious of her own recklessness and madness, and of an end to it all that could not but be dreadful to some one of them or all of them. But she was content willfully to flutter far above such deeps and to refuse to consider their existence. Alone, looking at herself in her mirror, she would shake her head in mock reproof and cry out, "Oh, you huntress! You huntress!" And when she did permit herself to think a little gravely, it was to admit that Shaw and the sages of the madrono grove might be right in their diatribes on the hunting proclivities of women.

She denied Dar Hyal's statement that woman was nature's failure to make a man; but again and again came to her Wilde's, "Woman attacks by sudden and strange surrenders." Had she so attacked Graham? she asked herself. Sudden and strange, to her, were the surrenders she had already made. Were there to be more? He wanted to go. With her, or without her, he wanted to go. But she held him—how? Was there a tacit promise of surrenders to come? And she would laugh away further consideration, confine herself to the fleeting present, and make her body more beautiful, and mood herself to be more fascinating, and glow with happiness in that she was living, thrilling, as she had never dreamed to live and thrill.

Chapter 27

But it is not the way for a man and a woman, in propinquity, to maintain a definite, unwavering distance asunder. Imperceptibly Paula and Graham drew closer. From lingering eye-gazings and hand-touchings the way led to permitted caresses, until there was a second clasping in the arms and a second kiss long on the lips. Nor this time did Paula flame in anger. Instead, she commanded:

"You must not go."

"I must not stay," Graham reiterated for the thousandth time. "Oh, I have kissed behind doors, and been guilty of all the rest of the silly rubbish," he complained. "But this is you, and this is Dick."

"It will work out, I tell you, Evan."

"Come with me then and of ourselves work it out. Come now."

She recoiled.

"Remember," Graham encouraged, "what Dick said at dinner the night Leo fought the dragons—that if it were you, Paula, his wife, who ran away, he would say 'Bless you, my children.'"

"And that is just why it is so hard, Evan. He *is* Great Heart. You named him well. Listen—you watch him now. He is as gentle as he said he would be that night—gentle toward me, I mean. And more. You watch him—"

"He knows?—he has spoken?" Graham broke in.

"He has not spoken, but I am sure he knows, or guesses. You watch him. He won't compete against you—"

"Compete!"

"Just that. He won't compete. Remember at the rodeo yesterday. He was breaking mustangs when our party arrived, but he never mounted again. Now he is a wonderful horse-breaker. You tried your hand. Frankly, while you did fairly well, you couldn't touch him. But he wouldn't show off against you. That alone would make me certain that he guesses.

"Listen. Of late haven't you noticed that he never questions a statement you make, as he used to question, as he questions every one else. He continues to play billiards with you, because there you best him. He fences and singlesticks with you—there you are even. But he won't box or wrestle with you."

"He *can* out-box and out-wrestle me," Graham muttered ruefully.

"You watch and you will see what I mean by not competing. He is treating me like a spirited colt, giving me my head to make a mess of things if I want to. Not for the world would he interfere. Oh, trust me, I know him. It is his own code that he is living up to. He could teach the philosophers what applied philosophy is.

"No, no; listen," she rushed over Graham's attempt to interrupt. "I want to tell you more. There is a secret staircase that goes up from the library to Dick's work room. Only he and I use it, and his secretaries. When you arrive at the head of it, you are right in his room, surrounded by shelves of books. I have just come from there. I was going in to see him when I heard voices. Of course it was ranch business, I thought, and they would soon be gone. So I waited. It *was* ranch business, but it was so interesting, so, what Hancock would call, illuminating, that I remained and eavesdropped. It was illuminating of Dick, I mean.

"It was the wife of one of the workmen Dick had on the carpet. Such things do arise on a large place like this. I wouldn't know the woman if I saw her, and I didn't recognize her name. She was whimpering out her trouble when Dick stopped her. 'Never mind all that,' he said. 'What I want to know is, did you give Smith any encouragement?'

"Smith isn't his name, but he is one of our foremen and has worked eight years for Dick.

"'Oh, no, sir,' I could hear her answer. 'He went out of his way from the first to bother me. I've tried to keep out of his way, always. Besides, my husband's a violent-tempered man, and I did so want him to hold his job here. He's worked nearly a year for you now, and there aren't any complaints, are there? Before that it was irregular work for a long time, and we had real hard times. It wasn't his fault. He ain't a drinking man. He always—'

"'That's all right,' Dick stopped her. 'His work and habits have nothing to do with the matter. Now you are sure you have never encouraged Mr. Smith in any way?' And she was so sure that she talked for ten minutes, detailing the foreman's persedition of her. She had a pleasant voice—one of those sweet, timid, woman's voices, and undoubtedly is quite attractive. It was all I could do to resist peeping. I wanted to see what she looked like.

"'Now this trouble, yesterday morning,' Dick said. 'Was it general? I mean, outside of your husband, and Mr. Smith, was the scene such that those who live around you knew of it?'

"'Yes, sir. You see, he had no right to come into my kitchen. My husband doesn't work under him anyway. And he had his arm around me and was trying to kiss me when my husband came in. My husband has a temper, but he ain't overly strong. Mr. Smith would make two of him. So he pulled a knife, and Mr. Smith got him by the arms, and they fought all over the kitchen. I knew there was murder going to be done and I run out screaming for help. The folks in the other cottages'd heard the racket already. They'd smashed the window and the cook stove, and the place was filled with smoke and ashes when the neighbors dragged them away from each other. I'd done nothing to deserve all that disgrace. You know, sir, the way the women will talk—'

"And Dick hushed her up there, and took all of five minutes more in getting rid of her. Her great fear was that her husband would lose his place. From what Dick told her, I waited. He had made no decision, and I knew the foreman was next on the carpet. In he came. I'd have given the world to see him. But I could only listen.

"Dick jumped right into the thick of it. He described the scene and uproar, and Smith acknowledged that it had been riotous for a while. 'She says she gave you no encouragement,' Dick said next.

"'Then she lies,' said Smith. 'She has that way of looking with her eyes that's an invitation. She looked at me that way from the first. But it was by word-of-mouth invitation that I was in her kitchen yesterday morning. We didn't expect the husband. But she began to struggle when he hove in sight. When she says she gave me no encouragement—'

"'Never mind all that,' Dick stopped him. 'It's not essential.' 'But it is, Mr. Forrest, if I am to clear myself,' Smith insisted.

"'No; it is not essential to the thing you can't clear yourself of,' Dick answered, and I could hear that cold, hard, judicial note come into his voice. Smith could not understand. Dick told him. 'The thing you have been guilty of, Mr. Smith, is the scene, the disturbance, the scandal, the wagging of the women's tongues now going on forty to the minute, the impairment of the discipline and order of the ranch, all of which is boiled down to the one grave thing, the hurt to the ranch efficiency.'

"And still Smith couldn't see. He thought the charge was of violating social morality by pursuing a married woman, and tried to mitigate the offense by showing the woman encouraged him and by pleading: 'And after all, Mr. Forrest, a man is only a man, and I admit she made a fool of me and I made a fool of myself.' "'Mr.

Smith,' Dick said. 'You've worked for me eight years. You've been a foreman six years of that time. I have no complaint against your work. You certainly do know how to handle labor. About your personal morality I don't care a damn. You can be a Mormon or a Turk for all it matters to me. Your private acts are your private acts, and are no concern of mine as long as they do not interfere with your work or my ranch. Any one of my drivers can drink his head off Saturday night, and every Saturday night. That's his business. But the minute he shows a hold-over on Monday morning that is taken out on my horses, that excites them, or injures them, or threatens to injure them, or that decreases in the slightest the work they should perform on Monday, that moment it is my business and the driver goes down the hill.'

"'You, you mean, Mr. Forrest,' Smith stuttered, 'that, that I'm to go down the hill?' 'That is just what I mean, Mr. Smith. You are to go down the hill, not because you climbed over another man's fence — that's your business and his; but because you were guilty of causing a disturbance that is an impairment of ranch efficiency.'

"Do you know, Evan," Paula broke in on her recital, "Dick can nose more human tragedy out of columns of ranch statistics than can the average fiction writer out of the whirl of a great city. Take the milk reports—the individual reports of the milkers—so many pounds of milk, morning and night, from cow so-and-so, so many pounds from cow so-and-so. He doesn't have to know the man. But there is a decrease in the weight of milk. 'Mr. Parkman,' he'll say to the head dairyman, 'is Barchi Peratta married?' 'Yes, sir.' 'Is he having trouble with his wife?' 'Yes, sir.'

"Or it will be: 'Mr. Parkman, Simpkins has the best long-time record of any of our milkers. Now he's slumped. What's up?' Mr. Parkman doesn't know. 'Investigate,' says Dick. 'There's something on his chest. Talk to him like an uncle and find out. We've got to get it off his chest.' And Mr. Parkman finds out. Simpkins' boy; working his way through Stanford University, has elected the joy-ride path and is in jail waiting trial for forgery. Dick put his own lawyers on the case, smoothed it over, got the boy out on probation, and Simpkins' milk reports came back to par. And the best of it is, the boy made good, Dick kept an eye on him, saw him through the college of engineering, and he's now working for Dick on the dredging end, earning a hundred and fifty a month, married, with a future before him, and his father still milks."

"You are right," Graham murmured sympathetically. "I well named him when I named him Great Heart."

"I call him my Rock of Ages," Paula said gratefully. "He is so solid. He stands in any storm.—Oh, you don't really know him. He is so sure. He stands right up. He's never taken a cropper in his life. God smiles on him. God has always smiled on him. He's never been beaten down to his knees... yet. I... I should not care to see that sight. It would be heartbreaking. And, Evan—" Her hand went out to his in a pleading gesture that merged into a half-caress. "—I am afraid for him now. That is why I don't know what to do. It is not for myself that I back and fill and hesitate. If he were ignoble, if he were narrow, if he were weak or had one tiniest shred of meanness, if he had ever been beaten to his knees before, why, my dear, my dear, I should have been gone with you long ago."

Her eyes filled with sudden moisture. She stilled him with a pressure of her hand, and, to regain herself, she went back to her recital:

"'Your little finger, Mr. Smith, I consider worth more to me and to the world,' Dick, told him, 'than the whole body of this woman's husband. Here's the report on him: willing, eager to please, not bright, not strong, an indifferent workman at best. Yet you have to go down the hill, and I am very, very sorry.'

"Oh, yes, there was more. But I've given you the main of it. You see Dick's code there. And he lives his code. He accords latitude to the individual. Whatever the individual may do, so long as it does not hurt the group of individuals in which he lives, is his own affair. He believed Smith had a perfect right to love the woman, and to be loved by her if it came to that. I have heard him always say that love could not be held nor enforced. Truly, did I go with you, he would say, 'Bless you, my children.' Though it broke his heart he would say it. Past love, he believes, gives no hold over the present. And every hour of love, I have heard him say, pays for itself, on both sides, quittance in full. He claims there can be no such thing as a love- debt, laughs at the absurdity of love-claims."

"And I agree with him," Graham said. "'You promised to love me always,' says the jilted one, and then strives to collect as if it were a promissory note for so many dollars. Dollars are dollars, but love lives or dies. When it is dead how can it be collected? We are all agreed, and the way is simple. We love. It is enough. Why delay another minute?"

His fingers strayed along her fingers on the keyboard as he bent to her, first kissing her hair, then slowly turning her face up to his and kissing her willing lips.

"Dick does not love me like you," she said; "not madly, I mean. He has had me so long, I think I have become a habit to him. And often and often, before I knew you, I used to puzzle whether he cared more for the ranch or more for me."

"It is so simple," Graham urged. "All we have to do is to be straightforward. Let us go."

He drew her to her feet and made as if to start.

But she drew away from him suddenly, sat down, and buried her flushed face in her hands.

"You do not understand, Evan. I love Dick. I shall always love him."

"And me?" Graham demanded sharply.

"Oh, without saying," she smiled. "You are the only man, besides Dick, that has ever kissed me this... way, and that I have kissed this way. But I can't make up my mind. The triangle, as you call it, must be solved for me. I can't solve it myself. I compare the two of you, weigh you, measure you. I remember Dick and all our past years. And I consult my heart for you. And I don't know. I don't know. You are a great man, my great lover. But Dick is a greater man than you. You— you are more clay, more—I grope to describe you—more human, I fancy. And that is why I love you more... or at least I think perhaps I do.

"But wait," she resisted him, prisoning his eager hand in hers. "There is more I want to say. I remember Dick and all our past years. But I remember him to-day, as well, and to-morrow. I cannot bear the thought that any man should pity my husband, that you should pity him, and pity him you must when I confess that I love you more. That is why I am not sure. That is why I so quickly take it back and do not know.

"I'd die of shame if through act of mine any man pitied Dick. Truly, I would. Of all things ghastly, I can think of none so ghastly as Dick being pitied. He has never been pitied in his life. He has always been top-dog—bright, light, strong, unassailable. And more, he doesn't deserve pity. And it's my fault... and yours, Evan."

She abruptly thrust Evan's hand away.

"And every act, every permitted touch of you, does make him pitiable. Don't you see how tangled it is for me? And then there is my own pride. That you should see me disloyal to him in little things, such as this—" (she caught his hand again and caressed it with soft finger-tips) "—hurts me in my love for you, diminishes me, must diminish me in your eyes. I shrink from the thought that my disloyalty to him in this I do—" (she laid his hand against her cheek) "—gives you reason to pity him and censure me."

She soothed the impatience of the hand on her cheek, and, almost absently, musingly scrutinizing it without consciously seeing it, turned it over and slowly kissed the palm. The next moment she was drawn to her feet and into his arms.

"There, you see," was her reproach as she disengaged herself.

"Why do you tell me all this about Dick?" Graham demanded another time, as they walked their horses side by side. "To keep me away? To protect yourself from me?"

Paula nodded, then quickly added, "No, not quite that. Because you know I don't want to keep you away ... too far. I say it because Dick is so much in my mind. For twelve years, you realize, he filled my mind. I say it because ... because I think it, I suppose. Think! The situation! You are trespassing on a perfect marriage."

"I know it," he answered. "And I do not like the role of trespasser. It is your insistence, instead of going away with me, that I should trespass. And I can't help it. I think away from you, try to force my thoughts elsewhere. I did half a chapter this morning, and I know it's rotten and will have to be rewritten. For I can't succeed in thinking away from you. What is South America and its ethnology compared to you? And when I come near you my arms go about you before I know what I am doing. And, by God, you want them there, you want them there, you know it."

Paula gathered her reins in signal for a gallop, but first, with a roguish smile, she acknowledged.

"I do want them there, dear trespasser."

Paula yielded and fought at the same time.

"I love my husband—never forget that," she would warn Graham, and within the minute be in his arms.

"There are only the three of us for once, thank goodness," Paula cried, seizing Dick and Graham by the hands and leading them toward Dick's favorite lounging couch in the big room. "Come, let us sit upon the ground and tell sad stories of the deaths of kings. Come, milords, and lordly perishers, and we will talk of Armageddon when the last sun goes down."

She was in a merry mood, and with surprise Dick observed her light a cigarette. He could count on his fingers the cigarettes she had smoked in a dozen years, and then, only under a hostess's provocation to give countenance to some smoking woman guest. Later, when he mixed a highball for himself and Graham, she again surprised him by asking him to mix her a "wee" one.

"This is Scotch," he warned.

"Oh, a very wee one," she insisted, "and then we'll be three good fellows together, winding up the world. And when you've got it all wound up and ready, I'll sing you the song of the Valkyries."

She took more part in the talk than usual, and strove to draw her husband out. Nor was Dick unaware of this, although he yielded and permitted himself to let go full tilt on the theme of the blond sun- perishers.

She is trying to make him compete—was Graham's thought. But Paula scarcely thought of that phase of it, her pleasure consisting in the spectacle of two such splendid men who were hers. They talk of big game hunting, she mused once to herself; but did ever one small woman capture bigger game than this?

She sat cross-legged on the couch, where, by a turn of the head, she could view Graham lounging comfortably in the big chair, or Dick, on his elbow, sprawled among the cushions. And ever, as they talked, her eyes roved from one to the other; and, as they spoke of struggle and battle, always in the cold iron terms of realists, her own thoughts became so colored, until she could look coolly at Dick with no further urge of the pity that had intermittently ached her heart for days.

She was proud of him—a goodly, eye-filling figure of a man to any woman; but she no longer felt sorry for him. They were right. It was a game. The race was to the swift, the battle to the strong. They had run such races, fought such battles. Then why not she? And as she continued to look, that self-query became reiterant.

They were not anchorites, these two men. Liberal-lived they must have been in that past out of which, like mysteries, they had come to her. They had had the days and nights that women were denied—women such as she. As for Dick, beyond all doubt—even had she heard whispers—there had been other women in that wild career of his over the world. Men were men, and they were two such men. She felt a burn of jealousy against those unknown women who must have been, and her heart hardened. They had taken their fun where they found it—Kipling's line ran through her head.

Pity? Why should she pity, any more than she should be pitied? The whole thing was too big, too natural, for pity. They were taking a hand in a big game, and all could not be winners. Playing with the fancy, she wandered on to a consideration of the outcome. Always she had avoided such consideration, but the tiny highball had given her daring. It came to her that she saw doom ahead, doom vague and formless but terrible.

She was brought back to herself by Dick's hand before her eyes and apparently plucking from the empty air the something upon which she steadfastly stared.

"Seeing things?" he teased, as her eyes turned to meet his.

His were laughing, but she glimpsed in them what, despite herself, made her veil her own with her long lashes. He knew. Beyond all possibility of error she knew now that he knew. That was what she had seen in his eyes and what had made her veil her own.

"'Cynthia, Cynthia, I've been a-thinking,'" she gayly hummed to him; and, as he resumed his talk, she reached and took a sip from his part- empty glass.

Let come what would, she asserted to herself, she would play it out. It was all a madness, but it was life, it was living. She had never so lived before, and it was worth it, no matter what inevitable payment must be made in the end. Love?—had she ever really loved Dick as she now felt herself capable of loving? Had she mistaken the fondness of affection for love all these years? Her eyes warmed as they rested on Graham, and she admitted that he had swept her as Dick never had.

Unused to alcohol in such strength, her heart was accelerated; and Dick, with casual glances, noted and knew the cause of the added brilliance, the flushed vividness of cheeks and lips.

He talked less and less, and the discussion of the sun-perishers died of mutual agreement as to its facts. Finally, glancing at his watch, he straightened up, yawned, stretched his arms and announced:

"Bed-time he stop. Head belong this fellow white man too much sleepy along him.—Nightcap, Evan?"

Graham nodded, for both felt the need of a stiffener.

"Mrs. Toper—nightcap?" Dick queried of Paula.

But she shook her head and busied herself at the piano putting away the music, while the men had their drink.

Graham closed down the piano for her, while Dick waited in the doorway, so that when they left he led them by a dozen feet. As they came along, Graham, under her instructions, turned off the lights in the halls. Dick waited where the ways diverged and where Graham would have to say good night on his way to the tower room.

The one remaining light was turned off.

"Oh, not that one, silly," Dick heard Paula cry out. "We keep it on all night."

Dick heard nothing, but the dark was fervent to him. He cursed himself for his own past embraces in the dark, for so the wisdom was given him to know the quick embrace that had occurred, ere, the next moment, the light flashed on again.

He found himself lacking the courage to look at their faces as they came toward him. He did not want to see Paula's frank eyes veiled by her lashes, and he fumbled to light a cigarette while he cudgeled his wits for the wording of an ordinary good night.

"How goes the book?—what chapter?" he called after Graham down his hall, as Paula put her hand in his.

Her hand in his, swinging his, hopping and skipping and all a-chatter in simulation of a little girl with a grown-up, Paula went on with Dick; while he sadly pondered what ruse she had in mind by which to avoid the long-avoided, good night kiss.

Evidently she had not found it when they reached the dividing of the ways that led to her quarters and to his. Still swinging his hand, still buoyantly chattering fun, she continued with him into his workroom. Here he surrendered. He had neither heart nor energy to wait for her to develop whatever she contemplated.

He feigned sudden recollection, deflected her by the hand to his desk, and picked up a letter.

"I'd promised myself to get a reply off on the first machine in the morning," he explained, as he pressed on the phonograph and began dictating.

For a paragraph she still held his hand. Then he felt the parting pressure of her fingers and her whispered good night.

"Good night, little woman," he answered mechanically, and continued dictating as if oblivious to her going.

Nor did he cease until he knew she was well out of hearing.

Chapter 28

A dozen times that morning, dictating to Blake or indicating answers, Dick had been on the verge of saying to let the rest of the correspondence go.

"Call up Hennessy and Mendenhall," he told Blake, when, at ten, the latter gathered up his notes and rose to go. "You ought to catch them at the stallion barn. Tell them not to come this morning but to-morrow morning."

Bonbright entered, prepared to shorthand Dick's conversations with his managers for the next hour.

"And—oh, Mr. Blake," Dick called. "Ask Hennessy about Alden Bessie.— The old mare was pretty bad last night," he explained to Bonbright.

"Mr. Hanley must see you right away, Mr. Forrest," Bonbright said, and added, at sight of the irritated drawing up of his employer's brows, "It's the piping from Buckeye Dam. Something's wrong with the plans—a serious mistake, he says."

Dick surrendered, and for an hour discussed ranch business with his foremen and managers.

Once, in the middle of a hot discussion over sheep-dips with Wardman, he left his desk and paced over to the window. The sound of voices and horses, and of Paula's laugh, had attracted him.

"Take that Montana report—I'll send you a copy to-day," he continued, as he gazed out. "They found the formula didn't get down to it. It was more a sedative than a germicide. There wasn't enough kick in it... "

Four horses, bunched, crossed his field of vision. Paula, teasing the pair of them, was between Martinez and Froelig, old friends of Dick, a painter and sculptor respectively, who had arrived on an early train. Graham, on Selim, made the fourth, and was slightly edged toward the rear. So the party went by, but Dick reflected that quickly enough it would resolve itself into two and two.

Shortly after eleven, restless and moody, he wandered out with a cigarette into the big patio, where he smiled grim amusement at the

216

various tell-tale signs of Paula's neglect of her goldfish. The sight of them suggested her secret patio in whose fountain pools she kept her selected and more gorgeous blooms of fish. Thither he went, through doors without knobs, by ways known only to Paula and the servants.

This had been Dick's one great gift to Paula. It was love-lavish as only a king of fortune could make it. He had given her a free hand with it, and insisted on her wildest extravagance; and it had been his delight to tease his quondam guardians with the stubs of the checkbook she had used. It bore no relation to the scheme and architecture of the Big House, and, for that matter, so deeply hidden was it that it played no part in jar of line or color. A show-place of show-places, it was not often shown. Outside Paula's sisters and intimates, on rare occasions some artist was permitted to enter and catch his breath. Graham had heard of its existence, but not even him had she invited to see.

It was round, and small enough to escape giving any cold hint of spaciousness. The Big House was of sturdy concrete, but here was marble in exquisite delicacy. The arches of the encircling arcade were of fretted white marble that had taken on just enough tender green to prevent any glare of reflected light. Palest of pink roses bloomed up the pillars and over the low flat roof they upheld, where Puck-like, humorous, and happy faces took the place of grinning gargoyles. Dick strolled the rosy marble pavement of the arcade and let the beauty of the place slowly steal in upon him and gentle his mood.

The heart and key of the fairy patio was the fountain, consisting of three related shallow basins at different levels, of white marble and delicate as shell. Over these basins rollicked and frolicked life-sized babies wrought from pink marble by no mean hand. Some peered over the edges into lower basins, one reached arms covetously toward the goldfish; one, on his back, laughed at the sky, another stood with dimpled legs apart stretching himself, others waded, others were on the ground amongst the roses white and blush, but all were of the fountain and touched it at some point. So good was the color of the marble, so true had been the sculptor, that the illusion was of life. No cherubs these, but live warm human babies.

Dick regarded the rosy fellowship pleasantly and long, finishing his cigarette and retaining it dead in his hand. That was what she had needed, he mused—babies, children. It had been her passion. Had she realized it... He sighed, and, struck by a fresh thought, looked to her favorite seat with certitude that he would not see the customary sewing lying on it in a pretty heap. She did not sew these days.

He did not enter the tiny gallery behind the arcade, which contained her chosen paintings and etchings, and copies in marble and bronze of her favorites of the European galleries. Instead he went up the stairway, past the glorious Winged Victory on the landing where the staircase divided, and on and up into her quarters that occupied the entire upper wing. But first, pausing by the Victory, he turned and gazed down into the fairy patio. The thing was a cut jewel in its perfectness and color, and he acknowledged, although he had made it possible for her, that it was entirely her own creation—her one masterpiece. It had long been her dream, and he had realized it for her. And yet now, he meditated, it meant nothing to her. She was not mercenary, that he knew; and if he could not hold her, mere baubles such as that would weigh nothing in the balance against her heart.

He wandered idly through her rooms, scarcely noting at what he gazed, but gazing with fondness at it all. Like everything else of hers, it was distinctive, different, eloquent of her. But when he glanced into the bathroom with its sunken Roman bath, for the life of him he was unable to avoid seeing a tiny drip and making a mental note for the ranch plumber.

As a matter of course, he looked to her easel with the expectation of finding no new work, but was disappointed; for a portrait of himself confronted him. He knew her trick of copying the pose and lines from a photograph and filling in from memory. The particular photograph she was using had been a fortunate snapshop of him on horseback. The Outlaw, for once and for a moment, had been at peace, and Dick, hat in hand, hair just nicely rumpled, face in repose, unaware of the impending snap, had at the instant looked squarely into the camera. No portrait photographer could have caught a better likeness. The head and shoulders Paula had had enlarged, and it was from this that she was working. But the portrait had already gone beyond the photograph, for Dick could see her own touches.

With a start he looked more closely. Was that expression of the eyes, of the whole face, his? He glanced at the photograph. It was not there. He walked over to one of the mirrors, relaxed his face, and led his thoughts to Paula and Graham. Slowly the expression came into his eyes and face. Not content, he returned to the easel and verified it. Paula knew. Paula knew that he knew. She had learned it from him, stolen it from him some time when it was unwittingly on his face, and carried it in her memory to the canvas.

Paula's Chinese maid, Oh Dear, entered from the wardrobe room, and Dick watched her unobserved as she came down the room toward him. Her eyes were down, and she seemed deep in thought. Dick remarked the sadness of her face, and that the little, solicitous contraction of the brows that had led to her naming was gone. She was not solicitous, that was patent. But cast down, she was, in heavy depression.

It would seem that all our faces are beginning to say things, he commented to himself.

"Good morning, Oh Dear," he startled her.

And as she returned the greeting, he saw compassion in her eyes as they dwelt on him. She knew. The first outside themselves. Trust her, a woman, so much in Paula's company when Paula was alone, to divine Paula's secret.

Oh Dear's lips trembled, and she wrung her trembling hands, nerving herself, as he could see, to speech.

"Mister Forrest," she began haltingly, "maybe you think me fool, but I like say something. You very kind man. You very kind my old mother. You very kind me long long time... "

She hesitated, moistening her frightened lips with her tongue, then braved her eyes to his and proceeded.

"Mrs. Forrest, she, I think... "

But so forbidding did Dick's face become that she broke off in confusion and blushed, as Dick surmised, with shame at the thoughts she had been about to utter.

"Very nice picture Mrs. Forrest make," he put her at her ease.

The Chinese girl sighed, and the same compassion returned into her eyes as she looked long at Dick's portrait.

She sighed again, but the coldness in her voice was not lost on Dick as she answered: "Yes, very nice picture Mrs. Forrest make."

She looked at him with sudden sharp scrutiny, studying his face, then turned to the canvas and pointed at the eyes.

"No good," she condemned.

Her voice was harsh, touched with anger.

"No good," she flung over her shoulder, more loudly, still more harshly, as she continued down the room and out of sight on Paula's sleeping porch.

Dick stiffened his shoulders, unconsciously bracing himself to face what was now soon to happen. Well, it was the beginning of the end. Oh Dear knew. Soon more would know, all would know. And in a way he was glad of it, glad that the torment of suspense would endure but little longer.

But when he started to leave he whistled a merry jingle to

advertise to Oh Dear that the world wagged very well with him so far as he knew anything about it.

The same afternoon, while Dick was out and away with Froelig and Martinez and Graham, Paula stole a pilgrimage to Dick's quarters. Out on his sleeping porch she looked over his rows of press buttons, his switchboard that from his bed connected him with every part of the ranch and most of the rest of California, his phonograph on the hinged and swinging bracket, the orderly array of books and magazines and agricultural bulletins waiting to be read, the ash tray, cigarettes, scribble pads, and thermos bottle.

Her photograph, the only picture on the porch, held her attention. It hung under his barometers and thermometers, which, she knew, was where he looked oftenest. A fancy came to her, and she turned the laughing face to the wall and glanced from the blankness of the back of the frame to the bed and back again. With a quick panic movement, she turned the laughing face out. It belonged, was her thought; it did belong.

The big automatic pistol in the holster on the wall, handy to one's hand from the bed, caught her eye. She reached to it and lifted gently at the butt. It was as she had expected—loose—Dick's way. Trust him, no matter how long unused, never to let a pistol freeze in its holster.

Back in the work room she wandered solemnly about, glancing now at the prodigious filing system, at the chart and blue-print cabinets, at the revolving shelves of reference books, and at the long rows of stoutly bound herd registers. At last she came to his books—a goodly row of pamphlets, bound magazine articles, and an even dozen ambitious tomes. She read the titles painstakingly: "Corn in California," "Silage Practice," "Farm Organization," "Farm Book-keeping," "The Shire in America," "Humus Destruction," "Soilage," "Alfalfa in California," "Cover Crops for California," "The Shorthorn in America"—at this last she smiled affectionately with memory of the great controversy he had waged for the beef cow and the milch cow as against the dual purpose cow.

She caressed, the backs of the books with her palm, pressed her cheek against them and leaned with closed eyes. Oh, Dick, Dick—a thought began that faded to a vagueness of sorrow and died because she did not dare to think it.

The desk was so typically Dick. There was no litter. Clean it was of all work save the wire tray with typed letters waiting his signature and an unusual pile of the flat yellow sheets on which his secretaries typed the telegrams relayed by telephone from Eldorado. Carelessly she ran her eyes over the opening lines of the uppermost sheet and chanced upon a reference that puzzled and interested her. She read closely, with in-drawn brows, then went deeper into the heap till she found confirmation. Jeremy Braxton was dead—big, genial, kindly Jeremy Braxton. A Mexican mob of pulque-crazed peons had killed him in the mountains through which he had been trying to escape from the Harvest into Arizona. The date of the telegram was two days old. Dick had known it for two days and never worried her with it. And it meant more. It meant money. It meant that the affairs of the Harvest Group were going from bad to worse. And it was Dick's way.

And Jeremy was dead. The room seemed suddenly to have grown cold. She shivered. It was the way of life—death always at the end of the road. And her own nameless dread came back upon her. Doom lay ahead. Doom for whom? She did not attempt to guess. Sufficient that it was doom. Her mind was heavy with it, and the quiet room was heavy with it as she passed slowly out.

Chapter 29

"'Tis a birdlike sensuousness that is all the Little Lady's own," Terrence was saying, as he helped himself to a cocktail from the tray Ah Ha was passing around.

It was the hour before dinner, and Graham, Leo and Terrence McFane had chanced together in the stag-room.

"No, Leo," the Irishman warned the young poet. "Let the one suffice you. Your cheeks are warm with it. A second one and you'll conflagrate. 'Tis no right you have to be mixing beauty and strong drink in that lad's head of yours. Leave the drink to your elders. There is such a thing as consanguinity for drink. You have it not. As for me—"

He emptied the glass and paused to turn the cocktail reminiscently on his tongue.

"'Tis women's drink," he shook his head in condemnation. "It likes me not. It bites me not. And devil a bit of a taste is there to it. —Ah Ha, my boy," he called to the Chinese, "mix me a highball in a long, long glass—a stiff one."

He held up four fingers horizontally to indicate the measure of liquor he would have in the glass, and, to Ah Ha's query as to what kind of whiskey, answered, "Scotch or Irish, bourbon or rye—whichever comes nearest to hand."

Graham shook his head to the Chinese, and laughed to the Irishman. "You'll never drink me down, Terrence. I've not forgotten what you did to O'Hay."

"'Twas an accident I would have you think," was the reply. "They say when a man's not feeling any too fit a bit of drink will hit him like a club."

"And you?" Graham questioned.

"Have never been hit by a club. I am a man of singularly few experiences."

"But, Terrence, you were saying... about Mrs. Forrest?" Leo begged. "It sounded as if it were going to be nice."

"As if it could be otherwise," Terrence censured. "But as I was saying, 'tis a bird-like sensuousness—oh, not the little, hoppy, wagtail kind, nor yet the sleek and solemn dove, but a merry sort of bird, like the wild canaries you see bathing in the fountains, always twittering and singing, flinging the water in the sun, and glowing the golden hearts of them on their happy breasts. 'Tis like that the Little Lady is. I have observed her much.

"Everything on the earth and under the earth and in the sky contributes to the passion of her days—the untoward purple of the ground myrtle when it has no right to aught more than pale lavender, a single red rose tossing in the bathing wind, one perfect Duchesse rose bursting from its bush into the sunshine, as she said to me, 'pink as the dawn, Terrence, and shaped like a kiss.'

"'Tis all one with her—the Princess's silver neigh, the sheep bells of a frosty morn, the pretty Angora goats making silky pictures on the hillside all day long, the drifts of purple lupins along the fences, the long hot grass on slope and roadside, the summer-burnt hills tawny as crouching lions—and even have I seen the sheer sensuous pleasure of the Little Lady with bathing her arms and neck in the blessed sun."

"She is the soul of beauty," Leo murmured. "One understands how men can die for women such as she."

"And how men can live for them, and love them, the lovely things," Terrence added. "Listen, Mr. Graham, and I'll tell you a secret. We philosophers of the madroño grove, we wrecks and wastages of life here in the quiet backwater and easement of Dick's munificence, are a brotherhood of lovers. And the lady of our hearts is all the one—the Little Lady. We, who merely talk and dream our days away, and who would lift never a hand for God, or country, or the devil, are pledged knights of the Little Lady."

"We would die for her," Leo affirmed, slowly nodding his head.

"Nay, lad, we would live for her and fight for her, dying is that easy."

Graham missed nothing of it. The boy did not understand, but in the blue eyes of the Celt, peering from under the mop of iron-gray hair, there was no mistaking the knowledge of the situation.

Voices of men were heard coming down the stairs, and, as Martinez and Dar Hyal entered, Terrence was saying:

"'Tis fine weather they say they're having down at Catalina now, and I hear the tunny fish are biting splendid."

Ah Ha served cocktails around, and was kept busy, for Hancock and Froelig followed along. Terrence impartially drank stiff highballs of whatever liquor the immobile-faced Chinese elected to serve him, and discoursed fatherly to Leo on the iniquities and abominations of the flowing bowl.

Oh My entered, a folded note in his hand, and looked about in doubt as to whom to give it.

"Hither, wing-heeled Celestial," Terrence waved him up.

"'Tis a petition, couched in very proper terms," Terrence explained, after a glance at its contents. "And Ernestine and Lute have arrived, for 'tis they that petition. Listen." And he read: "'Oh, noble and glorious stags, two poor and lowly meek-eyed does, wandering lonely in the forest, do humbly entreat admission for the brief time before dinner to the stamping ground of the herd.'

"The metaphor is mixed," said Terrence. "Yet have they acted well. 'Tis the rule—Dick's rule—and a good rule it is: no petticoats in the stag-room save by the stags' unanimous consent.—Is the herd ready for the question? All those in favor will say 'Aye.'—Contrary minded?—The ayes have it.

"Oh My, fleet with thy heels and bring in the ladies."

"'With sandals beaten from the crowns of kings,'" Leo added, murmuring the words reverently, loving them with his lips as his lips formed them and uttered them.

"'Shall he tread down the altars of their night,'" Terrence completed the passage. "The man who wrote that is a great man. He is Leo's friend, and Dick's friend, and proud am I that he is my friend."

"And that other line," Leo said. "From the same sonnet," he explained to Graham. "Listen to the sound of it: 'To hear what song the star of morning sings'—oh, listen," the boy went on, his voice hushed low with beauty-love for the words: "'With perished beauty in his hands as clay, Shall he restore futurity its dream—'"

He broke off as Paula's sisters entered, and rose shyly to greet them.

Dinner that night was as any dinner at which the madroño sages were present. Dick was as robustly controversial as usual, locking horns with Aaron Hancock on Bergson, attacking the latter's metaphysics in sharp realistic fashion.

"Your Bergson is a charlatan philosopher, Aaron," Dick concluded. "He has the same old medicine-man's bag of metaphysical tricks, all decked out and frilled with the latest ascertained facts of science."

"'Tis true," Terrence agreed. "Bergson is a charlatan thinker. 'Tis why he is so popular—"

"I deny—" Hancock broke in.

"Wait a wee, Aaron. 'Tis a thought I have glimmered. Let me

catch it before it flutters away into the azure. Dick's caught Bergson with the goods on him, filched straight from the treasure-house of science. His very cocksureness is filched from Darwin's morality of strength based on the survival of the fittest. And what did Bergson do with it? Touched it up with a bit of James' pragmatism, rosied it over with the eternal hope in man's breast that he will live again, and made it all a-shine with Nietzsche's 'nothing succeeds like excess—'"

"Wilde's, you mean," corrected Ernestine.

"Heaven knows I should have filched it for myself had you not been present," Terrence sighed, with a bow to her. "Some day the antiquarians will decide the authorship. Personally I would say it smacked of Methuselah—But as I was saying, before I was delightfully interrupted… "

"Who more cocksure than Dick?" Aaron was challenging a little later; while Paula glanced significantly to Graham.

"I was looking at the herd of yearling stallions but yesterday," Terrence replied, "and with the picture of the splendid beasties still in my eyes I'll ask: And who more delivers the goods?"

"But Hancock's objection is solid," Martinez ventured. "It would be a mean and profitless world without mystery. Dick sees no mystery."

"There you wrong him," Terrence defended. "I know him well. Dick recognizes mystery, but not of the nursery-child variety. No cock-and- bull stories for him, such as you romanticists luxuriate in."

"Terrence gets me," Dick nodded. "The world will always be mystery. To me man's consciousness is no greater mystery than the reaction of the gases that make a simple drop of water. Grant that mystery, and all the more complicated phenomena cease to be mysteries. That simple chemical reaction is like one of the axioms on which the edifice of geometry is reared. Matter and force are the everlasting mysteries, manifesting themselves in the twin mysteries of space and time. The manifestations are not mysteries—only the stuff of the manifestations, matter and force; and the theater of the manifestations, space and time."

Dick ceased and idly watched the expressionless Ah Ha and Ah Me who chanced at the moment to be serving opposite him. Their faces did not talk, was his thought; although ten to one was a fair bet that they were informed with the same knowledge that had perturbed Oh Dear.

"And there you are," Terrence was triumphing. "'Tis the perfect joy of him—never up in the air with dizzy heels. Flat on the good ground he stands, four square to fact and law, set against all airy fancies and bubbly speculations... ."

And as at table, so afterward that evening no one could have guessed from Dick that all was not well with him. He seemed bent on celebrating Lute's and Ernestine's return, refused to tolerate the heavy talk of the philosophers, and bubbled over with pranks and tricks. Paula yielded to the contagion, and aided and abetted him in his practical jokes which none escaped.

Choicest among these was the kiss of welcome. No man escaped it. To Graham was accorded the honor of receiving it first so that he might witness the discomfiture of the others, who, one by one, were ushered in by Dick from the patio.

Hancock, Dick's arm guiding him, came down the room to confront Paula and her sisters standing in a row on three chairs in the middle of the floor. He scanned them suspiciously, and insisted upon walking around behind them. But there seemed nothing unusual about them save that each wore a man's felt hat.

"Looks good to me," Hancock announced, as he stood on the floor before them and looked up at them.

"And it is good," Dick assured him. "As representing the ranch in its fairest aspects, they are to administer the kiss of welcome. Make your choice, Aaron."

Aaron, with a quick whirl to catch some possible lurking disaster at his back, demanded, "They are all three to kiss me?"

"No, make your choice which is to give you the kiss."

"The two I do not choose will not feel that I have discriminated against them?" Aaron insisted.

"Whiskers no objection?" was his next query.

"Not in the way at all," Lute told him. "I have always wondered what it would be like to kiss black whiskers."

"Here's where all the philosophers get kissed tonight, so hurry up," Ernestine said. "The others are waiting. I, too, have yet to be kissed by an alfalfa field."

"Whom do you choose?" Dick urged.

"As if, after that, there were any choice about it," Hancock returned jauntily. "I kiss my lady—the Little Lady."

As he put up his lips, Paula bent her head forward, and, nicely directed, from the indented crown of her hat canted a glassful of water into his face.

When Leo's turn came, he bravely made his choice of Paula and nearly spoiled the show by reverently bending and kissing the hem of her gown.

"It will never do," Ernestine told him. "It must be a real kiss. Put up your lips to be kissed."

"Let the last be first and kiss me, Leo," Lute begged, to save him from his embarrassment.

He looked his gratitude, put up his lips, but without enough tilt of his head, so that he received the water from Lute's hat down the back of his neck.

"All three shall kiss me and thus shall paradise be thrice multiplied," was Terrence's way out of the difficulty; and simultaneously he received three crowns of water for his gallantry.

Dick's boisterousness waxed apace. His was the most care-free seeming in the world as he measured Froelig and Martinez against the door to settle the dispute that had arisen as to whether Froelig or Martinez was the taller.

"Knees straight and together, heads back," Dick commanded.

And as their heads touched the wood, from the other side came a rousing thump that jarred them. The door swung open, revealing Ernestine with a padded gong-stick in either hand.

Dick, a high-heeled satin slipper in his hand, was under a sheet with Terrence, teaching him "Brother Bob I'm bobbed" to the uproarious joy of the others, when the Masons and Watsons and all their Wickenberg following entered upon the scene.

Whereupon Dick insisted that the young men of their party receive the kiss of welcome. Nor did he miss, in the hubbub of a dozen persons meeting as many more, Lottie Mason's: "Oh, good evening, Mr. Graham. I thought you had gone."

And Dick, in the midst of the confusion of settling such an influx of guests, still maintaining his exuberant jolly pose, waited for that sharp scrutiny that women have only for women. Not many moments later he saw Lottie Mason steal such a look, keen with speculation, at Paula as she chanced face to face with Graham, saying something to him.

Not yet, was Dick's conclusion. Lottie did not know. But suspicion was rife, and nothing, he was certain, under the circumstances, would gladden her woman's heart more than to discover the unimpeachable Paula as womanly weak as herself.

Lottie Mason was a tall, striking brunette of twenty-five, undeniably beautiful, and, as Dick had learned, undeniably daring. In the not remote past, attracted by her, and, it must be submitted, subtly invited by her, he had been guilty of a philandering that he had not allowed to go as far as her wishes. The thing had not been serious on his part. Nor had he permitted it to become serious on her side. Nevertheless, sufficient flirtatious passages had taken place to impel him this night to look to her, rather than to the other Wickenberg women, for the first signals of suspicion.

"Oh, yes, he's a beautiful dancer," Dick, as he came up to them half an hour later, heard Lottie Mason telling little Miss Maxwell. "Isn't he, Dick?" she appealed to him, with innocent eyes of candor through which disguise he knew she was studying him.

"Who?—Graham, you must mean," he answered with untroubled directness. "He certainly is. What do you say we start dancing and let Miss Maxwell see? Though there's only one woman here who can give him full swing to show his paces."

"Paula, of course," said Lottie.

"Paula, of course. Why, you young chits don't know how to waltz. You never had a chance to learn."—Lottie tossed her fine head. "Perhaps you learned a little before the new dancing came in," he amended. "Anyway, I'll get Evan and Paula started, you take me on, and I'll wager we'll be the only couples on the floor."

Half through the waltz, he broke it off with: "Let them have the floor to themselves. It's worth seeing."

And, glowing with appreciation, he stood and watched his wife and Graham finish the dance, while he knew that Lottie, beside him, stealing side glances at him, was having her suspicions allayed.

The dancing became general, and, the evening being warm, the big doors to the patio were thrown open. Now one couple, and now another, danced out and down the long arcades where the moonlight streamed, until it became the general thing.

"What a boy he is," Paula said to Graham, as they listened to Dick descanting to all and sundry on the virtues of his new night camera. "You heard Aaron complaining at table, and Terrence explaining, his sureness. Nothing terrible has ever happened to him in his life. He has never been overthrown. His sureness has always been vindicated. As Terrence said, it has always delivered the goods. He does know, he does know, and yet he is so sure of himself, so sure of me."

Graham taken away to dance with Miss Maxwell, Paula continued her train of thought to herself. Dick was not suffering so much after all. And she might have expected it. He was the coolhead, the philosopher. He would take her loss with the same equanimity as he would take the loss of Mountain Lad, as he had taken the death of Jeremy Braxton and the flooding of the Harvest mines. It was difficult, she smiled to herself, aflame as she was toward Graham, to be married to a philosopher who would not lift a hand to hold her. And it came to her afresh that one phase of

Graham's charm for her was his humanness, his flamingness. They met on common ground. At any rate, even in the heyday of their coming together in Paris, Dick had not so inflamed her. A wonderful lover he had been, too, with his gift of speech and lover's phrases, with his love-chants that had so delighted her; but somehow it was different from this what she felt for Graham and what Graham must feel for her. Besides, she had been most young in experience of love and lovers in that long ago when Dick had burst so magnificently upon her.

And so thinking, she hardened toward him and recklessly permitted herself to flame toward Graham. The crowd, the gayety, the excitement, the closeness and tenderness of contact in the dancing, the summer- warm of the evening, the streaming moonlight, and the night-scents of flowers—all fanned her ardency, and she looked forward eagerly to the at least one more dance she might dare with Graham.

"No flash light is necessary," Dick was explaining. "It's a German invention. Half a minute exposure under the ordinary lighting is sufficient. And the best of it is that the plate can be immediately developed just like an ordinary blue print. Of course, the drawback is one cannot print from the plate."

"But if it's good, an ordinary plate can be copied from it from which prints can be made," Ernestine amplified.

She knew the huge, twenty-foot, spring snake coiled inside the camera and ready to leap out like a jack-in-the-box when Dick squeezed the bulb. And there were others who knew and who urged Dick to get the camera and make an exposure.

He was gone longer than he expected, for Bonbright had left on his desk several telegrams concerning the Mexican situation that needed immediate replies. Trick camera in hand, Dick returned by a short cut across the house and patio. The dancing couples were ebbing down the arcade and disappearing into the hall, and he leaned against a pillar and watched them go by. Last of all came Paula and Evan, passing so close that he could have reached out and touched them. But, though the moon shone full on him, they did not see him. They saw only each other in the tender sport of gazing.

The last preceding couple was already inside when the music ceased. Graham and Paula paused, and he was for giving her his arm and leading her inside, but she clung to him in sudden impulse. Man-like, cautious, he slightly resisted for a moment, but with one arm around his neck she drew his head willingly down to the kiss. It was a flash of quick passion. The next instant, Paula on his arm, they were passing in and Paula's laugh was ringing merrily and naturally.

Dick clutched at the pillar and eased himself down abruptly until he sat flat on the pavement. Accompanying violent suffocation, or causing it, his heart seemed rising in his chest. He panted for air. The cursed thing rose and choked and stifled him until, in the grim turn his fancy took, it seemed to him that he chewed it between his teeth and gulped it back and down his throat along with the reviving air. He felt chilled, and was aware that he was wet with sudden sweat.

"And who ever heard of heart disease in the Forrests?" he muttered, as, still sitting, leaning against the pillar for support, he mopped his face dry. His hand was shaking, and he felt a slight nausea from an internal quivering that still persisted.

It was not as if Graham had kissed her, he pondered. It was Paula who had kissed Graham. That was love, and passion. He had seen it, and as it burned again before his eyes, he felt his heart surge, and the premonitory sensation of suffocation seized him. With a sharp effort of will he controlled himself and got to his feet.

"By God, it came up in my mouth and I chewed it," he muttered. "I chewed it."

Returning across the patio by the round-about way, he entered the lighted room jauntily enough, camera in hand, and unprepared for the reception he received.

"Seen a ghost?" Lute greeted.

"Are you sick?"—"What's the matter?" were other questions.

"What *is* the matter?" he countered.

"Your face—the look of it," Ernestine said. "Something has happened. What is it?"

And while he oriented himself he did not fail to note Lottie Mason's quick glance at the faces of Graham and Paula, nor to note that Ernestine had observed Lottie's glance and followed it up for herself.

"Yes," he lied. "Bad news. Just got the word. Jeremy Braxton is dead. Murdered. The Mexicans got him while he was trying to escape into Arizona."

"Old Jeremy, God love him for the fine man he was," Terrence said, tucking his arm in Dick's. "Come on, old man, 'tis a stiffener you're wanting and I'm the lad to lead you to it."

"Oh, I'm all right," Dick smiled, shaking his shoulders and squaring himself as if gathering himself together. "It did hit me hard for the moment. I hadn't a doubt in the world but Jeremy would make it out all right. But they got him, and two engineers with him. They put up a devil of a fight first. They got under a cliff and stood off a mob of half a thousand for a day and night. And then the Mexicans tossed dynamite down from above. Oh, well, all flesh is grass, and there is no grass of yesteryear. Terrence, your suggestion is a good one. Lead on."

After a few steps he turned his head over his shoulder and called back: "Now this isn't to stop the fun. I'll be right back to take that photograph. You arrange the group, Ernestine, and be sure to have them under the strongest light."

Terrence pressed open the concealed buffet at the far end of the room and set out the glasses, while Dick turned on a wall light and studied his face in the small mirror inside the buffet door.

"It's all right now, quite natural," he announced.

"'Twas only a passing shade," Terrence agreed, pouring the whiskey. "And man has well the right to take it hard the going of old friends."

They toasted and drank silently.

"Another one," Dick said, extending his glass.

"Say 'when,'" said the Irishman, and with imperturbable eyes he watched the rising tide of liquor in the glass.

Dick waited till it was half full.

Again they toasted and drank silently, eyes to eyes, and Dick was grateful for the offer of all his heart that he read in Terrence's eyes.

Back in the middle of the hall, Ernestine was gayly grouping the victims, and privily, from the faces of Lottie, Paula, and Graham, trying to learn more of the something untoward that she sensed. Why had Lottie looked so immediately and searchingly at Graham and Paula? —she asked herself. And something was wrong with Paula now. She was worried, disturbed, and not in the way to be expected from the announcement of Jeremy Braxton's death. From Graham, Ernestine could glean nothing. He was quite his ordinary self, his facetiousness the cause of much laughter to Miss Maxwell and Mrs. Watson.

Paula was disturbed. What had happened? Why had Dick lied? He had known of Jeremy's death for two days. And she had never known anybody's death so to affect him. She wondered if he had been drinking unduly. In the course of their married life she had seen him several times in liquor. He carried it well, the only noticeable effects being a flush in his eyes and a loosening of his tongue to whimsical fancies and extemporized chants. Had he, in his trouble, been drinking with the iron-headed Terrence down in the stag room? She had found them all assembled there just before dinner. The real cause for Dick's strangeness never crossed her mind, if, for no other reason, than that he was not given to spying.

He came back, laughing heartily at a joke of Terrence's, and beckoned Graham to join them while Terrence repeated it. And when the three had had their laugh, he prepared to take the picture. The burst of the huge snake from the camera and the genuine screams of the startled women served to dispel the gloom that threatened, and next Dick was arranging a tournament of peanut-carrying.

From chair to chair, placed a dozen yards apart, the feat was with a table knife to carry the most peanuts in five minutes. After the preliminary try-out, Dick chose Paula for his partner, and challenged the world, Wickenberg and the madroño grove included. Many boxes of candy were wagered, and in the end he and Paula won out against Graham and Ernestine, who had proved the next best couple. Demands for a speech changed to clamor for a peanut song. Dick complied, beating the accent, Indian fashion, with stiff-legged hops and hand-slaps on thighs.

"I am Dick Forrest, son of Richard the Lucky, Son of Jonathan the Puritan, son of John who was a sea-rover, as his father Albert before him, who was the son of Mortimer, a pirate who was hanged in chains and died without issue.

"I am the last of the Forrests, but first of the peanut-carriers. Neither Nimrod nor Sandow has anything on me. I carry the peanuts on a knife, a silver knife. The peanuts are animated by the devil. I carry the peanuts with grace and celerity and in quantity. The peanut never sprouted that can best me.

"The peanuts roll. The peanuts roll. Like Atlas who holds the world, I never let them fall. Not every one can carry peanuts. I am God-gifted. I am master of the art. It is a fine art. The peanuts roll, the peanuts roll, and I carry them on forever.

"Aaron is a philosopher. He cannot carry peanuts. Ernestine is a blonde. She cannot carry peanuts. Evan is a sportsman. He drops peanuts. Paula is my partner. She fumbles peanuts. Only I, I, by the grace of God and my own cleverness, carry peanuts.

"When anybody has had enough of my song, throw something at me. I am proud. I am tireless. I can sing on forever. I shall sing on forever.

"Here beginneth the second canto. When I die, bury me in a peanut patch. While I live—"

The expected avalanche of cushions quenched his song but not his ebullient spirits, for he was soon in a corner with Lottie Mason and Paula concocting a conspiracy against Terrence.

And so the evening continued to be danced and joked and played away. At midnight supper was served, and not till two in the morning were the Wickenbergers ready to depart. While they were getting on their wraps, Paula was proposing for the following afternoon a trip down to the Sacramento River to look over Dick's experiment in rice-raising.

"I had something else in view," he told her. "You know the mountain pasture above Sycamore Creek. Three yearlings have been killed there in the last ten days."

"Mountain lions!" Paula cried.

"Two at least.—Strayed in from the north," he explained to Graham. "They sometimes do that. We got three five years ago.—Moss and Hartley will be there with the dogs waiting. They've located two of the beasts. What do you say all of you join me. We can leave right after lunch."

"Let me have Mollie?" Lute asked.

"And you can ride Altadena," Paula told Ernestine.

Quickly the mounts were decided upon, Froelig and Martinez agreeing to go, but promising neither to shoot well nor ride well.

All went out to see the Wickenbergers off, and, after the machines were gone, lingered to make arrangements for the hunting.

"Good night, everybody," Dick said, as they started to move inside. "I'm going to take a look at Alden Bessie before I turn in. Hennessy is sitting up with her. Remember, you girls, come to lunch in your riding togs, and curses on the head of whoever's late."

The ancient dam of the Fotherington Princess was in a serious way, but Dick would not have made the visit at such an hour, save that he wanted to be by himself and that he could not nerve himself for a chance moment alone with Paula so soon after what he had overseen in the patio.

Light steps in the gravel made him turn his head. Ernestine caught up with him and took his arm.

"Poor old Alden Bessie," she explained. "I thought I'd go along."

Dick, still acting up to his night's rôle, recalled to her various funny incidents of the evening, and laughed and chuckled with reminiscent glee.

"Dick," she said in the first pause, "you are in trouble." She could feel him stiffen, and hurried on: "What can I do? You know you can depend on me. Tell me."

"Yes, I'll tell you," he answered. "Just one thing." She pressed his arm gratefully. "I'll have a telegram sent you to-morrow. It will be urgent enough, though not too serious. You will just bundle up and depart with Lute."

"Is that all?" she faltered.

"It will be a great favor."

"You won't talk with me?" she protested, quivering under the rebuff.

"I'll have the telegram come so as to rout you out of bed. And now never mind Alden Bessie. You run a long in. Good night."

He kissed her, gently thrust her toward the house, and went on his way.

Chapter 30

On the way back from the sick mare, Dick paused once to listen to the restless stamp of Mountain Lad and his fellows in the stallion barn. In the quiet air, from somewhere up the hills, came the ringing of a single bell from some grazing animal. A cat's-paw of breeze fanned him with sudden balmy warmth. All the night was balmy with the faint and almost aromatic scent of ripening grain and drying grass. The stallion stamped again, and Dick, with a deep breath and realization that never had he more loved it all, looked up and circled the sky-line where the crests of the mountains blotted the field of stars.

"No, Cato," he mused aloud. "One cannot agree with you. Man does not depart from life as from an inn. He departs as from a dwelling, the one dwelling he will ever know. He departs ... nowhere. It is good night. For him the Noiseless One ... and the dark."

He made as if to start, but once again the stamp of the stallions held him, and the hillside bell rang out. He drew a deep inhalation through his nostrils of the air of balm, and loved it, and loved the fair land of his devising.

"'I looked into time and saw none of me there,'" he quoted, then capped it, smiling, with a second quotation: "'She gat me nine great sons... . The other nine were daughters.'"

Back at the house, he did not immediately go in, but stood a space gazing at the far flung lines of it. Nor, inside, did he immediately go to his own quarters. Instead, he wandered through the silent rooms, across the patios, and along the dim-lit halls. His frame of mind was as of one about to depart on a journey. He pressed on the lights in Paula's fairy patio, and, sitting in an austere Roman seat of marble, smoked a cigarette quite through while he made his plans.

Oh, he would do it nicely enough. He could pull off a hunting accident that would fool the world. Trust him not to bungle it. Next day would be the day, in the woods above Sycamore Creek.

Grandfather Jonathan Forrest, the straight-laced Puritan, had died of a hunting accident. For the first time Dick doubted that accident. Well, if it hadn't been an accident, the old fellow had done it well. It had never been hinted in the family that it was aught but an accident.

His hand on the button to turn off the lights, Dick delayed a moment for a last look at the marble babies that played in the fountain and among the roses.

"So long, younglings," he called softly to them. "You're the nearest I ever came to it."

From his sleeping porch he looked across the big patio to Paula's porch. There was no light. The chance was she slept.

On the edge of the bed, he found himself with one shoe unlaced, and, smiling at his absentness, relaced it. What need was there for him to sleep? It was already four in the morning. He would at least watch his last sunrise. Last things were coming fast. Already had he not dressed for the last time? And the bath of the previous morning would be his last. Mere water could not stay the corruption of death. He would have to shave, however—a last vanity, for the hair did continue to grow for a time on dead men's faces.

He brought a copy of his will from the wall-safe to his desk and read it carefully. Several minor codicils suggested themselves, and he wrote them out in long-hand, pre-dating them six months as a precaution. The last was the endowment of the sages of the madroño grove with a fellowship of seven.

He ran through his life insurance policies, verifying the permitted suicide clause in each one; signed the tray of letters that had waited his signature since the previous morning; and dictated a letter into the phonograph to the publisher of his books. His desk cleaned, he scrawled a quick summary of income and expense, with all earnings from the Harvest mines deducted. He transposed the summary into a second summary, increasing the expense margins, and cutting down the income items to an absurdest least possible. Still the result was satisfactory.

He tore up the sheets of figures and wrote out a program for the future handling of the Harvest situation. He did it sketchily, with casual tentativeness, so that when it was found among the papers there would be no suspicions. In the same fashion he worked out a line- breeding program for the Shires, and an in-breeding table, up and down, for Mountain Lad and the Fotherington Princess and certain selected individuals of their progeny.

When Oh My came in with coffee at six, Dick was on his last paragraph of his scheme for rice-growing.

"Although the Italian rice may be worth experimenting with for quick maturity," he wrote, "I shall for a time confine the main plantings in equal proportions to Moti, Ioko, and the Wateribune. Thus, with different times of maturing, the same crews and the same machinery, with the same overhead, can work a larger acreage than if only one variety is planted."

Oh My served the coffee at his desk, and made no sign even after a glance to the porch at the bed which had not been slept in—all of which control Dick permitted himself privily to admire.

At six-thirty the telephone rang and he heard Hennessy's tired voice: "I knew you'd be up and glad to know Alden Bessie's pulled through. It was a squeak, though. And now it's me for the hay."

When Dick had shaved, he looked at the shower, hesitated a moment, then his face set stubbornly. I'm darned if I will, was his thought; a sheer waste of time. He did, however, change his shoes to a pair of heavy, high-laced ones fit for the roughness of hunting.

He was at his desk again, looking over the notes in his scribble pads for the morning's work, when Paula entered. She did not call her "Good morning, merry gentleman"; but came quite close to him before she greeted him softly with:

"The Acorn-planter. Ever tireless, never weary Red Cloud."

He noted the violet-blue shadows under her eyes, as he arose, without offering to touch her. Nor did she offer invitation.

"A white night?" he asked, as he placed a chair.

"A white night," she answered wearily. "Not a second's sleep, though I tried so hard."

Both were reluctant of speech, and they labored under a mutual inability to draw their eyes away from each other.

"You ... you don't look any too fit yourself," she said.

"Yes, my face," he nodded. "I was looking at it while I shaved. The expression won't come off."

"Something happened to you last night," she probed, and he could not fail to see the same compassion in her eyes that he had seen in Oh Dear's. "Everybody remarked your expression. What was it?"

He shrugged his shoulders. "It has been coming on for some time," he evaded, remembering that the first hint of it had been given him by Paula's portrait of him. "You've noticed it?" he inquired casually.

She nodded, then was struck by a sudden thought. He saw the idea leap to life ere her words uttered it.

"Dick, you haven't an affair?"

It was a way out. It would straighten all the tangle. And hope was in her voice and in her face.

He smiled, shook his head slowly, and watched her disappointment.

"I take it back," he said. "I have an affair."

"Of the heart?"

She was eager, as he answered, "Of the heart."

But she was not prepared for what came next. He abruptly drew his chair close, till his knees touched hers, and, leaning forward, quickly but gently prisoned her hands in his resting on her knees.

"Don't be alarmed, little bird-woman," he quieted her. "I shall not kiss you. It is a long time since I have. I want to tell you about that affair. But first I want to tell you how proud I am—proud of myself. I am proud that I am a lover. At my age, a lover! It is unbelievable, and it is wonderful. And such a lover! Such a curious, unusual, and quite altogether remarkable lover. In fact, I have laughed all the books and all biology in the face. I am a monogamist. I love the woman, the one woman. After a dozen years of possession I love her quite madly, oh, so sweetly madly."

Her hands communicated her disappointment to him, making a slight, impulsive flutter to escape; but he held them more firmly.

"I know her every weakness, and, weakness and strength and all, I love her as madly as I loved her at the first, in those mad moments when I first held her in my arms."

Her hands were mutinous of the restraint he put upon them, and unconsciously she was beginning to pull and tug to be away from him. Also, there was fear in her eyes. He knew her fastidiousness, and he guessed, with the other man's lips recent on hers, that she feared a more ardent expression on his part.

"And please, please be not frightened, timid, sweet, beautiful, proud, little bird-woman. See. I release you. Know that I love you most dearly, and that I am considering you as well as myself, and before myself, all the while."

He drew his chair away from her, leaned back, and saw confidence grow in her eyes.

"I shall tell you all my heart," he continued, "and I shall want you to tell me all your heart."

"This love for me is something new?" she asked. "A recrudescence?"

"Yes, a recrudescence, and no."

"I thought that for a long time I had been a habit to you," she said.

"But I was loving you all the time."

"Not madly."

"No," he acknowledged. "But with certainty. I was so sure of you, of myself. It was, to me, all a permanent and forever established thing. I plead guilty. But when that permanency was shaken, all my love for you fired up. It was there all the time, a steady, long-married flame."

"But about me?" she demanded.

"That is what we are coming to. I know your worry right now, and of a minute ago. You are so intrinsically honest, so intrinsically true, that the thought of sharing two men is abhorrent to you. I have not misread you. It is a long time since you have permitted me any love- touch." He shrugged his shoulders "And an equally long time since I offered you a love-touch."

"Then you *have* known from the first?" she asked quickly.

He nodded.

"Possibly," he added, with an air of judicious weighing, "I sensed it coming before even you knew it. But we will not go into that or other things."

"You have seen… " she attempted to ask, stung almost to shame at thought of her husband having witnessed any caress of hers and Graham's.

"We will not demean ourselves with details, Paula. Besides, there was and is nothing wrong about any of it. Also, it was not necessary for me to see anything. I have my memories of when I, too, kissed stolen kisses in the pause of the seconds between the frank, outspoken 'Good nights.' When all the signs of ripeness are visible—the love-shades and love-notes that cannot be hidden, the unconscious caress of the eyes in a fleeting glance, the involuntary softening of voices, the cuckoo-sob in the throat—why, the night-parting kiss does not need to be seen. It has to be. Still further, oh my woman, know that I justify you in everything."

"It… it was not ever… much," she faltered.

"I should have been surprised if it had been. It couldn't have been you. As it is, I have been surprised. After our dozen years it was unexpected—"

"Dick," she interrupted him, leaning toward him and searching him. She paused to frame her thought, and then went on with directness. "In our dozen years, will you say it has never been any more with you?"

"I have told you that I justify you in everything," he softened his reply.

"But you have not answered my question," she insisted. "Oh, I do not mean mere flirtatious passages, bits of primrose philandering. I mean unfaithfulness and I mean it technically. In the past you have?"

"In the past," he answered, "not much, and not for a long, long time."

"I often wondered," she mused.

"And I have told you I justify you in everything," he reiterated. "And now you know where lies the justification."

"Then by the same token I had a similar right," she said. "Though I haven't, Dick, I haven't," she hastened to add. "Well, anyway, you always did preach the single standard."

"Alas, not any longer," he smiled. "One's imagination will conjure, and in the past few weeks I've been forced to change my mind."

"You mean that you demand I must be faithful?"

He nodded and said, "So long as you live with me."

"But where's the equity?"

"There isn't any equity," he shook his head. "Oh, I know it seems a preposterous change of view. But at this late day I have made the discovery of the ancient truth that women are different from men. All I have learned of book and theory goes glimmering before the everlasting fact that the women are the mothers of our children. I... I still had my hopes of children with you, you see. But that's all over and done with. The question now is, what's in your heart? I have told you mine. And afterward we can determine what is to be done."

"Oh, Dick," she breathed, after silence had grown painful, "I do love you, I shall always love you. You are my Red Cloud. Why, do you know, only yesterday, out on your sleeping porch, I turned my face to the wall. It was terrible. It didn't seem right. I turned it out again, oh so quickly."

He lighted a cigarette and waited.

"But you have not told me what is in your heart, all of it," he chided finally.

"I do love you," she repeated.

"And Evan?"

"That is different. It is horrible to have to talk this way to you. Besides, I don't know. I can't make up my mind what is in my heart."

"Love? Or amorous adventure? It must be one or the other."

She shook her head.

"Can't you understand?" she asked. "That I don't understand? You see, I am a woman. I have never sown any wild oats. And now that all this has happened, I don't know what to make of it. Shaw and the rest must be right. Women are hunting animals. You are both big game. I can't help it. It is a challenge to me. And I find I am a puzzle to myself. All my concepts have been toppled over by my conduct. I want you. I want Evan. I want both of you. It is not amorous adventure, oh believe me. And if by any chance it is, and I do not know it—no, it isn't, I know it isn't."

"Then it is love."

"But I do love you, Red Cloud."

"And you say you love him. You can't love both of us."

"But I can. I do. I do love both of you.—Oh, I am straight. I shall be straight. I must work this out. I thought you might help me. That is why I came to you this morning. There must be some solution."

She looked at him appealingly as he answered, "It is one or the other, Evan or me. I cannot imagine any other solution."

"That's what he says. But I can't bring myself to it. He was for coming straight to you. I would not permit him. He has wanted to go, but I held him here, hard as it was on both of you, in order to have you together, to compare you two, to weigh you in my heart. And I get nowhere. I want you both. I can't give either of you up."

"Unfortunately, as you see," Dick began, a slight twinkle in his eyes, "while you may be polyandrously inclined, we stupid male men cannot reconcile ourselves to such a situation."

"Don't be cruel, Dick," she protested.

"Forgive me. It was not so meant. It was out of my own hurt—an effort to bear it with philosophical complacence."

"I have told him that he was the only man I had ever met who is as great as my husband, and that my husband is greater."

"That was loyalty to me, yes, and loyalty to yourself," Dick explained. "You were mine until I ceased being the greatest man in the world. He then became the greatest man in the world."

She shook her head.

"Let me try to solve it for you," he continued. "You don't know your mind, your desire. You can't decide between us because you equally want us both?"

"Yes," she whispered. "Only, rather, differently want you both."

"Then the thing is settled," he concluded shortly.

"What do you mean?"

"This, Paula. I lose. Graham is the winner. Don't you see. Here am I, even with him, even and no more, while my advantage over him is our dozen years together—the dozen years of past love, the ties and bonds of heart and memory. Heavens! If all this weight were thrown in the balance on Evan's side, you wouldn't hesitate an instant in your decision. It is the first time you have ever been bowled over in your life, and the experience, coming so late, makes it hard for you to realize."

"But, Dick, you bowled me over."

He shook his head.

"I have always liked to think so, and sometimes I have believed —but never really. I never took you off your feet, not even in the very beginning, whirlwind as the affair was. You may have been glamoured. You were never mad as I was mad, never swept as I was swept. I loved you first—"

"And you were a royal lover."

"I loved you first, Paula, and, though you did respond, it was not in the same way. I never took you off your feet. It seems pretty clear that Evan has."

"I wish I could be sure," she mused. "I have a feeling of being bowled over, and yet I hesitate. The two are not compatible. Perhaps I never shall be bowled over by any man. And you don't seem to help me in the least."

"You, and you alone, can solve it, Paula," he said gravely.

"But if you would help, if you would try—oh, such a little, to hold me," she persisted.

"But I am helpless. My hands are tied. I can't put an arm to hold you. You can't share two. You have been in his arms—" He put up his hand to hush her protest. "Please, please, dear, don't. You have been in his arms. You flutter like a frightened bird at thought of my caressing you. Don't you see? Your actions decide against me. You have decided, though you may not know it. Your very flesh has decided. You can bear his arms. The thought of mine you cannot bear."

She shook her head with slow resoluteness.

"And still I do not, cannot, make up my mind," she persisted.

"But you must. The present situation is intolerable. You must decide quickly, for Evan must go. You realize that. Or you must go. You both cannot continue on here. Take all the time in the world. Send Evan away. Or, suppose you go and visit Aunt Martha for a while. Being away from both of us might aid you to get somewhere. Perhaps it will be better to call off the hunting. I'll go alone, and you stay and talk it over with Evan. Or come on along and talk it over with him as you ride. Whichever way, I won't be in till late. I may sleep out all night in one of the herder's cabins. When I come back, Evan must be gone. Whether or not you are gone with him will also have been decided."

"And if I should go?" she queried.

Dick shrugged his shoulders, and stood up, glancing at his wristwatch.

"I have sent word to Blake to come earlier this morning," he explained, taking a step toward the door in invitation for her to go.

At the door she paused and leaned toward him.

"Kiss me, Dick," she said, and, afterward: "This is not a... love-touch." Her voice had become suddenly husky. "It's just in case I do decide to... to go."

The secretary approached along the hall, but Paula lingered.

"Good morning, Mr. Blake," Dick greeted him. "Sorry to rout you out so early. First of all, will you please telephone Mr. Agar and Mr. Pitts. I won't be able to see them this morning. Oh, and put the rest off till to-morrow, too. Make a point of getting Mr. Hanley. Tell him I approve of his plan for the Buckeye spillway, and to go right ahead. I will see Mr. Mendenhall, though, and Mr. Manson. Tell them nine- thirty."

"One thing, Dick," Paula said. "Remember, I made him stay. It was not his fault or wish. I wouldn't let him go."

"You've bowled *him* over right enough," Dick smiled. "I could not reconcile his staying on, under the circumstances, with what I knew of him. But with you not permitting him to go, and he as mad as a man has a right to be where you are concerned, I can understand. He's a whole lot better than a good sort. They don't make many like him. He will make you happy—"

She held up her hand.

"I don't know that I shall ever be happy again, Red Cloud. When I see what I have brought into your face... . And I was so happy and contented all our dozen years. I can't forget it. That is why I have been unable to decide. But you are right. The time has come for me to solve the ... " She hesitated and could not utter the word "triangle" which he saw forming on her lips. "The situation," her voice trailed away. "We'll all go hunting. I'll talk with him as we ride, and I'll send him away, no matter what I do."

"I shouldn't be precipitate, Paul," Dick advised. "You know I don't care a hang for morality except when it is useful. And in this case it is exceedingly useful. There may be children.—Please, please," he hushed her. "And in such case even old scandal is not exactly good for them. Desertion takes too long. I'll arrange to give you the real statutory grounds, which will save a year in the divorce."

"If I so make up my mind," she smiled wanly.

He nodded.

"But I may not make up my mind that way. I don't know it myself. Perhaps it's all a dream, and soon I shall wake up, and Oh Dear will come in and tell me how soundly and long I have slept."

She turned away reluctantly, and paused suddenly when she had made half a dozen steps.

"Dick," she called. "You have told me your heart, but not what's in your mind. Don't do anything foolish. Remember Denny Holbrook—no hunting accident, mind."

He shook his head, and twinkled his eyes in feigned amusement, and marveled to himself that her intuition should have so squarely hit the mark.

"And leave all this?" he lied, with a gesture that embraced the ranch and all its projects. "And that book on in-and-in-breeding? And my first annual home sale of stock just ripe to come off?"

"It would be preposterous," she agreed with brightening face. "But, Dick, in this difficulty of making up my mind, please, please know that—" She paused for the phrase, then made a gesture in mimicry of his, that included the Big House and its treasures, and said, "All this does not influence me a particle. Truly not."

"As if I did not know it," he assured her. "Of all unmercenary women— "

"Why, Dick," she interrupted him, fired by a new thought, "if I loved Evan as madly as you think, you would mean so little that I'd be content, if it were the only way out, for you to have a hunting accident. But you see, I don't. Anyway, there's a brass tack for you to ponder."

She made another reluctant step away, then called back in a whisper, her face over her shoulder:

"Red Cloud, I'm dreadfully sorry... . And through it all I'm so glad that you do still love me."

Before Blake returned, Dick found time to study his face in the glass. Printed there was the expression that had startled his company the preceding evening. It had come to stay. Oh, well, was his thought, one cannot chew his heart between his teeth without leaving some sign of it.

He strolled out on the sleeping porch and looked at Paula's picture under the barometers. He turned it to the wall, and sat on the bed and regarded the blankness for a space. Then he turned it back again.

"Poor little kid," he murmured, "having a hard time of it just waking up at this late day."

But as he continued to gaze, abruptly there leaped before his eyes the vision of her in the moonlight, clinging to Graham and drawing his lips down to hers.

Dick got up quickly, with a shake of head to shake the vision from his eyes.

By half past nine his correspondence was finished and his desk cleaned save for certain data to be used in his talks with his Shorthorn and Shire managers. He was over at the window and waving a smiling farewell to Lute and Ernestine in the limousine, as Mendenhall entered. And to him, and to Manson next, Dick managed, in casual talk, to impress much of his bigger breeding plans.

"We've got to keep an eagle eye on the bull-get of King Polo," he told Manson. "There's all the promise in the world for a greater than he from Bleakhouse Fawn, or Alberta Maid, or Moravia's Nellie Signal. We missed it this year so far, but next year, or the year after, soon or late, King Polo is going to be responsible for a real humdinger of winner."

And as with Manson, with much more talk, so with Mendenhall, Dick succeeded in emphasizing the far application of his breeding theories.

With their departure, he got Oh Joy on the house 'phone and told him to take Graham to the gun room to choose a rifle and any needed gear.

At eleven he did not know that Paula had come up the secret stairway from the library and was standing behind the shelves of books listening. She had intended coming in but had been deterred by the sound of his voice. She could hear him talking over the telephone to Hanley about the spillway of the Buckeye dam.

"And by the way," Dick's voice went on, "you've been over the reports on the Big Miramar?... Very good. Discount them. I disagree with them flatly. The water is there. I haven't a doubt we'll find a fairly shallow artesian supply. Send up the boring outfit at once and start prospecting. The soil's ungodly rich, and if we don't make that dry hole ten times as valuable in the next five years ... "

Paula sighed, and turned back down the spiral to the library.

Red Cloud the incorrigible, always planting his acorns—was her thought. There he was, with his love-world crashing around him, calmly considering dams and well-borings so that he might, in the years to come, plant more acorns.

Nor was Dick ever to know that Paula had come so near to him with her need and gone away. Again, not aimlessly, but to run through for the last time the notes of the scribble pad by his bed, he was out on his sleeping porch. His house was in order. There was nothing left but to sign up the morning's dictation, answer several telegrams, then would come lunch and the hunting in the Sycamore hills. Oh, he would do it well. The Outlaw would bear the blame. And he would have an eye- witness, either Froelig or Martinez. But not both of them. One pair of eyes would be enough to satisfy when the martingale parted and the mare reared and toppled backward upon him into the brush. And from that screen of brush, swiftly linking accident to catastrophe, the witness would hear the rifle go off.

Martinez was more emotional than the sculptor and would therefore make a more satisfactory witness, Dick decided. Him would he maneuver to have with him in the narrow trail when the Outlaw should be made the scapegoat. Martinez was no horseman. All the better. It would be well, Dick judged, to make the Outlaw act up in real devilishness for a minute or two before the culmination. It would give verisimilitude. Also, it would excite Martinez's horse, and, therefore, excite Martinez so that he would not see occurrences too clearly.

He clenched his hands with sudden hurt. The Little Lady was mad, she must be mad; on no other ground could he understand such arrant cruelty, listening to her voice and Graham's from the open windows of the music room as they sang together the "Gypsy Trail."

Nor did he unclench his hands during all the time they sang. And they sang the mad, reckless song clear through to its mad reckless end. And he continued to stand, listening to her laugh herself merrily away from Graham and on across the house to her wing, from the porches of which she continued to laugh as she teased and chided Oh Dear for fancied derelictions.

From far off came the dim but unmistakable trumpeting of Mountain Lad. King Polo asserted his lordly self, and the harems of mares and heifers sent back their answering calls. Dick listened to all the whinnying and nickering and bawling of sex, and sighed aloud: "Well, the land is better for my having been. It is a good thought to take to bed."

=

Chapter 31

A ring of his bed 'phone made Dick sit on the bed to take up the receiver. As he listened, he looked out across the patio to Paula's porches. Bonbright was explaining that it was a call from Chauncey Bishop who was at Eldorado in a machine. Chauncey Bishop, editor and owner of the San Francisco *Dispatch*, was sufficiently important a person, in Bonbright's mind, as well as old friend of Dick's, to be connected directly to him.

"You can get here for lunch," Dick told the newspaper owner. "And, say, suppose you put up for the night... . Never mind your special writers. We're going hunting mountain lions this afternoon, and there's sure to be a kill. Got them located... . Who? What's she write?... What of it? She can stick around the ranch and get half a dozen columns out of any of half a dozen subjects, while the writer chap can get the dope on lion-hunting... . Sure, sure. I'll put him on a horse a child can ride."

The more the merrier, especially newspaper chaps, Dick grinned to himself—and grandfather Jonathan Forrest would have nothing on him when it came to pulling off a successful finish.

But how could Paula have been so wantonly cruel as to sing the "Gypsy Trail" so immediately afterward? Dick asked himself, as, receiver near to ear, he could distantly hear Chauncey Bishop persuading his writer man to the hunting.

"All right then, come a running," Dick told Bishop in conclusion. "I'm giving orders now for the horses, and you can have that bay you rode last time."

Scarcely had he hung up, when the bell rang again. This time it was Paula.

"Red Cloud, dear Red Cloud," she said, "your reasoning is all wrong. I think I love you best. I am just about making up my mind, and it's for you. And now, just to help me to be sure, tell me what you told me a little while ago—you know—' I love the woman, the one woman. After a dozen years of possession I love her quite madly, oh, so sweetly madly.' Say it to me, Red Cloud."

"I do truly love the woman, the one woman," Dick repeated. "After a dozen years of possession I do love her quite madly, oh, so sweetly madly."

There was a pause when he had finished, which, waiting, he did not dare to break.

"There is one little thing I almost forgot to tell you," she said, very softly, very slowly, very clearly. "I do love you. I have never loved you so much as right now. After our dozen years you've bowled me over at last. And I was bowled over from the beginning, although I did not know it. I have made up my mind now, once and for all."

She hung up abruptly.

With the thought that he knew how a man felt receiving a reprieve at the eleventh hour, Dick sat on, thinking, forgetful that he had not hooked the receiver, until Bonbright came in from the secretaries' room to remind him.

"It was from Mr. Bishop," Bonbright explained. "Sprung an axle. I took the liberty of sending one of our machines to bring them in."

"And see what our men can do with repairing theirs," Dick nodded.

Alone again, he got up and stretched, walked absently the length of the room and back.

"Well, Martinez, old man," he addressed the empty air, "this afternoon you'll be defrauded out of as fine a histrionic stunt as you will never know you've missed."

He pressed the switch for Paula's telephone and rang her up.

Oh Dear answered, and quickly brought her mistress.

"I've a little song I want to sing to you, Paul," he said, then chanted the old negro 'spiritual':

"'Fer itself, fer itself, Fer itself, fer itself, Every soul got ter confess Fer itself.'

"And I want you to tell me again, fer yourself, fer yourself, what you just told me."

Her laughter came in a merry gurgle that delighted him.

"Red Cloud, I do love you," she said. "My mind is made up. I shall never have any man but you in all this world. Now be good, and let me dress. I'll have to rush for lunch as it is."

"May I come over?—for a moment?" he begged.

"Not yet, eager one. In ten minutes. Let me finish with Oh Dear first. Then I'll be all ready for the hunt. I'm putting on my Robin Hood outfit—you know, the greens and russets and the long feather. And I'm taking my 30-30. It's heavy enough for mountain lions."

"You've made me very happy," Dick continued.

"And you're making me late. Ring off.—Red Cloud, I love you more this minute—"

He heard her hang up, and was surprised, the next moment, that somehow he was reluctant to yield to the happiness that he had claimed was his. Rather, did it seem that he could still hear her voice and Graham's recklessly singing the "Gypsy Trail."

Had she been playing with Graham? Or had she been playing with him? Such conduct, for her, was unprecedented and incomprehensible. As he groped for a solution, he saw her again in the moonlight, clinging to Graham with upturned lips, drawing Graham's lips down to hers.

Dick shook his head in bafflement, and glanced at his watch. At any rate, in ten minutes, in less than ten minutes, he would hold her in his arms and know.

So tedious was the brief space of time that he strolled slowly on the way, pausing to light a cigarette, throwing it away with the first inhalation, pausing again to listen to the busy click of typewriters from the secretaries' room. With still two minutes to spare, and knowing that one minute would take him to the door without a knob, he stopped in the patio and gazed at the wild canaries bathing in the fountain.

When they startled into the air, a cloud of fluttering gold and crystal droppings in the sunshine, Dick startled. The report of the rifle had come from Paula's wing above, and he identified it as her 30-30 as he dashed across the patio. *She beat me to it*, was his next thought, and what had been incomprehensible the moment before was as sharply definite as the roar of her rifle.

And across the patio, up the stairs, through the door left wide-flung behind him, continued to pulse in his brain: *She beat me to it. She beat me to it.*

She lay, crumpled and quivering, in hunting costume complete, save for the pair of tiny bronze spurs held over her in anguished impotence by the frightened maid.

His examination was quick. Paula breathed, although she was unconscious. From front to back, on the left side, the bullet had torn through. His next spring was to the telephone, and as he waited the delay of connecting through the house central he prayed that Hennessy would be at the stallion barn. A stable boy answered, and, while he ran to fetch the veterinary, Dick ordered Oh Joy to stay by the switches, and to send Oh My to him at once.

From the tail of his eye he saw Graham rush into the room and on to Paula.

"Hennessy," Dick commanded. "Come on the jump. Bring the needful for first aid. It's a rifle shot through the lungs or heart or both. Come right to Mrs. Forrest's rooms. Now jump."

"Don't touch her," he said sharply to Graham. "It might make it worse, start a worse hemorrhage."

Next he was back at Oh Joy.

"Start Callahan with the racing car for Eldorado. Tell him he'll meet Doctor Robinson on the way, and that he is to bring Doctor Robinson back with him on the jump. Tell him to jump like the devil was after him. Tell him Mrs. Forrest is hurt and that if he makes time he'll save her life."

Receiver to ear, he turned to look at Paula. Graham, bending over her but not touching her, met his eyes.

"Forrest," he began, "if you have done—"

But Dick hushed him with a warning glance directed toward Oh Dear who still held the bronze spurs in speechless helplessness.

"It can be discussed later," Dick said shortly, as he turned his mouth to the transmitter.

"Doctor Robinson?... Good. Mrs. Forrest has a rifle-shot through lungs or heart or maybe both. Callahan is on his way to meet you in the racing car. Keep coming as fast as God'll let you till you meet Callahan. Good-by."

Back to Paula, Graham stepped aside as Dick, on his knees, bent over her. His examination was brief. He looked up at Graham with a shake of the head and said:

"It's too ticklish to fool with."

He turned to Oh Dear.

"Put down those spurs and bring pillows.—Evan, lend a hand on the other side, and lift gently and steadily.—Oh Dear, shove that pillow under—easy, easy."

He looked up and saw Oh My standing silently, awaiting orders.

"Get Mr. Bonbright to relieve Oh Joy at the switches," Dick commanded. "Tell Oh Joy to stand near to Mr. Bonbright to rush orders. Tell Oh Joy to have all the house boys around him to rush the orders. As soon as Saunders comes back with Mr. Bishop's crowd, tell Oh Joy to start him out on the jump to Eldorado to look for Callahan in case Callahan has a smash up. Tell Oh Joy to get hold of Mr. Manson, and Mr. Pitts or any two of the managers who have machines and have them, with their machines, waiting here at the house. Tell Oh Joy to take care of Mr. Bishop's crowd as usual. And you come back here where I can call you."

Dick turned to Oh Dear.

"Now tell me how it happened."

Oh Dear shook her head and wrung her hands.

"Where were you when the rifle went off?"

The Chinese girl swallowed and pointed toward the wardrobe room.

"Go on, talk," Dick commanded harshly.

"Mrs. Forrest tell me to get spurs. I forget before. I go quick. I hear gun. I come back quick. I run."

She pointed to Paula to show what she had found.

"But the gun?" Dick asked.

"Some trouble. Maybe gun no work. Maybe four minutes, maybe five minutes, Mrs. Forrest try make gun work."

"Was she trying to make the gun work when you went for the spurs?"

Oh Dear nodded.

"Before that I say maybe Oh Joy can fix gun. Mrs. Forrest say never mind. She say you can fix. She put gun down. Then she try once more fix gun. Then she tell me get spurs. Then... gun go off."

Hennessy's arrival shut off further interrogation. His examination was scarcely less brief than Dick's. He looked up with a shake of the head.

"Nothing I can dare tackle, Mr. Forrest. The hemorrhage has eased of itself, though it must be gathering inside. You've sent for a doctor?"

"Robinson. I caught him in his office.—He's young, a good surgeon," Dick explained to Graham. "He's nervy and daring, and I'd trust him in this farther than some of the old ones with reputations.—What do you think, Mr. Hennessy? What chance has she?"

"Looks pretty bad, though I'm no judge, being only a horse doctor. Robinson'll know. Nothing to do but wait."

Dick nodded and walked out on Paula's sleeping porch to listen for the exhaust of the racing machine Callahan drove. He heard the ranch limousine arrive leisurely and swiftly depart. Graham came out on the porch to him.

"I want to apologize, Forrest," he said. "I was rather off for the moment. I found you here, and I thought you were here when it happened. It must have been an accident.'"

"Poor little kid," Dick agreed. "And she so prided herself on never being careless with guns."

"I've looked at the rifle," Graham said, "but I couldn't find anything wrong with it."

"And that's how it happened. Whatever was wrong got right. That's how it went off."

And while Dick talked, building the fabric of the lie so that even Graham should be fooled, to himself he was understanding how well Paula had played the trick. That last singing of the "Gypsy Trail" had been her farewell to Graham and at the same time had provided against any suspicion on his part of what she had intended directly to do. It had been the same with him. She had had her farewell with him, and, the last thing, over the telephone, had assured him that she would never have any man but him in all the world.

He walked away from Graham to the far end of the porch.

"She had the grit, she had the grit," he muttered to himself with quivering lips. "Poor kid. She couldn't decide between the two, and so she solved it this way."

The noise of the racing machine drew him and Graham together, and together they entered the room to wait for the doctor. Graham betrayed unrest, reluctant to go, yet feeling that he must.

"Please stay on, Evan," Dick told him. "She liked you much, and if she does open her eyes she'll be glad to see you."

Dick and Graham stood apart from Paula while Doctor Robinson made his examination. When he arose with an air of finality, Dick looked his question. Robinson shook his head.

"Nothing to be done," he said. "It is a matter of hours, maybe of minutes." He hesitated, studying Dick's face for a moment. "I can ease her off if you say the word. She might possibly recover consciousness and suffer for a space."

Dick took a turn down the room and back, and when he spoke it was to Graham.

"Why not let her live again, brief as the time may be? The pain is immaterial. It will have its inevitable quick anodyne. It is what I would wish, what you would wish. She loved life, every moment of it. Why should we deny her any of the little left her?"

Graham bent his head in agreement, and Dick turned to the doctor.

"Perhaps you can stir her, stimulate her, to a return of consciousness. If you can, do so. And if the pain proves too severe, then you can ease her."

When her eyes fluttered open, Dick nodded Graham up beside him. At first bewilderment was all she betrayed, then her eyes focused first on Dick's face, then on Graham's, and, with recognition, her lips parted in a pitiful smile.

"I... I thought at first that I was dead," she said.

But quickly another thought was in her mind, and Dick divined it in her eyes as they searched him. The question was if he knew it was no accident. He gave no sign. She had planned it so, and she must pass believing it so.

"I... was... wrong," she said. She spoke slowly, faintly, in evident pain, with a pause for strength of utterance between each word. "I was always so cocksure I'd never have an accident, and look what I've gone and done."

"It's a darn shame," Dick said, sympathetically. "What was it? A jam?"

She nodded, and again her lips parted in the pitiful brave smile as she said whimsically: "Oh, Dick, go call the neighbors in and show them what little Paula's din.

"How serious is it?" she asked. "Be honest, Red Cloud, you know *me*," she added, after the briefest of pauses in which Dick had not replied.

He shook his head.

"How long?" she queried.

"Not long," came his answer. "You can ease off any time."

"You mean... ?" She glanced aside curiously at the doctor and back to Dick, who nodded.

"It's only what I should have expected from you, Red Cloud," she murmured gratefully. "But is Doctor Robinson game for it?"

The doctor stepped around so that she could see him, and nodded.

"Thank you, doctor. And remember, I am to say when."

"Is there much pain?" Dick queried.

Her eyes were wide and brave and dreadful, and her lips quivered for the moment ere she replied, "Not much, but dreadful, quite dreadful. I won't care to stand it very long. I'll say when."

Once more the smile on her lips announced a whimsey.

"Life is queer, most queer, isn't it? And do you know, I want to go out with love-songs in my ears. You first, Evan, sing the 'Gypsy Trail.'—Why, I was singing it with you less than an hour ago. Think of it! Do, Evan, please."

Graham looked to Dick for permission, and Dick gave it with his eyes.

"Oh, and sing it robustly, gladly, madly, just as a womaning Gypsy man should sing it," she urged. "And stand back there, so, where I can see you."

And while Graham sang the whole song through to its:

"The heart of a man to the heart of a maid, light of my tents be fleet, Morning waits at the end of the world and the world is all at our feet,"

Oh My, immobile-faced, a statue, stood in the far doorway awaiting commands. Oh Dear, grief-stricken, stood at her mistress's head, no longer wringing her hands, but holding them so tightly clasped that the finger-tips and nails showed white. To the rear, at Paula's dressing table, Doctor Robinson noiselessly dissolved in a glass the anodyne pellets and filled his hypodermic.

When Graham had finished, Paula thanked him with her eyes, closed them, and lay still for a space.

"And now, Red Cloud," she said when next she opened them, "the song of Ai-kut, and of the Dew-Woman, the Lush-Woman. Stand where Evan did, so that I can see you well."

And Dick chanted:

"I am Ai-kut, the first man of the Nishinam. Ai-kut is the short for Adam, and my father and my mother were the coyote and the moon. And this is Yo-to-to-wi, my wife. Yo-to-to-wi is the short for Eve. She is the first woman of the Nishinam.

"Me, I am Ai-kut. This is my dew of women. This is my honey-dew of women. Her father and her mother were the Sierra dawn and the summer east wind of the mountains. Together they conspired, and from the air and earth they sweated all sweetness till in a mist of their own love the leaves of the chaparral and the manzanita were dewed with the honey dew.

"Yo-to-to-wi is my honey-dew woman. Hear me! I am Ai-kut! Yo-to-to-wi is my quail-woman, my deer-woman, my lush-woman of all soft rain and fat soil. She was born of the thin starlight and the brittle dawn- light, in the morning of the world, and she is the one woman of all women to me."

Again, with closed eyes, she lay silent for a while. Once she attempted to draw a deeper breath, which caused her to cough slightly several times.

"Try not to cough," Dick said.

They could see her brows contract with the effort of will to control the irritating tickle that might precipitate a paroxysm.

"Oh Dear, come around where I can see you," she said, when she opened her eyes.

The Chinese girl obeyed, moving blindly, so that Robinson, with a hand on her arm, was compelled to guide her.

"Good-by, Oh Dear. You've been very good to me always. And sometimes, maybe, I have not been good to you. I am sorry. Remember, Mr. Forrest will always be your father and your mother... . And all my jade is yours."

She closed her eyes in token that the brief audience was over.

Again she was vexed by the tickling cough that threatened to grow more pronounced.

"I am ready, Dick," she said faintly, still with closed eyes. "I want to make my sleepy, sleepy noise. Is the doctor ready? Come closer. Hold my hand like you did before in the little death."

She turned her eyes to Graham, and Dick did not look, for he knew love was in that last look of hers, as he knew it would be when she looked into his eyes at the last.

"Once," she explained to Graham, "I had to go on the table, and I made Dick go with me into the anaesthetic chamber and hold my hand until I went under. You remember, Henley called it the drunken dark, the little death in life. It was very easy."

In the silence she continued her look, then turned her face and eyes back to Dick, who knelt close to her, holding her hand.

With a pressure of her fingers on his and a beckoning of her eyes, she drew his ear down to her lips.

"Red Cloud," she whispered, "I love you best. And I am proud I belonged to you for such a long, long time." Still closer she drew him with the pressure of her fingers. "I'm sorry there were no babies, Red Cloud."

With the relaxing of her fingers she eased him from her so that she could look from one to the other.

"Two bonnie, bonnie men. Good-by, bonnie men. Good-by, Red Cloud."

In the pause, they waited, while the doctor bared her arm for the needle.

"Sleepy, sleepy," she twittered in mimicry of drowsy birds. "I am ready, doctor. Stretch the skin tight, first. You know I don't like to be hurt.—Hold me tight, Dick."

Robinson, receiving the eye permission from Dick, easily and quickly thrust the needle through the stretched skin, with steady hand sank the piston home, and with the ball of the finger soothingly rubbed the morphine into circulation.

"Sleepy, sleepy, boo'ful sleepy," she murmured drowsily, after a time.

Semi-consciously she half-turned on her side, curved her free arm on the pillow and nestled her head on it, and drew her body up in nestling curves in the way Dick knew she loved to sleep.

After a long time, she sighed faintly, and began so easily to go that she was gone before they guessed. From without, the twittering of the canaries bathing in the fountain penetrated the silence of the room, and from afar came the trumpeting of Mountain Lad and the silver whinny of the Fotherington Princess.

www.ingramcontent.com/pod-product-compliance
Lightning Source LLC
LaVergne TN
LVHW040044080526
838202LV00045B/3488